big NATE

BEWARE OF LOW - FLYING CORN MUFFINS

Complete Your *Big Nate* Collection

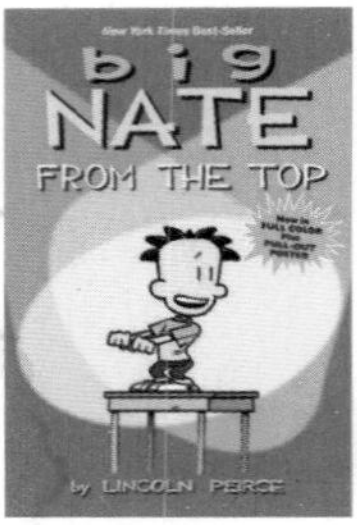
New York Times Best-Seller
big NATE
FROM THE TOP
by LINCOLN PEIRCE

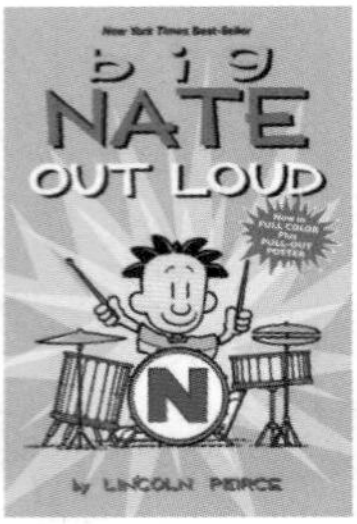
New York Times Best-Seller
big NATE
OUT LOUD
by LINCOLN PEIRCE

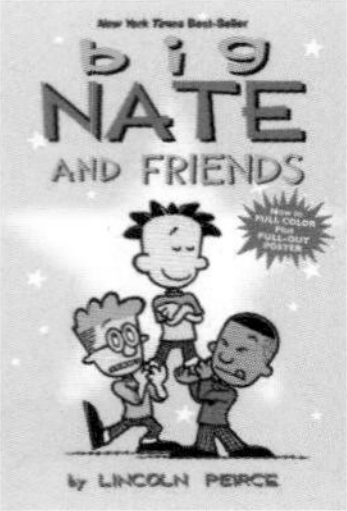
New York Times Best-Seller
big NATE
AND FRIENDS
by LINCOLN PEIRCE

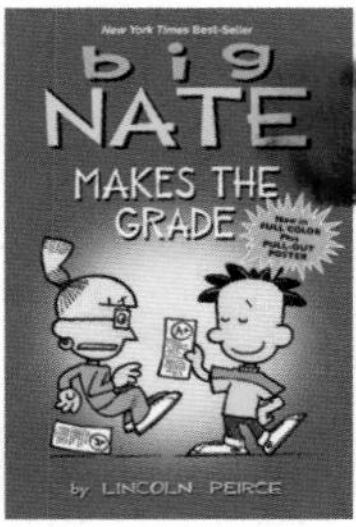
New York Times Best-Seller
big NATE
MAKES THE GRADE
by LINCOLN PEIRCE

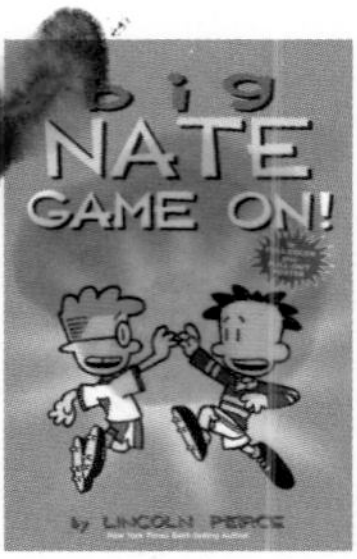
big NATE
GAME ON!
by LINCOLN PEIRCE

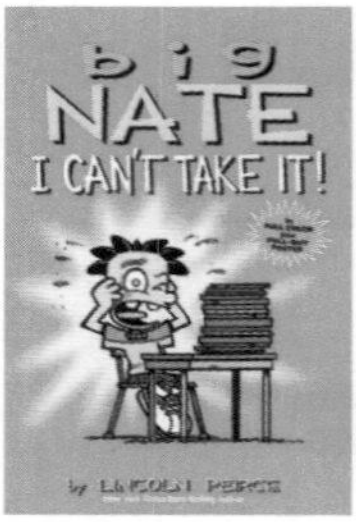
big NATE
I CAN'T TAKE IT!
by LINCOLN PEIRCE

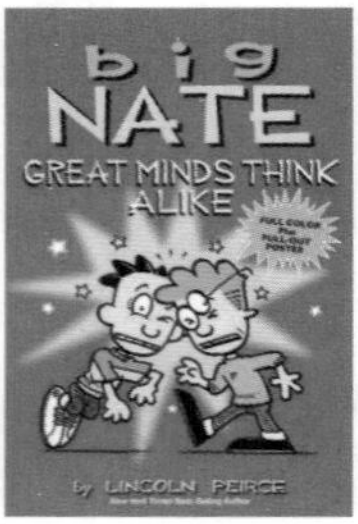
big NATE
GREAT MINDS THINK ALIKE
by LINCOLN PEIRCE

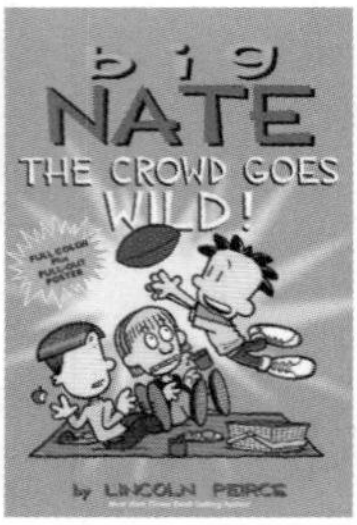
big NATE
THE CROWD GOES WILD!
by LINCOLN PEIRCE

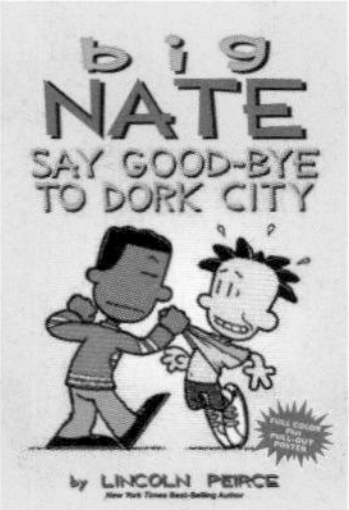
big NATE
SAY GOOD-BYE TO DORK CITY
by LINCOLN PEIRCE

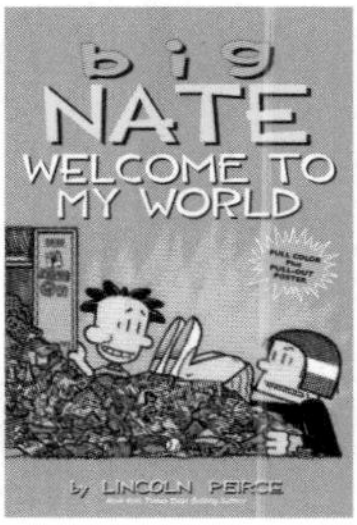
big NATE
WELCOME TO MY WORLD
by LINCOLN PEIRCE

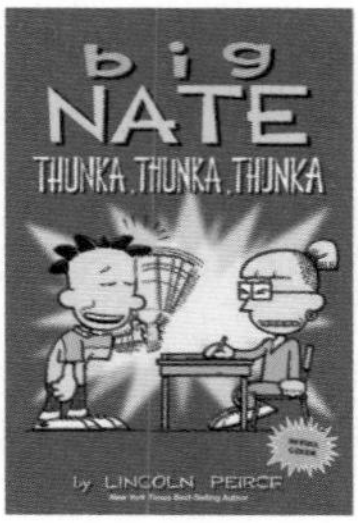
big NATE
THUNKA, THUNKA, THUNKA
by LINCOLN PEIRCE

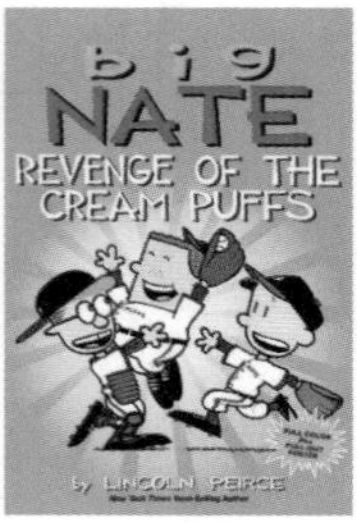
big NATE
REVENGE OF THE CREAM PUFFS
by LINCOLN PEIRCE

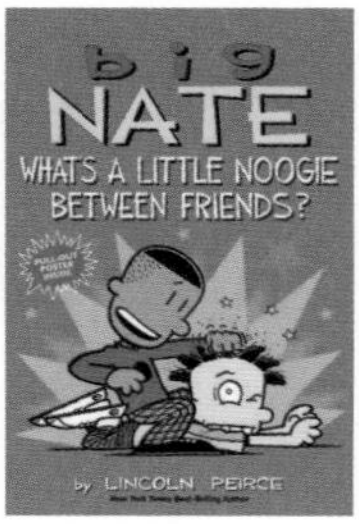
big NATE
WHAT'S A LITTLE NOOGIE BETWEEN FRIENDS?
by LINCOLN PEIRCE

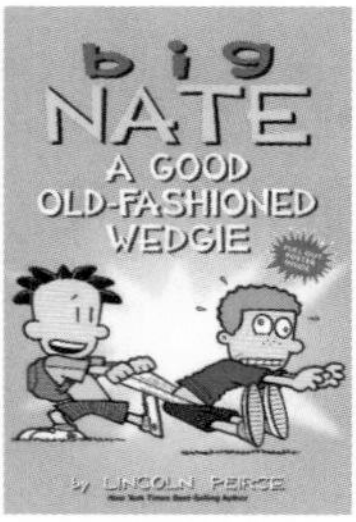
big NATE
A GOOD OLD-FASHIONED WEDGIE
by LINCOLN PEIRCE

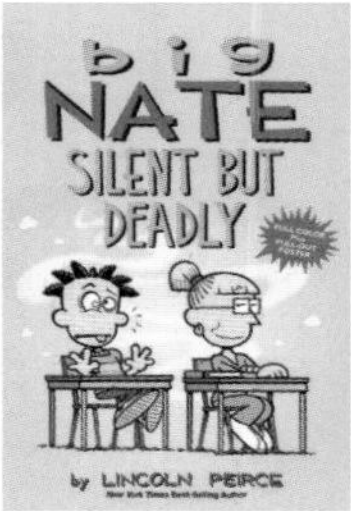
big NATE
SILENT BUT DEADLY
by LINCOLN PEIRCE

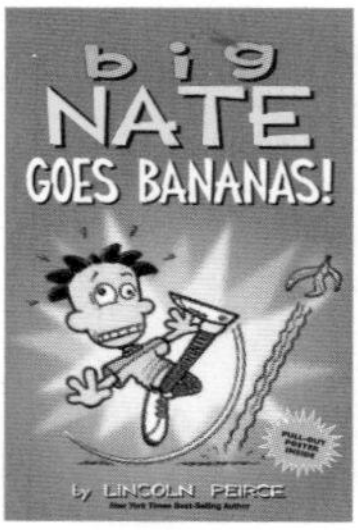
big NATE
GOES BANANAS!
by LINCOLN PEIRCE

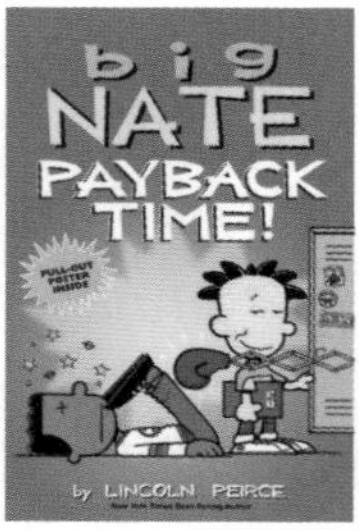
big NATE
PAYBACK TIME!
by LINCOLN PEIRCE

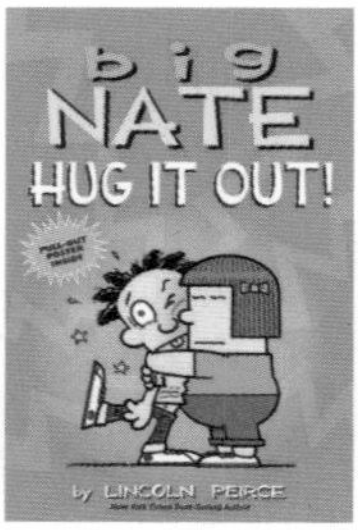
big NATE
HUG IT OUT!
by LINCOLN PEIRCE

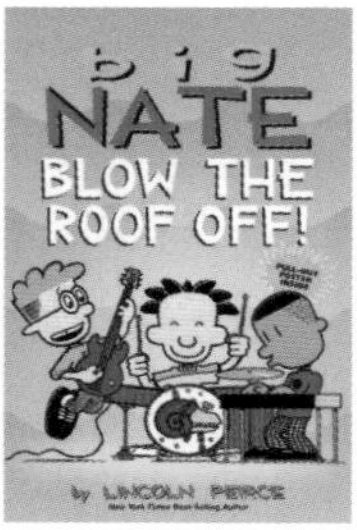
big NATE
BLOW THE ROOF OFF!
by LINCOLN PEIRCE

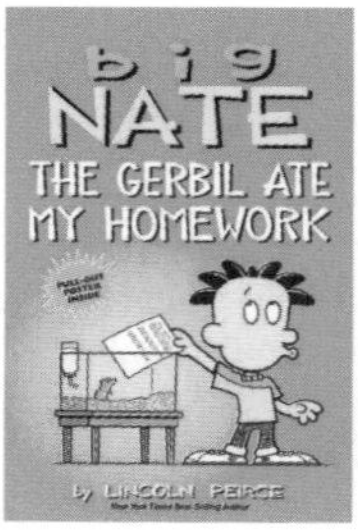
big NATE
THE GERBIL ATE MY HOMEWORK
by LINCOLN PEIRCE

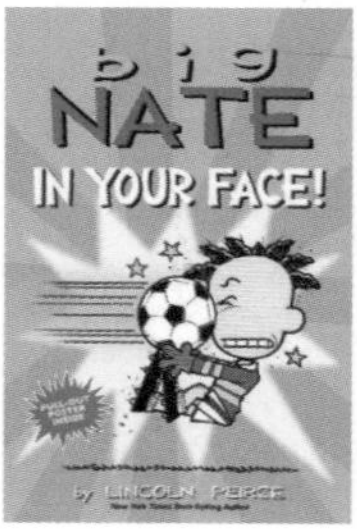
big NATE
IN YOUR FACE!
by LINCOLN PEIRCE

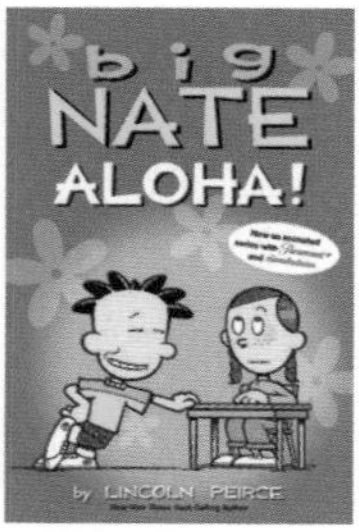
big NATE
ALOHA!
by LINCOLN PEIRCE

Big NATE

BEWARE OF LOW-FLYING CORN MUFFINS

by LINCOLN PEIRCE

Andrews McMeel
PUBLISHING®

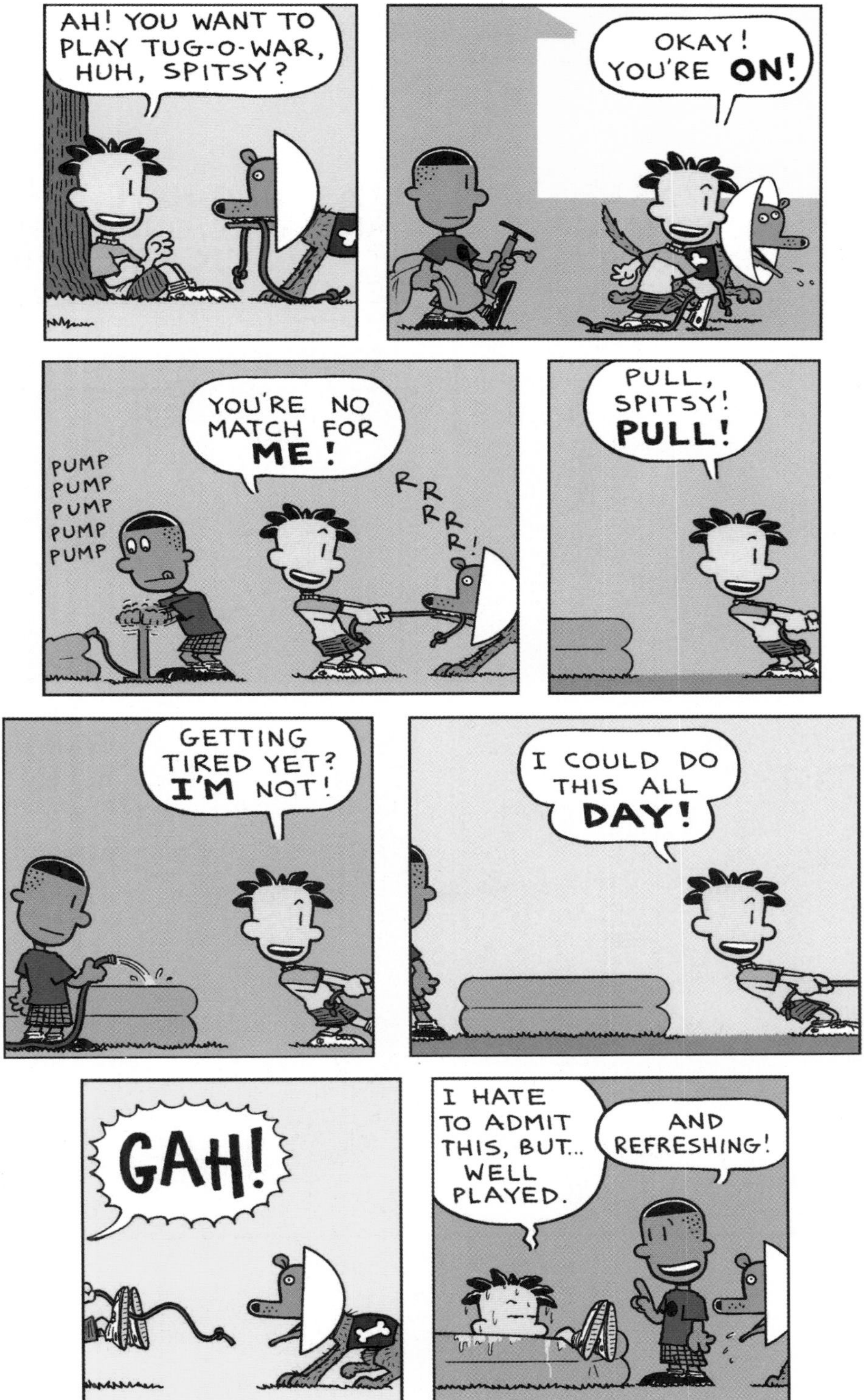
AH! YOU WANT TO PLAY TUG-O-WAR, HUH, SPITSY?
OKAY! YOU'RE **ON**!
PUMP PUMP PUMP PUMP PUMP
YOU'RE NO MATCH FOR **ME**!
RRRRR!
PULL, SPITSY! **PULL**!
GETTING TIRED YET? **I'M** NOT!
I COULD DO THIS ALL **DAY**!
GAH!
I HATE TO ADMIT THIS, BUT... WELL PLAYED.
AND REFRESHING!
Peirce

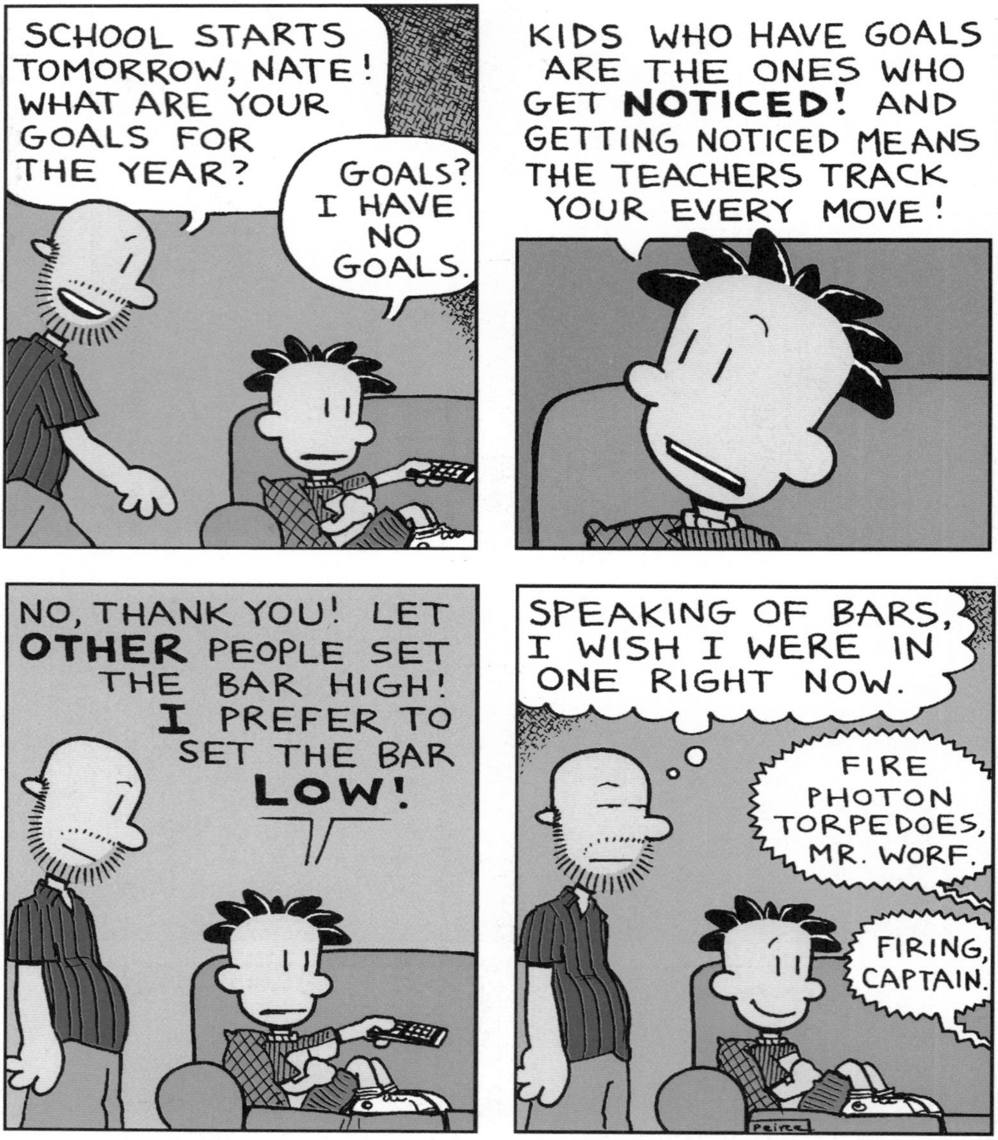
SCHOOL STARTS TOMORROW, NATE! WHAT ARE YOUR GOALS FOR THE YEAR?
GOALS? I HAVE NO GOALS.
KIDS WHO HAVE GOALS ARE THE ONES WHO GET **NOTICED!** AND GETTING NOTICED MEANS THE TEACHERS TRACK YOUR EVERY MOVE!
NO, THANK YOU! LET **OTHER** PEOPLE SET THE BAR HIGH! **I** PREFER TO SET THE BAR **LOW!**
SPEAKING OF BARS, I WISH I WERE IN ONE RIGHT NOW.
FIRE PHOTON TORPEDOES, MR. WORF.
FIRING, CAPTAIN.
Peirce

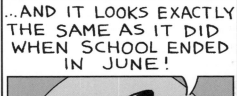

WELCOME BACK, NATE!

HI, PRINCIPAL NICHOLS. HEY, I JUST POPPED INTO THE STUDENT LOUNGE...

...AND IT LOOKS EXACTLY THE SAME AS IT DID WHEN SCHOOL ENDED IN JUNE!

WELL, WHY WOULDN'T IT?

BECAUSE I EMAILED YOU OVER THE SUMMER AND ASKED FOR A FOOSBALL TABLE.

I MUST HAVE MISSED THAT.

Peirce

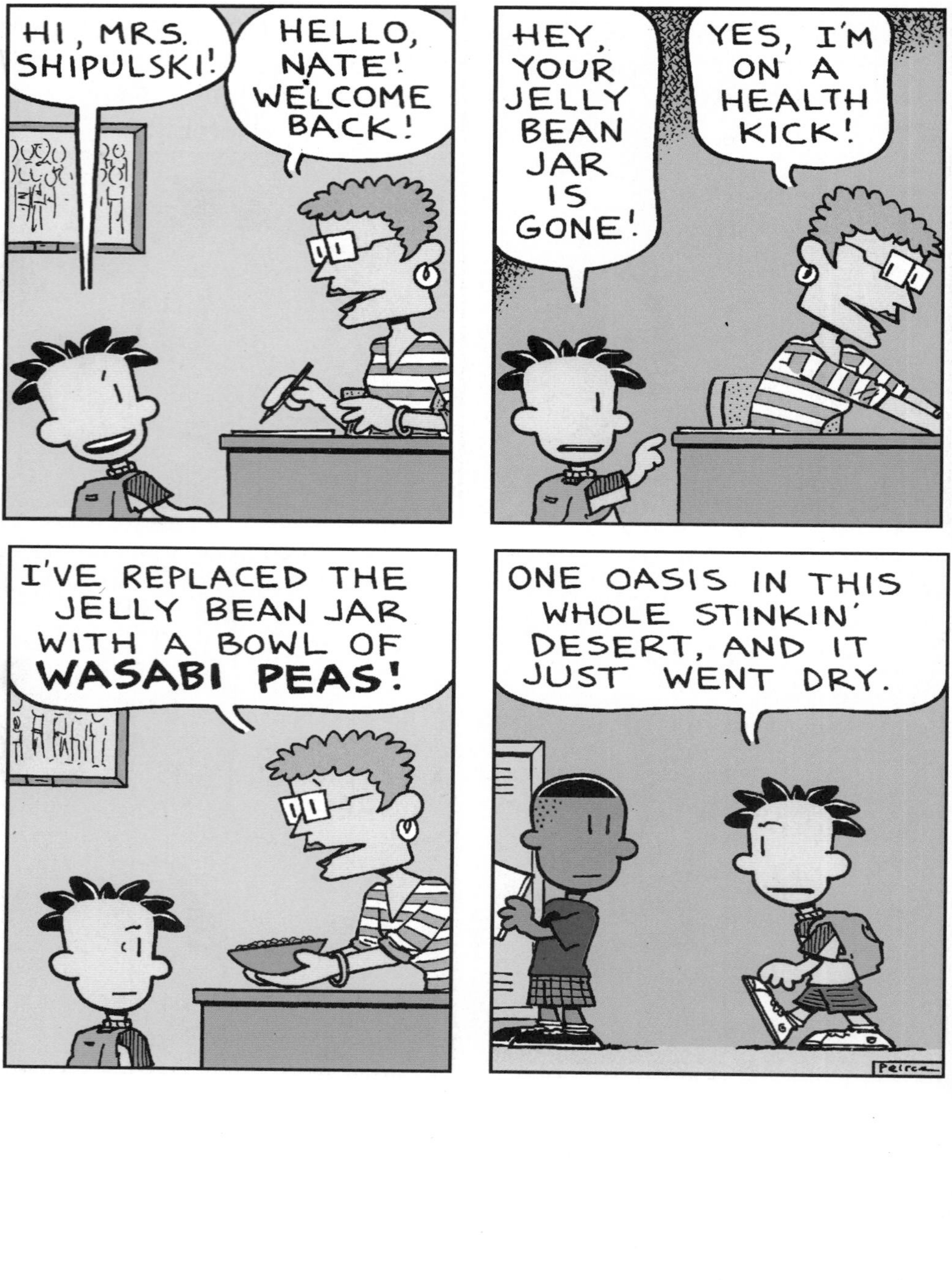
HI, MRS. SHIPULSKI!
HELLO, NATE! WELCOME BACK!
HEY, YOUR JELLY BEAN JAR IS GONE!
YES, I'M ON A HEALTH KICK!
I'VE REPLACED THE JELLY BEAN JAR WITH A BOWL OF WASABI PEAS!
ONE OASIS IN THIS WHOLE STINKIN' DESERT, AND IT JUST WENT DRY.
Peirce

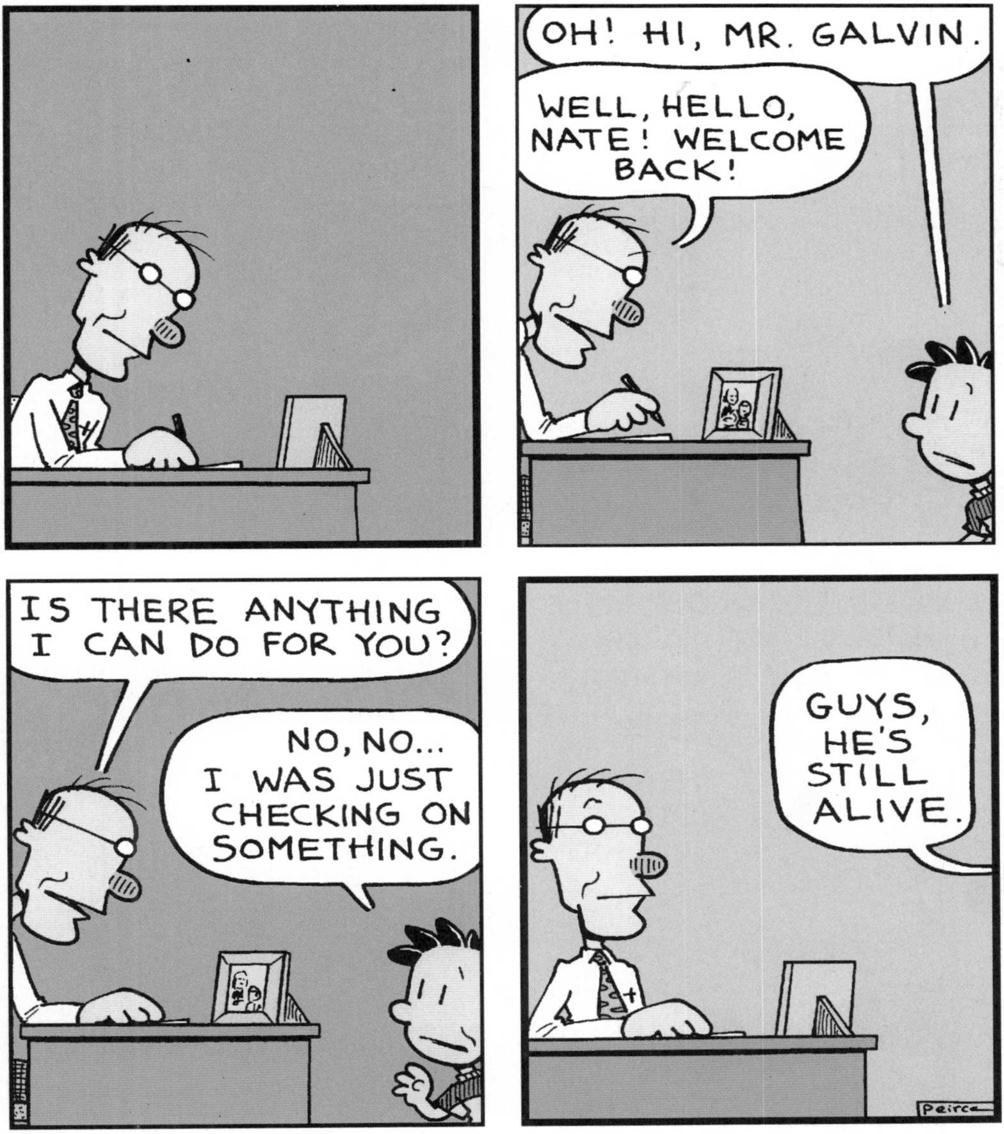
OH! HI, MR. GALVIN.
WELL, HELLO, NATE! WELCOME BACK!
IS THERE ANYTHING I CAN DO FOR YOU?
NO, NO... I WAS JUST CHECKING ON SOMETHING.
GUYS, HE'S STILL ALIVE.
Peirce

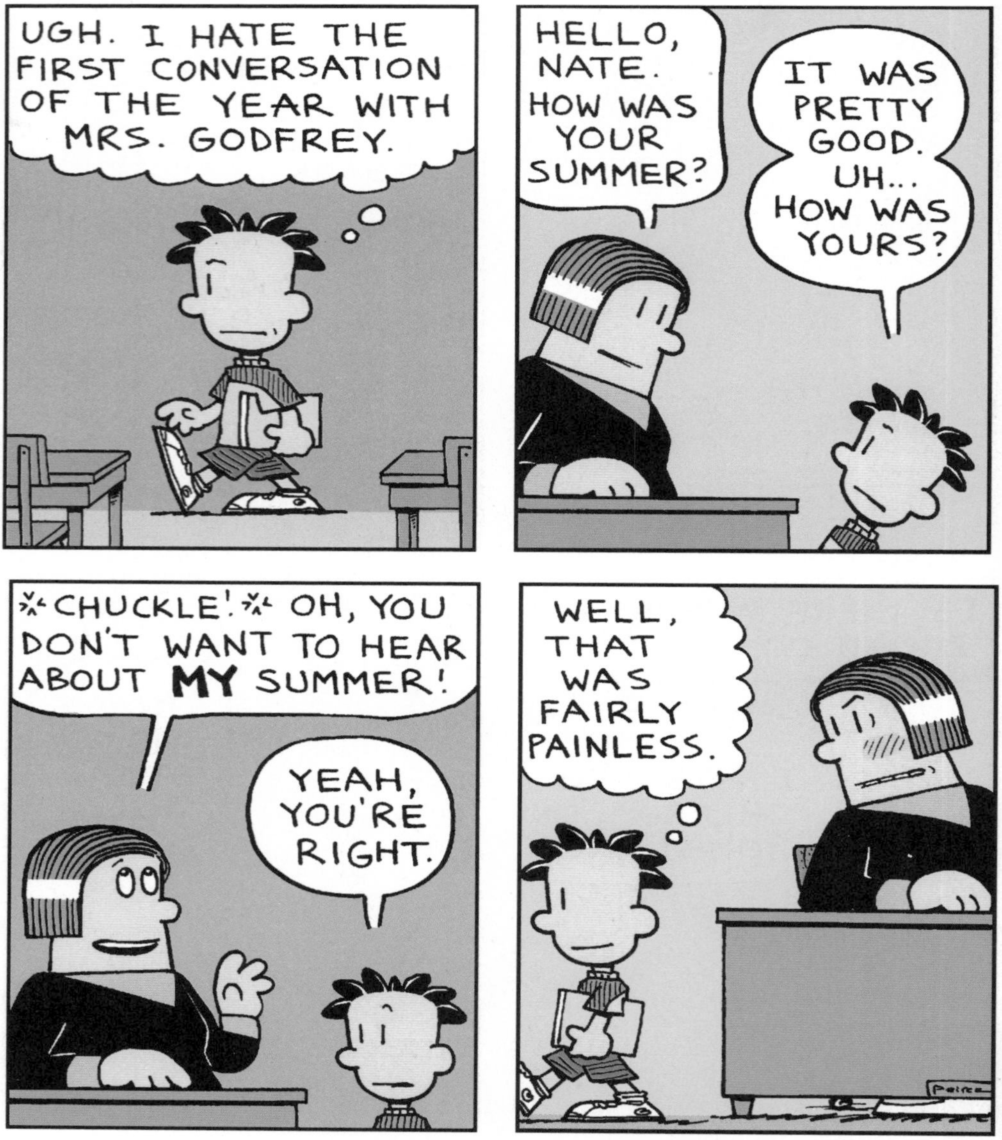
UGH. I HATE THE FIRST CONVERSATION OF THE YEAR WITH MRS. GODFREY.
HELLO, NATE. HOW WAS YOUR SUMMER?
IT WAS PRETTY GOOD. UH... HOW WAS YOURS?
CHUCKLE! OH, YOU DON'T WANT TO HEAR ABOUT **MY** SUMMER!
YEAH, YOU'RE RIGHT.
WELL, THAT WAS FAIRLY PAINLESS.

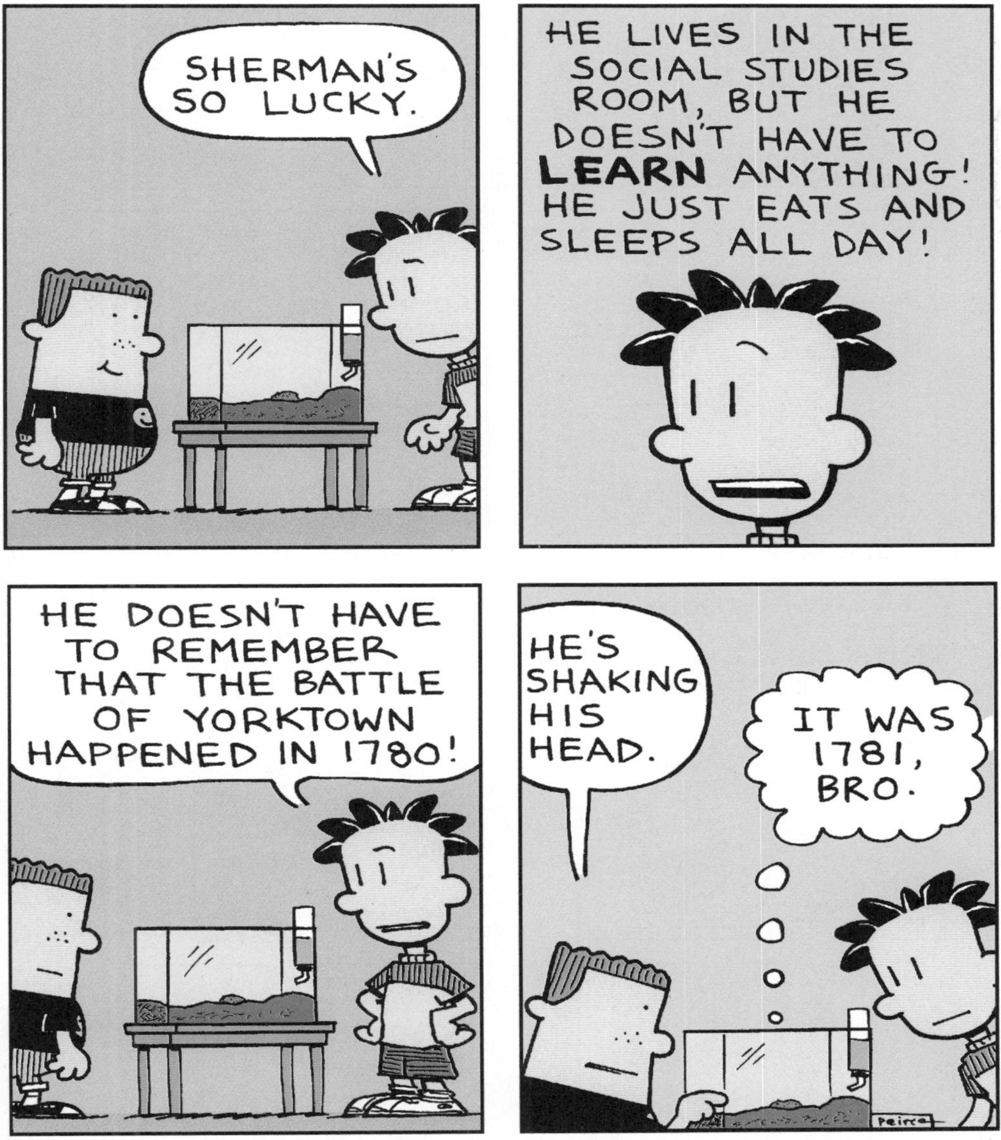
SHERMAN'S SO LUCKY.
HE LIVES IN THE SOCIAL STUDIES ROOM, BUT HE DOESN'T HAVE TO **LEARN** ANYTHING! HE JUST EATS AND SLEEPS ALL DAY!
HE DOESN'T HAVE TO REMEMBER THAT THE BATTLE OF YORKTOWN HAPPENED IN 1780!
HE'S SHAKING HIS HEAD.
IT WAS 1781, BRO.
Peirce

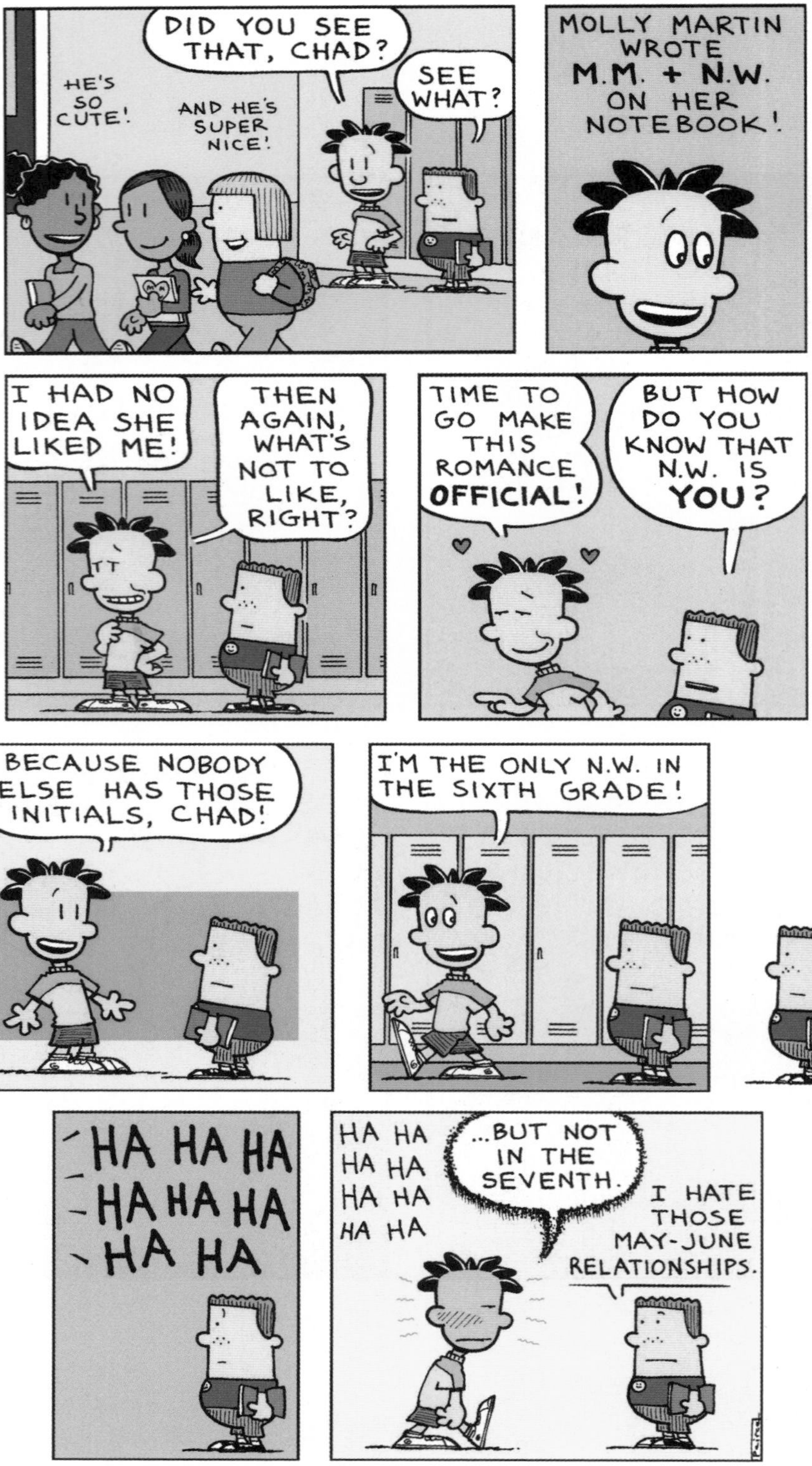
HE'S SO CUTE!
AND HE'S SUPER NICE!
DID YOU SEE THAT, CHAD?
SEE WHAT?
MOLLY MARTIN WROTE M.M. + N.W. ON HER NOTEBOOK!
I HAD NO IDEA SHE LIKED ME!
THEN AGAIN, WHAT'S NOT TO LIKE, RIGHT?
TIME TO GO MAKE THIS ROMANCE OFFICIAL!
BUT HOW DO YOU KNOW THAT N.W. IS YOU?
BECAUSE NOBODY ELSE HAS THOSE INITIALS, CHAD!
I'M THE ONLY N.W. IN THE SIXTH GRADE!
HA HA HA HA HA HA HA HA
HA HA HA HA HA HA HA HA
...BUT NOT IN THE SEVENTH.
I HATE THOSE MAY-JUNE RELATIONSHIPS.

HI, MRS. CZERWICKI.
OH, DEAR. DETENTION, NATE? ON THE SECOND DAY OF SCHOOL?
ET
SE
YEAH, BUT I'M BEING **RAILROADED**! THIS IS A TOTAL MIS-CARRIAGE OF JUSTICE!
SIGH LET ME SEE YOUR SLIP.
THIS SAYS YOU HIT COACH JOHN IN THE HEAD WITH A BRAN MUFFIN.
I DENY IT. THAT'S 100% WRONG.
IT WAS A **CORN** MUFFIN.
WELL, THEN, LET'S START THE APPEAL PROCESS.
Peirce

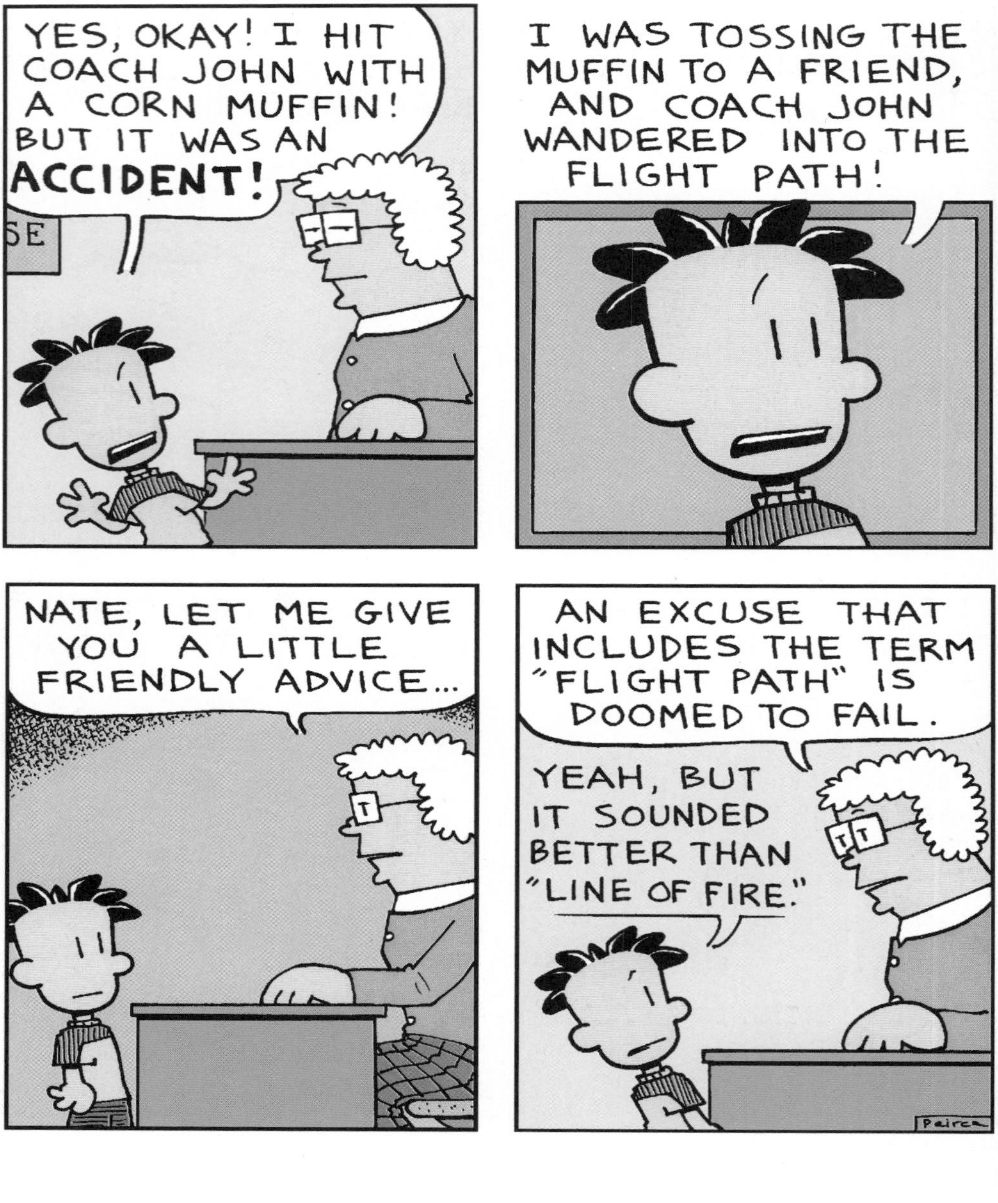
YES, OKAY! I HIT COACH JOHN WITH A CORN MUFFIN! BUT IT WAS AN **ACCIDENT!**
SE
I WAS TOSSING THE MUFFIN TO A FRIEND, AND COACH JOHN WANDERED INTO THE FLIGHT PATH!
NATE, LET ME GIVE YOU A LITTLE FRIENDLY ADVICE...
AN EXCUSE THAT INCLUDES THE TERM "FLIGHT PATH" IS DOOMED TO FAIL.
YEAH, BUT IT SOUNDED BETTER THAN "LINE OF FIRE."
Peirce

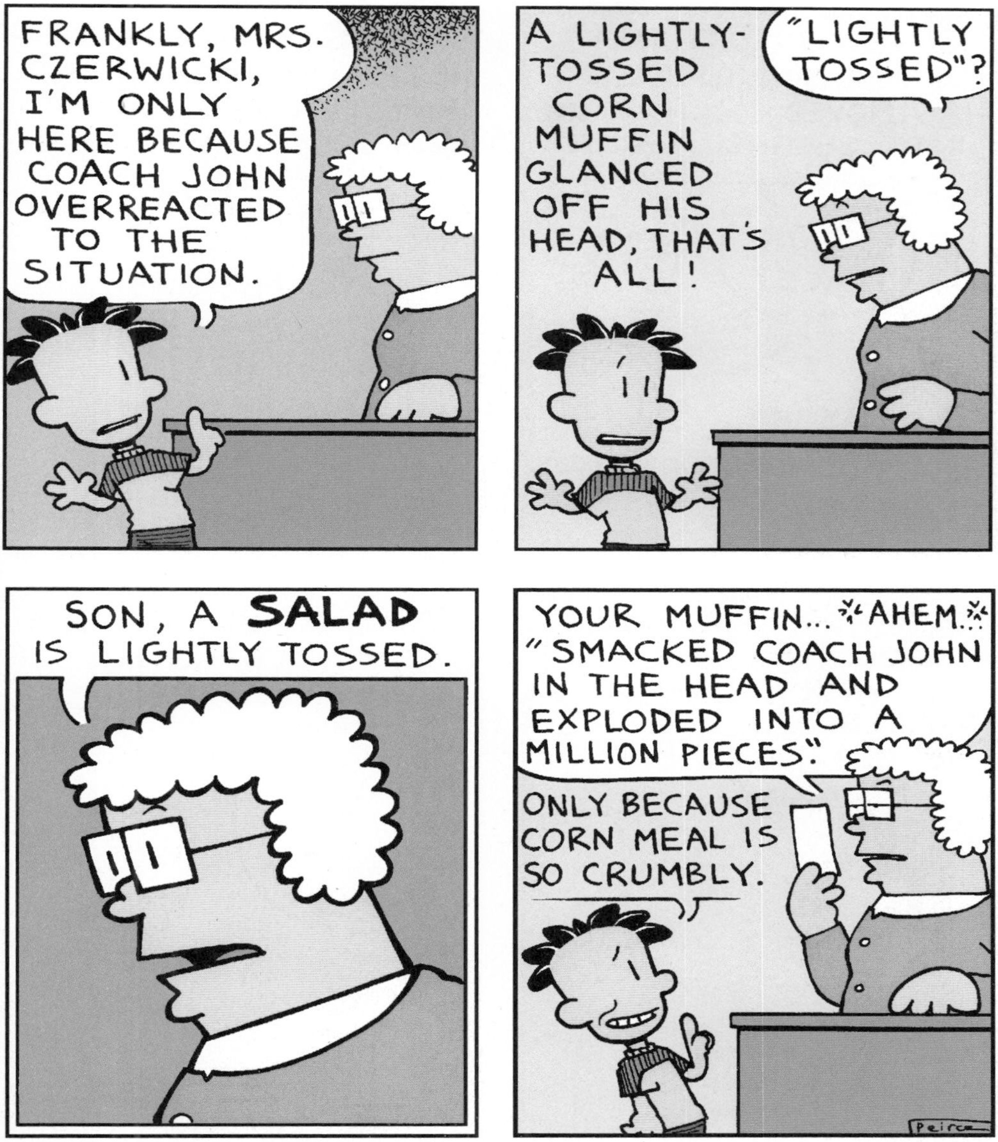
FRANKLY, MRS. CZERWICKI, I'M ONLY HERE BECAUSE COACH JOHN OVERREACTED TO THE SITUATION.
A LIGHTLY-TOSSED CORN MUFFIN GLANCED OFF HIS HEAD, THAT'S ALL!
"LIGHTLY TOSSED"?
SON, A **SALAD** IS LIGHTLY TOSSED.
YOUR MUFFIN... *AHEM.* "SMACKED COACH JOHN IN THE HEAD AND EXPLODED INTO A MILLION PIECES."
ONLY BECAUSE CORN MEAL IS SO CRUMBLY.
Peirce

THIS UNFORTUNATE CORN MUFFIN INCIDENT HAS MOVED COACH JOHN INTO SECOND PLACE.

SECOND PLACE?

HE'S GIVEN ME DETENTION MORE THAN ANY TEACHER EXCEPT MRS. GODFREY! SHE'S IN FIRST, HE'S IN SECOND!

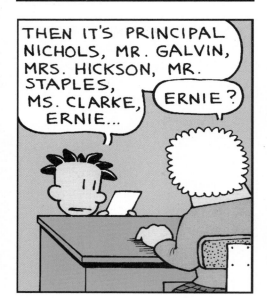

THEN IT'S PRINCIPAL NICHOLS, MR. GALVIN, MRS. HICKSON, MR. STAPLES, MS. CLARKE, ERNIE...

ERNIE?

NATE, ERNIE IS THE **COPY MACHINE REPAIRMAN!**

RIGHT. SO OBVIOUSLY HE'S GOT NO PEOPLE SKILLS.

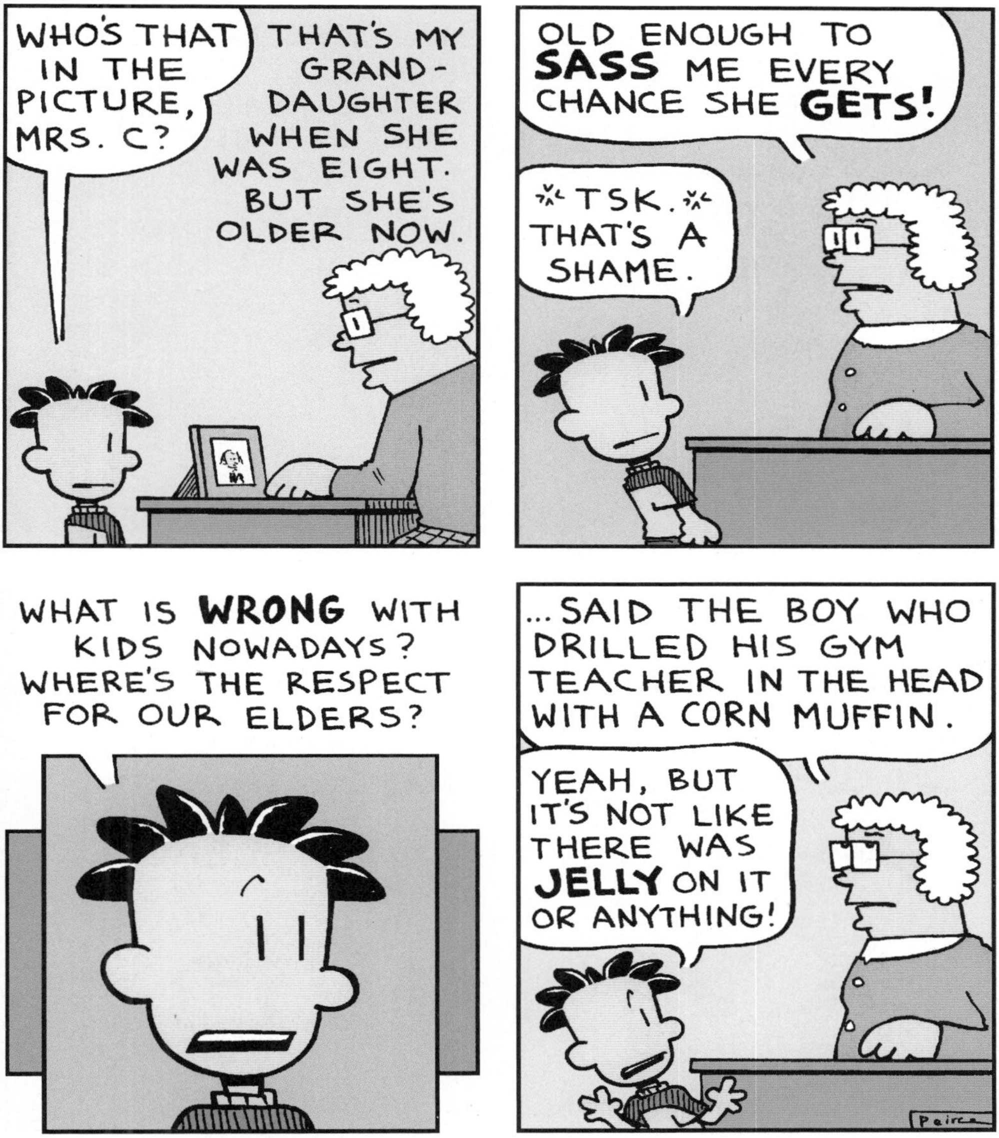
WHO'S THAT IN THE PICTURE, MRS. C?
THAT'S MY GRAND-DAUGHTER WHEN SHE WAS EIGHT. BUT SHE'S OLDER NOW.
OLD ENOUGH TO **SASS** ME EVERY CHANCE SHE **GETS!**
TSK. THAT'S A SHAME.
WHAT IS **WRONG** WITH KIDS NOWADAYS? WHERE'S THE RESPECT FOR OUR ELDERS?
...SAID THE BOY WHO DRILLED HIS GYM TEACHER IN THE HEAD WITH A CORN MUFFIN.
YEAH, BUT IT'S NOT LIKE THERE WAS **JELLY** ON IT OR ANYTHING!
Peirce

MRS. CZERWICKI! HALLO!
WHA-? ARTUR!
HA! WHO WOULDA THUNK IT? WELCOME TO THE REAL WORLD, ARTUR! WHAT DID YOU DO?
WHAT I DID DO?
TO END UP IN DETENTION! WHY ARE YOU HERE?
AH! TO GIVE TO MRS. CZERWICKI A TASTY HOMEMADE COOKIE!
OF COURSE YOU ARE.
BUT INSTEAD OF STAY HERE WITH YOU, I NOW CAN LEAVE!
Peirce

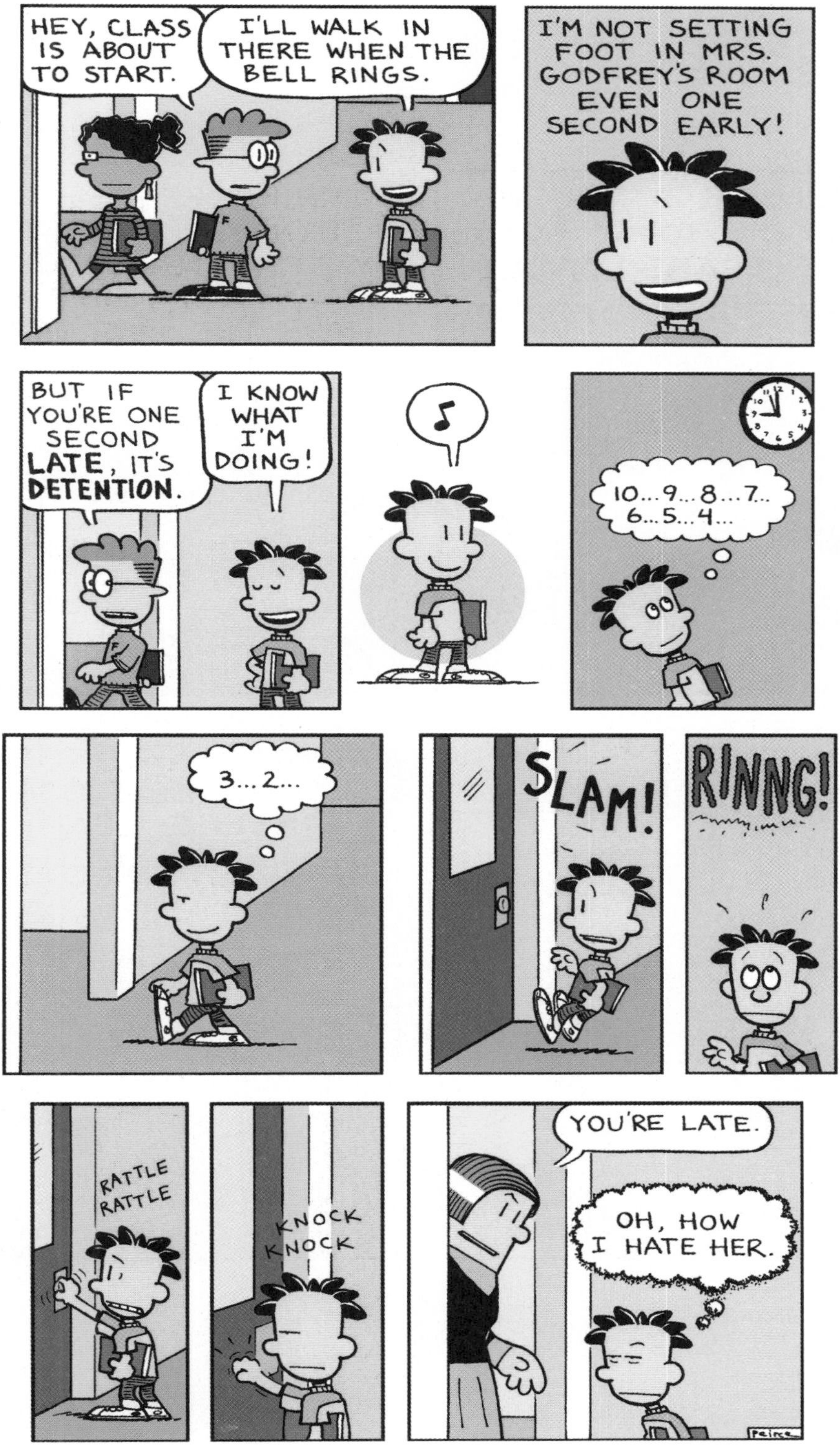
HEY, CLASS IS ABOUT TO START.
I'LL WALK IN THERE WHEN THE BELL RINGS.
I'M NOT SETTING FOOT IN MRS. GODFREY'S ROOM EVEN ONE SECOND EARLY!
BUT IF YOU'RE ONE SECOND LATE, IT'S DETENTION.
I KNOW WHAT I'M DOING!
10... 9... 8... 7... 6... 5... 4...
3... 2...
SLAM!
RINNG!
RATTLE RATTLE
KNOCK KNOCK
YOU'RE LATE.
OH, HOW I HATE HER.
peirce

COULD BE A TOUGH MATCHUP TODAY, BOYS. THIS TEAM'S **LOADED.**

THEIR OFFENSE IS DYNAMIC, THEIR MIDFIELDERS ARE VERY FAST, AND THEY HAVE THE BEST GOALIE IN THE —

THEY HAVE THE SECOND BEST GOALIE IN THE LEAGUE.

THAT'S WHAT I'M TALKIN' ABOUT.

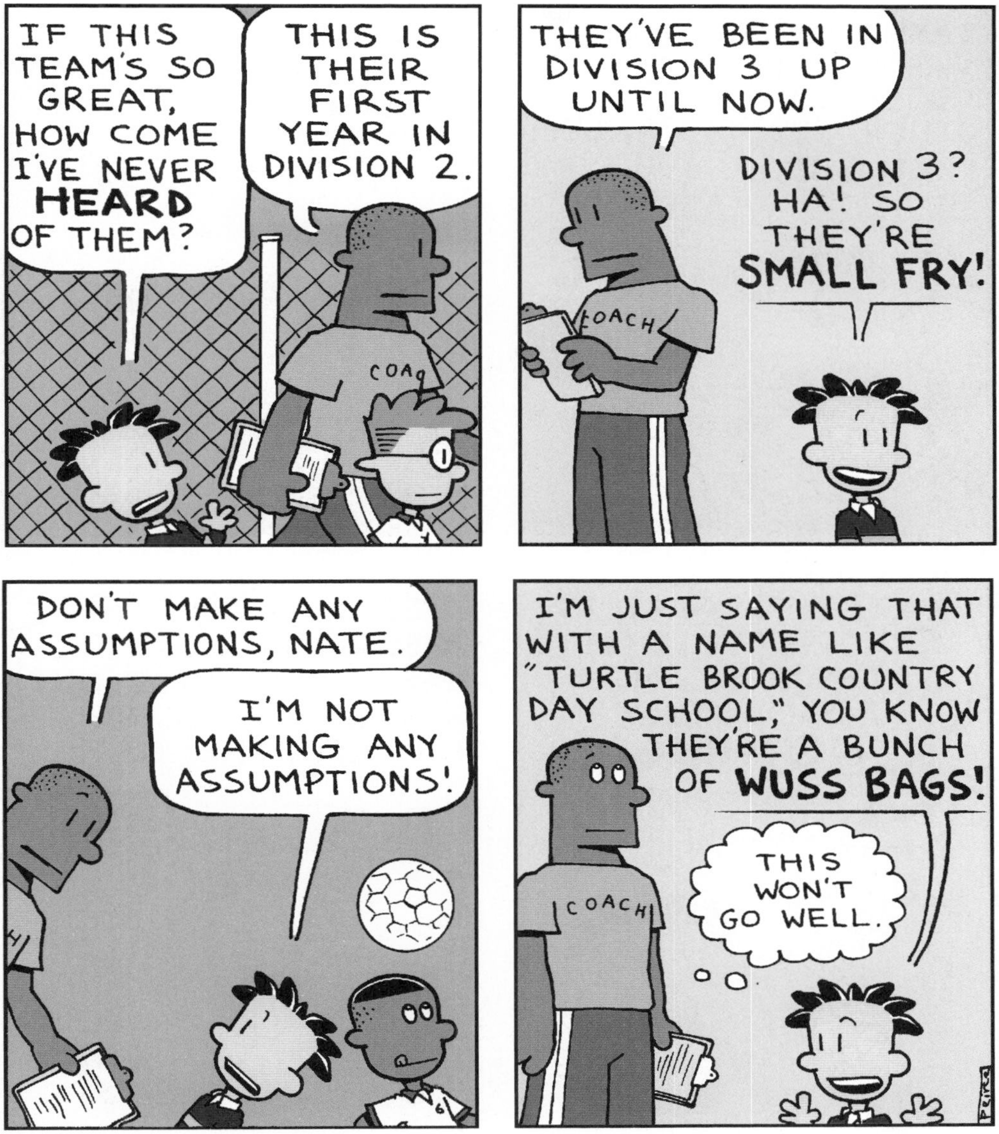
IF THIS TEAM'S SO GREAT, HOW COME I'VE NEVER **HEARD** OF THEM?
THIS IS THEIR FIRST YEAR IN DIVISION 2.
COAC
THEY'VE BEEN IN DIVISION 3 UP UNTIL NOW.
DIVISION 3? HA! SO THEY'RE **SMALL FRY!**
COACH
DON'T MAKE ANY ASSUMPTIONS, NATE.
I'M NOT MAKING ANY ASSUMPTIONS!
I'M JUST SAYING THAT WITH A NAME LIKE "TURTLE BROOK COUNTRY DAY SCHOOL," YOU KNOW THEY'RE A BUNCH OF **WUSS BAGS!**
THIS WON'T GO WELL.
COACH
PEIRCE

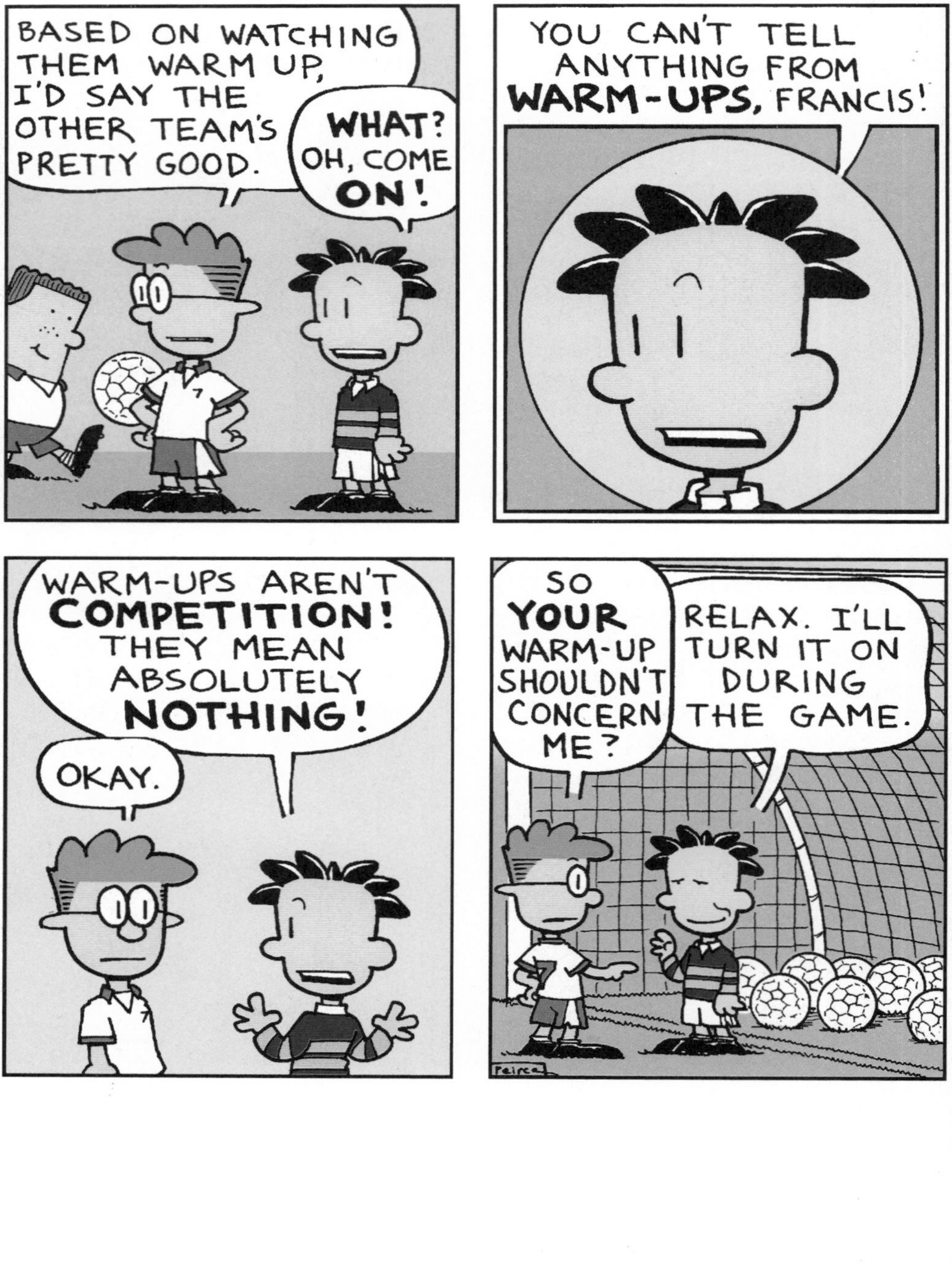
BASED ON WATCHING THEM WARM UP, I'D SAY THE OTHER TEAM'S PRETTY GOOD.
WHAT? OH, COME ON!
YOU CAN'T TELL ANYTHING FROM WARM-UPS, FRANCIS!
WARM-UPS AREN'T COMPETITION! THEY MEAN ABSOLUTELY NOTHING!
OKAY.
SO YOUR WARM-UP SHOULDN'T CONCERN ME?
RELAX. I'LL TURN IT ON DURING THE GAME.
Peirce

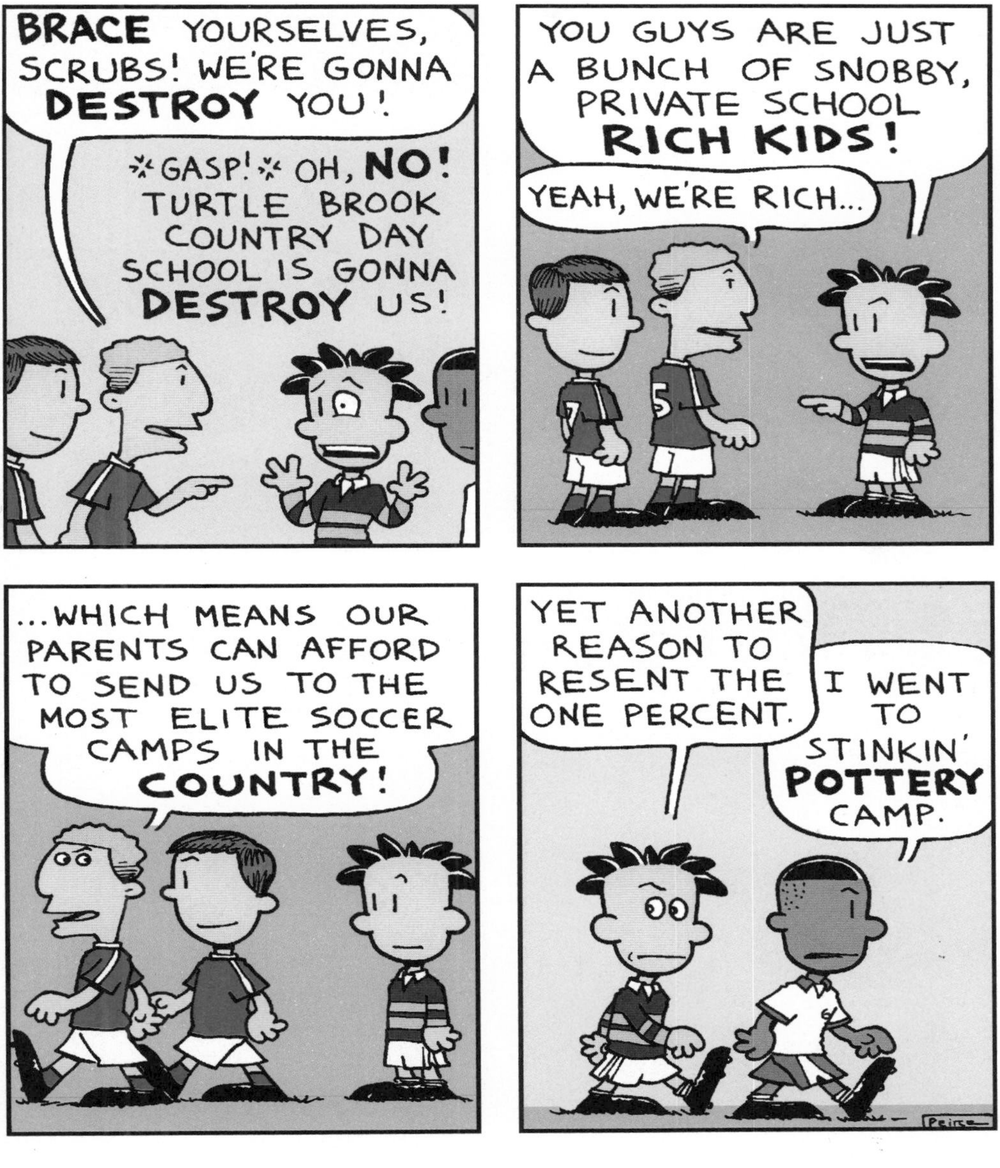
BRACE YOURSELVES, SCRUBS! WE'RE GONNA DESTROY YOU!
GASP! OH, NO! TURTLE BROOK COUNTRY DAY SCHOOL IS GONNA DESTROY US!
YOU GUYS ARE JUST A BUNCH OF SNOBBY, PRIVATE SCHOOL RICH KIDS!
YEAH, WE'RE RICH...
...WHICH MEANS OUR PARENTS CAN AFFORD TO SEND US TO THE MOST ELITE SOCCER CAMPS IN THE COUNTRY!
YET ANOTHER REASON TO RESENT THE ONE PERCENT.
I WENT TO STINKIN' POTTERY CAMP.
Peirce

30:00
BUMP
29:59... 29:58... 29:57...
29:56... 29:55... 29:54...
29:53... 29:52... 29:51...
29:50... 29:49... 29:48...
DOOF!
AT THIS RATE, THEY'RE GOING TO BEAT US, 300 TO 0.
DON'T TELL ME THE MATH.
Peirce

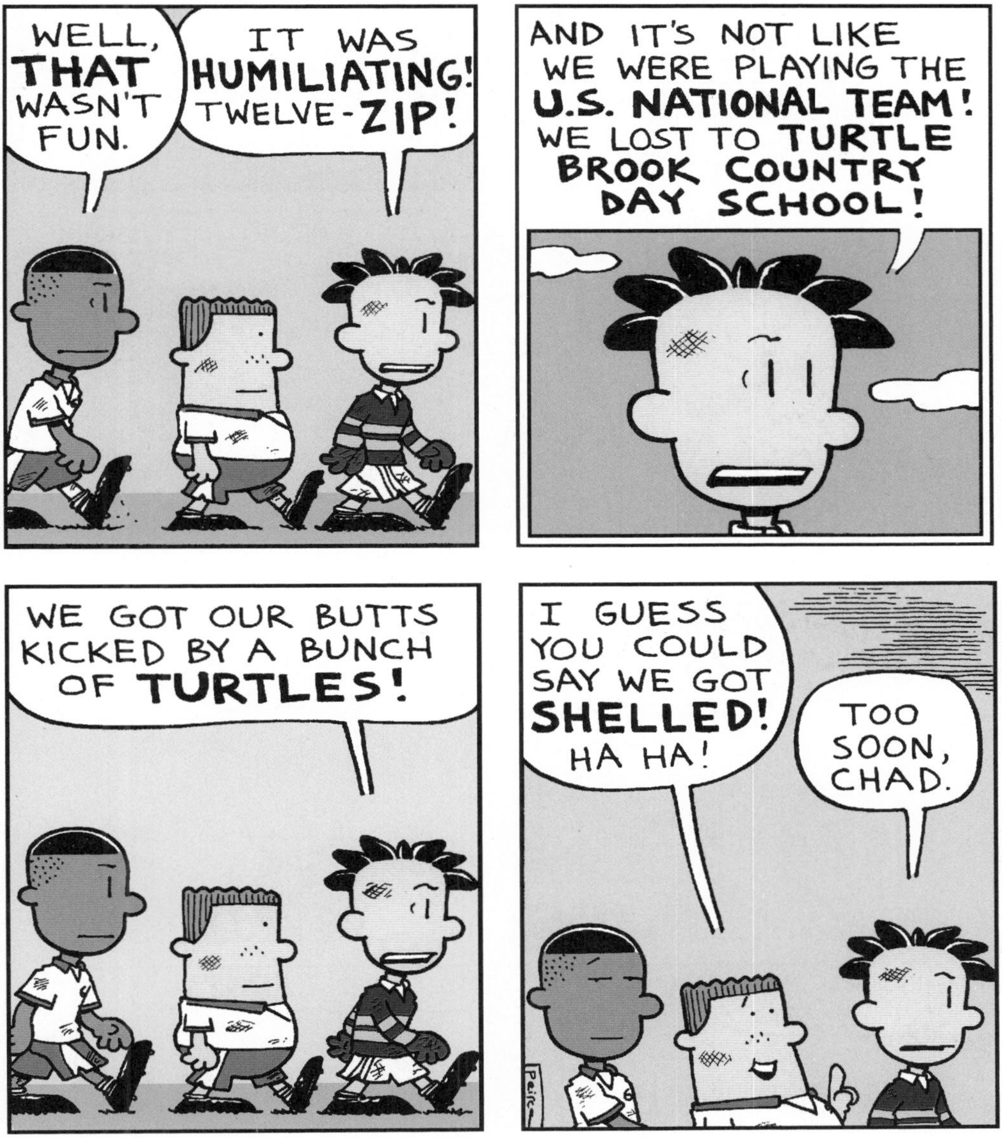
WELL, THAT WASN'T FUN.
IT WAS HUMILIATING! TWELVE-ZIP!
AND IT'S NOT LIKE WE WERE PLAYING THE U.S. NATIONAL TEAM! WE LOST TO TURTLE BROOK COUNTRY DAY SCHOOL!
WE GOT OUR BUTTS KICKED BY A BUNCH OF TURTLES!
I GUESS YOU COULD SAY WE GOT SHELLED! HA HA!
TOO SOON, CHAD.
Peirce

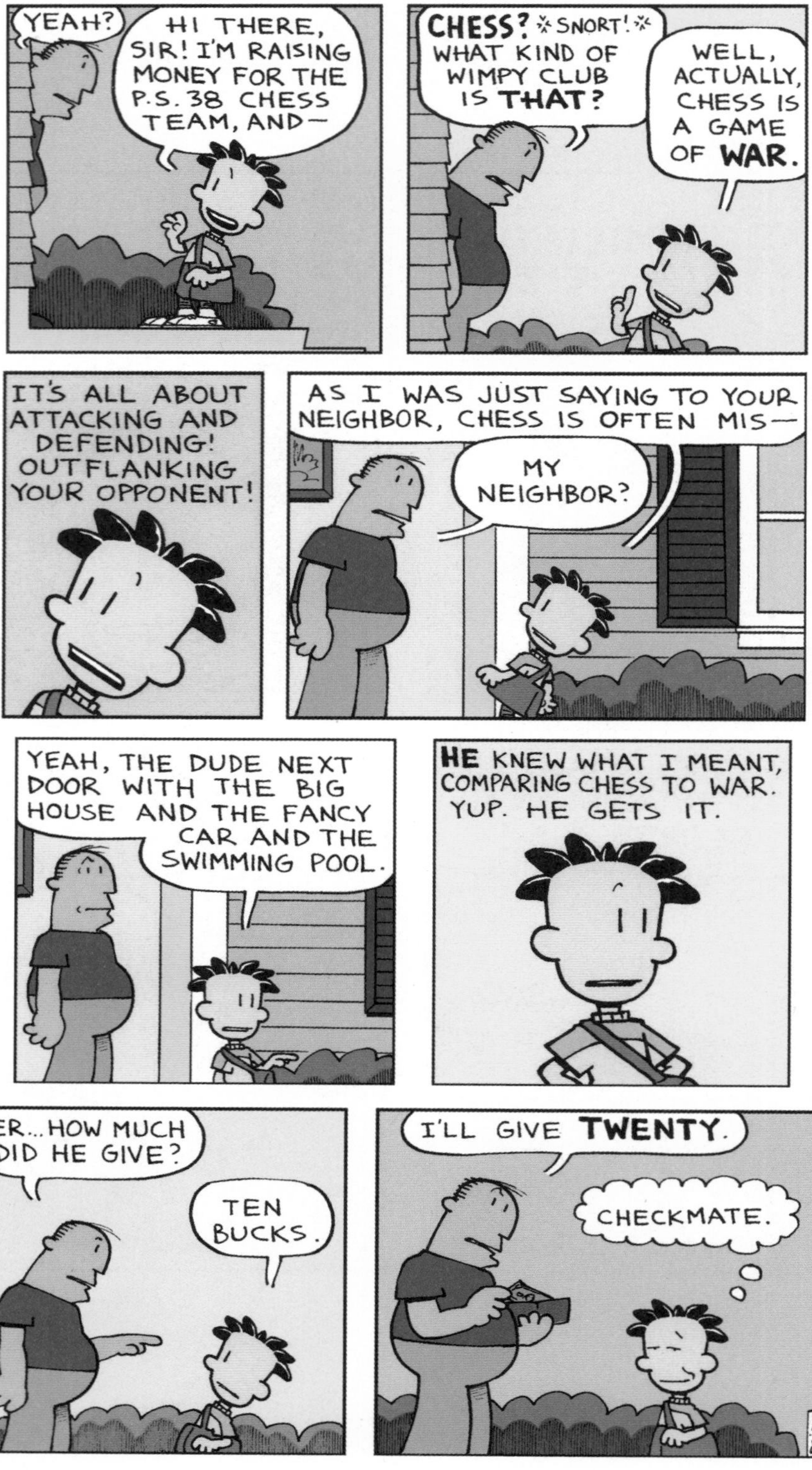
YEAH?
HI THERE, SIR! I'M RAISING MONEY FOR THE P.S. 38 CHESS TEAM, AND—
CHESS? *SNORT!* WHAT KIND OF WIMPY CLUB IS THAT?
WELL, ACTUALLY, CHESS IS A GAME OF WAR.
IT'S ALL ABOUT ATTACKING AND DEFENDING! OUTFLANKING YOUR OPPONENT!
AS I WAS JUST SAYING TO YOUR NEIGHBOR, CHESS IS OFTEN MIS—
MY NEIGHBOR?
YEAH, THE DUDE NEXT DOOR WITH THE BIG HOUSE AND THE FANCY CAR AND THE SWIMMING POOL.
HE KNEW WHAT I MEANT, COMPARING CHESS TO WAR. YUP. HE GETS IT.
ER... HOW MUCH DID HE GIVE?
TEN BUCKS.
I'LL GIVE TWENTY.
CHECKMATE.
Peirce

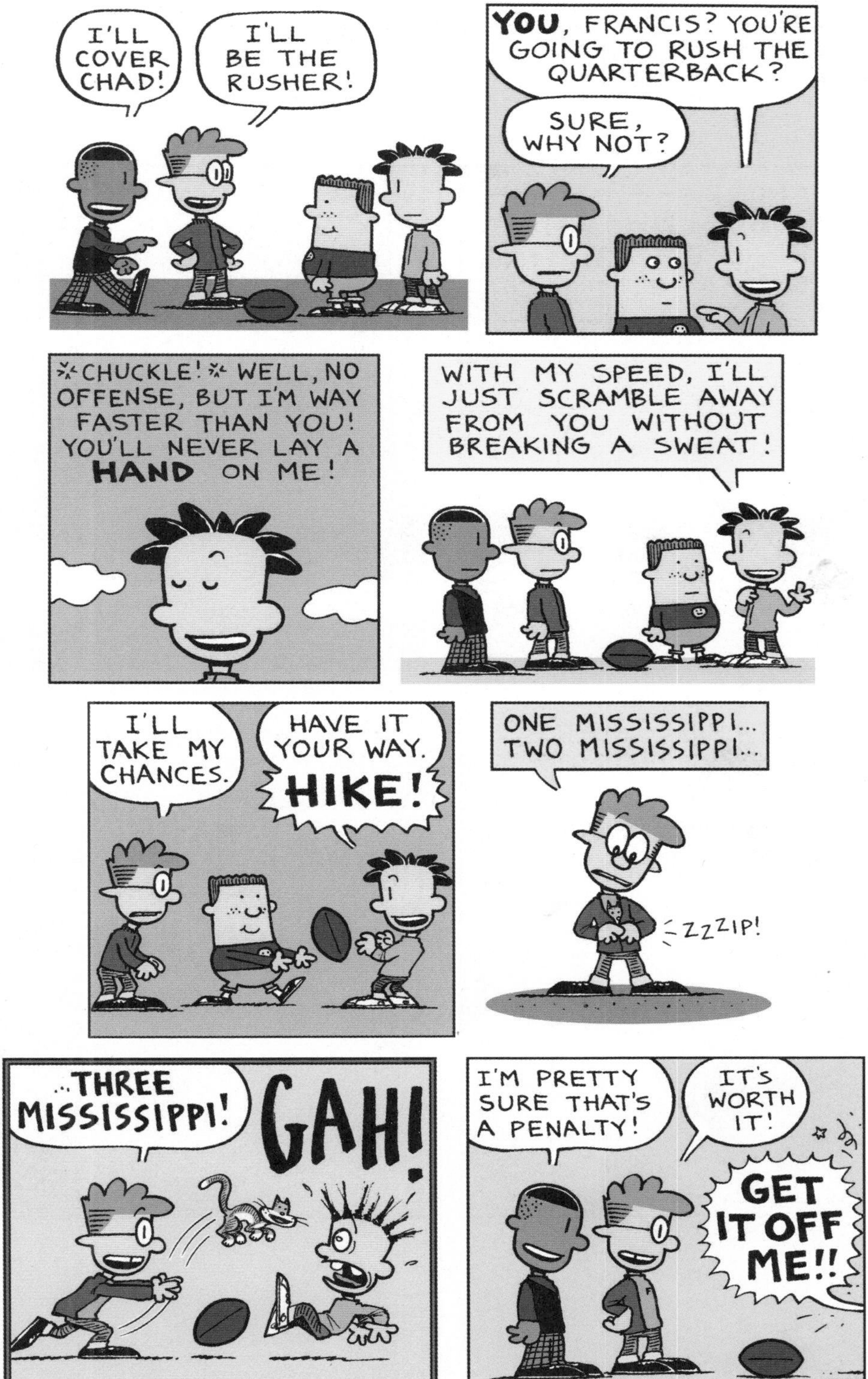
I'LL COVER CHAD!
I'LL BE THE RUSHER!
YOU, FRANCIS? YOU'RE GOING TO RUSH THE QUARTERBACK?
SURE, WHY NOT?
CHUCKLE! WELL, NO OFFENSE, BUT I'M WAY FASTER THAN YOU! YOU'LL NEVER LAY A HAND ON ME!
WITH MY SPEED, I'LL JUST SCRAMBLE AWAY FROM YOU WITHOUT BREAKING A SWEAT!
I'LL TAKE MY CHANCES.
HAVE IT YOUR WAY.
HIKE!
ONE MISSISSIPPI... TWO MISSISSIPPI...
ZZZIP!
...THREE MISSISSIPPI!
GAH!
I'M PRETTY SURE THAT'S A PENALTY!
IT'S WORTH IT!
GET IT OFF ME!!

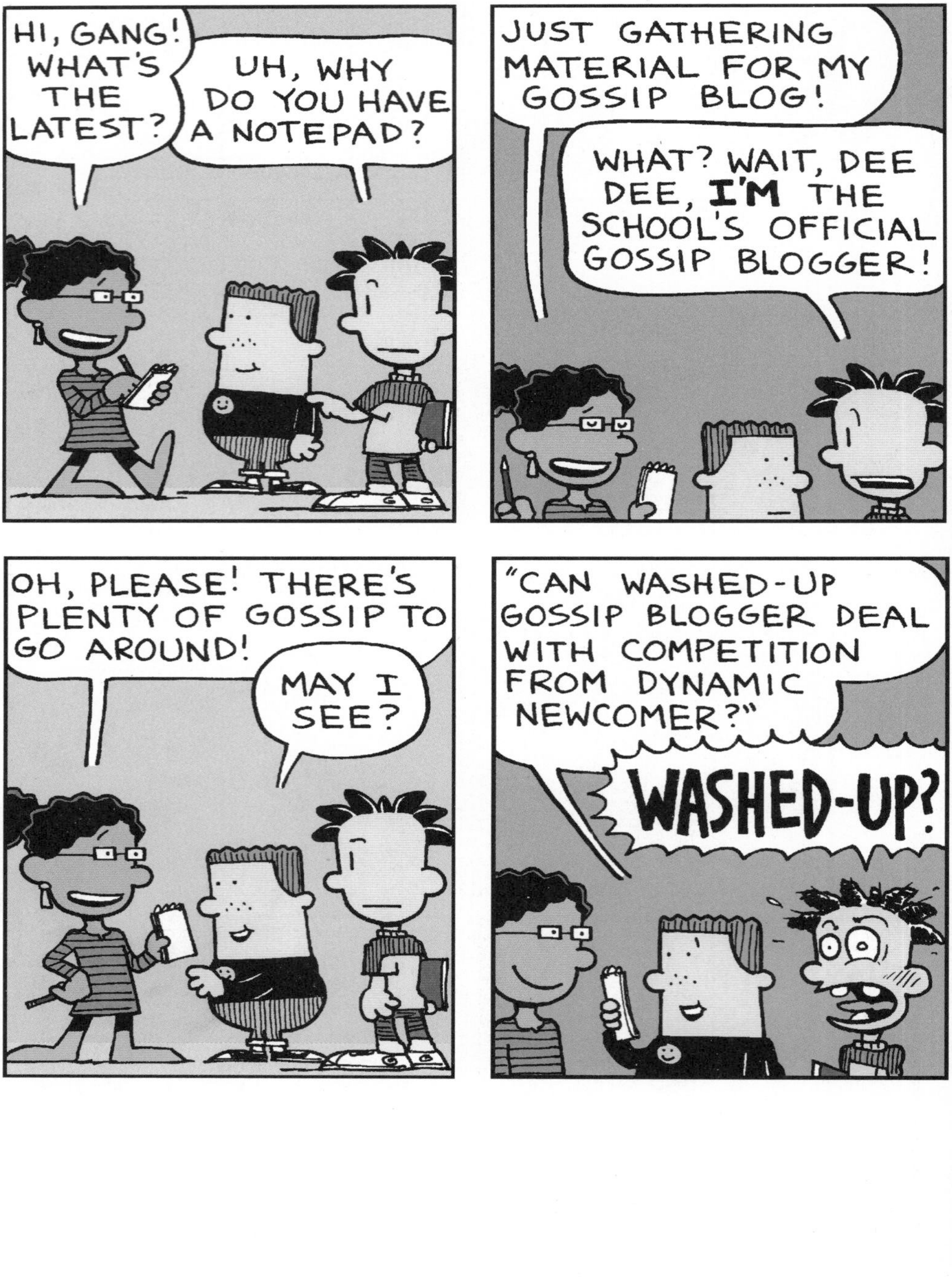
HI, GANG! WHAT'S THE LATEST?
UH, WHY DO YOU HAVE A NOTEPAD?
JUST GATHERING MATERIAL FOR MY GOSSIP BLOG!
WHAT? WAIT, DEE DEE, I'M THE SCHOOL'S OFFICIAL GOSSIP BLOGGER!
OH, PLEASE! THERE'S PLENTY OF GOSSIP TO GO AROUND!
MAY I SEE?
"CAN WASHED-UP GOSSIP BLOGGER DEAL WITH COMPETITION FROM DYNAMIC NEWCOMER?"
WASHED-UP?

DEE DEE, WHAT **GIVES**? HOW COME YOU STARTED A **GOSSIP BLOG**?
BECAUSE I LOVE GOSSIP! I LOVE BEING PLUGGED IN!
BUT I'M **ALREADY** PLUGGED IN! I'VE BEEN WRITING "CLASSROOM CHATTER" SINCE—
NATE, "CLASSROOM CHATTER" IS **TIRED**!
IT IS **NOT**! I'M STILL BRINGIN' MY "A" GAME!
OH, **REALLY**? SHALL WE TAKE A LOOK AT YOUR LATEST ENTRY?
"CHAD IS THINKING OF CHANGING HIS FAVORITE COLOR FROM PURPLE TO BLUE."
ACTUALLY, I'VE DECIDED TO GO WITH SEA FOAM!

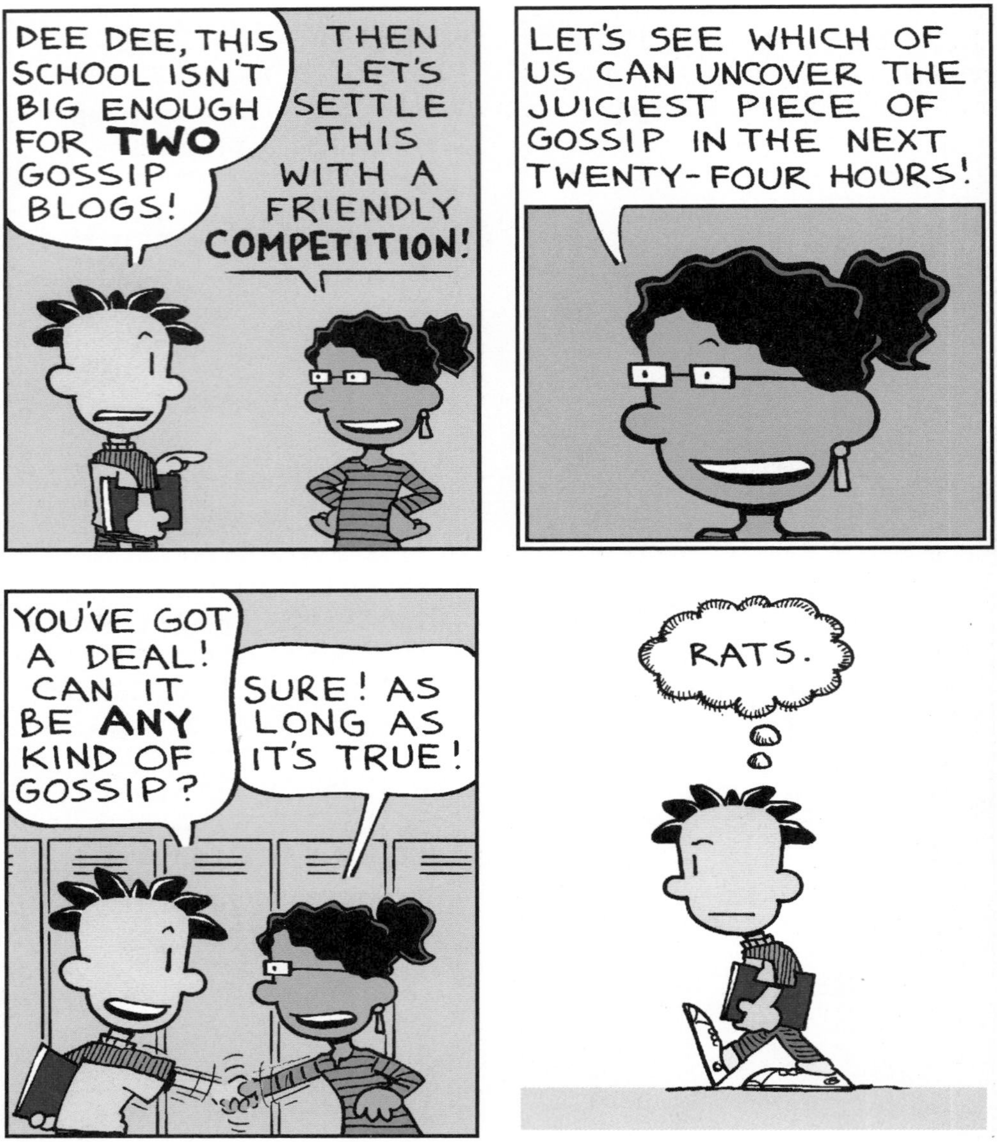
DEE DEE, THIS SCHOOL ISN'T BIG ENOUGH FOR **TWO** GOSSIP BLOGS!
THEN LET'S SETTLE THIS WITH A FRIENDLY **COMPETITION**!
LET'S SEE WHICH OF US CAN UNCOVER THE JUICIEST PIECE OF GOSSIP IN THE NEXT TWENTY-FOUR HOURS!
YOU'VE GOT A DEAL! CAN IT BE **ANY** KIND OF GOSSIP?
SURE! AS LONG AS IT'S TRUE!
RATS.

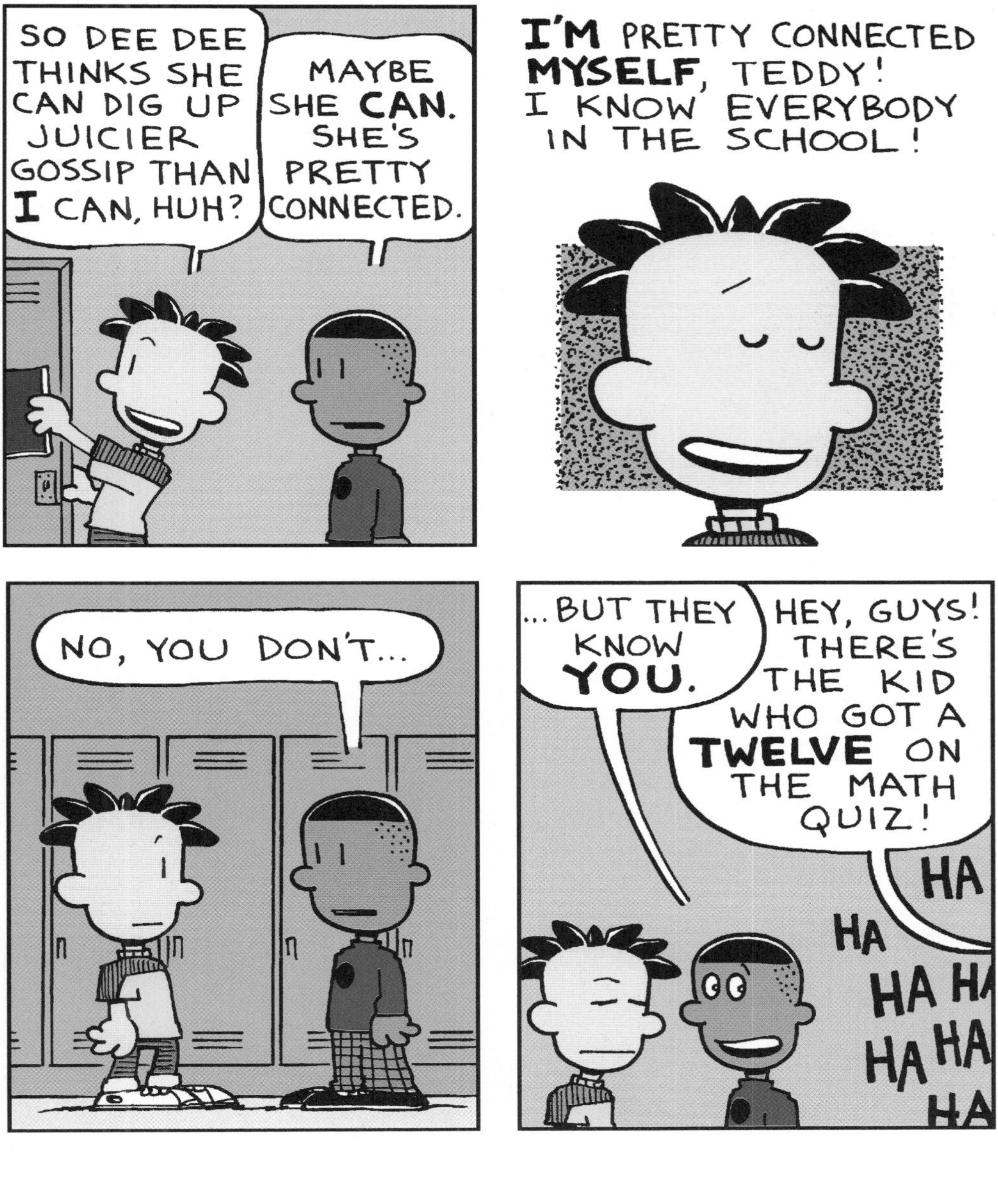
SO DEE DEE THINKS SHE CAN DIG UP JUICIER GOSSIP THAN I CAN, HUH?
MAYBE SHE CAN. SHE'S PRETTY CONNECTED.
I'M PRETTY CONNECTED MYSELF, TEDDY! I KNOW EVERYBODY IN THE SCHOOL!
NO, YOU DON'T...
...BUT THEY KNOW YOU.
HEY, GUYS! THERE'S THE KID WHO GOT A TWELVE ON THE MATH QUIZ!
HA HA HA HA HA HA HA

DEE DEE'S TALKING TO **EVERYONE**, NATE. SHE'S PROBABLY COLLECTING TONS OF GOOD GOSSIP.

DO I LOOK WORRIED? NO.

IT'S **QUALITY**, NOT **QUANTITY!** I DON'T NEED TO TALK TO A ZILLION PEOPLE TO GET GOSSIP! I JUST NEED TO TALK TO **ONE**: STEVE THE JANITOR!

HE KNOWS **EVERYTHING!** HE'S AN UNIMPEACHABLE SOURCE! HE'S MY SECRET WEAPON!... HE'S MY TRUSTIEST INFORMANT!...

HE RETIRED LAST SPRING.

HE'S MY— WAIT, WHAT?

YOU'RE NOT VERY GOOD AT THIS.

HOW ARE YOU GOING TO BEAT DEE DEE IN THE GOSSIP WARS?
BY GOING TO SEE MRS. SHIPULSKI!
SHE'S THE SCHOOL SECRETARY! NOTHING HAPPENS AROUND HERE WITHOUT HER KNOWING ABOUT IT!
Join
AND **NOBODY** CAN GET HER TALKING LIKE **I** CAN!
NOBODY?

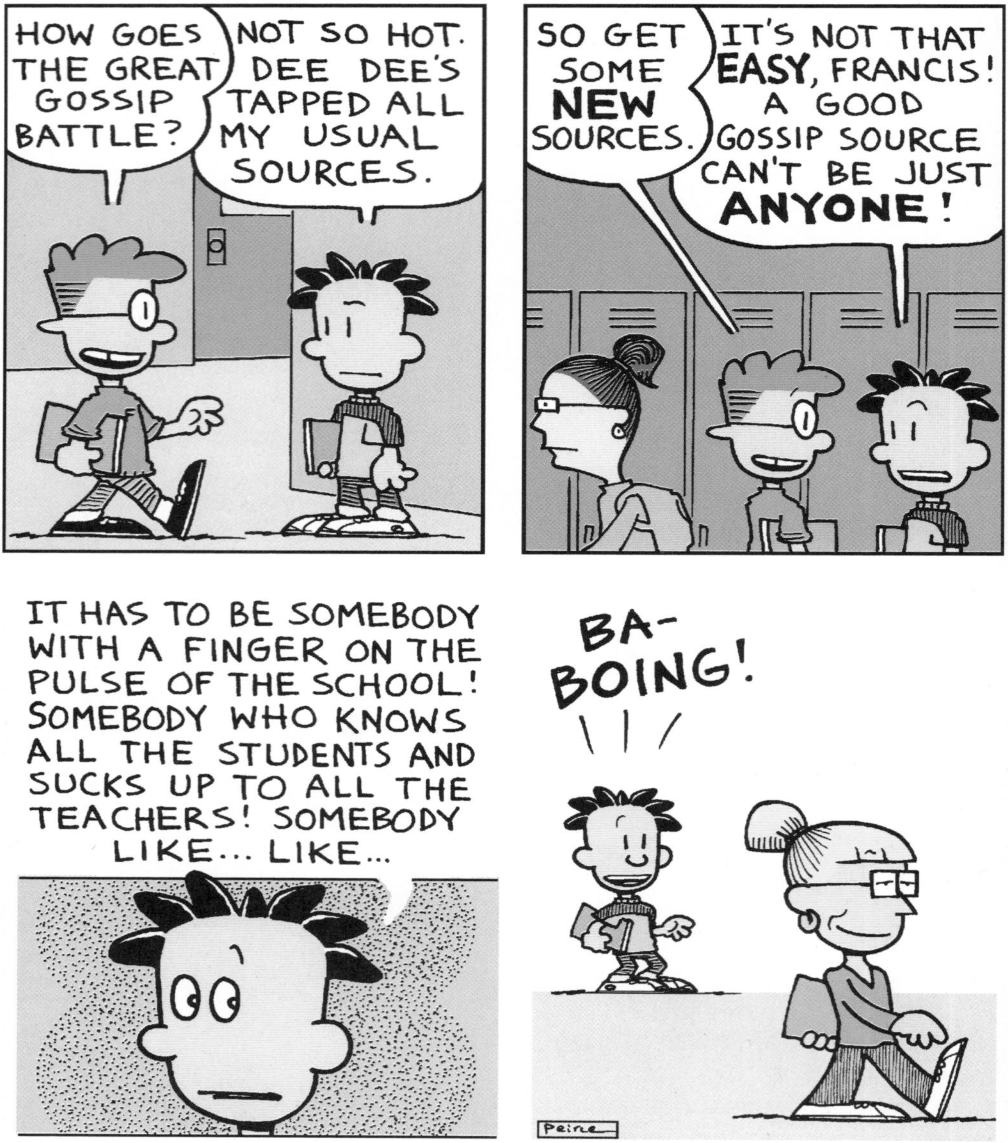
HOW GOES THE GREAT GOSSIP BATTLE?
NOT SO HOT. DEE DEE'S TAPPED ALL MY USUAL SOURCES.
SO GET SOME **NEW** SOURCES.
IT'S NOT THAT **EASY**, FRANCIS! A GOOD GOSSIP SOURCE CAN'T BE JUST **ANYONE**!
IT HAS TO BE SOMEBODY WITH A FINGER ON THE PULSE OF THE SCHOOL! SOMEBODY WHO KNOWS ALL THE STUDENTS AND SUCKS UP TO ALL THE TEACHERS! SOMEBODY LIKE... LIKE...
BA-BOING!
Peirce

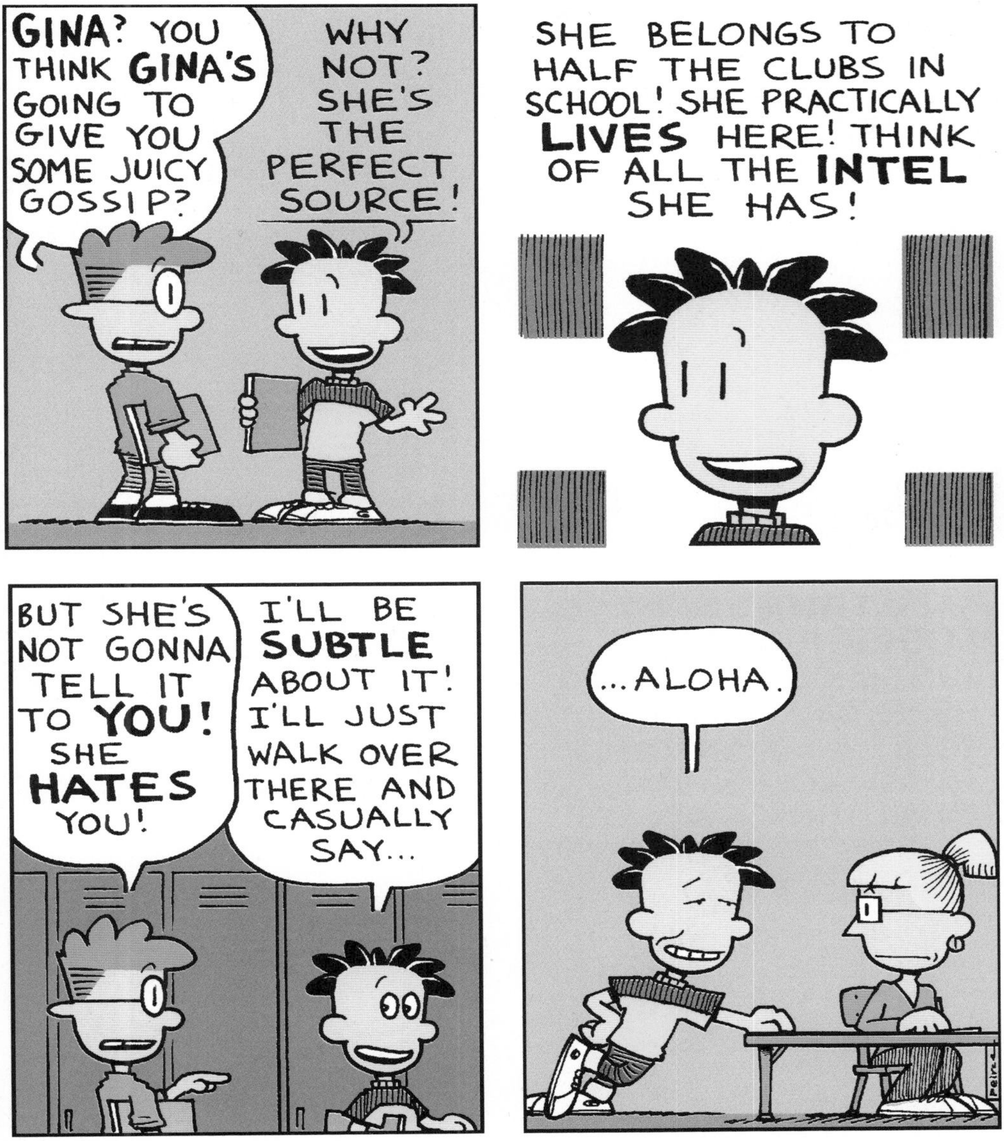
GINA? YOU THINK GINA'S GOING TO GIVE YOU SOME JUICY GOSSIP?
WHY NOT? SHE'S THE PERFECT SOURCE!
SHE BELONGS TO HALF THE CLUBS IN SCHOOL! SHE PRACTICALLY LIVES HERE! THINK OF ALL THE INTEL SHE HAS!
BUT SHE'S NOT GONNA TELL IT TO YOU! SHE HATES YOU!
I'LL BE SUBTLE ABOUT IT! I'LL JUST WALK OVER THERE AND CASUALLY SAY...
...ALOHA.

MIND IF I SIT HERE?
WHY WOULD YOU AND I WANT TO SIT TOGETHER?
TO GET CAUGHT UP! THE TWO OF US DON'T CHAT ANYMORE!
"ANYMORE"? WE'VE NEVER CHATTED! WE HAVE NOTHING TO SAY TO EACH OTHER!
GINA, GINA! WHY SO SUSPICIOUS? I'M JUST INTERESTED TO HEAR WHAT'S NEW WITH YOU!... AND ANYONE ELSE YOU KNOW SOMETHING ABOUT!
BEEP!
ARE YOU RECORDING ME?
NOT RECORDING! PRESERVING FOR POSTERITY!
peirce

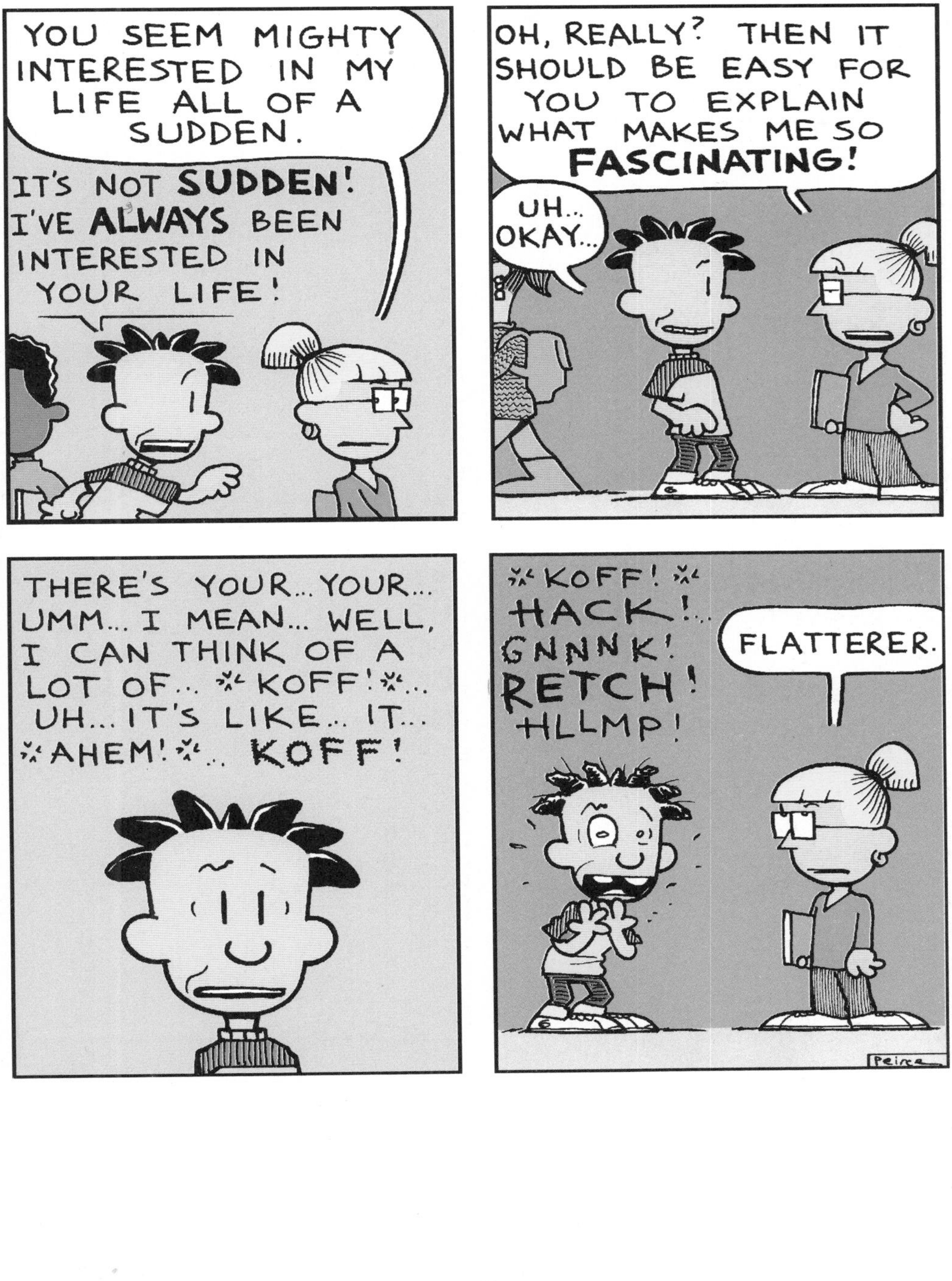
YOU SEEM MIGHTY INTERESTED IN MY LIFE ALL OF A SUDDEN.
IT'S NOT SUDDEN! I'VE ALWAYS BEEN INTERESTED IN YOUR LIFE!
OH, REALLY? THEN IT SHOULD BE EASY FOR YOU TO EXPLAIN WHAT MAKES ME SO FASCINATING!
UH... OKAY...
THERE'S YOUR... YOUR... UMM... I MEAN... WELL, I CAN THINK OF A LOT OF... *KOFF!*... UH... IT'S LIKE... IT... *AHEM!*... KOFF!
KOFF! HACK!.. GNNNK! RETCH! HLLMP!
FLATTERER.
Peirce

DO YOU THINK I'M AN IDIOT, NATE? I KNOW ALL ABOUT YOUR LITTLE CONTEST WITH DEE DEE!
YOU'RE COMPETING TO SEE WHO CAN COME UP WITH THE JUICIEST GOSSIP! AND FOR SOME REASON, YOU WANT ME TO HELP YOU!
...WHICH I MIGHT CONSIDER...
...IF YOU BEG.
!
SAY HELLO TO ROCK BOTTOM.
LOWER.
Peirce

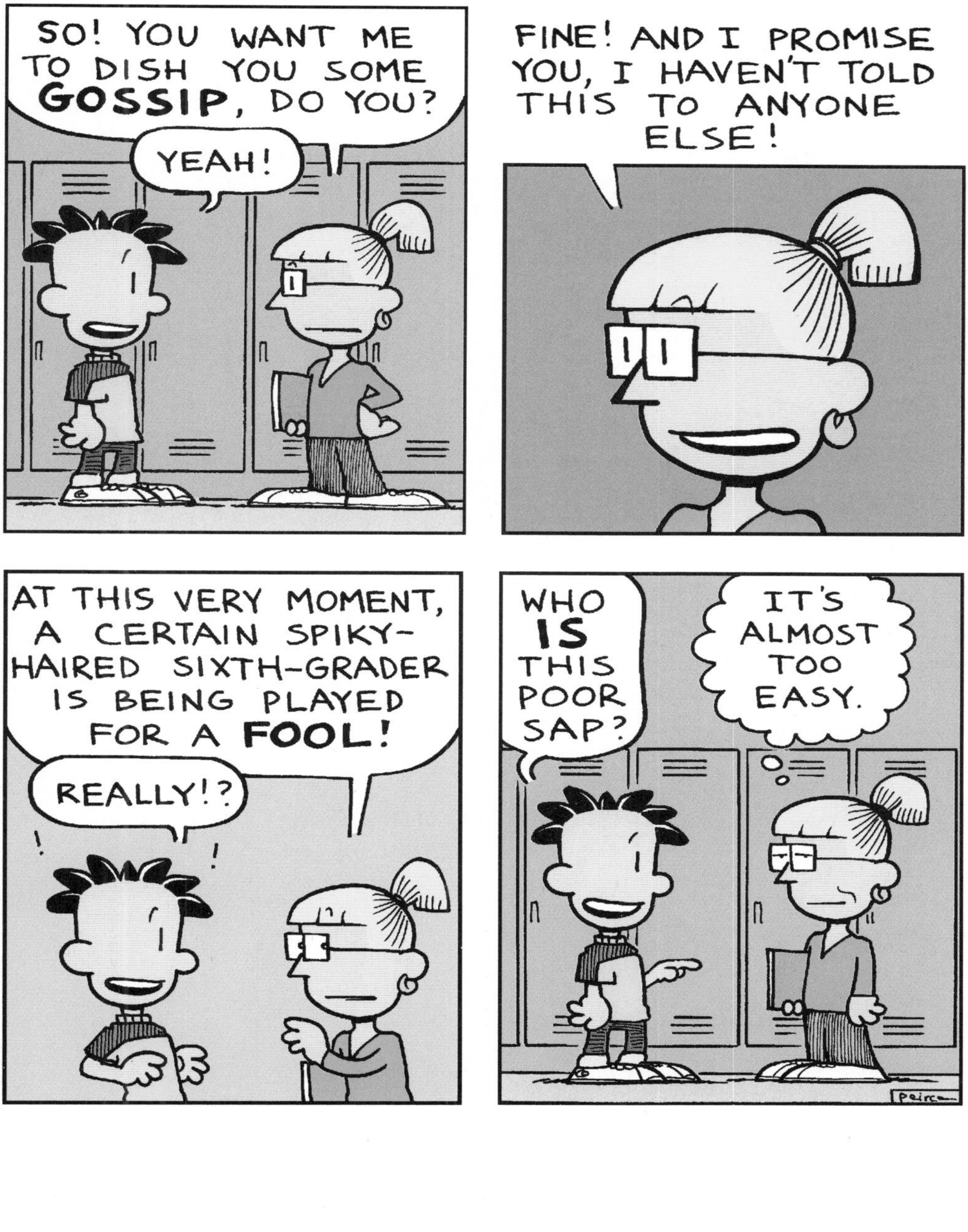
SO! YOU WANT ME TO DISH YOU SOME **GOSSIP**, DO YOU?
YEAH!
FINE! AND I PROMISE YOU, I HAVEN'T TOLD THIS TO ANYONE ELSE!
AT THIS VERY MOMENT, A CERTAIN SPIKY-HAIRED SIXTH-GRADER IS BEING PLAYED FOR A **FOOL**!
REALLY!?
! !
WHO **IS** THIS POOR SAP?
IT'S ALMOST TOO EASY.
Peirce

SO? DID GINA DISH YOU SOME DIRT?

✳ SNORT. ✳ NO.

I HAD 24 HOURS TO COME UP WITH BETTER GOSSIP THAN DEE DEE... **GAH!** AND I'VE ONLY GOT FIVE MINUTES LEFT!

ARTUR! DO YOU KNOW ANY JUICY GOSSIP?

OH, ABSOLUTE!

I AM ENJOY **MANY** KINDS OF JUICE! APPLE, ORANGE, GRAPEFRUIT...

I CAN'T TAKE IT.

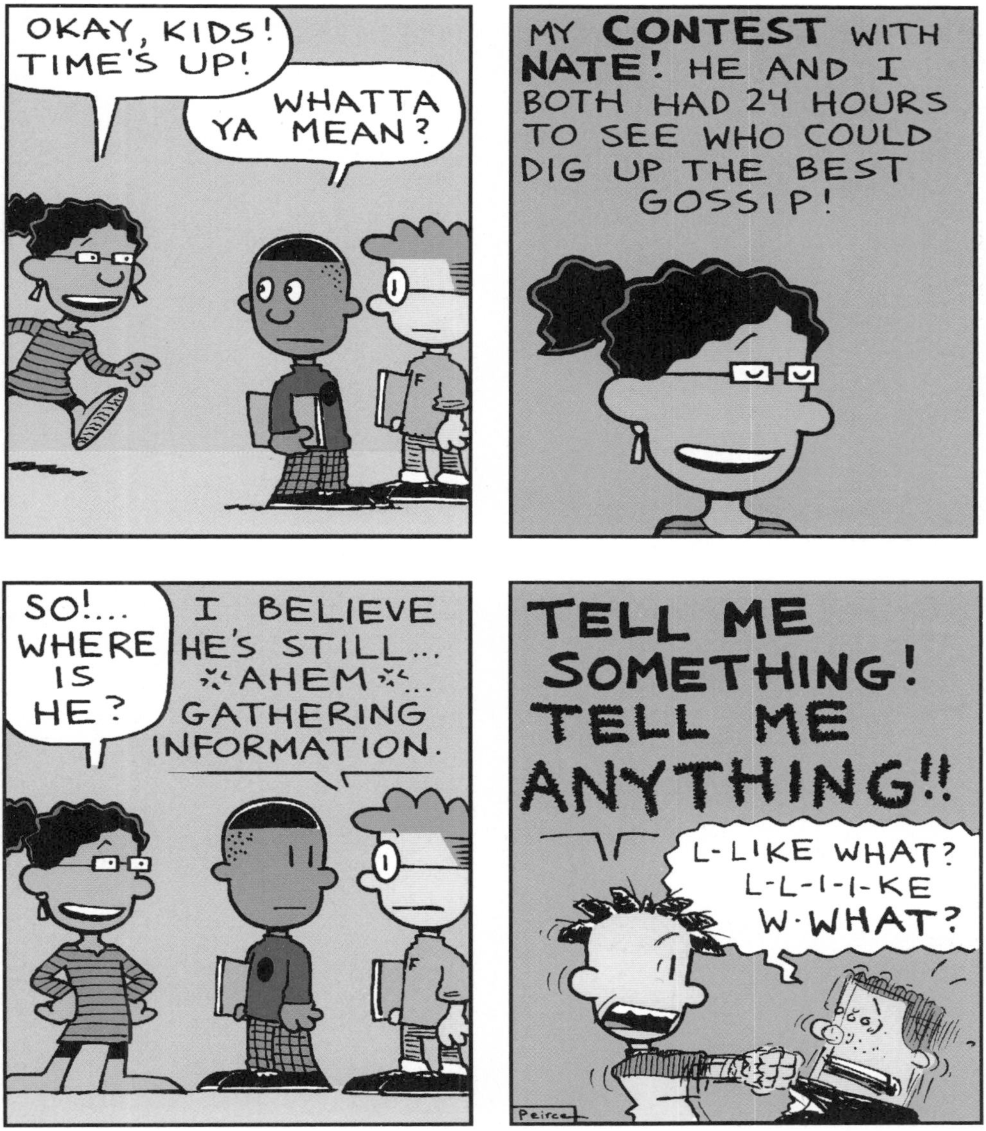
OKAY, KIDS! TIME'S UP!
WHATTA YA MEAN?
MY CONTEST WITH NATE! HE AND I BOTH HAD 24 HOURS TO SEE WHO COULD DIG UP THE BEST GOSSIP!
SO!... WHERE IS HE?
I BELIEVE HE'S STILL... AHEM... GATHERING INFORMATION.
TELL ME SOMETHING! TELL ME ANYTHING!!
L-LIKE WHAT? L-L-I-I-KE W-WHAT?
Peirce

AH, **THERE** YOU ARE! METHINKS YOU'VE BEEN **AVOIDING** ME!

I HAVE **NOT**.

THEN LET'S **HEAR** IT, NATE! WHAT'S THE BEST GOSSIP YOU DUG UP?

OKAY! HOLD ONTO YOUR HAT!

JONAH IS ABOUT TO BREAK UP WITH **MINDY**!

HE **ALREADY** BROKE UP WITH HER! HE'S WITH **AMBER** NOW!

IT'S TRUE. I AM.

YOU SNOOZE, YOU LOSE, GOSSIP BOY!

ARRRGH!

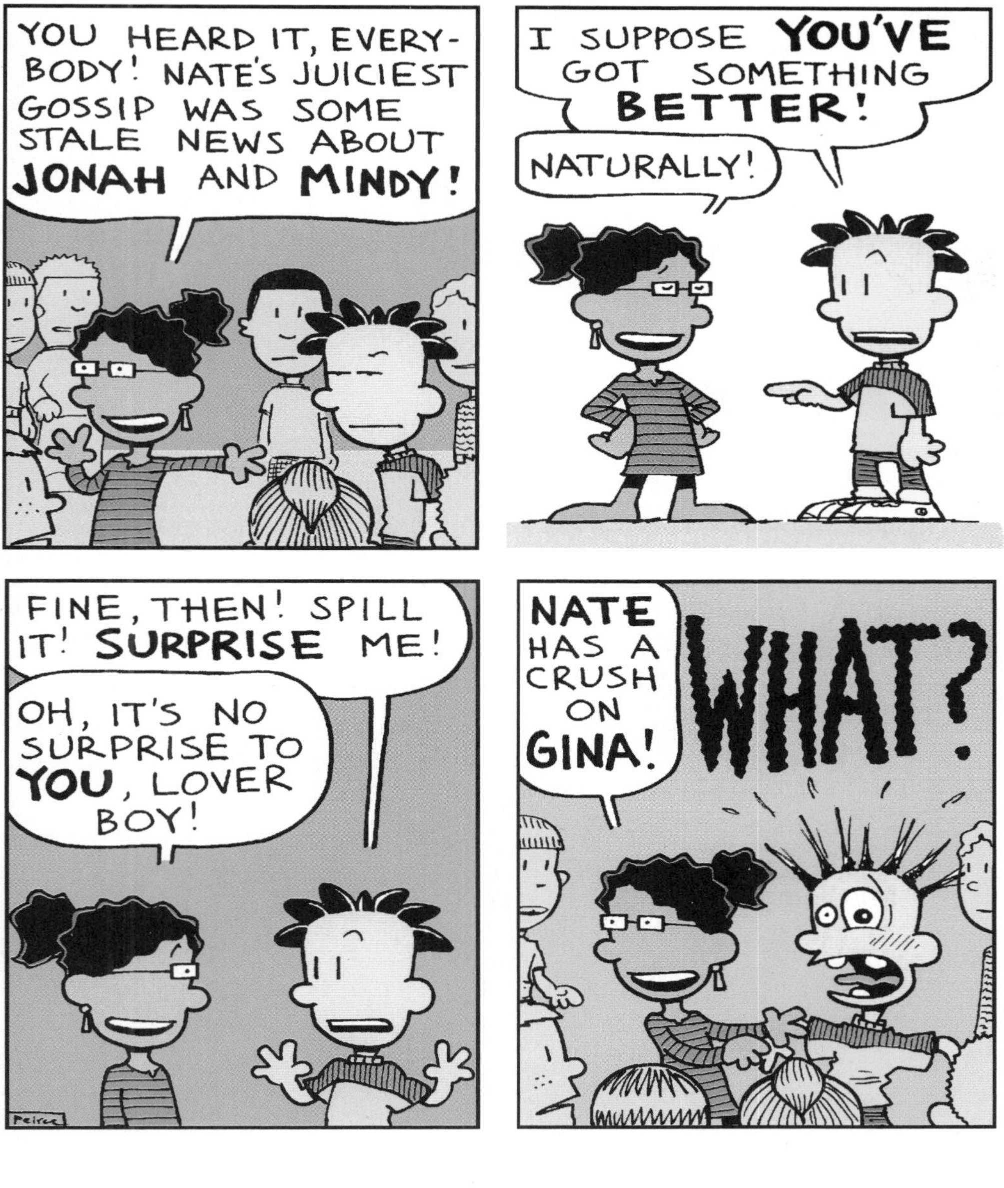
YOU HEARD IT, EVERYBODY! NATE'S JUICIEST GOSSIP WAS SOME STALE NEWS ABOUT JONAH AND MINDY!
I SUPPOSE YOU'VE GOT SOMETHING BETTER!
NATURALLY!
FINE, THEN! SPILL IT! SURPRISE ME!
OH, IT'S NO SURPRISE TO YOU, LOVER BOY!
NATE HAS A CRUSH ON GINA!
WHAT?
Peirce

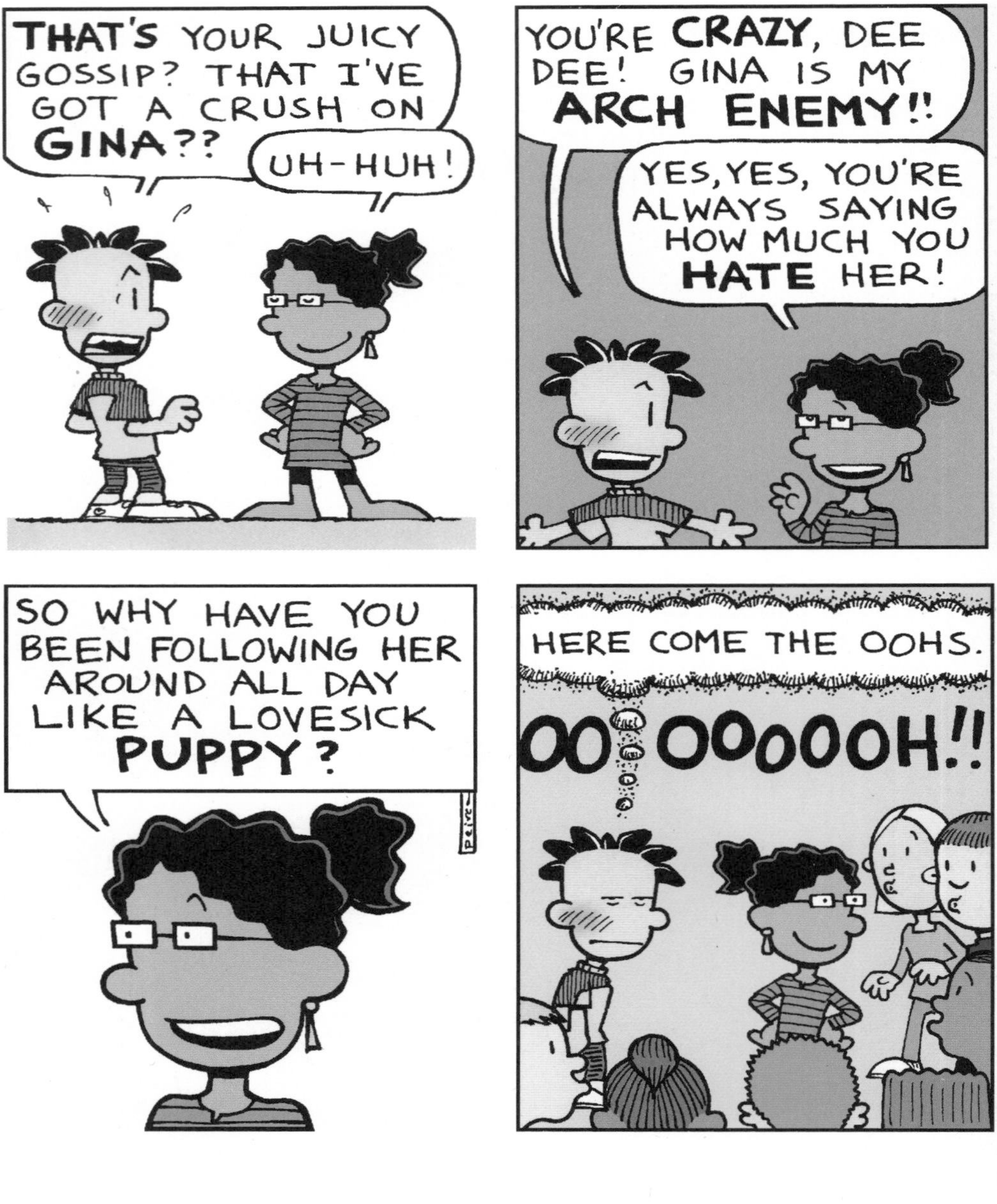
THAT'S YOUR JUICY GOSSIP? THAT I'VE GOT A CRUSH ON GINA??
UH-HUH!
YOU'RE CRAZY, DEE DEE! GINA IS MY ARCH ENEMY!!
YES, YES, YOU'RE ALWAYS SAYING HOW MUCH YOU HATE HER!
SO WHY HAVE YOU BEEN FOLLOWING HER AROUND ALL DAY LIKE A LOVESICK PUPPY?
HERE COME THE OOHS.
OOOOOOOH!!

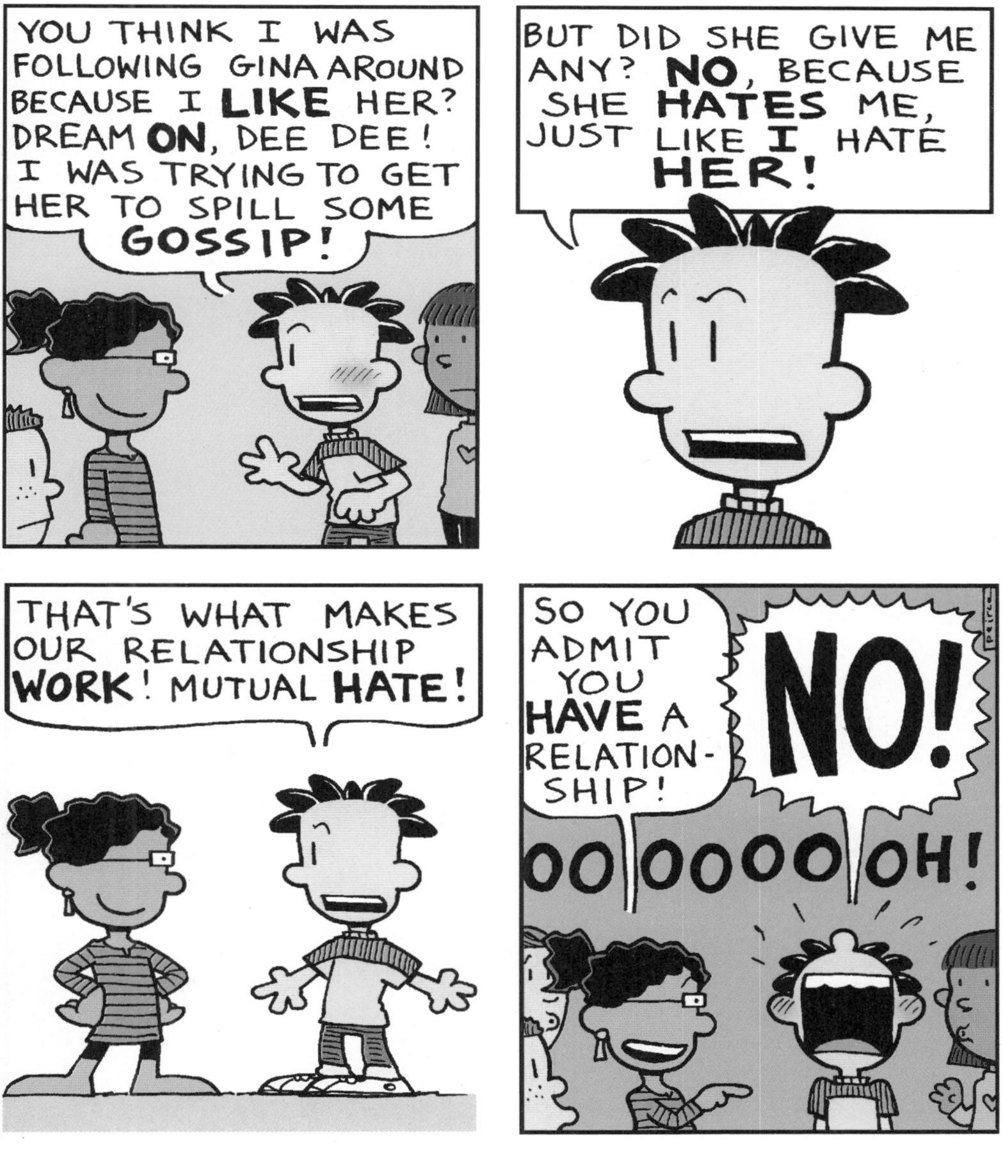
YOU THINK I WAS FOLLOWING GINA AROUND BECAUSE I LIKE HER? DREAM ON, DEE DEE! I WAS TRYING TO GET HER TO SPILL SOME GOSSIP!
BUT DID SHE GIVE ME ANY? NO, BECAUSE SHE HATES ME, JUST LIKE I HATE HER!
THAT'S WHAT MAKES OUR RELATIONSHIP WORK! MUTUAL HATE!
SO YOU ADMIT YOU HAVE A RELATION-SHIP!
NO!
OOOOOOOH!

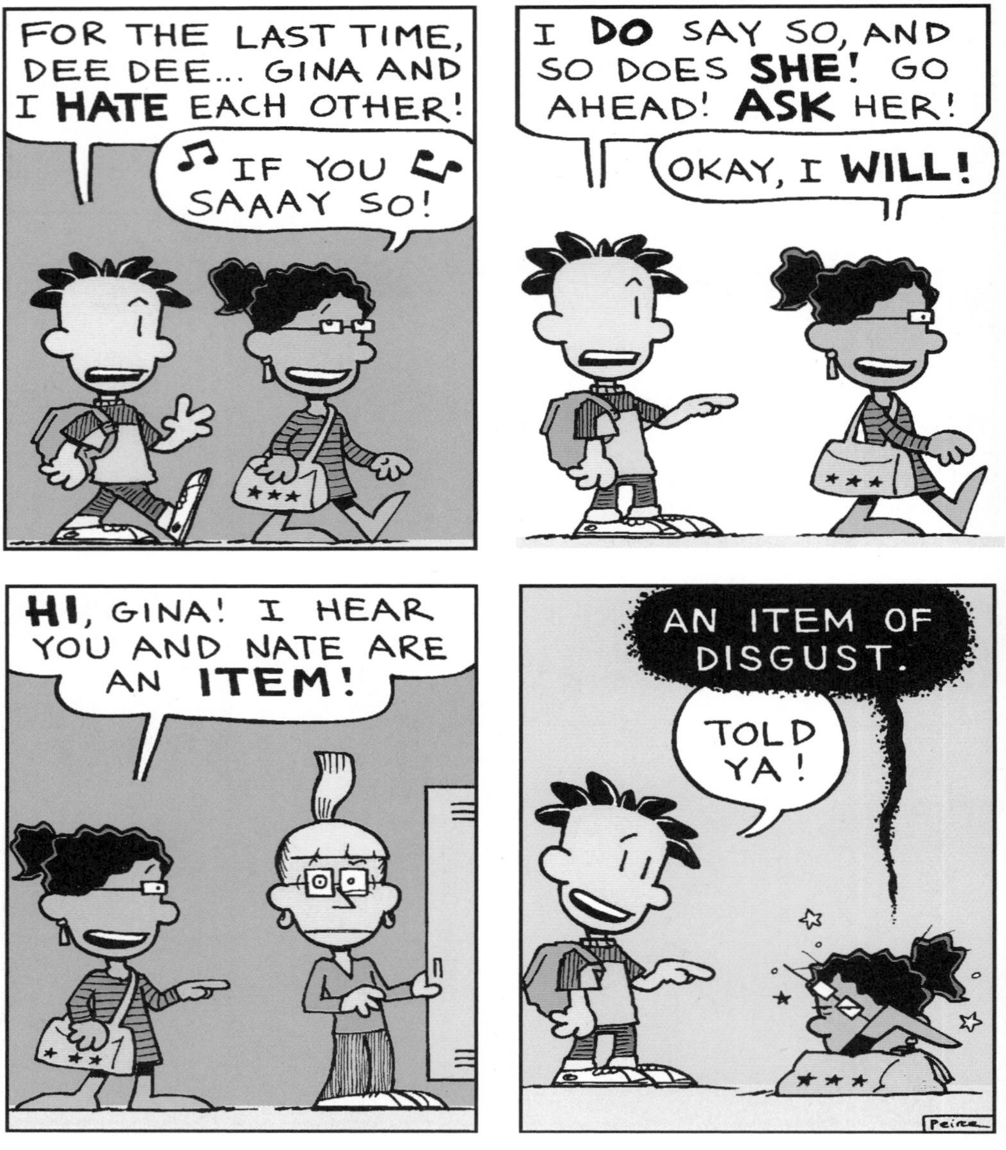
FOR THE LAST TIME, DEE DEE... GINA AND I **HATE** EACH OTHER!
IF YOU SAAAY SO!
I **DO** SAY SO, AND SO DOES **SHE**! GO AHEAD! **ASK** HER!
OKAY, I **WILL**!
HI, GINA! I HEAR YOU AND NATE ARE AN **ITEM**!
AN ITEM OF DISGUST.
TOLD YA!
Peirce

I'M OFFICIALLY DECLARING OUR GOSSIP COMPETITION A **TIE**, DEE DEE!

MY GOSSIP WAS OUTDATED, AND **YOURS** WAS TOTALLY **WRONG**.

HEY, WHY DON'T WE WRITE A GOSSIP BLOG **TOGETHER**?

WE'LL POOL OUR RESOURCES, SHARE INFORMATION, AND TAKE TURNS TALKING TO PEOPLE WITH GOSSIP TO SPILL!

HANNAH BROKE UP WITH ME BECAUSE OF MY CHRONIC B.O.

WHY DON'T YOU HANDLE THIS ONE?

MR. ROSA! CAN I INTERVIEW YOU FOR MY "CLASSROOM CHATTER" BLOG?

I HEARD YOU WEREN'T WRITING THAT ANYMORE.

UNTRUE! DEE DEE AND I ARE WORKING ON IT TOGETHER!

SHE'S HANDLING THE **STUDENT** GOSSIP, AND I'M HANDLING THE **TEACHER** DIRT!

DIRT. CHARMING.

SO! BROKEN ANY MARRIAGE VOWS LATELY?

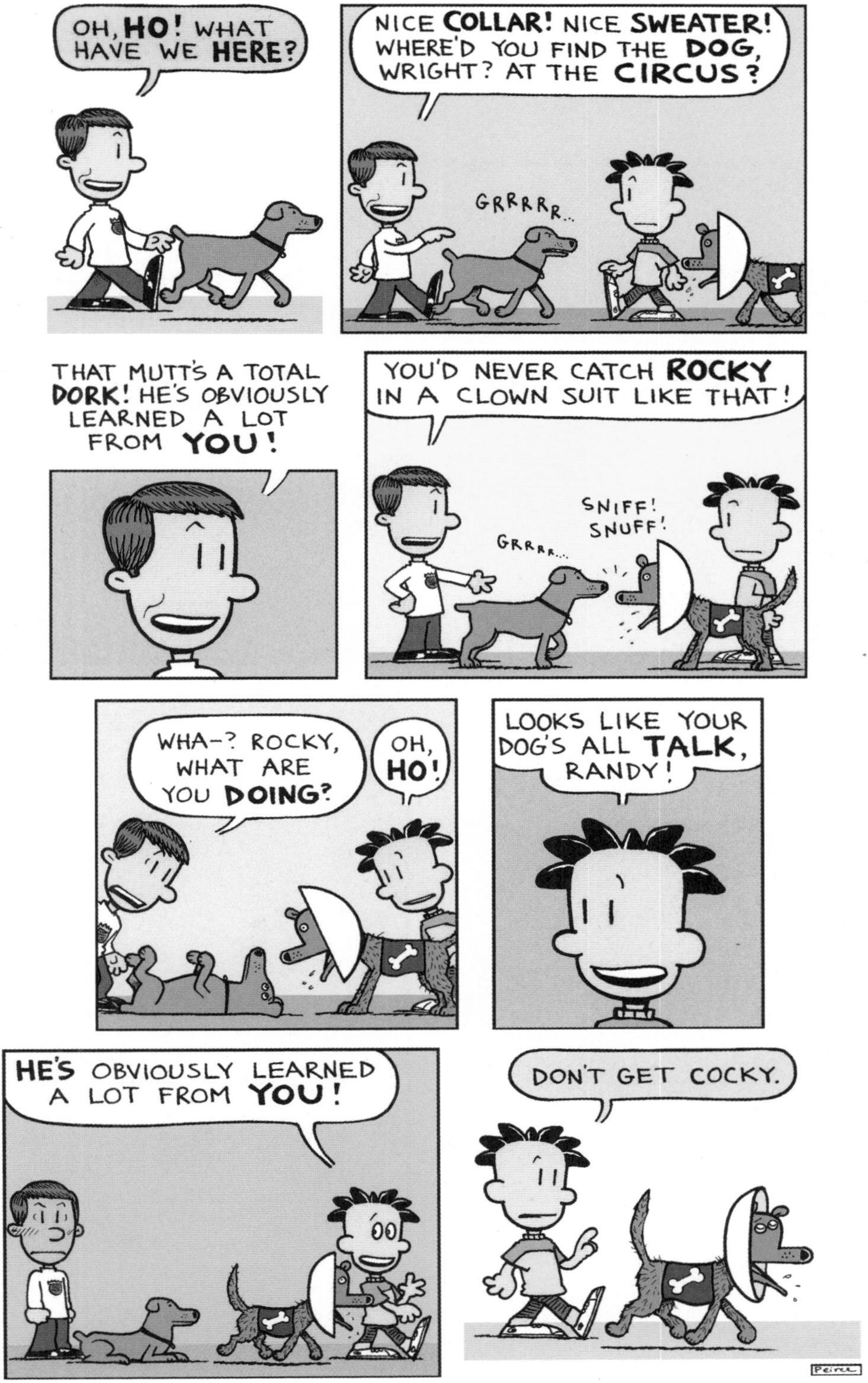
OH, HO! WHAT HAVE WE HERE?
NICE COLLAR! NICE SWEATER! WHERE'D YOU FIND THE DOG, WRIGHT? AT THE CIRCUS?
GRRRRR...
THAT MUTT'S A TOTAL DORK! HE'S OBVIOUSLY LEARNED A LOT FROM YOU!
YOU'D NEVER CATCH ROCKY IN A CLOWN SUIT LIKE THAT!
GRRRR...
SNIFF! SNUFF!
WHA-? ROCKY, WHAT ARE YOU DOING?
OH, HO!
LOOKS LIKE YOUR DOG'S ALL TALK, RANDY!
HE'S OBVIOUSLY LEARNED A LOT FROM YOU!
DON'T GET COCKY.
Peirce

...AND THEN CAP'N PICARD YELLS AT THE GUY: "THERE... ARE... FOUR... LIGHTS!"
AH!
YOU'RE TALKING ABOUT "CHAIN OF COMMAND," PART 2! I LOVE THAT EPISODE!
WHA-? YOU WATCH "STAR TREK: THE NEXT GENERATION"?
WATCH IT? IT'S MY FAVORITE TV SHOW OF ALL TIME!
!
!
RED ALERT.
Peirce

WHAT'S WITH YOU?
I JUST FOUND OUT THAT MRS. GODFREY'S FAVORITE TV SHOW IS "STAR TREK: THE NEXT GENERATION."
HEY, THAT'S YOUR FAVORITE SHOW!
OH, REALLY? GEE, THANKS, TEDDY! I DIDN'T KNOW THAT!
YOU AND MRS. GODFREY HAVE SOMETHING IN COMMON!
SHUT UP.
THE TWO OF YOU THINK ALIKE!
SHUT UP.
YOU'VE BECOME ONE WITH THE BORG!
RESISTANCE IS FUTILE.
Peirce

MAYBE WHEN MRS. GODFREY CALLED "STAR TREK: THE NEXT GENERATION" HER FAVORITE TV SHOW, IT WAS JUST... Y'KNOW... AN **EXPRESSION**.

UH... JUST HOW INTO "THE NEXT GENERATION" **ARE** YOU?

SO INTO IT!

ONE HALLOWEEN, I DRESSED UP LIKE COUNSELOR DEANNA TROI!

AN ESSENTIAL PART OF MY PRE-ADOLESCENT FANTASY LIFE WAS JUST BLOWN TO SMITHEREENS.

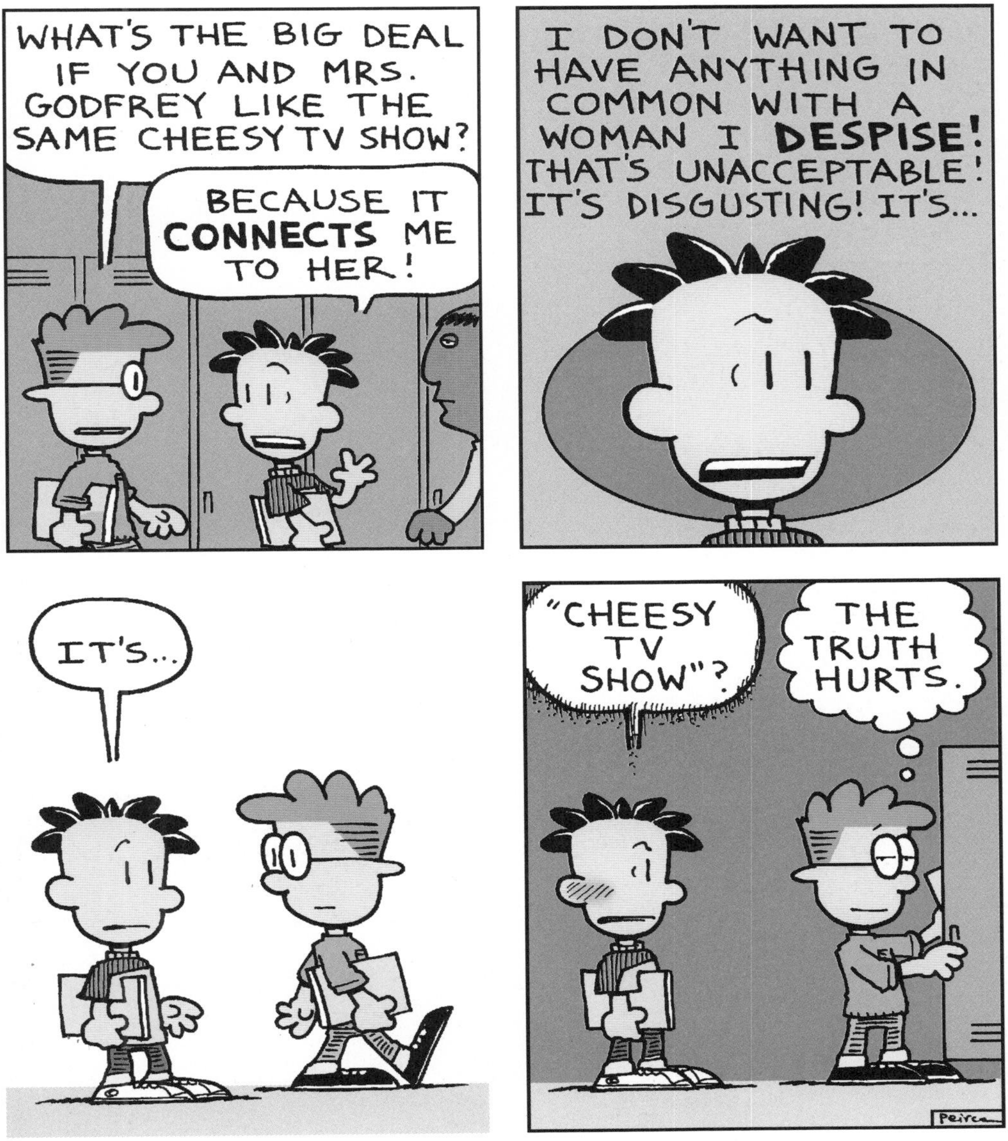
WHAT'S THE BIG DEAL IF YOU AND MRS. GODFREY LIKE THE SAME CHEESY TV SHOW?
BECAUSE IT **CONNECTS** ME TO HER!
I DON'T WANT TO HAVE ANYTHING IN COMMON WITH A WOMAN I **DESPISE!** THAT'S UNACCEPTABLE! IT'S DISGUSTING! IT'S...
IT'S...
"CHEESY TV SHOW"?
THE TRUTH HURTS.
Peirce

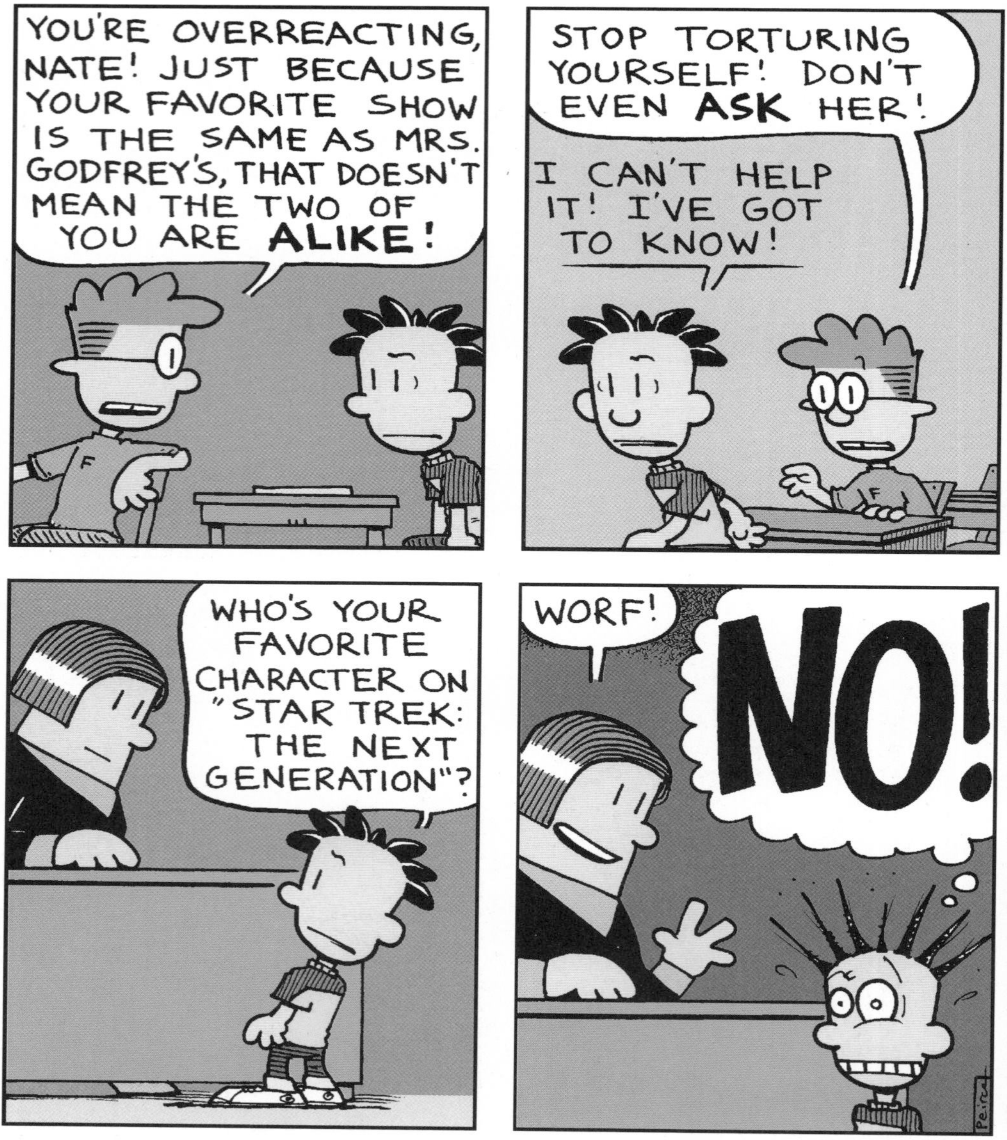
YOU'RE OVERREACTING, NATE! JUST BECAUSE YOUR FAVORITE SHOW IS THE SAME AS MRS. GODFREY'S, THAT DOESN'T MEAN THE TWO OF YOU ARE ALIKE!
STOP TORTURING YOURSELF! DON'T EVEN ASK HER!
I CAN'T HELP IT! I'VE GOT TO KNOW!
WHO'S YOUR FAVORITE CHARACTER ON "STAR TREK: THE NEXT GENERATION"?
WORF!
NO!
Peirce

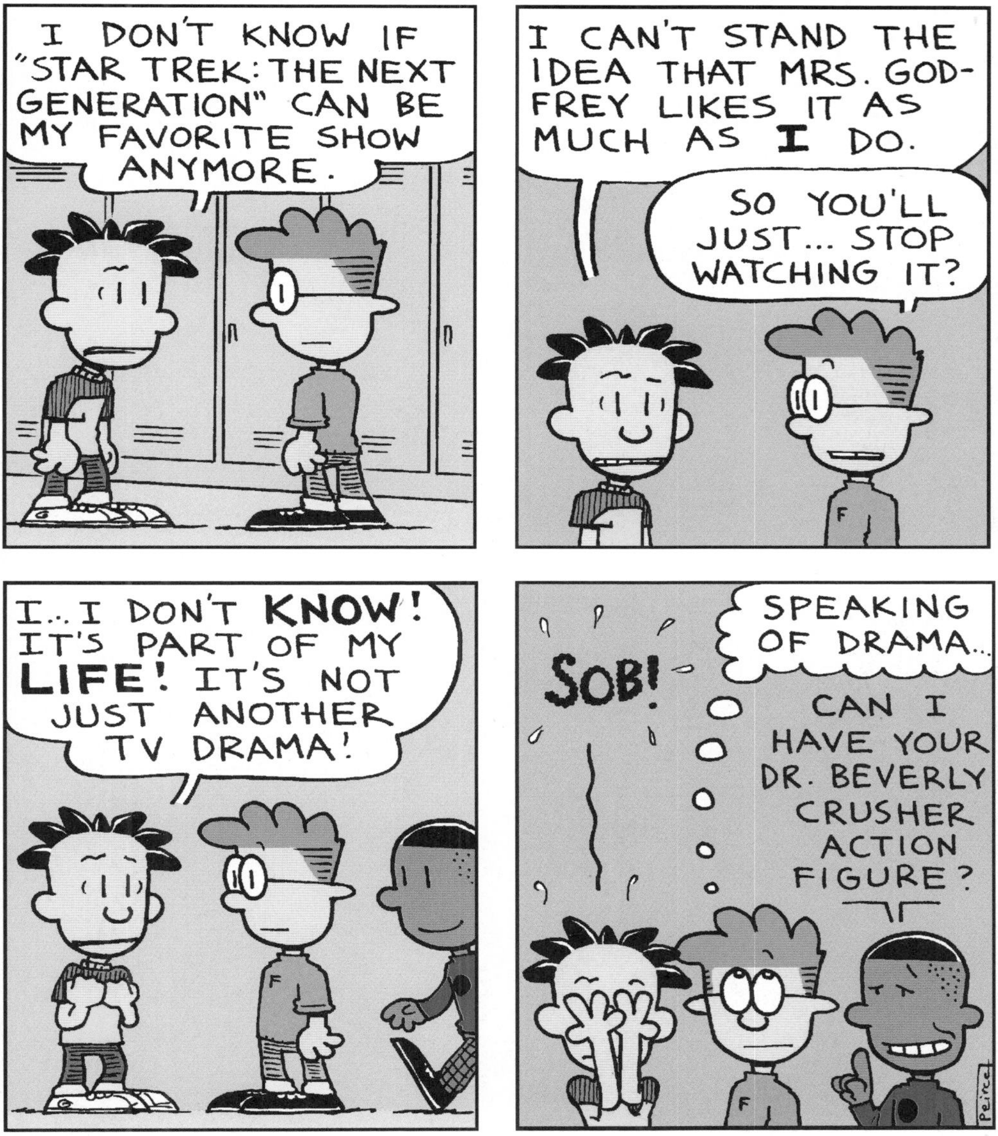
I DON'T KNOW IF "STAR TREK: THE NEXT GENERATION" CAN BE MY FAVORITE SHOW ANYMORE.
I CAN'T STAND THE IDEA THAT MRS. GODFREY LIKES IT AS MUCH AS I DO.
SO YOU'LL JUST... STOP WATCHING IT?
I... I DON'T KNOW! IT'S PART OF MY LIFE! IT'S NOT JUST ANOTHER TV DRAMA!
SOB!
SPEAKING OF DRAMA...
CAN I HAVE YOUR DR. BEVERLY CRUSHER ACTION FIGURE?
Peirce

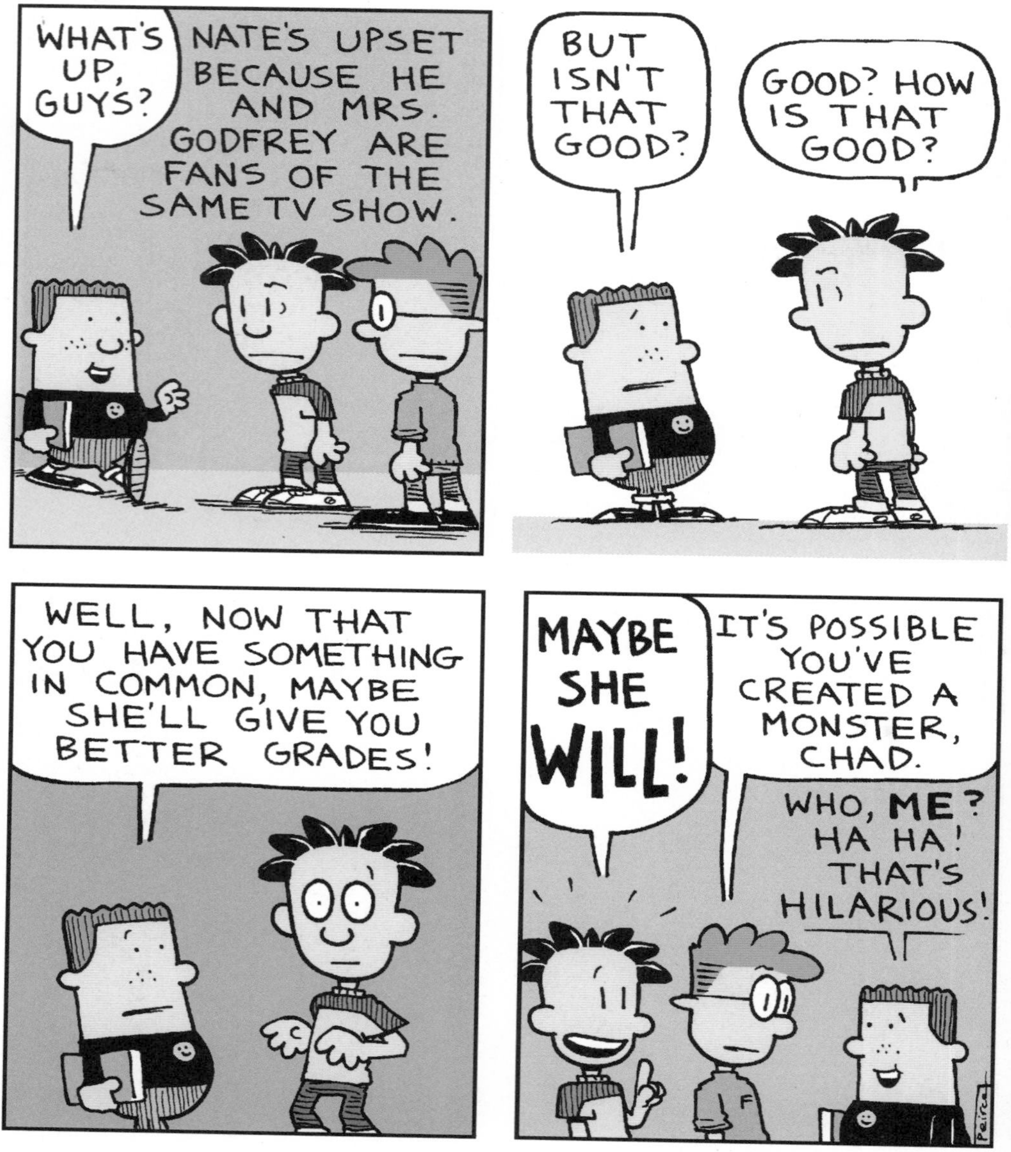
WHAT'S UP, GUYS?
NATE'S UPSET BECAUSE HE AND MRS. GODFREY ARE FANS OF THE SAME TV SHOW.
BUT ISN'T THAT GOOD?
GOOD? HOW IS THAT GOOD?
WELL, NOW THAT YOU HAVE SOMETHING IN COMMON, MAYBE SHE'LL GIVE YOU BETTER GRADES!
MAYBE SHE WILL!
IT'S POSSIBLE YOU'VE CREATED A MONSTER, CHAD.
WHO, ME? HA HA! THAT'S HILARIOUS!
Peirce

NATE, YOU HAVEN'T HANDED IN YOUR HOMEWORK.
I KNOW!
I WAS WATCHING A TWO-PART EPISODE OF... *AHEM*... "STAR TREK: THE NEXT GENERATION," AND I GUESS I GOT CAUGHT UP IN IT!
I'M SURE YOU, A FELLOW FAN, CAN UNDERSTAND!
I UNDERSTAND THAT YOU'RE USING THE FINEST TV SHOW OF ALL TIME AS AN EXCUSE!
HOW DARE YOU SULLY ITS NAME?
THIS ISN'T GOING WELL.
Peirce

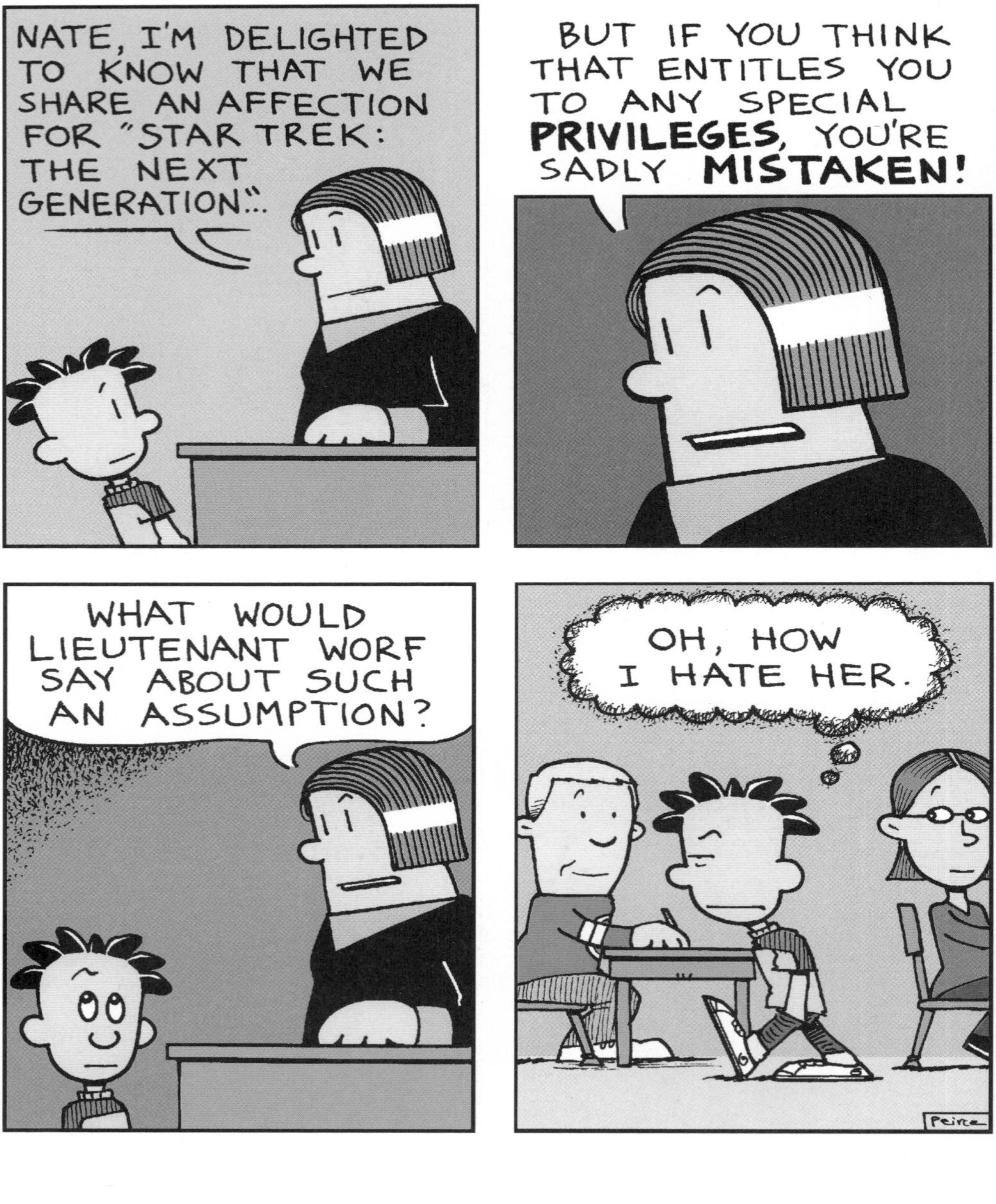
NATE, I'M DELIGHTED TO KNOW THAT WE SHARE AN AFFECTION FOR "STAR TREK: THE NEXT GENERATION."...
BUT IF YOU THINK THAT ENTITLES YOU TO ANY SPECIAL **PRIVILEGES**, YOU'RE SADLY **MISTAKEN!**
WHAT WOULD LIEUTENANT WORF SAY ABOUT SUCH AN ASSUMPTION?
OH, HOW I HATE HER.
Peirce

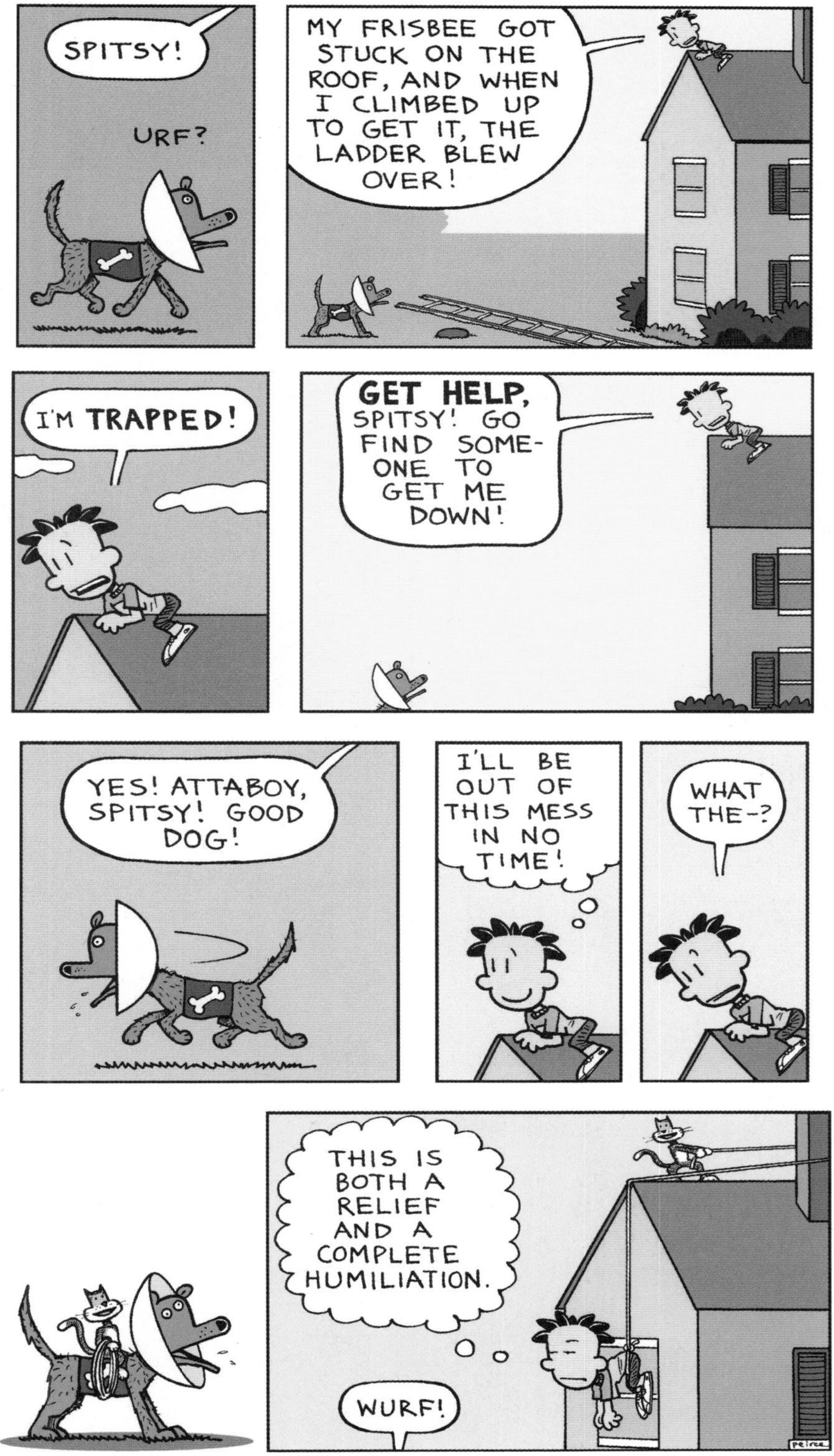
SPITSY!
URF?
MY FRISBEE GOT STUCK ON THE ROOF, AND WHEN I CLIMBED UP TO GET IT, THE LADDER BLEW OVER!
I'M **TRAPPED!**
GET HELP, SPITSY! GO FIND SOME-ONE TO GET ME DOWN!
YES! ATTABOY, SPITSY! GOOD DOG!
I'LL BE OUT OF THIS MESS IN NO TIME!
WHAT THE-?
THIS IS BOTH A RELIEF AND A COMPLETE HUMILIATION.
WURF!
peirce

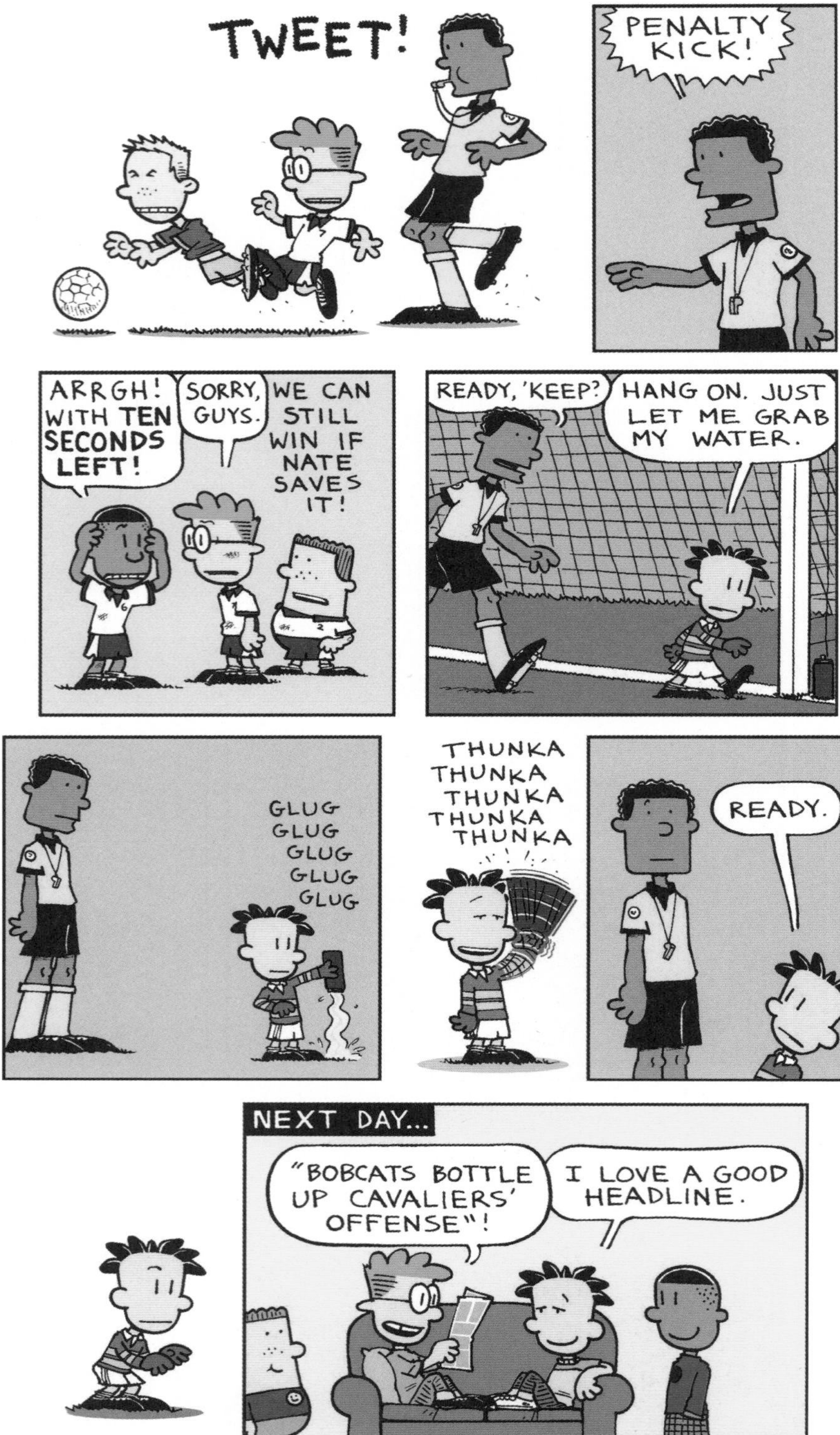

TWEET!
PENALTY KICK!
ARRGH! WITH TEN SECONDS LEFT!
SORRY, GUYS.
WE CAN STILL WIN IF NATE SAVES IT!
READY, 'KEEP?
HANG ON. JUST LET ME GRAB MY WATER.
GLUG GLUG GLUG GLUG GLUG
THUNKA THUNKA THUNKA THUNKA THUNKA
READY.
NEXT DAY...
"BOBCATS BOTTLE UP CAVALIERS' OFFENSE"!
I LOVE A GOOD HEADLINE.

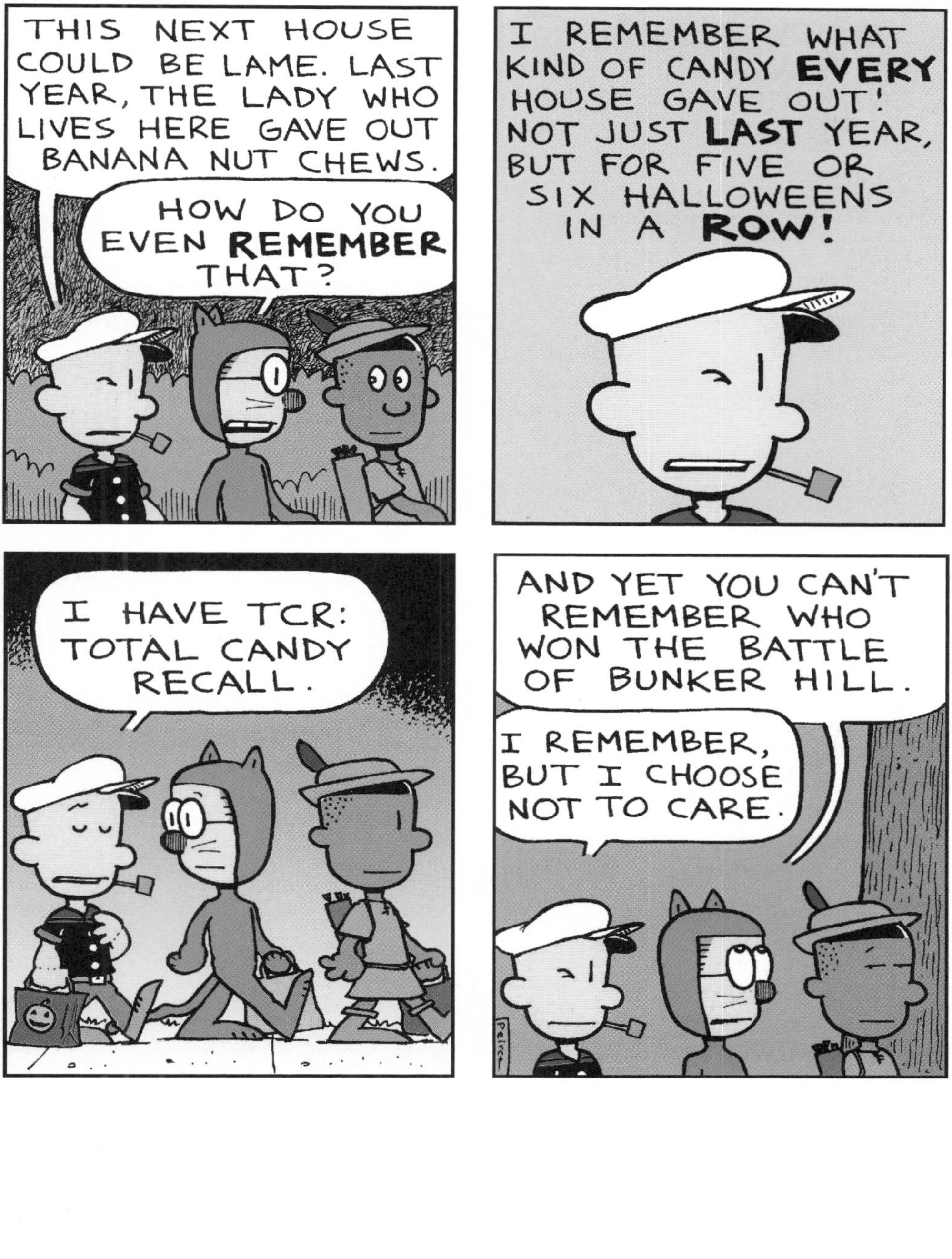
THIS NEXT HOUSE COULD BE LAME. LAST YEAR, THE LADY WHO LIVES HERE GAVE OUT BANANA NUT CHEWS.
HOW DO YOU EVEN REMEMBER THAT?
I REMEMBER WHAT KIND OF CANDY EVERY HOUSE GAVE OUT! NOT JUST LAST YEAR, BUT FOR FIVE OR SIX HALLOWEENS IN A ROW!
I HAVE TCR: TOTAL CANDY RECALL.
AND YET YOU CAN'T REMEMBER WHO WON THE BATTLE OF BUNKER HILL.
I REMEMBER, BUT I CHOOSE NOT TO CARE.
Peirce

I DON'T BELIEVE YOU HAVE "TOTAL CANDY RECALL," NATE! **PROVE** IT!

OKAY, MR. **DOUBTING THOMAS!**

THIS GRAY HOUSE GIVES OUT MILK DUDS AND SKITTLES. THIS PLACE ON THE CORNER GIVES OUT BITE-SIZE MILKY WAYS. AT THIS HOUSE, EITHER BUTTERFINGERS OR SNICKERS.

THAT ONE IS TOOTSIE POPS, THAT ONE'S A CHOICE BETWEEN KIT KATS AND BABY RUTHS, AND **THIS** HOUSE OFFERS A WHIMSICAL ASSORTMENT OF NUT-FREE CANDY BARS.

WHIMSICAL ASSORTMENT?

OVER THERE: JOLLY RANCHERS.

EW.

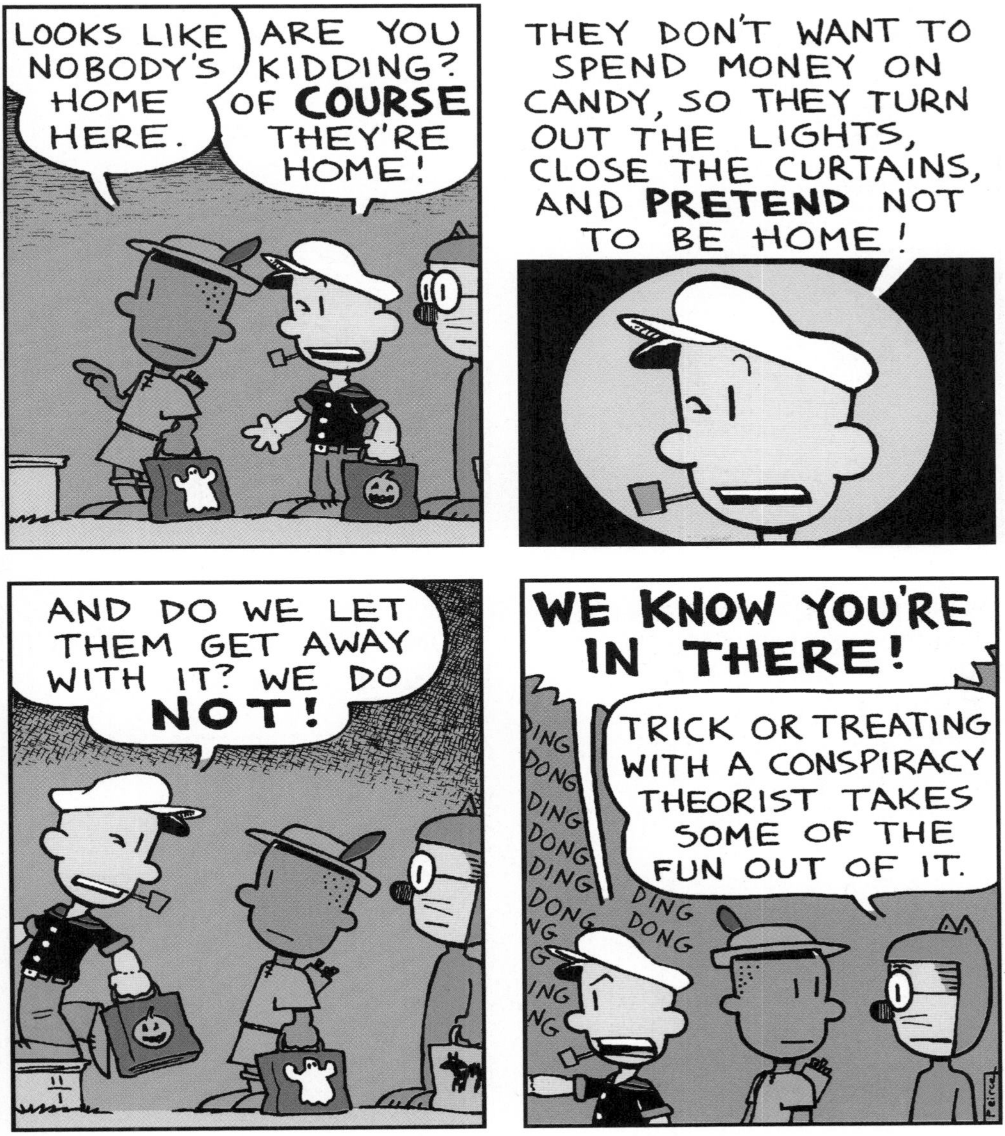
LOOKS LIKE NOBODY'S HOME HERE.
ARE YOU KIDDING? OF **COURSE** THEY'RE HOME!
THEY DON'T WANT TO SPEND MONEY ON CANDY, SO THEY TURN OUT THE LIGHTS, CLOSE THE CURTAINS, AND **PRETEND** NOT TO BE HOME!
AND DO WE LET THEM GET AWAY WITH IT? WE DO **NOT!**
WE KNOW YOU'RE IN THERE!
DING DONG DING DONG DING DONG
DING DONG
TRICK OR TREATING WITH A CONSPIRACY THEORIST TAKES SOME OF THE FUN OUT OF IT.
Peirce

PTOO! ARRGH! IT HAPPENED **AGAIN!**

WHAT DID?

I PUT A GREEN CANDY IN MY MOUTH, AND IT WAS THE **WRONG FLAVOR!** GREEN CANDY IS SUPPOSED TO BE **LIME!**

WHEN I EAT A GREEN CANDY, I'M EXPECTING IT TO BE **LIME!** I **DESERVE** THAT! IT'S MY CONSTITUTIONAL **RIGHT!**

I'M PRETTY SURE THE CONSTITUTION DOESN'T MENTION CANDY OF **ANY** COLOR.

WHEN DID "SOUR APPLE" HIJACK GREEN??

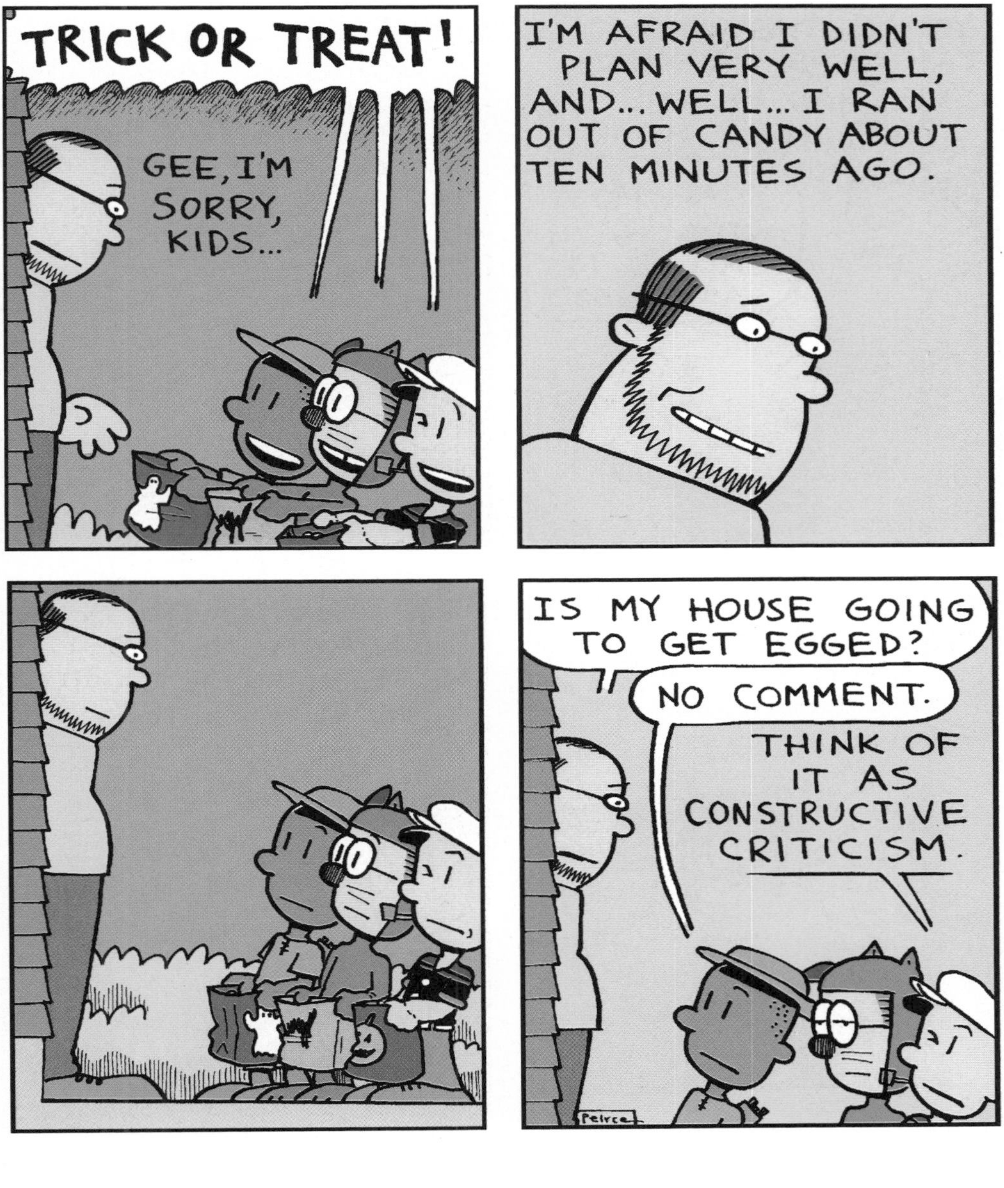
TRICK OR TREAT!
GEE, I'M SORRY, KIDS...
I'M AFRAID I DIDN'T PLAN VERY WELL, AND... WELL... I RAN OUT OF CANDY ABOUT TEN MINUTES AGO.
IS MY HOUSE GOING TO GET EGGED?
NO COMMENT.
THINK OF IT AS CONSTRUCTIVE CRITICISM.
Peirce

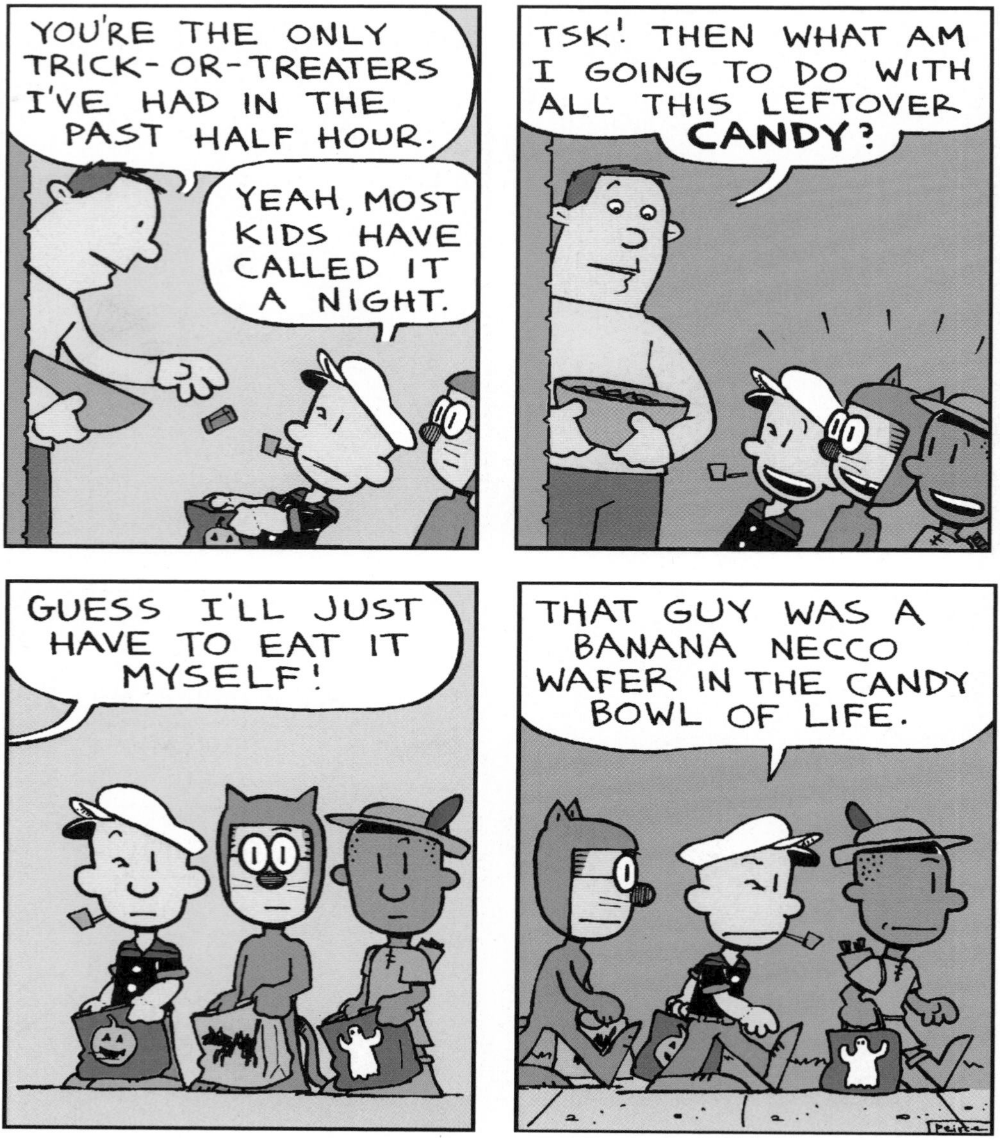
YOU'RE THE ONLY TRICK-OR-TREATERS I'VE HAD IN THE PAST HALF HOUR.
YEAH, MOST KIDS HAVE CALLED IT A NIGHT.
TSK! THEN WHAT AM I GOING TO DO WITH ALL THIS LEFTOVER **CANDY**?
GUESS I'LL JUST HAVE TO EAT IT MYSELF!
THAT GUY WAS A BANANA NECCO WAFER IN THE CANDY BOWL OF LIFE.

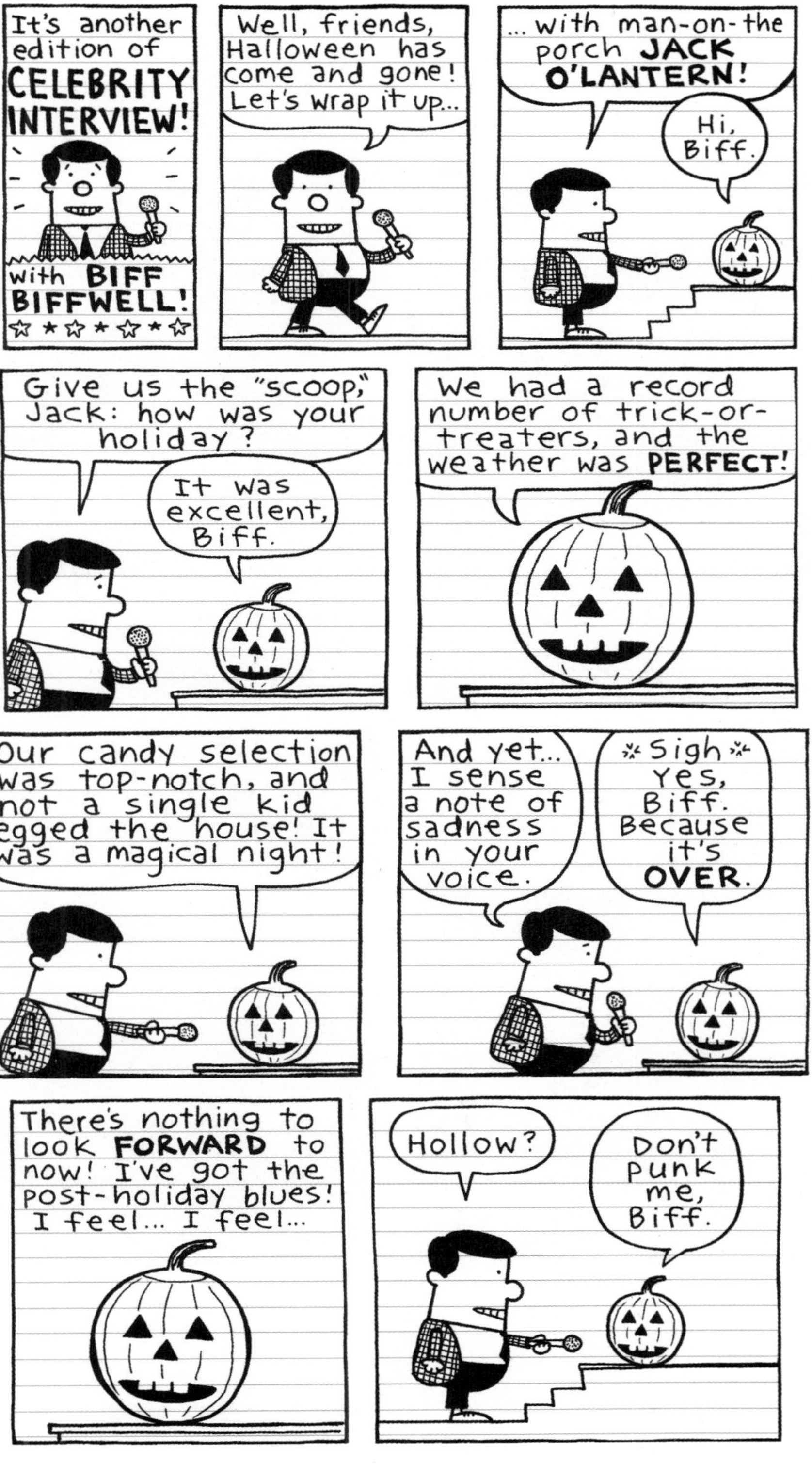
It's another edition of CELEBRITY INTERVIEW!
with BIFF BIFFWELL!
Well, friends, Halloween has come and gone! Let's wrap it up...
... with man-on-the porch JACK O'LANTERN!
Hi, Biff.
Give us the "scoop," Jack: how was your holiday?
It was excellent, Biff.
We had a record number of trick-or-treaters, and the weather was PERFECT!
Our candy selection was top-notch, and not a single kid egged the house! It was a magical night!
And yet... I sense a note of sadness in your voice.
Sigh Yes, Biff. Because it's OVER.
There's nothing to look FORWARD to now! I've got the post-holiday blues! I feel... I feel...
Hollow?
Don't punk me, Biff.

CAN I SEE THE FUNNIES, DAD?

JUST A SEC. I'M DOING THE KEN KEN.

WHY DO NEWSPAPERS PUT MATH PUZZLES ALONGSIDE THE COMICS, ANYWAY?

I MEAN, WHAT DO THE **COMICS PAGE** AND **MATH** HAVE IN COMMON?

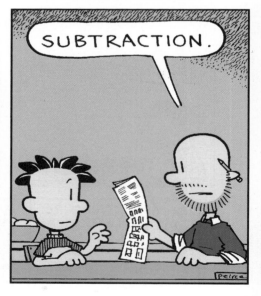

SUBTRACTION.

EVER NOTICE HOW PRACTICALLY EVERY NEWSPAPER IN THE WORLD INCLUDES KEN KEN AND SUDOKU?

SO?

SO WHOEVER INVENTED THOSE PUZZLES IS PROBABLY A **GAZILLIONAIRE**!

IF **I** COULD INVENT THE NEXT GREAT MATH PUZZLE, I COULD BE **RICH**!

YOU?

AND MATH?

HA HA HA HA HA A HA HA H HA HA HA HA

MAYBE I'LL WRITE THE NEXT GREAT ADVICE COLUMN INSTEAD.

MR. STAPLES, DO YOU LIKE KEN KEN?
I SURE DO! AND SUDOKU, TOO!
WELL, HOW HARD DO YOU THINK IT WOULD BE TO INVENT A PUZZLE LIKE THAT?
AH! SEE WHAT YOU'RE DOING, NATE?
YOU'RE IMAGINING FUN APPLICATIONS FOR BASIC ARITH-METIC! YOU'RE THINKING LIKE A REAL MATHEMATICIAN!!
THAT'S THE NASTIEST THING ANYONE'S EVER SAID TO ME.
Peirce

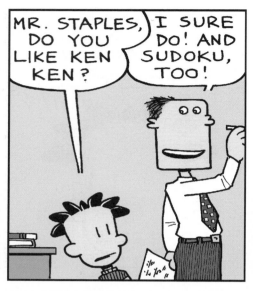

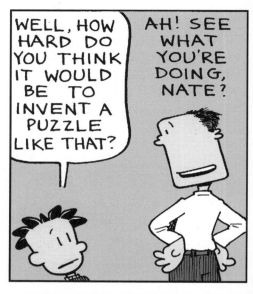

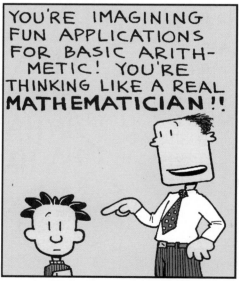

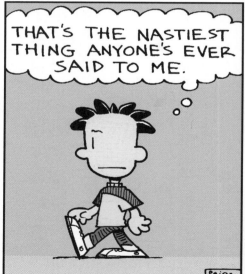

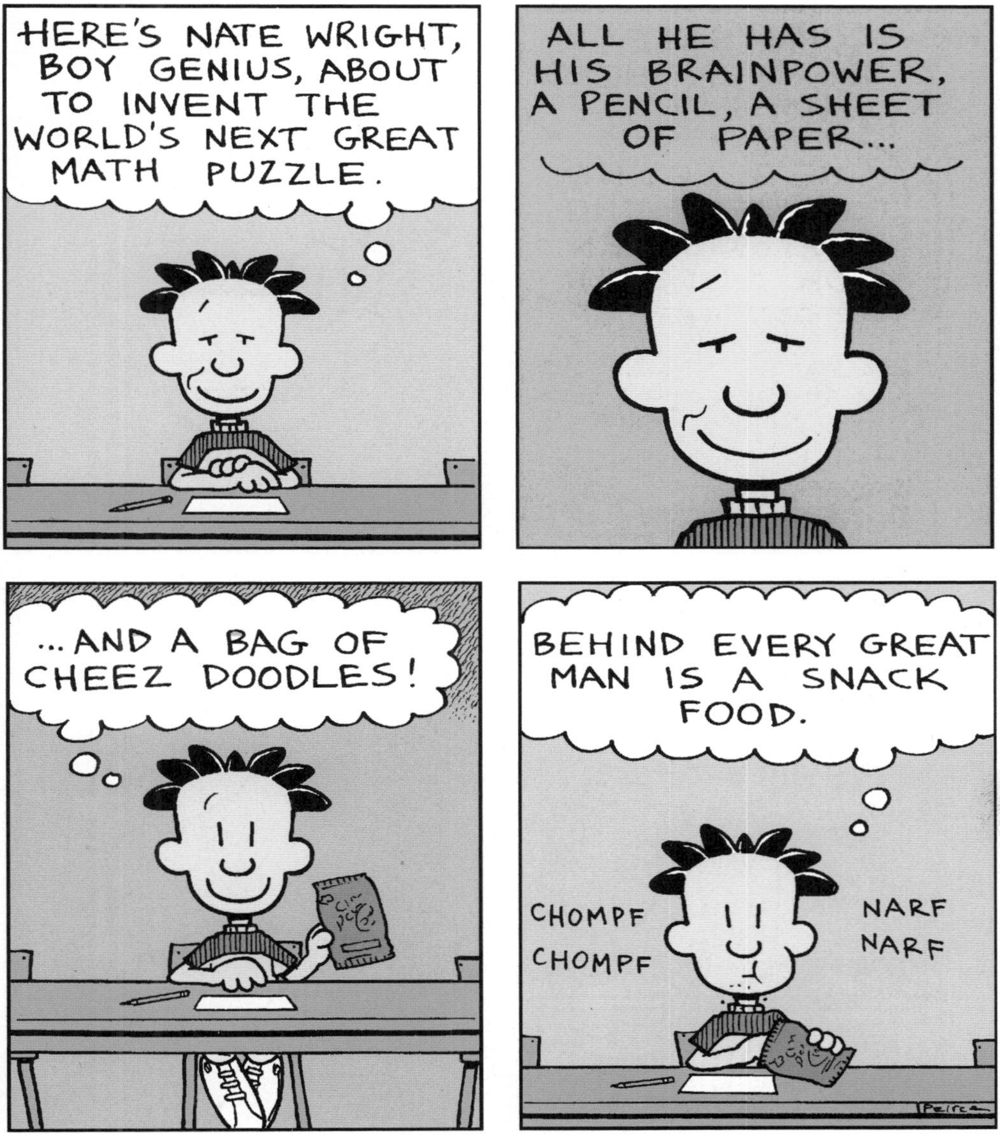
HERE'S NATE WRIGHT, BOY GENIUS, ABOUT TO INVENT THE WORLD'S NEXT GREAT MATH PUZZLE.
ALL HE HAS IS HIS BRAINPOWER, A PENCIL, A SHEET OF PAPER...
...AND A BAG OF CHEEZ DOODLES!
BEHIND EVERY GREAT MAN IS A SNACK FOOD.
CHOMPF
CHOMPF
NARF
NARF
Peirce

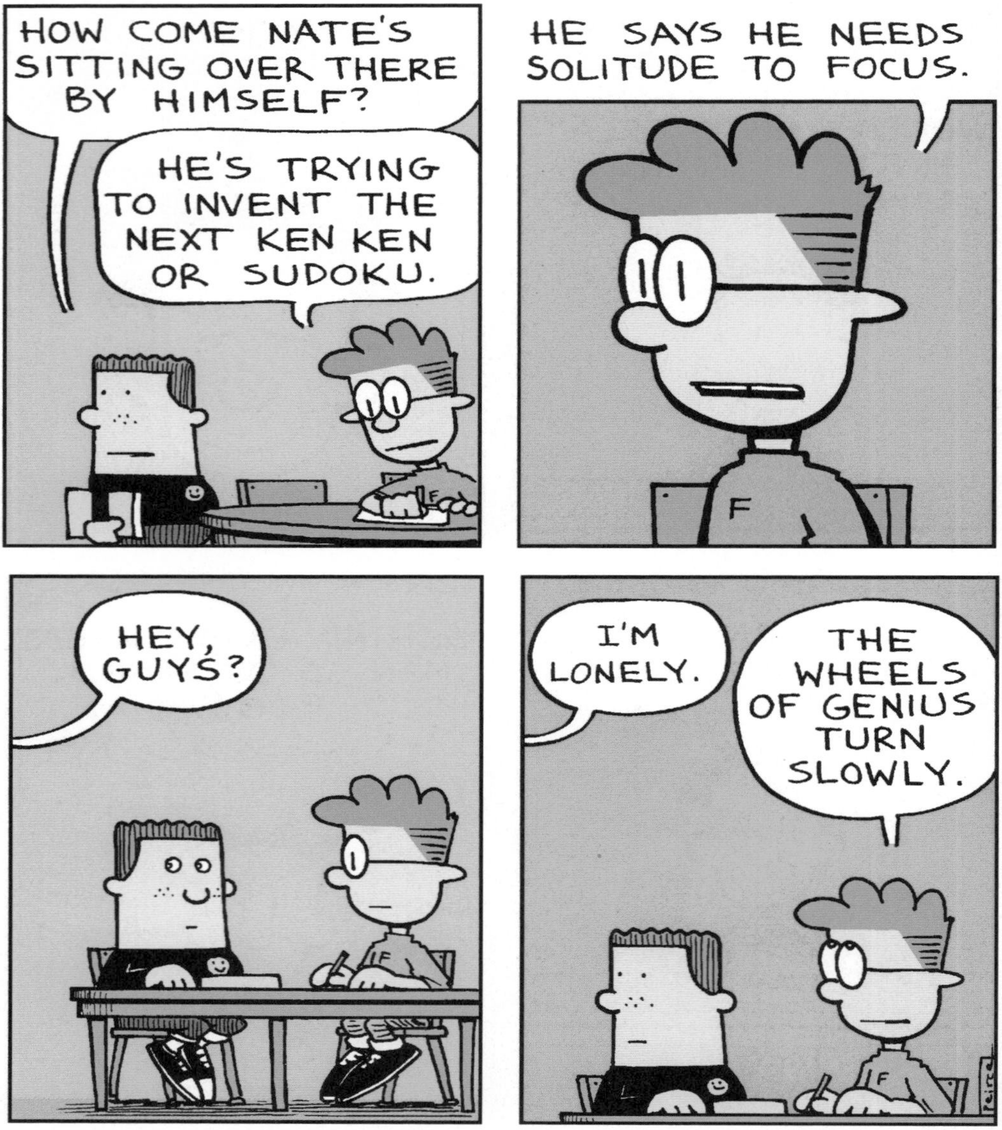
HOW COME NATE'S SITTING OVER THERE BY HIMSELF?
HE'S TRYING TO INVENT THE NEXT KEN KEN OR SUDOKU.
HE SAYS HE NEEDS SOLITUDE TO FOCUS.
HEY, GUYS?
I'M LONELY.
THE WHEELS OF GENIUS TURN SLOWLY.

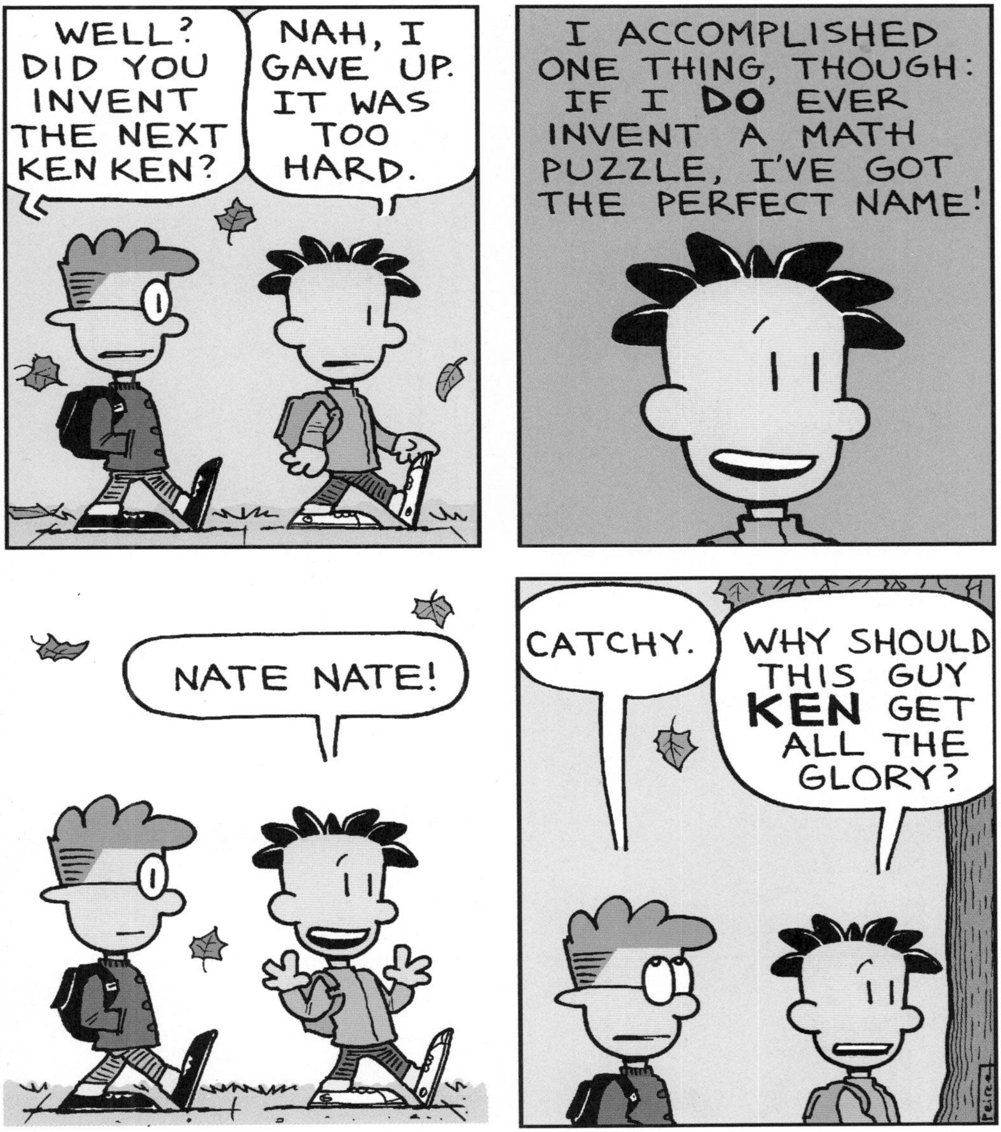
WELL? DID YOU INVENT THE NEXT KEN KEN?
NAH, I GAVE UP. IT WAS TOO HARD.
I ACCOMPLISHED ONE THING, THOUGH: IF I **DO** EVER INVENT A MATH PUZZLE, I'VE GOT THE PERFECT NAME!
NATE NATE!
CATCHY.
WHY SHOULD THIS GUY **KEN** GET ALL THE GLORY?
Peirce

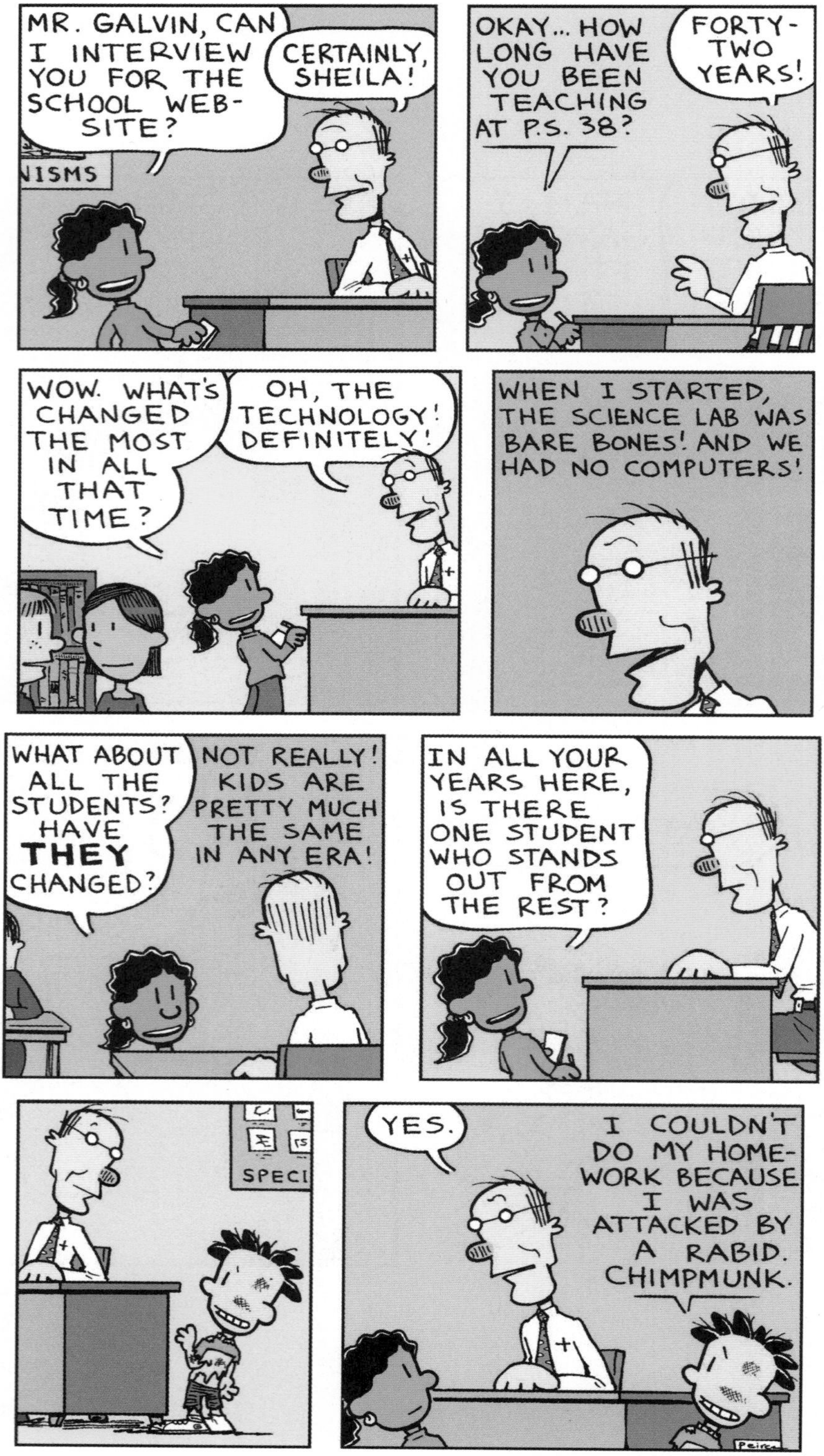

MR. GALVIN, CAN I INTERVIEW YOU FOR THE SCHOOL WEB-SITE?
CERTAINLY, SHEILA!
NISMS
OKAY... HOW LONG HAVE YOU BEEN TEACHING AT P.S. 38?
FORTY-TWO YEARS!
WOW. WHAT'S CHANGED THE MOST IN ALL THAT TIME?
OH, THE TECHNOLOGY! DEFINITELY!
WHEN I STARTED, THE SCIENCE LAB WAS BARE BONES! AND WE HAD NO COMPUTERS!
WHAT ABOUT ALL THE STUDENTS? HAVE **THEY** CHANGED?
NOT REALLY! KIDS ARE PRETTY MUCH THE SAME IN ANY ERA!
IN ALL YOUR YEARS HERE, IS THERE ONE STUDENT WHO STANDS OUT FROM THE REST?
SPECI
YES.
I COULDN'T DO MY HOME-WORK BECAUSE I WAS ATTACKED BY A RABID CHIMPMUNK.
Peirce

C'MON, NATE! CARTOONING CLUB MEETING!
UH... JUST A SEC.
I CAN'T FIND THE NOTEBOOK THAT HAS ALL MY **COMICS** IN IT! I HAD IT WITH ME JUST A MINUTE AGO IN...
...SOCIAL STUDIES.
PEIRCE

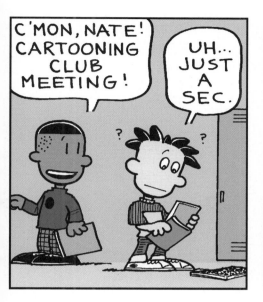

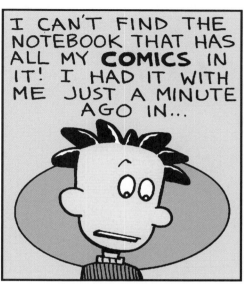

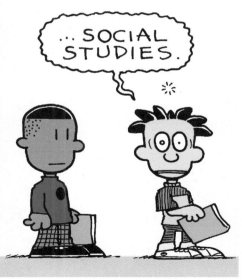

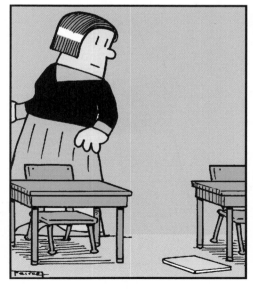

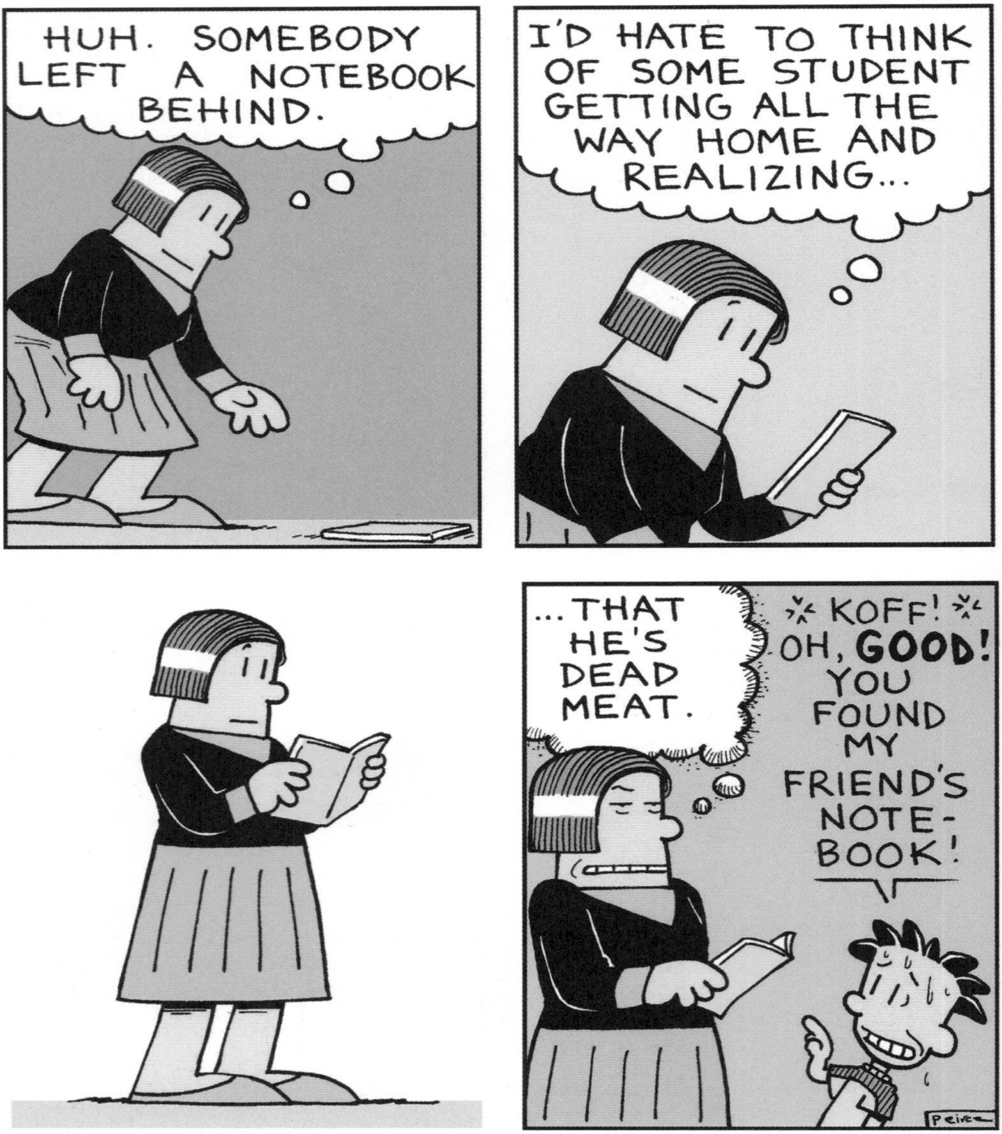
HUH. SOMEBODY LEFT A NOTEBOOK BEHIND.
I'D HATE TO THINK OF SOME STUDENT GETTING ALL THE WAY HOME AND REALIZING...
...THAT HE'S DEAD MEAT.
KOFF! OH, **GOOD!** YOU FOUND MY FRIEND'S NOTE-BOOK!
Peirce

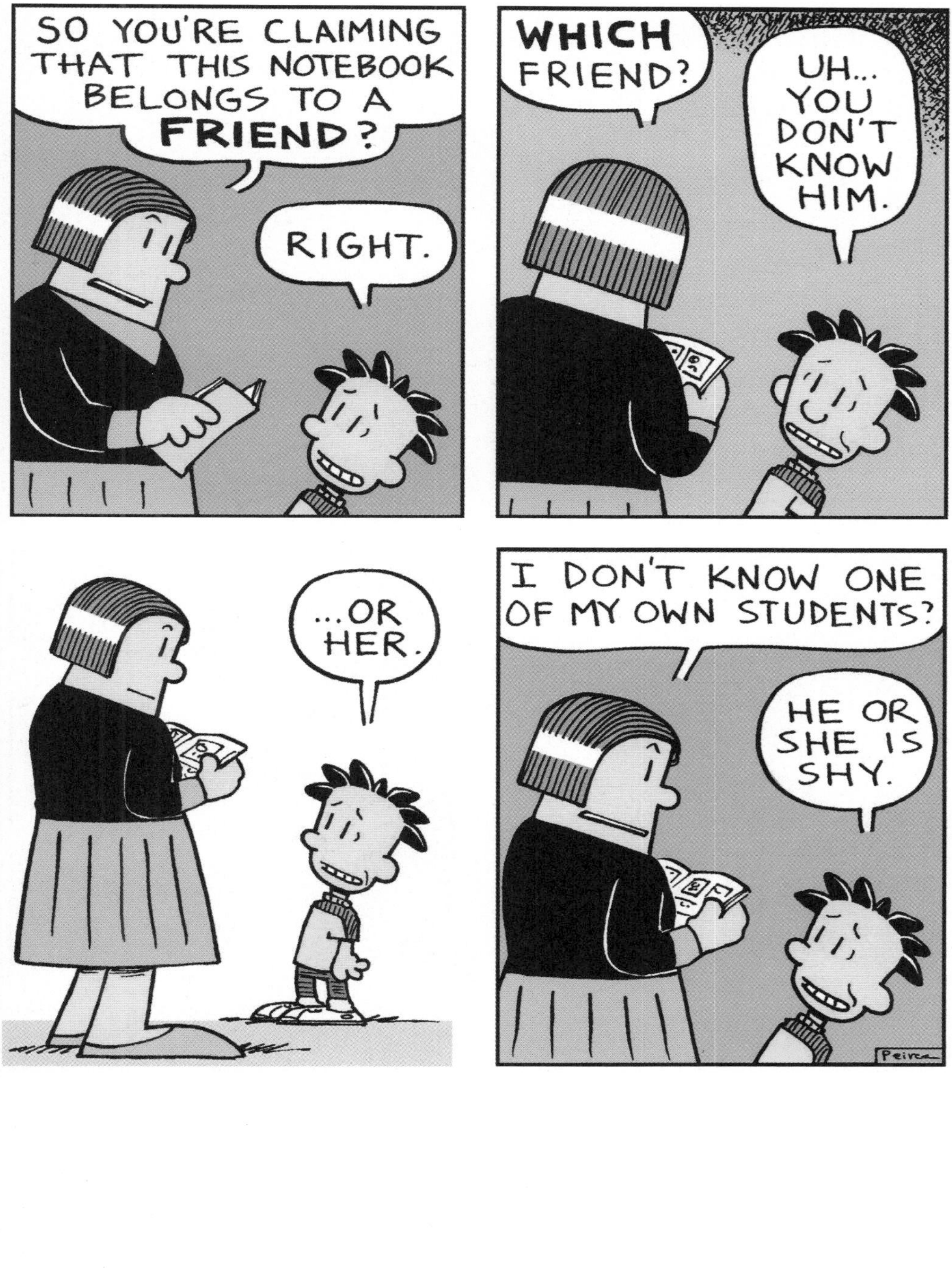
SO YOU'RE CLAIMING THAT THIS NOTEBOOK BELONGS TO A **FRIEND**?
RIGHT.
WHICH FRIEND?
UH... YOU DON'T KNOW HIM.
...OR HER.
I DON'T KNOW ONE OF MY OWN STUDENTS?
HE OR SHE IS SHY.
Peirce

NATE, LET'S END THIS CHARADE. WE BOTH KNOW THIS NOTEBOOK IS YOURS.
WHO ELSE BUT YOU WOULD DRAW A COMIC STRIP CALLED "MRS. GODFREY: ADVENTURES IN SUMO"?
MMPH.
I'M SO **PLEASED** I **AMUSE** YOU!
MY IMPULSE CONTROL NEEDS WORK.
Peirce

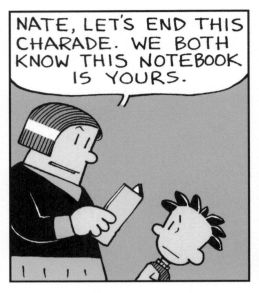

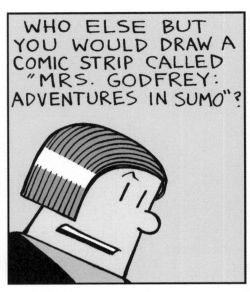

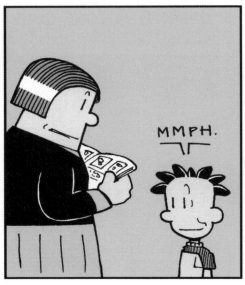

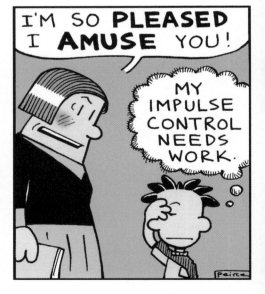

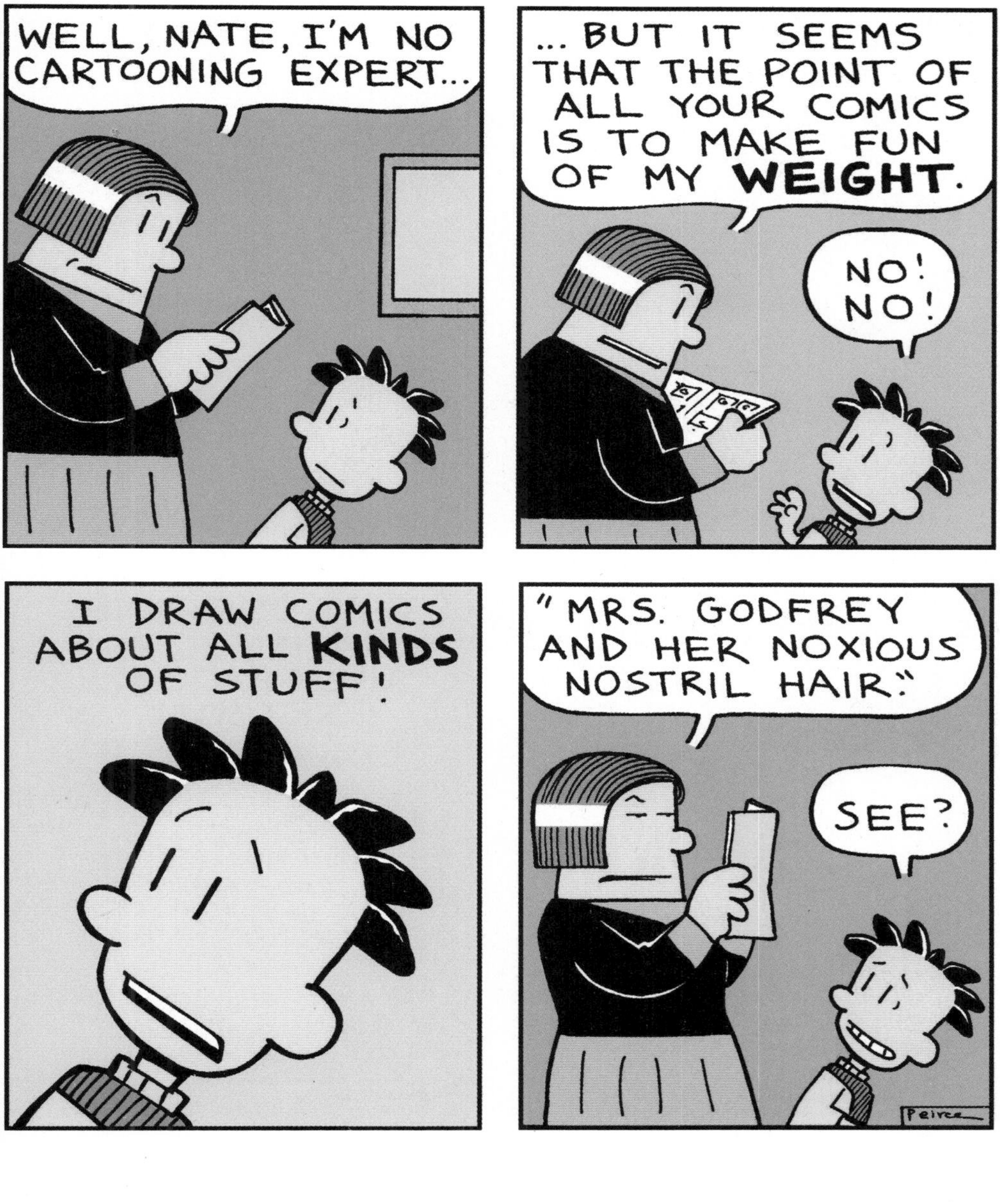
WELL, NATE, I'M NO CARTOONING EXPERT...
... BUT IT SEEMS THAT THE POINT OF ALL YOUR COMICS IS TO MAKE FUN OF MY **WEIGHT**.
NO! NO!
I DRAW COMICS ABOUT ALL **KINDS** OF STUFF!
"MRS. GODFREY AND HER NOXIOUS NOSTRIL HAIR."
SEE?
Peirce

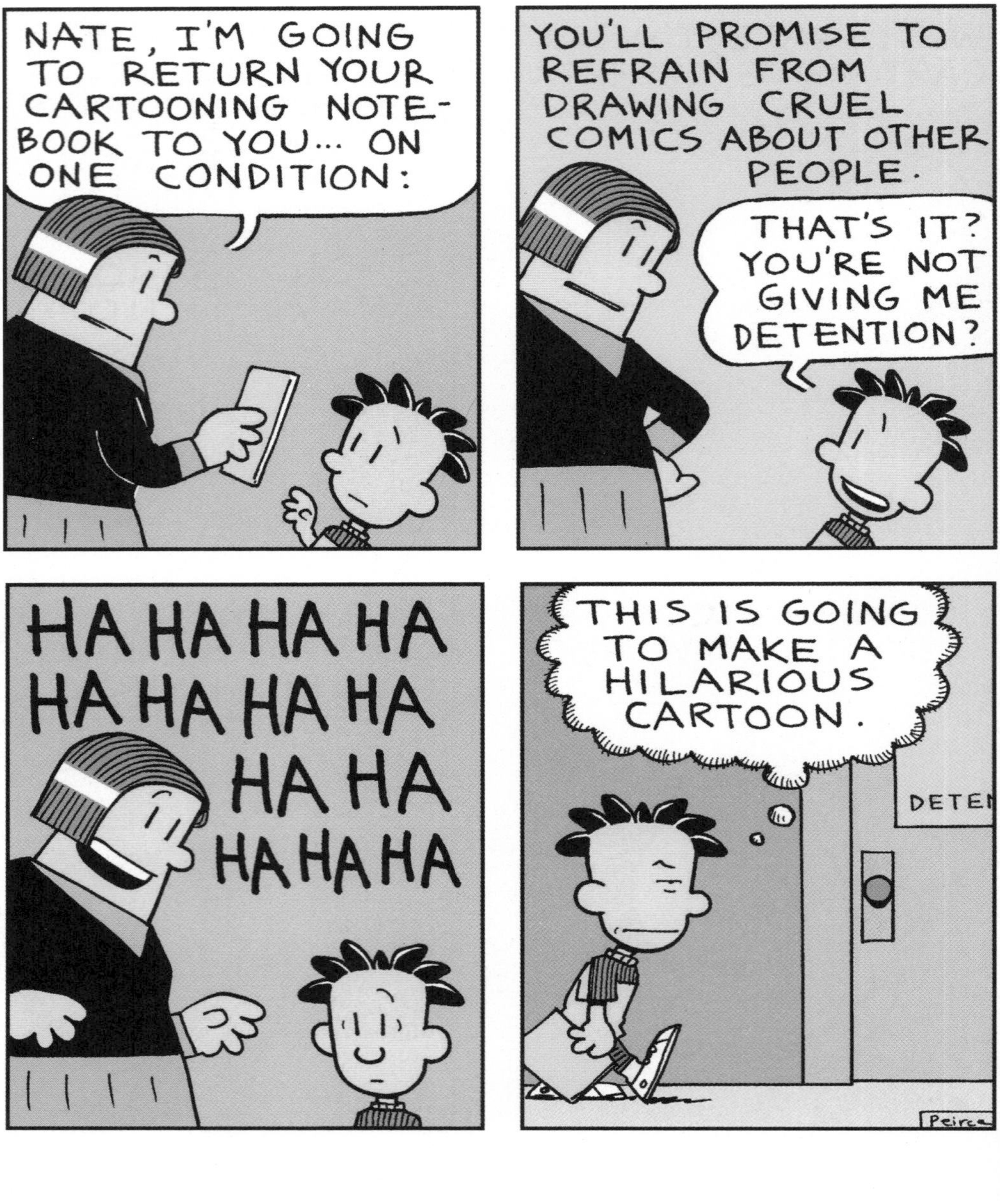
NATE, I'M GOING TO RETURN YOUR CARTOONING NOTE-BOOK TO YOU... ON ONE CONDITION:
YOU'LL PROMISE TO REFRAIN FROM DRAWING CRUEL COMICS ABOUT OTHER PEOPLE.
THAT'S IT? YOU'RE NOT GIVING ME DETENTION?
HA HA HA HA HA
HA HA HA HA HA
HA HA
HA HA HA HA
THIS IS GOING TO MAKE A HILARIOUS CARTOON.
DETEN
Peirce

MRS. GODFREY CHEWED ME OUT ABOUT MY COMICS. SHE SAID THEY'RE TOO MEAN.
WELL... THEY **ARE** KINDA MEAN.
ALL YOU DO IS MOCK PEOPLE YOU DON'T LIKE.
BUT IT'S **FUNNY!**
FUNNY, YES. BUT DEFINITELY OVER THE TOP.
WHAT? WHEN HAVE I EVER BEEN OVER THE TOP?
YOU ONCE CREATED A 300-PAGE GRAPHIC NOVEL ABOUT COACH JOHN'S TOUPÉE.
I WANTED TO BE THOROUGH.

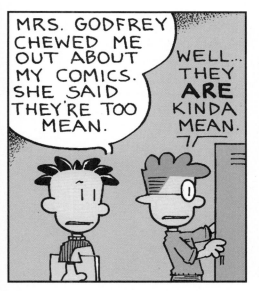

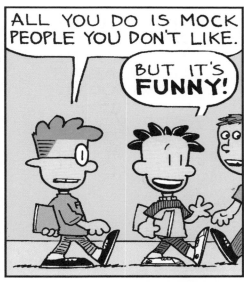

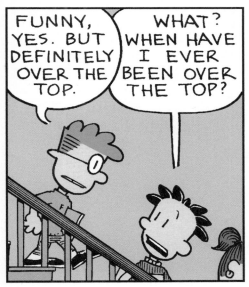

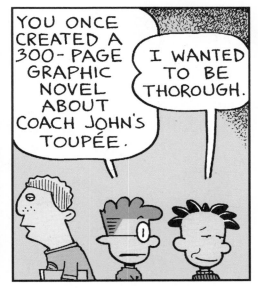

I DON'T SEE WHY IT'S A BIG DEAL IF I DRAW A MEAN CARTOON ABOUT SOMEBODY!

LOOK AT POLITICAL CARTOONISTS! THEY RIP PEOPLE ALL THE **TIME**!

BUT THEY'RE DOING IT FOR A **REASON**!

THEY'RE USING CARTOONS TO TELL PEOPLE ABOUT ISSUES THEY SHOULD BE AWARE OF!

WHICH IS EXACTLY WHAT **I'M** DOING!

PEOPLE NEED TO BE AWARE OF MRS. GODFREY'S TOXIC TUNA BREATH?

THINK OF IT AS A PUBLIC SERVICE!

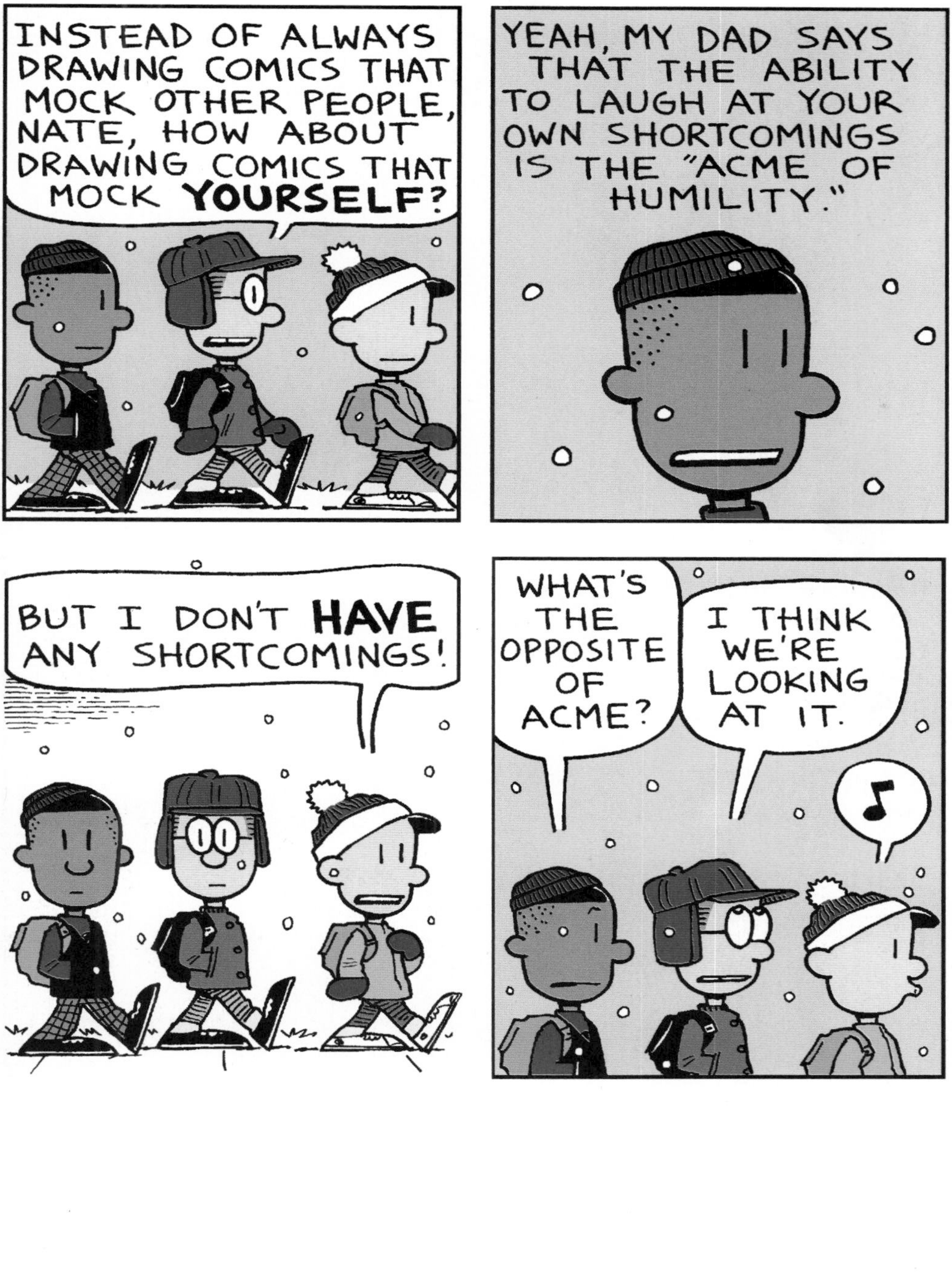
INSTEAD OF ALWAYS DRAWING COMICS THAT MOCK OTHER PEOPLE, NATE, HOW ABOUT DRAWING COMICS THAT MOCK **YOURSELF**?
YEAH, MY DAD SAYS THAT THE ABILITY TO LAUGH AT YOUR OWN SHORTCOMINGS IS THE "ACME OF HUMILITY."
BUT I DON'T **HAVE** ANY SHORTCOMINGS!
WHAT'S THE OPPOSITE OF ACME?
I THINK WE'RE LOOKING AT IT.

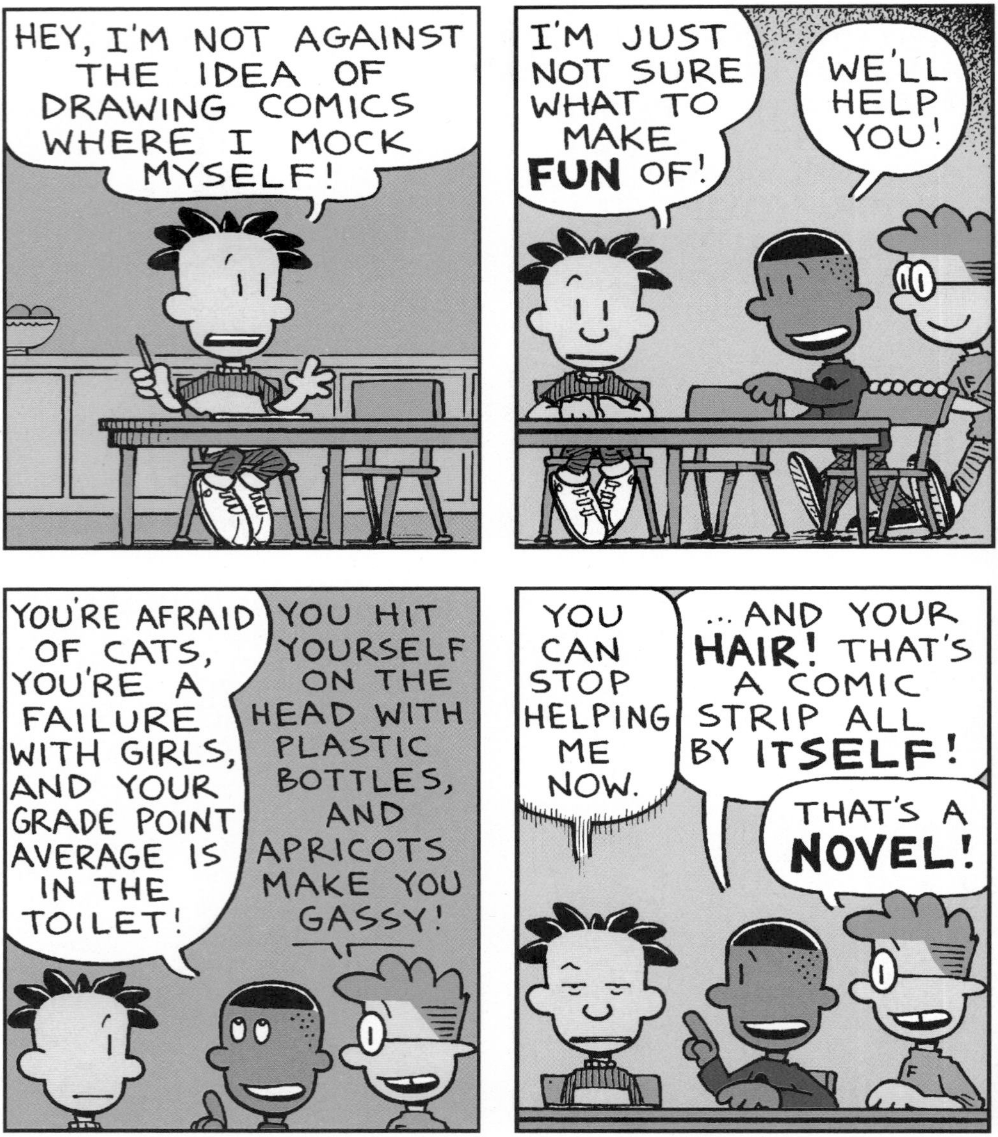
HEY, I'M NOT AGAINST THE IDEA OF DRAWING COMICS WHERE I MOCK MYSELF!
I'M JUST NOT SURE WHAT TO MAKE **FUN** OF!
WE'LL HELP YOU!
YOU'RE AFRAID OF CATS, YOU'RE A FAILURE WITH GIRLS, AND YOUR GRADE POINT AVERAGE IS IN THE TOILET!
YOU HIT YOURSELF ON THE HEAD WITH PLASTIC BOTTLES, AND APRICOTS MAKE YOU GASSY!
YOU CAN STOP HELPING ME NOW.
... AND YOUR **HAIR!** THAT'S A COMIC STRIP ALL BY **ITSELF!**
THAT'S A **NOVEL!**

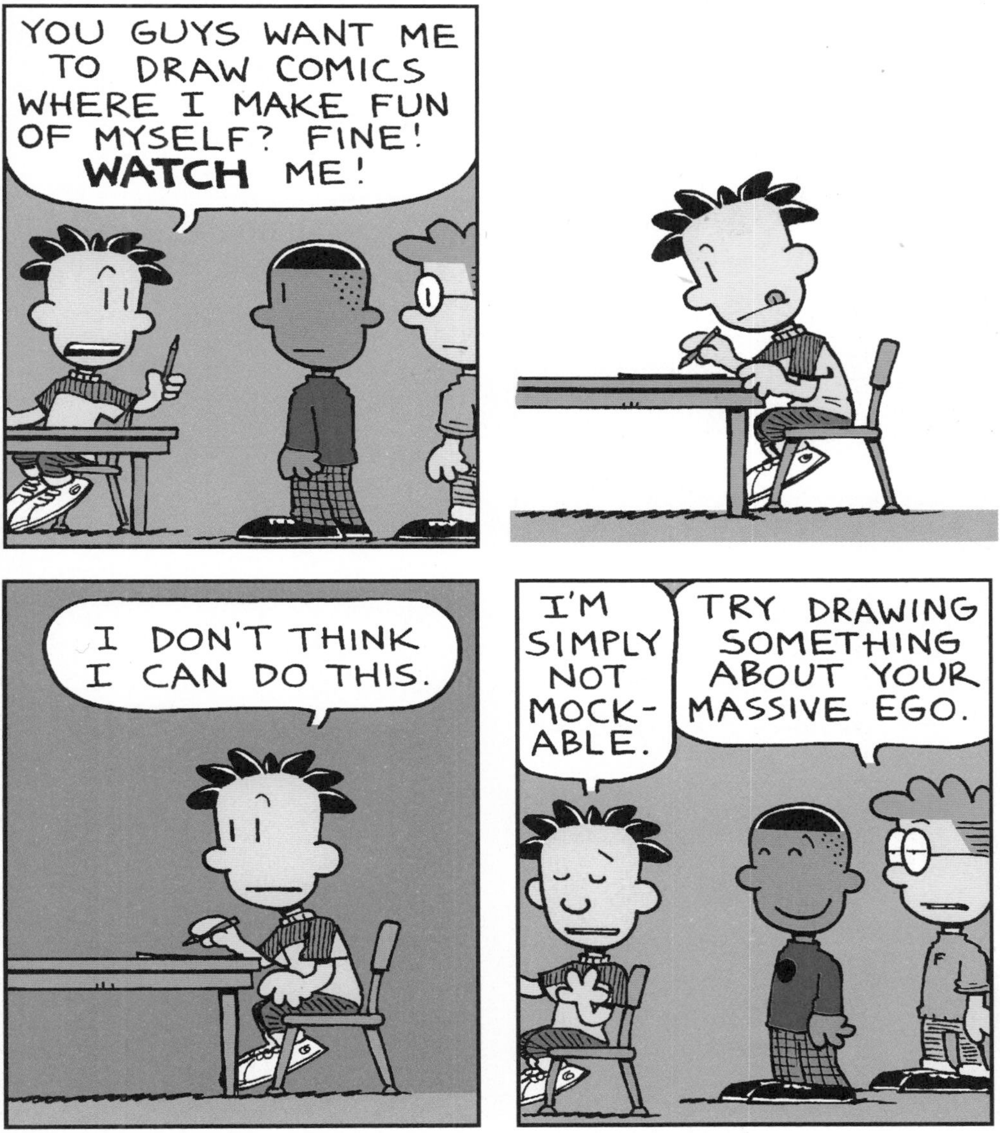
YOU GUYS WANT ME TO DRAW COMICS WHERE I MAKE FUN OF MYSELF? FINE! **WATCH** ME!
I DON'T THINK I CAN DO THIS.
I'M SIMPLY NOT MOCK-ABLE.
TRY DRAWING SOMETHING ABOUT YOUR MASSIVE EGO.

WELL, I DID IT!
JUST LIKE YOU SUGGESTED, I DREW COMICS WHERE **I'M** THE BUTT OF THE JOKE!
AND WHAT **IS** THE JOKE?
THE JOKE IS: I'M COMPLETELY UNAWARE OF HOW **EXCEPTIONAL** I AM!
IT'S FUNNY BECAUSE IT'S **TRUE**!
I'M LAUGHING ALREADY.

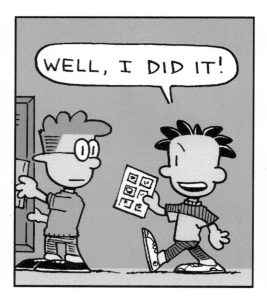

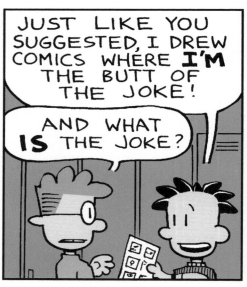

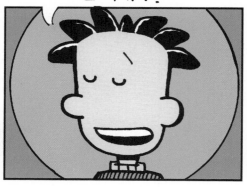

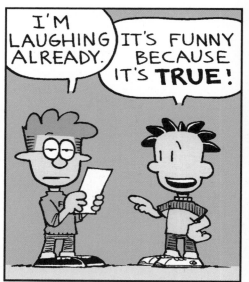

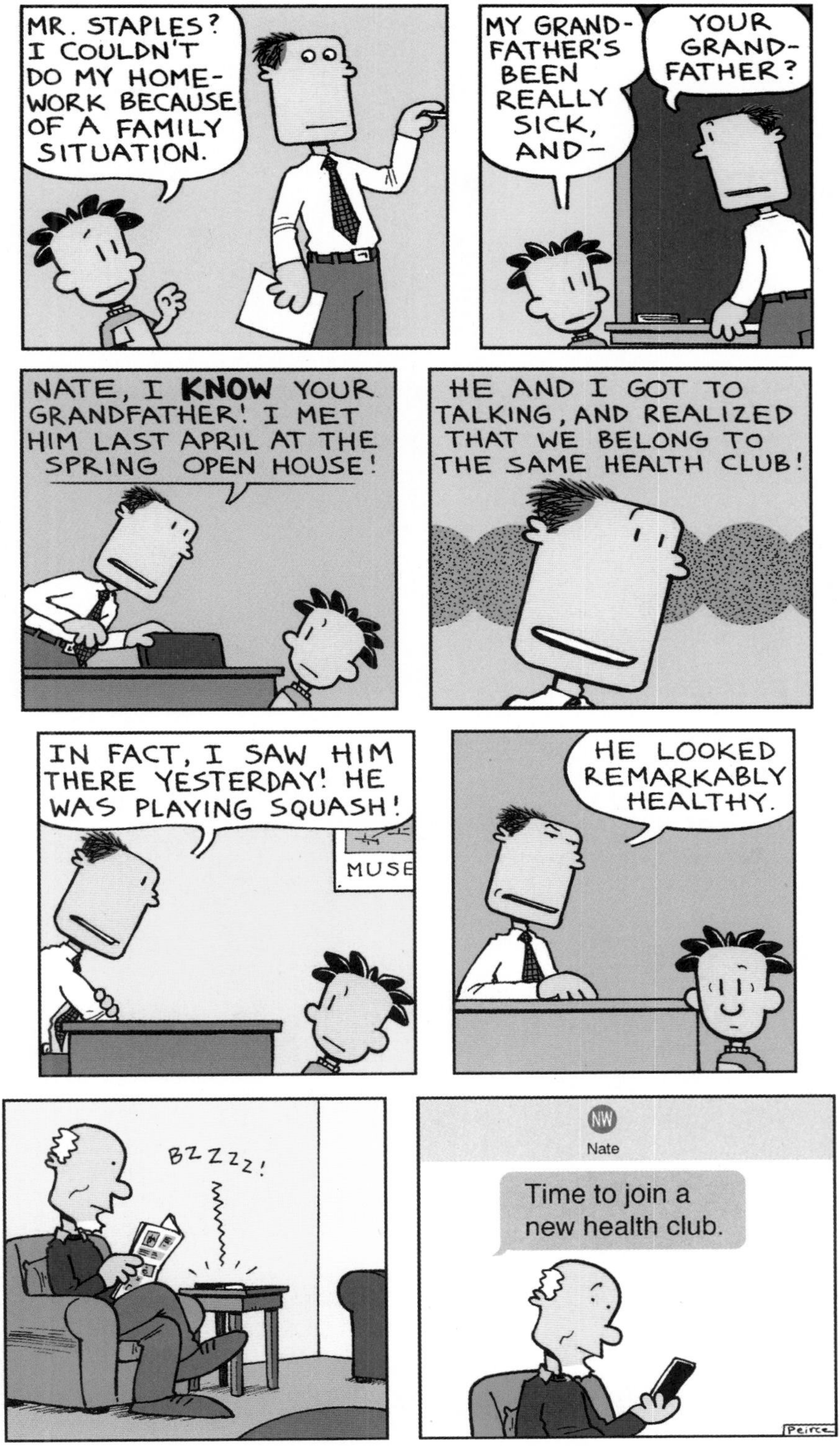
MR. STAPLES? I COULDN'T DO MY HOME-WORK BECAUSE OF A FAMILY SITUATION.
MY GRAND-FATHER'S BEEN REALLY SICK, AND-
YOUR GRAND-FATHER?
NATE, I KNOW YOUR GRANDFATHER! I MET HIM LAST APRIL AT THE SPRING OPEN HOUSE!
HE AND I GOT TO TALKING, AND REALIZED THAT WE BELONG TO THE SAME HEALTH CLUB!
IN FACT, I SAW HIM THERE YESTERDAY! HE WAS PLAYING SQUASH!
MUSE
HE LOOKED REMARKABLY HEALTHY.
BZZZZ!
NW
Nate
Time to join a new health club.
Peirce

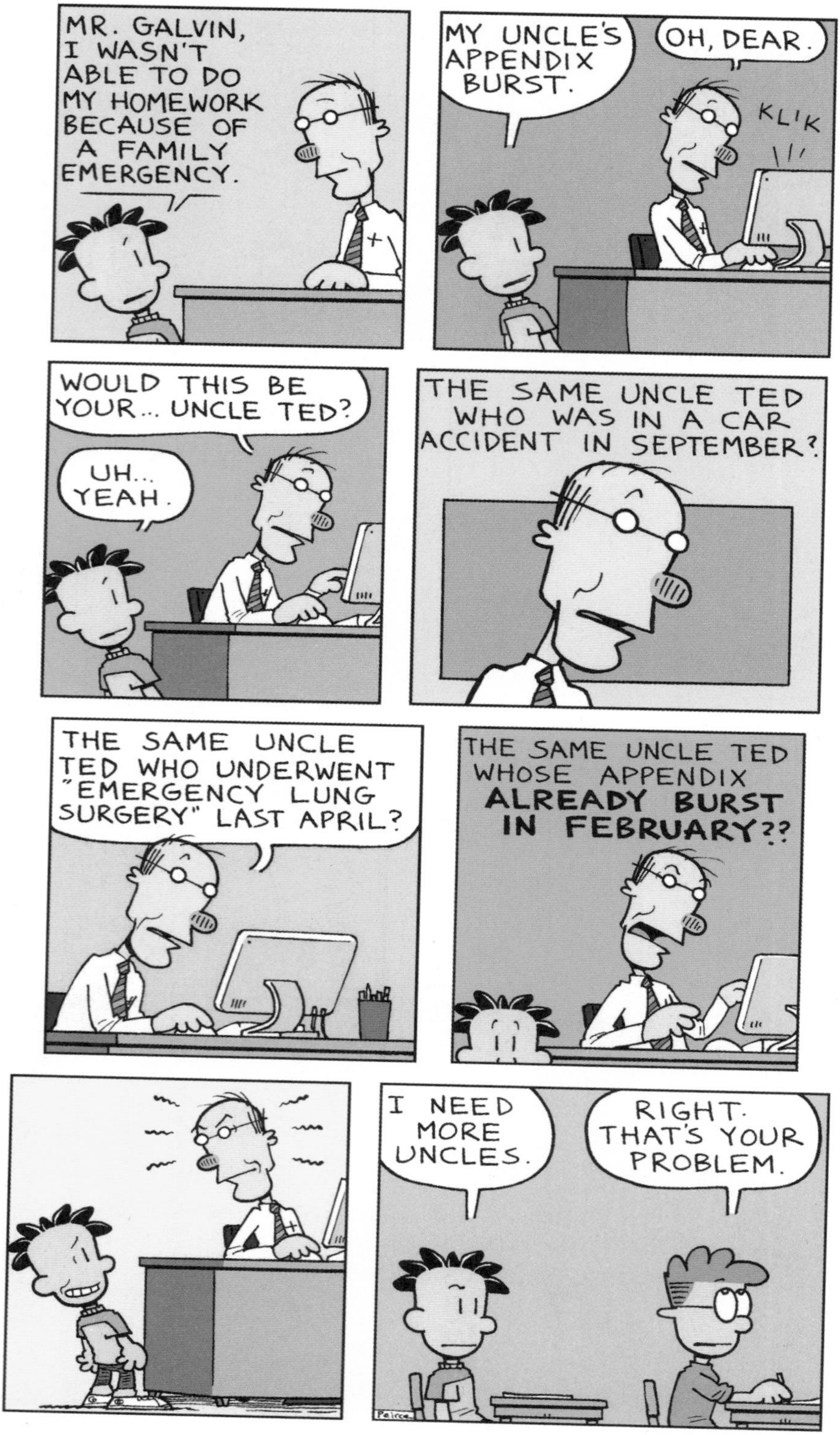
MR. GALVIN, I WASN'T ABLE TO DO MY HOMEWORK BECAUSE OF A FAMILY EMERGENCY.
MY UNCLE'S APPENDIX BURST.
OH, DEAR.
KLIK
WOULD THIS BE YOUR... UNCLE TED?
UH... YEAH.
THE SAME UNCLE TED WHO WAS IN A CAR ACCIDENT IN SEPTEMBER?
THE SAME UNCLE TED WHO UNDERWENT "EMERGENCY LUNG SURGERY" LAST APRIL?
THE SAME UNCLE TED WHOSE APPENDIX **ALREADY BURST IN FEBRUARY??**
I NEED MORE UNCLES.
RIGHT. THAT'S YOUR PROBLEM.
Peirce

MR. GALVIN BUSTED ME THE OTHER DAY FOR USING A BOGUS HOMEWORK EXCUSE.

THEN HE POINTED OUT **ALL** THE BOGUS EXCUSES I USED OVER THE PAST FEW MONTHS.

HE MADE ME SEE HOW WRONG I'VE BEEN. HE INSPIRED ME TO TRY A COMPLETELY NEW APPROACH.

WAIT FOR IT.

HELP ME COME UP WITH SOME FRESH EXCUSES.

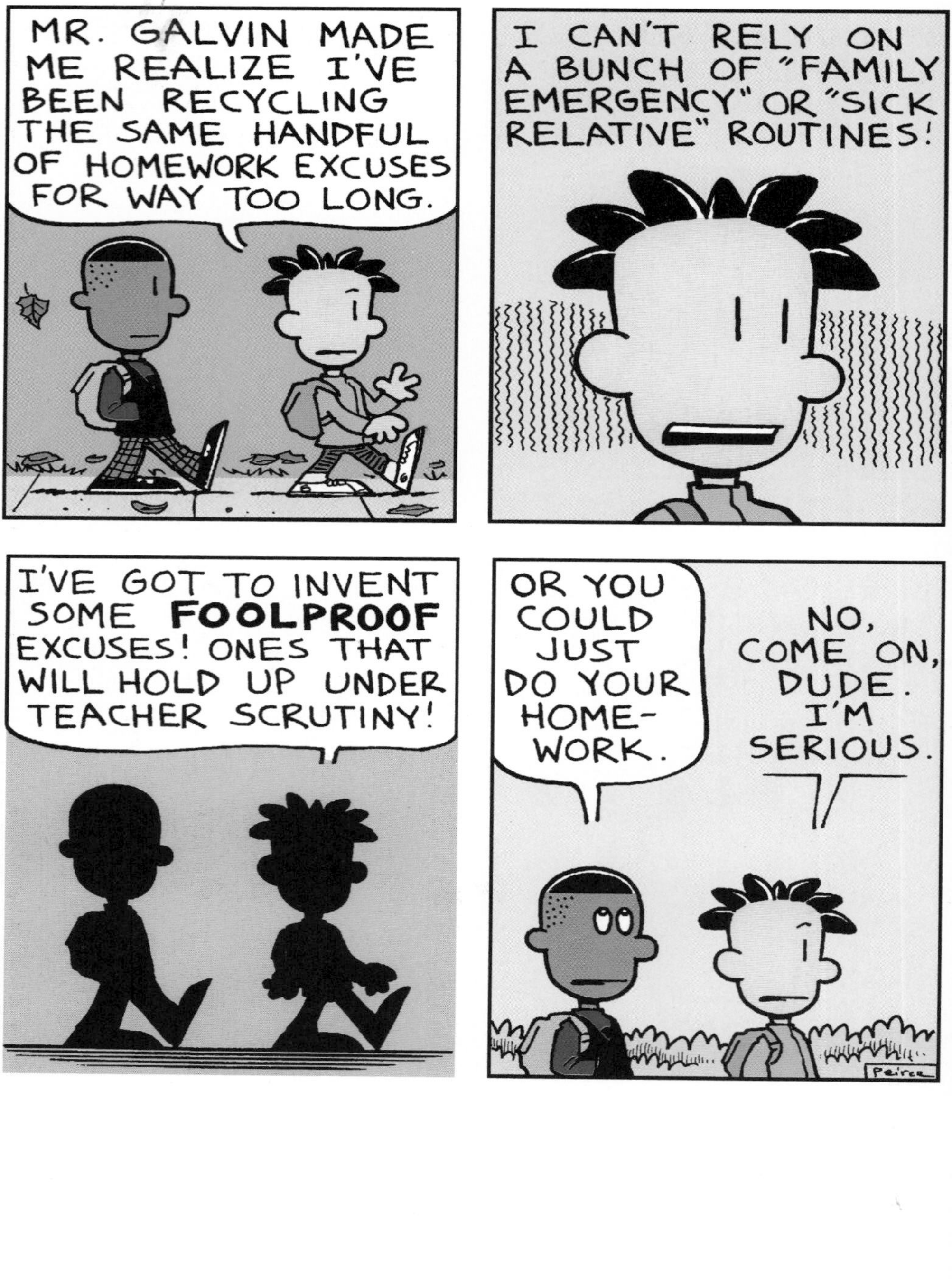
MR. GALVIN MADE ME REALIZE I'VE BEEN RECYCLING THE SAME HANDFUL OF HOMEWORK EXCUSES FOR WAY TOO LONG.
I CAN'T RELY ON A BUNCH OF "FAMILY EMERGENCY" OR "SICK RELATIVE" ROUTINES!
I'VE GOT TO INVENT SOME **FOOLPROOF** EXCUSES! ONES THAT WILL HOLD UP UNDER TEACHER SCRUTINY!
OR YOU COULD JUST DO YOUR HOME-WORK.
NO, COME ON, DUDE. I'M SERIOUS.
Peirce

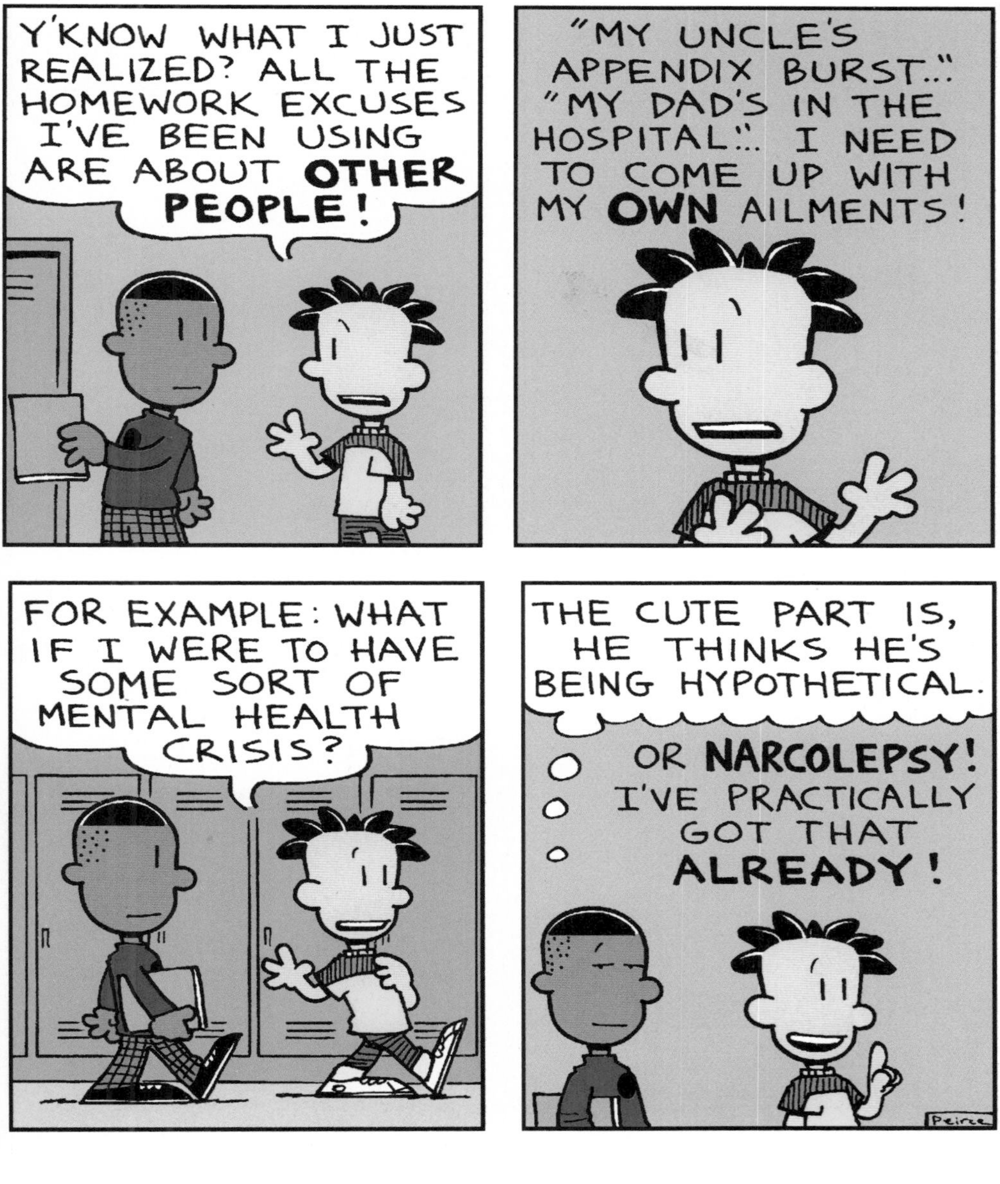
Y'KNOW WHAT I JUST REALIZED? ALL THE HOMEWORK EXCUSES I'VE BEEN USING ARE ABOUT **OTHER PEOPLE**!
"MY UNCLE'S APPENDIX BURST..." "MY DAD'S IN THE HOSPITAL!"... I NEED TO COME UP WITH MY **OWN** AILMENTS!
FOR EXAMPLE: WHAT IF I WERE TO HAVE SOME SORT OF MENTAL HEALTH CRISIS?
THE CUTE PART IS, HE THINKS HE'S BEING HYPOTHETICAL.
OR **NARCOLEPSY**! I'VE PRACTICALLY GOT THAT **ALREADY**!
PEIRCE

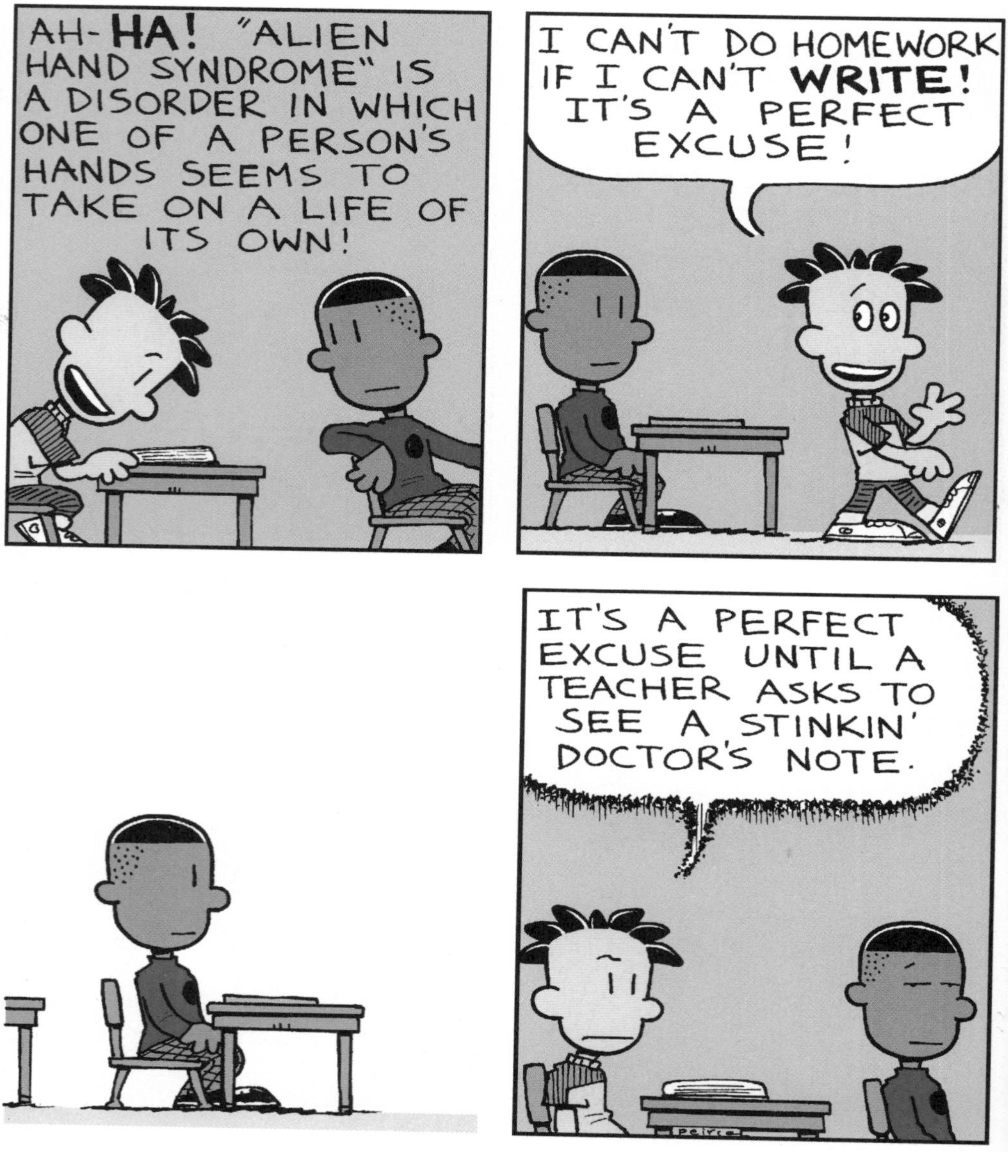
AH-**HA!** "ALIEN HAND SYNDROME" IS A DISORDER IN WHICH ONE OF A PERSON'S HANDS SEEMS TO TAKE ON A LIFE OF ITS OWN!
I CAN'T DO HOMEWORK IF I CAN'T **WRITE!** IT'S A PERFECT EXCUSE!
IT'S A PERFECT EXCUSE UNTIL A TEACHER ASKS TO SEE A STINKIN' DOCTOR'S NOTE.
peirce

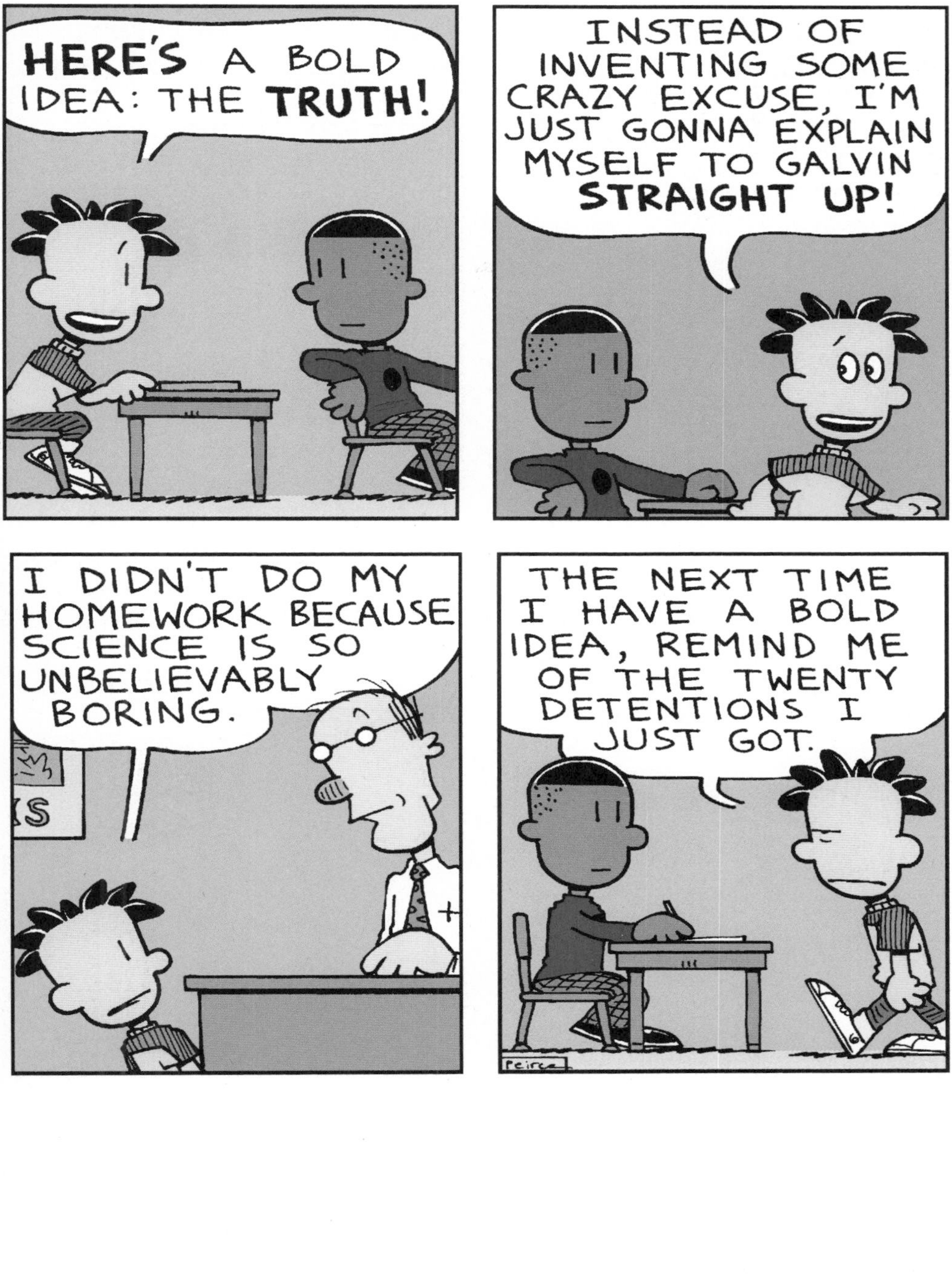
HERE'S A BOLD IDEA: THE TRUTH!
INSTEAD OF INVENTING SOME CRAZY EXCUSE, I'M JUST GONNA EXPLAIN MYSELF TO GALVIN STRAIGHT UP!
I DIDN'T DO MY HOMEWORK BECAUSE SCIENCE IS SO UNBELIEVABLY BORING.
THE NEXT TIME I HAVE A BOLD IDEA, REMIND ME OF THE TWENTY DETENTIONS I JUST GOT.
Peirce

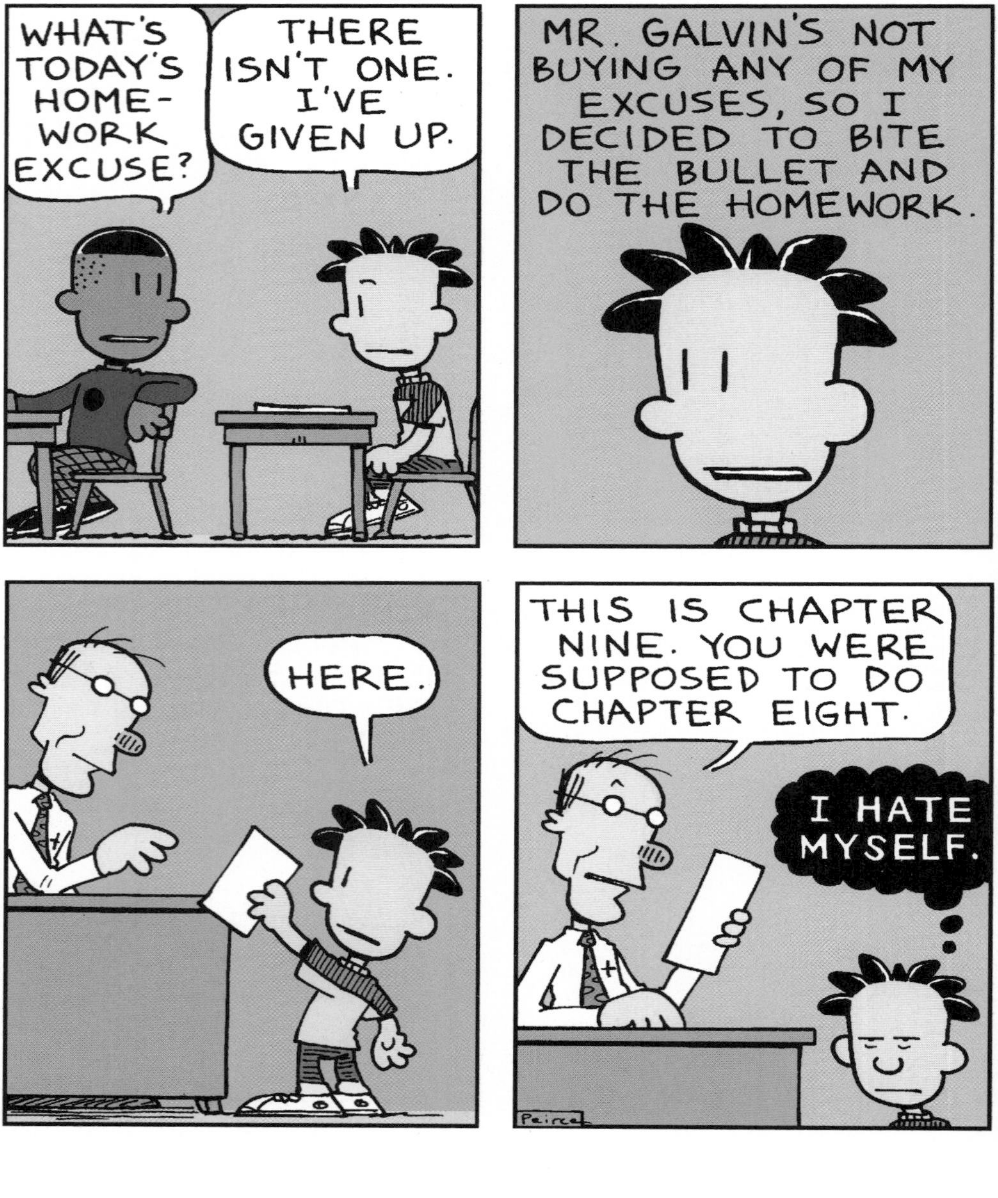
WHAT'S TODAY'S HOME-WORK EXCUSE?
THERE ISN'T ONE. I'VE GIVEN UP.
MR. GALVIN'S NOT BUYING ANY OF MY EXCUSES, SO I DECIDED TO BITE THE BULLET AND DO THE HOMEWORK.
HERE.
THIS IS CHAPTER NINE. YOU WERE SUPPOSED TO DO CHAPTER EIGHT.
I HATE MYSELF.
Peirce

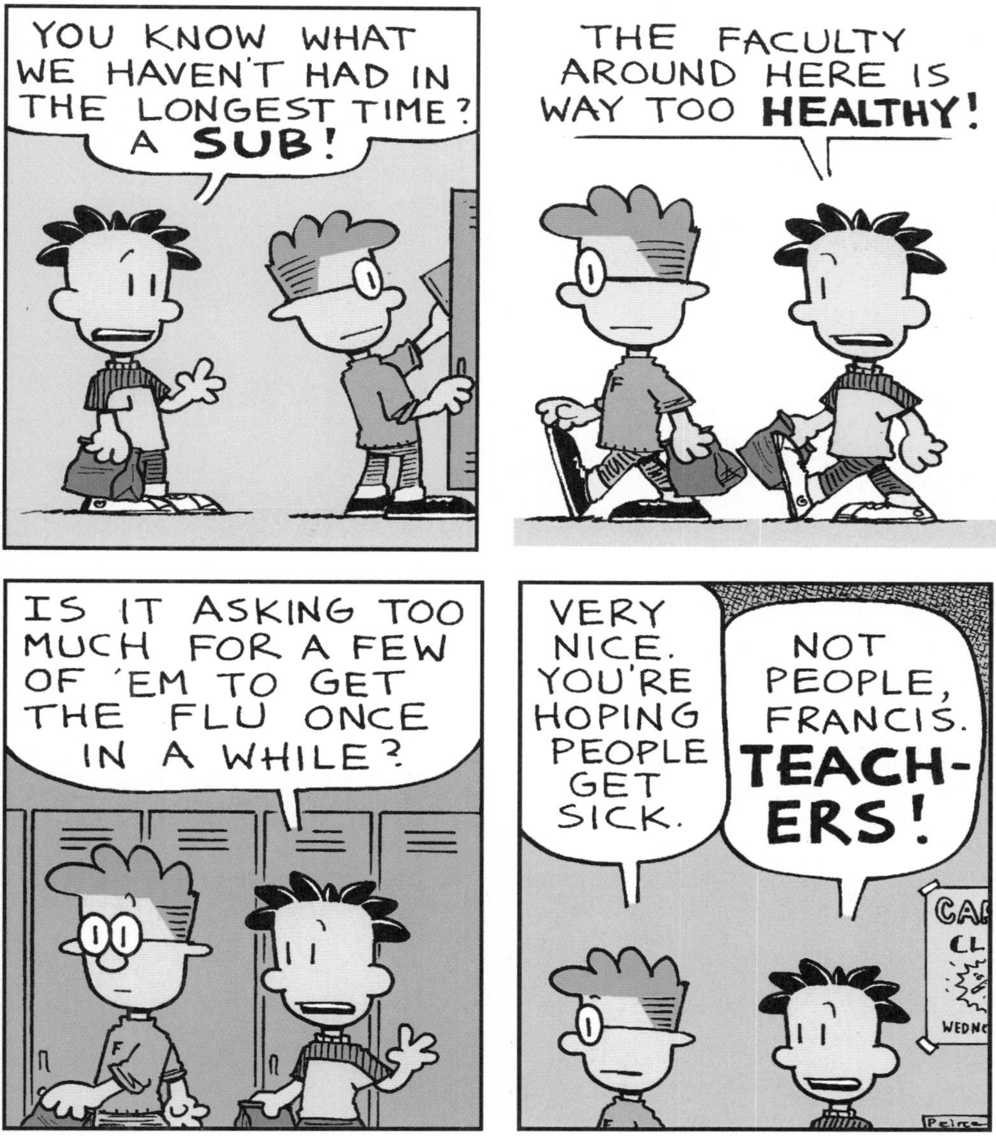
YOU KNOW WHAT WE HAVEN'T HAD IN THE LONGEST TIME? A **SUB**!
THE FACULTY AROUND HERE IS WAY TOO **HEALTHY**!
IS IT ASKING TOO MUCH FOR A FEW OF 'EM TO GET THE FLU ONCE IN A WHILE?
VERY NICE. YOU'RE HOPING PEOPLE GET SICK.
NOT PEOPLE, FRANCIS. **TEACHERS!**
Peirce

WHAT'S UP, GENTS?
NATE'S HOPING ALL THE TEACHERS GET SICK.
I JUST WANT A SUB EVERY NOW AND THEN! AND FOR THERE TO BE A SUB, A TEACHER HAS TO BE ABSENT!
HEY, I'M NOT ASKING FOR SOME SORT OF DEADLY DISEASE! A BASIC SLIP-AND-FALL WOULD BE FINE!
YOU'RE ALL HEART.
OOH! MINOR HEART ATTACK! GOOD ONE!
peirce

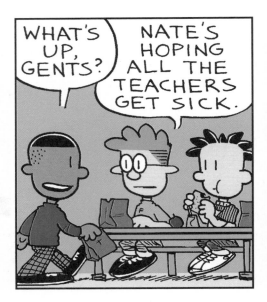

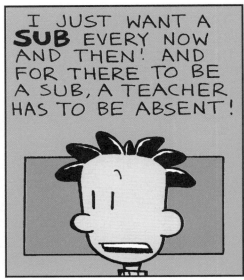

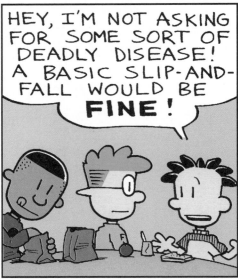

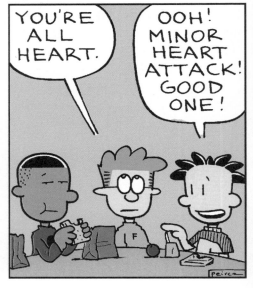

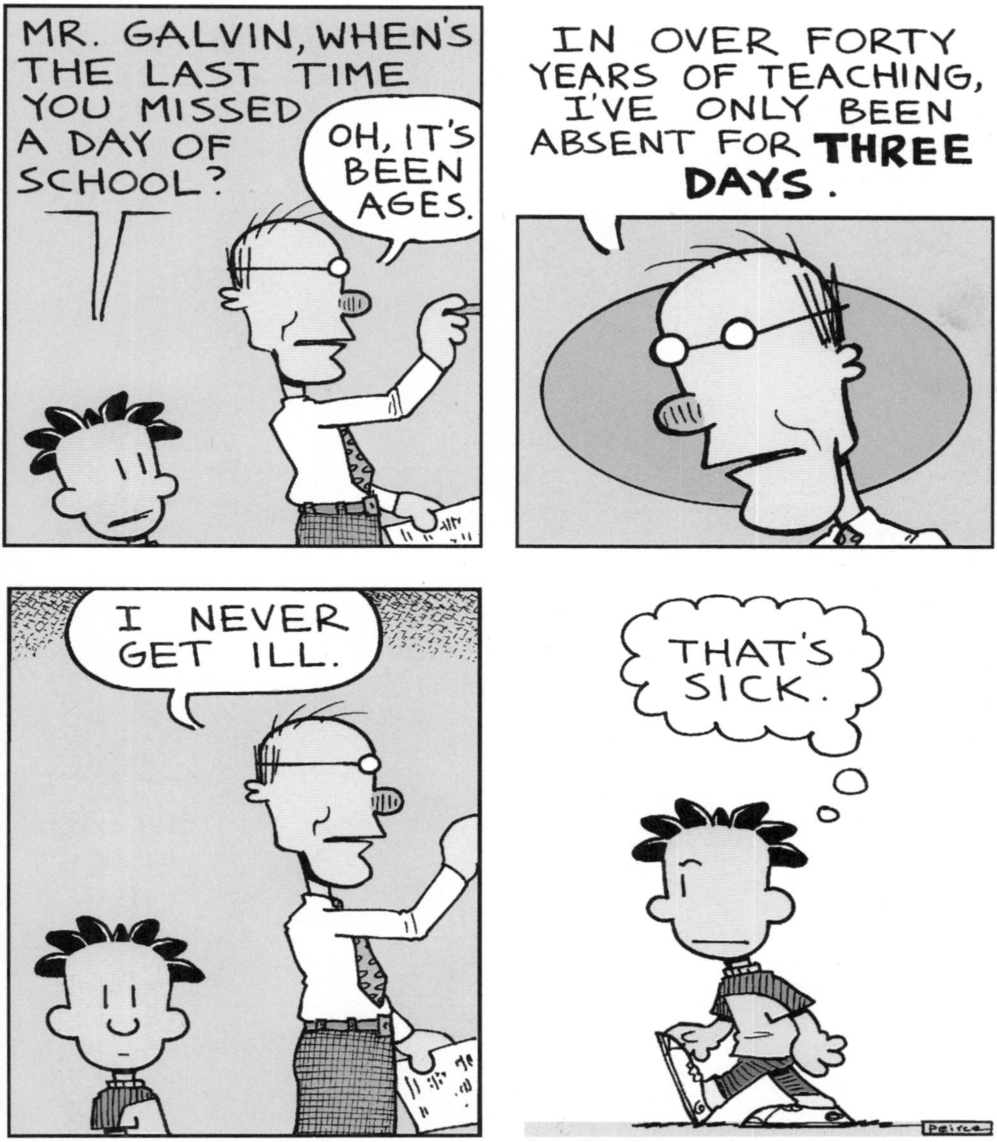
MR. GALVIN, WHEN'S THE LAST TIME YOU MISSED A DAY OF SCHOOL?
OH, IT'S BEEN AGES.
IN OVER FORTY YEARS OF TEACHING, I'VE ONLY BEEN ABSENT FOR **THREE DAYS**.
I NEVER GET ILL.
THAT'S SICK.
PEIRCE

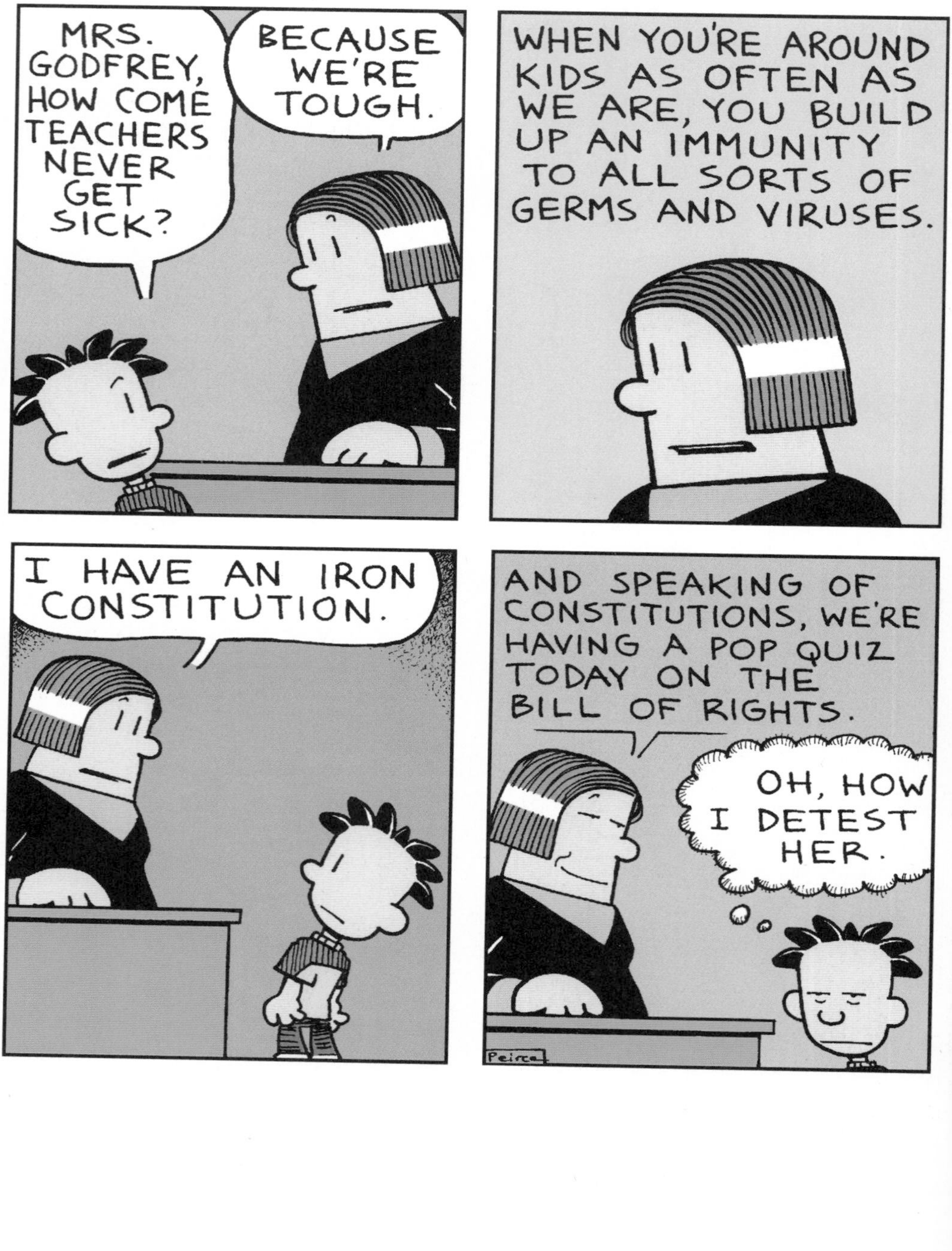
MRS. GODFREY, HOW COME TEACHERS NEVER GET SICK?
BECAUSE WE'RE TOUGH.
WHEN YOU'RE AROUND KIDS AS OFTEN AS WE ARE, YOU BUILD UP AN IMMUNITY TO ALL SORTS OF GERMS AND VIRUSES.
I HAVE AN IRON CONSTITUTION.
AND SPEAKING OF CONSTITUTIONS, WE'RE HAVING A POP QUIZ TODAY ON THE BILL OF RIGHTS.
OH, HOW I DETEST HER.
Peirce

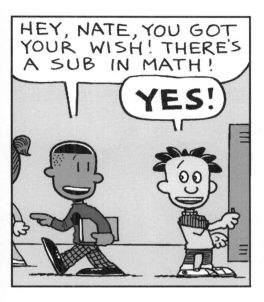

HEY, NATE, YOU GOT YOUR WISH! THERE'S A SUB IN MATH!

YES!

SEE? THERE SHE IS!

SO NOW THE QUESTION IS: WHAT KIND OF SUB IS SHE?

IS SHE AN EXPERIENCED SUB WHO'S GOING TO MAKE US **WORK**, OR A NEWBIE WHO WANTS TO BE OUR FRIEND?

HI, KIDS! WHO WANTS TWIZZLERS?

WE NOW HAVE CONTROL OF THIS ROOM.

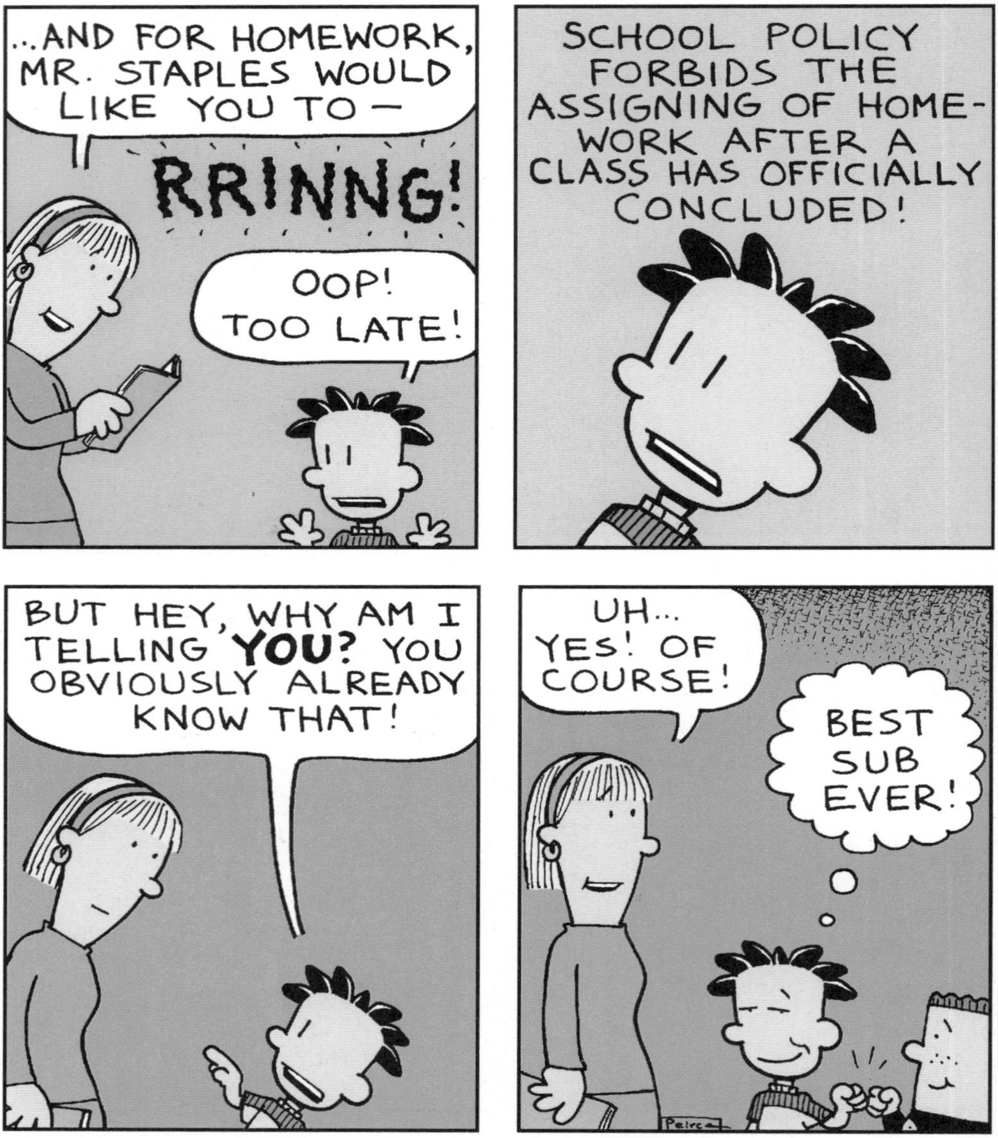
...AND FOR HOMEWORK, MR. STAPLES WOULD LIKE YOU TO —
RRINNG!
OOP! TOO LATE!
SCHOOL POLICY FORBIDS THE ASSIGNING OF HOME-WORK AFTER A CLASS HAS OFFICIALLY CONCLUDED!
BUT HEY, WHY AM I TELLING **YOU?** YOU OBVIOUSLY ALREADY KNOW THAT!
UH... YES! OF COURSE!
BEST SUB EVER!
Peirce

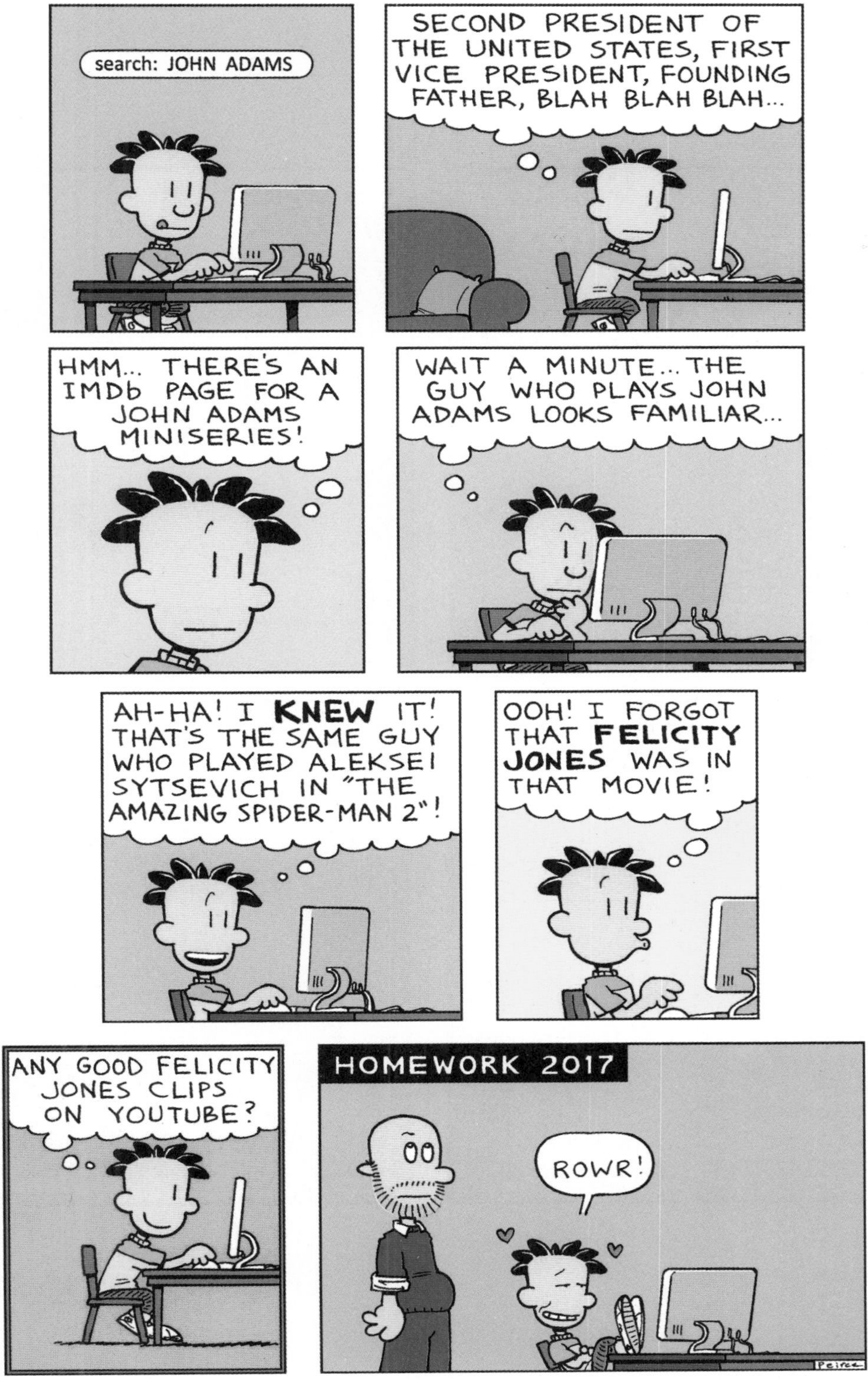
search: JOHN ADAMS
SECOND PRESIDENT OF THE UNITED STATES, FIRST VICE PRESIDENT, FOUNDING FATHER, BLAH BLAH BLAH...
HMM... THERE'S AN IMDb PAGE FOR A JOHN ADAMS MINISERIES!
WAIT A MINUTE... THE GUY WHO PLAYS JOHN ADAMS LOOKS FAMILIAR...
AH-HA! I KNEW IT! THAT'S THE SAME GUY WHO PLAYED ALEKSEI SYTSEVICH IN "THE AMAZING SPIDER-MAN 2"!
OOH! I FORGOT THAT FELICITY JONES WAS IN THAT MOVIE!
ANY GOOD FELICITY JONES CLIPS ON YOUTUBE?
HOMEWORK 2017
ROWR!
Peirce

HI, NATE!
GORDIE, MY MAN! I'M READY FOR WORK!
CHANGE OF PLANS, NATE. WE CANCELED YOUR SHIFT FOR TODAY.
HUH? HOW COME?
WE LOANED YOU OUT! YOU'LL BE WORKING IN ANOTHER PART OF THE MALL!
SO... WHERE DO I GO?
NORTH.
SANTA NEEDS AN ELF, AMIGO!

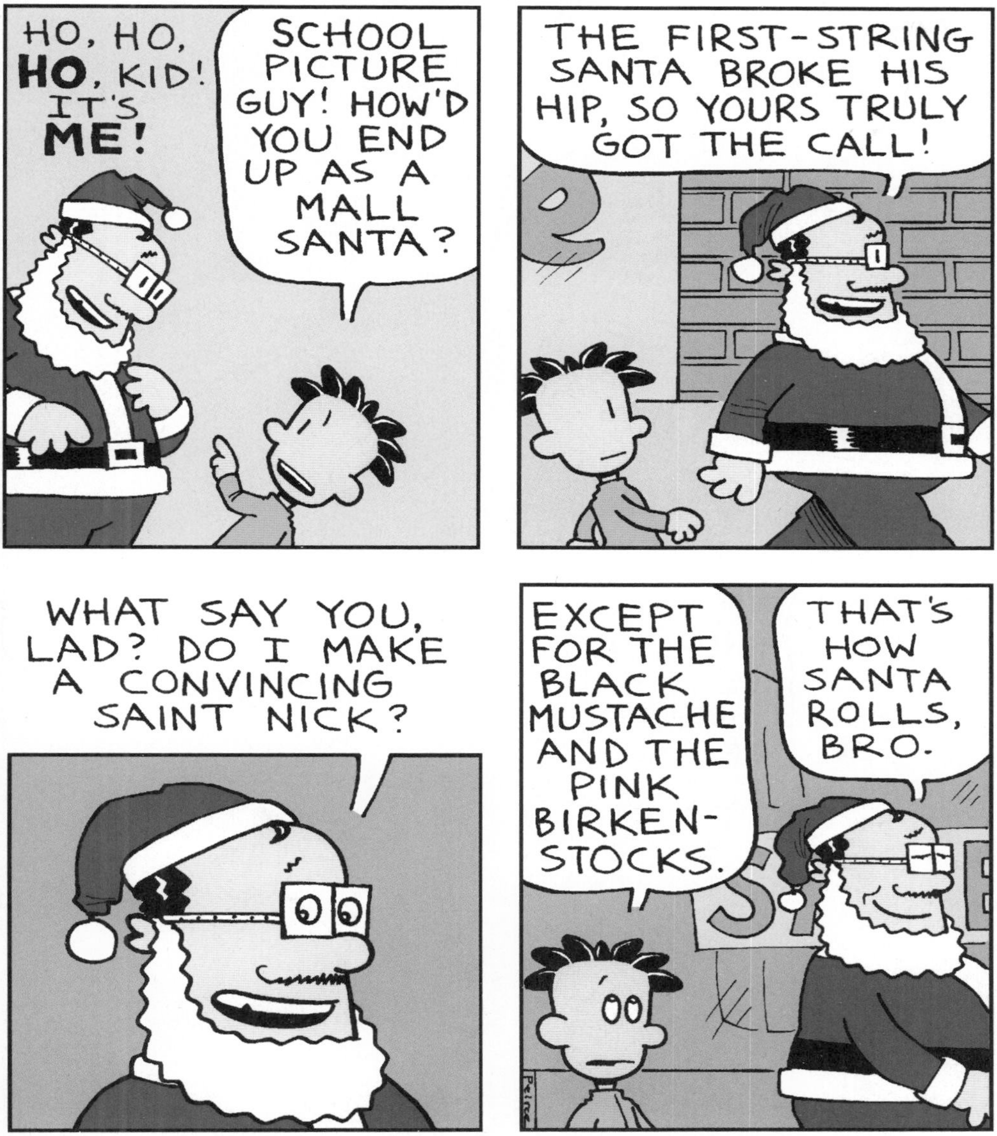
HO, HO, HO, KID! IT'S ME!
SCHOOL PICTURE GUY! HOW'D YOU END UP AS A MALL SANTA?
THE FIRST-STRING SANTA BROKE HIS HIP, SO YOURS TRULY GOT THE CALL!
WHAT SAY YOU, LAD? DO I MAKE A CONVINCING SAINT NICK?
EXCEPT FOR THE BLACK MUSTACHE AND THE PINK BIRKEN-STOCKS.
THAT'S HOW SANTA ROLLS, BRO.
PEIRCE

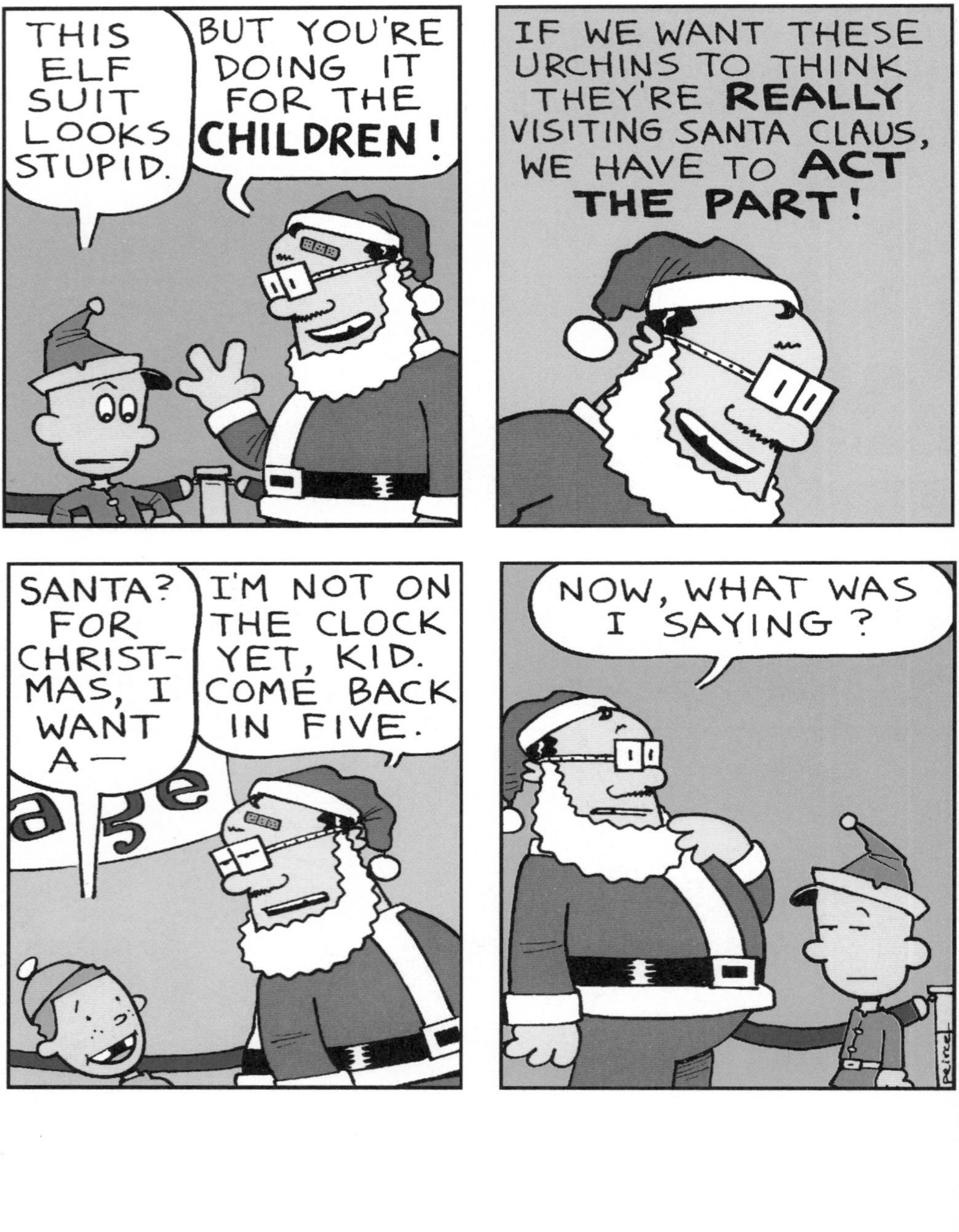
THIS ELF SUIT LOOKS STUPID.
BUT YOU'RE DOING IT FOR THE CHILDREN!
IF WE WANT THESE URCHINS TO THINK THEY'RE REALLY VISITING SANTA CLAUS, WE HAVE TO ACT THE PART!
SANTA? FOR CHRISTMAS, I WANT A—
I'M NOT ON THE CLOCK YET, KID. COME BACK IN FIVE.
NOW, WHAT WAS I SAYING?
PEIRCE

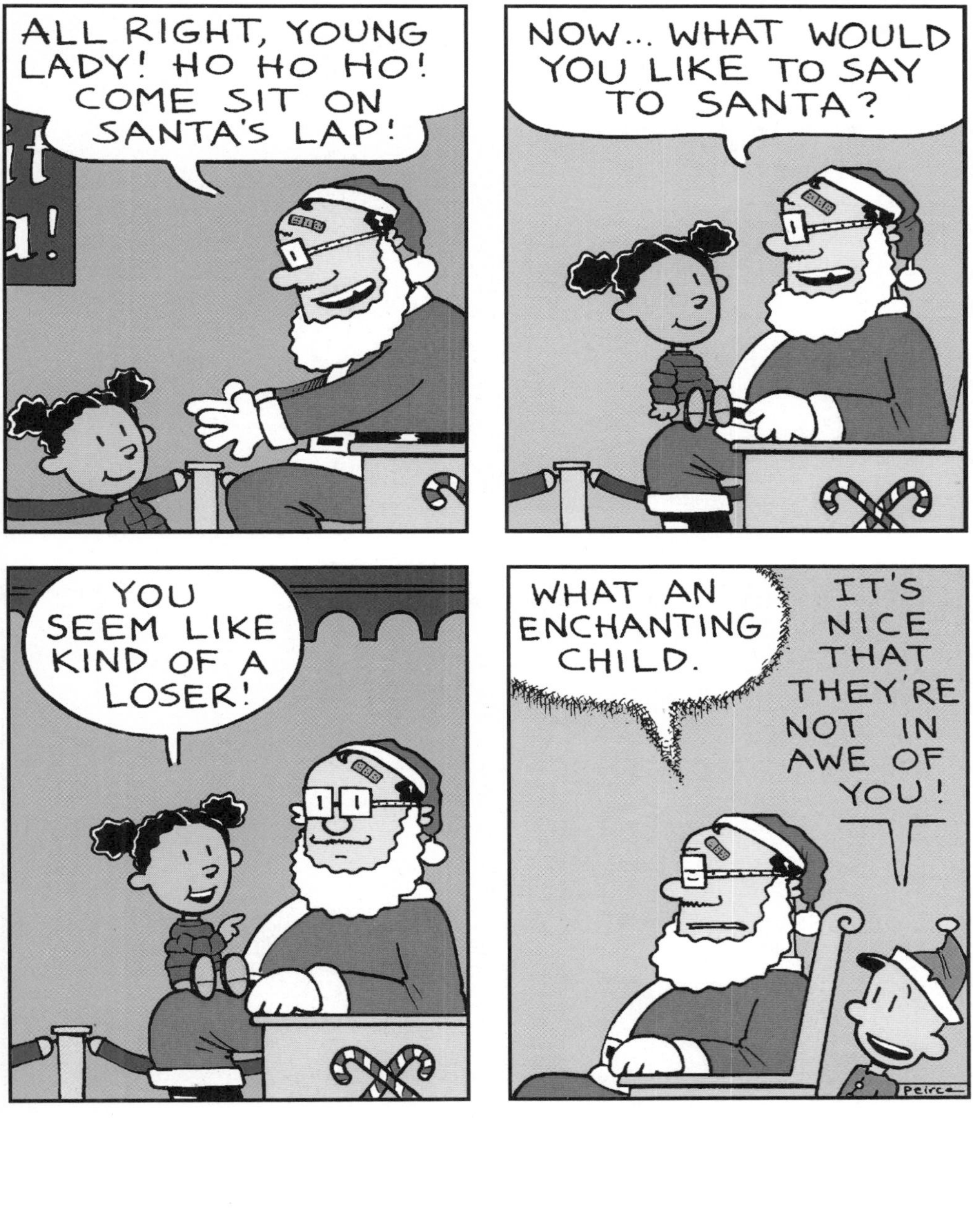
ALL RIGHT, YOUNG LADY! HO HO HO! COME SIT ON SANTA'S LAP!
NOW... WHAT WOULD YOU LIKE TO SAY TO SANTA?
YOU SEEM LIKE KIND OF A LOSER!
WHAT AN ENCHANTING CHILD.
IT'S NICE THAT THEY'RE NOT IN AWE OF YOU!
peirce

...AND THEIR NAMES ARE DASHER, DANCER, PRANCER, VIXEN, COMET, CUPID, DONNER, AND BLITZEN!

BUT WHAT ABOUT RUDOLPH?

RUDOLPH? HE'S JUST A CHARACTER CREATED IN 1939 FOR A DEPARTMENT STORE **BOOK GIVEAWAY!**

UNLIKE THE ORIGINAL EIGHT REINDEER, THAT RED-NOSED GLORY BOY IS NOTHING MORE THAN A GIANT **MERCHANDISING MACHINE!**

WAAAAH!

NICE MOVE, KRINGLE.

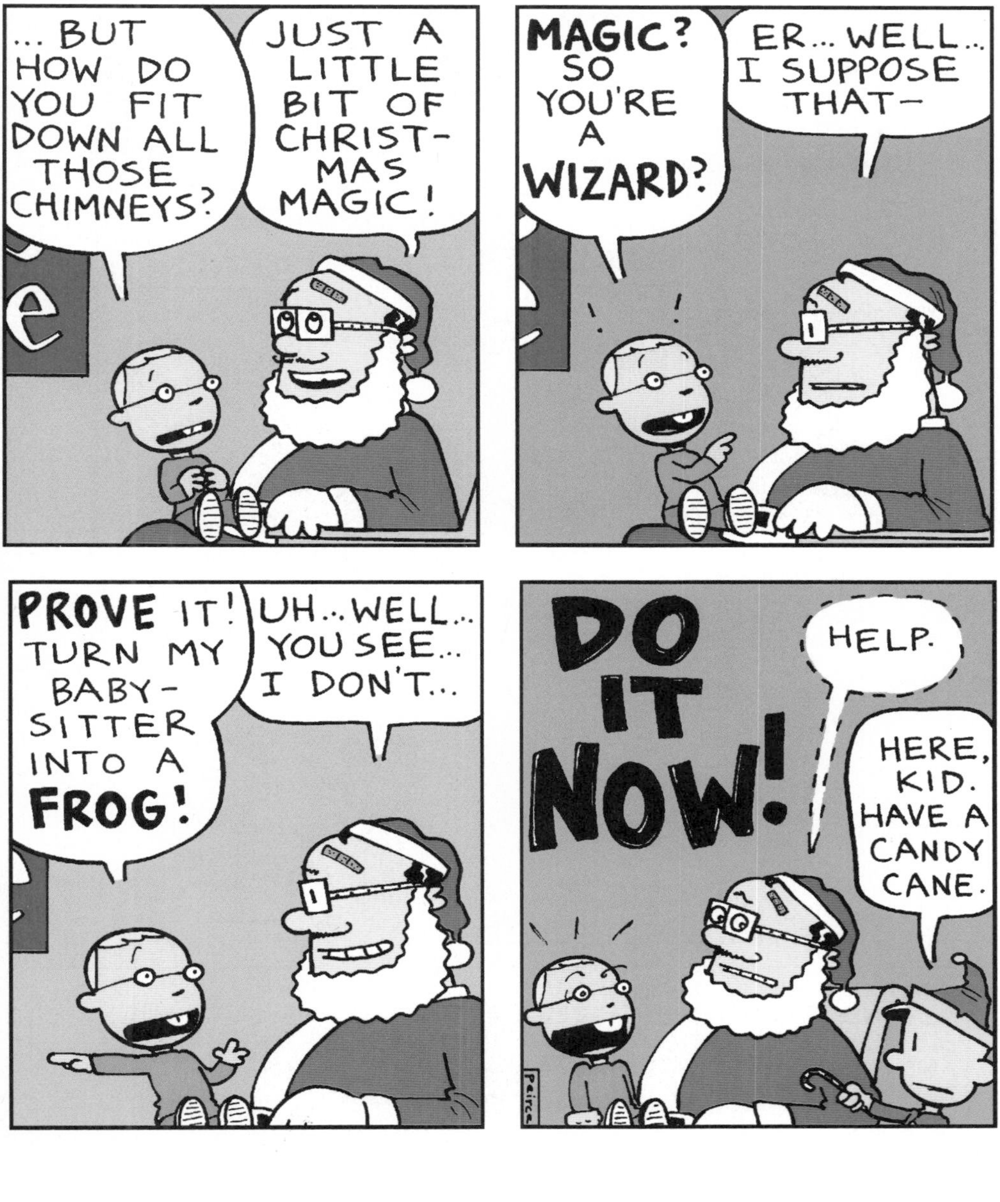
... BUT HOW DO YOU FIT DOWN ALL THOSE CHIMNEYS?
JUST A LITTLE BIT OF CHRIST-MAS MAGIC!
MAGIC? SO YOU'RE A WIZARD?
ER... WELL... I SUPPOSE THAT–
PROVE IT! TURN MY BABY-SITTER INTO A FROG!
UH... WELL... YOU SEE... I DON'T...
DO IT NOW!
HELP.
HERE, KID. HAVE A CANDY CANE.
Peirce

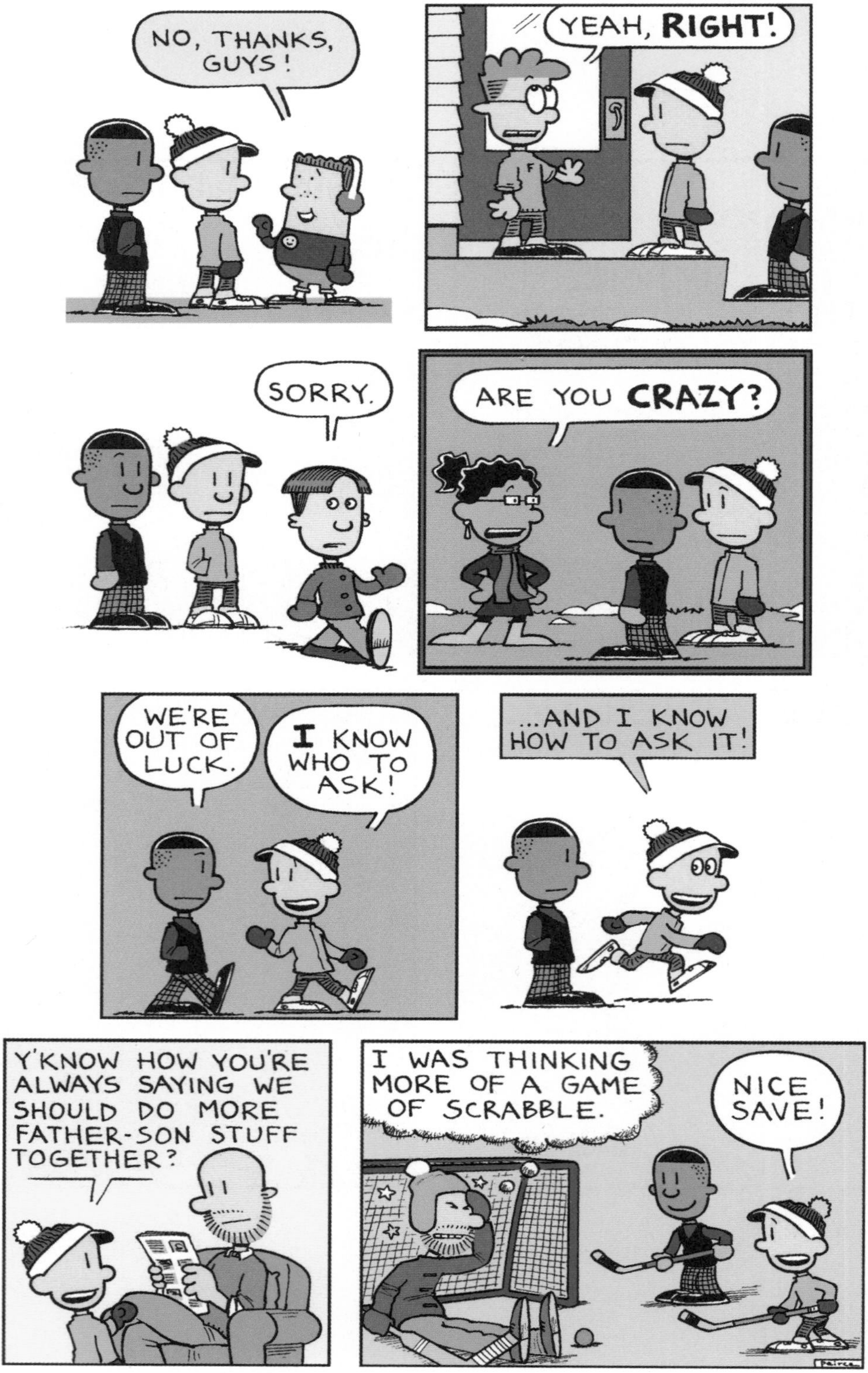
NO, THANKS, GUYS!
YEAH, RIGHT!
SORRY.
ARE YOU CRAZY?
WE'RE OUT OF LUCK.
I KNOW WHO TO ASK!
...AND I KNOW HOW TO ASK IT!
Y'KNOW HOW YOU'RE ALWAYS SAYING WE SHOULD DO MORE FATHER-SON STUFF TOGETHER?
I WAS THINKING MORE OF A GAME OF SCRABBLE.
NICE SAVE!

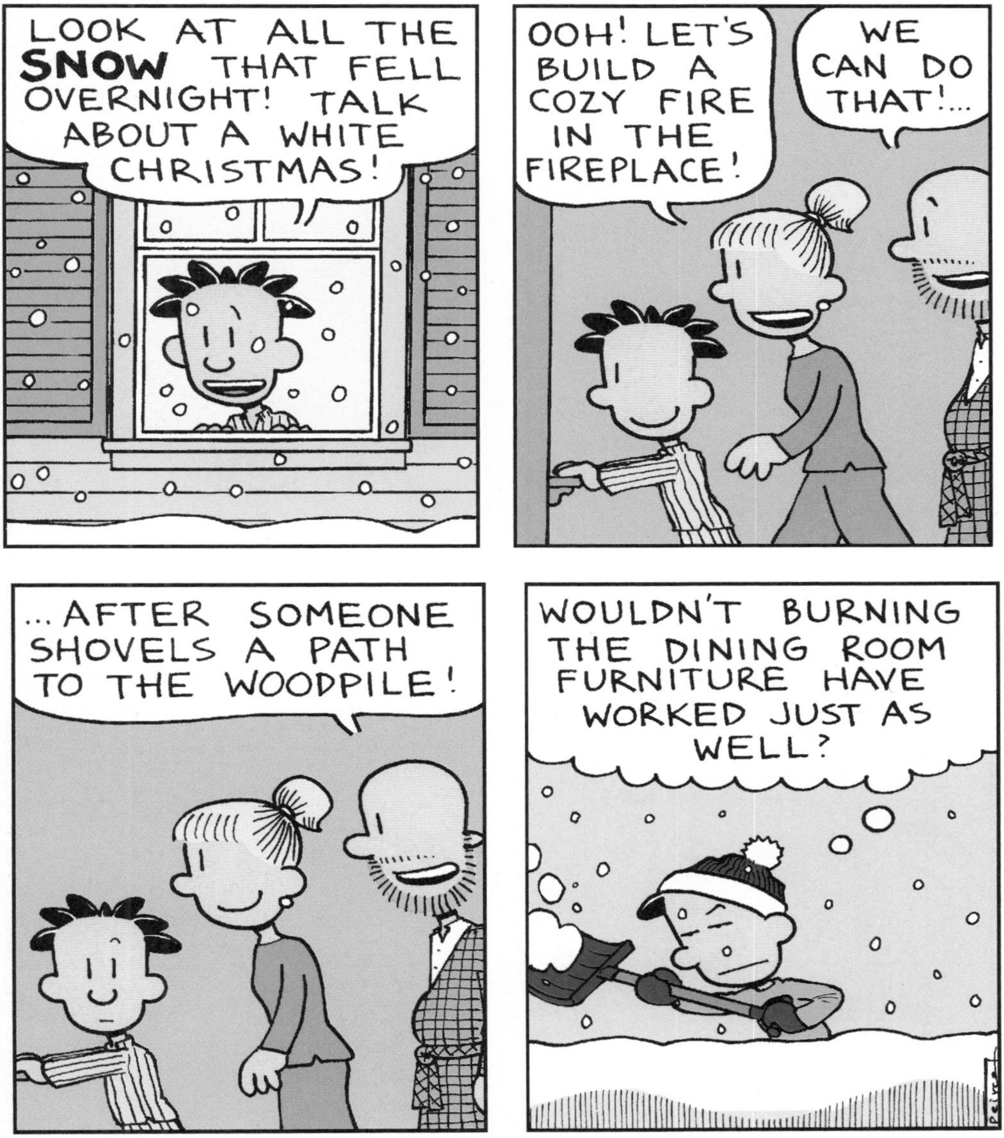
LOOK AT ALL THE SNOW THAT FELL OVERNIGHT! TALK ABOUT A WHITE CHRISTMAS!
OOH! LET'S BUILD A COZY FIRE IN THE FIREPLACE!
WE CAN DO THAT!...
...AFTER SOMEONE SHOVELS A PATH TO THE WOODPILE!
WOULDN'T BURNING THE DINING ROOM FURNITURE HAVE WORKED JUST AS WELL?
Peirce

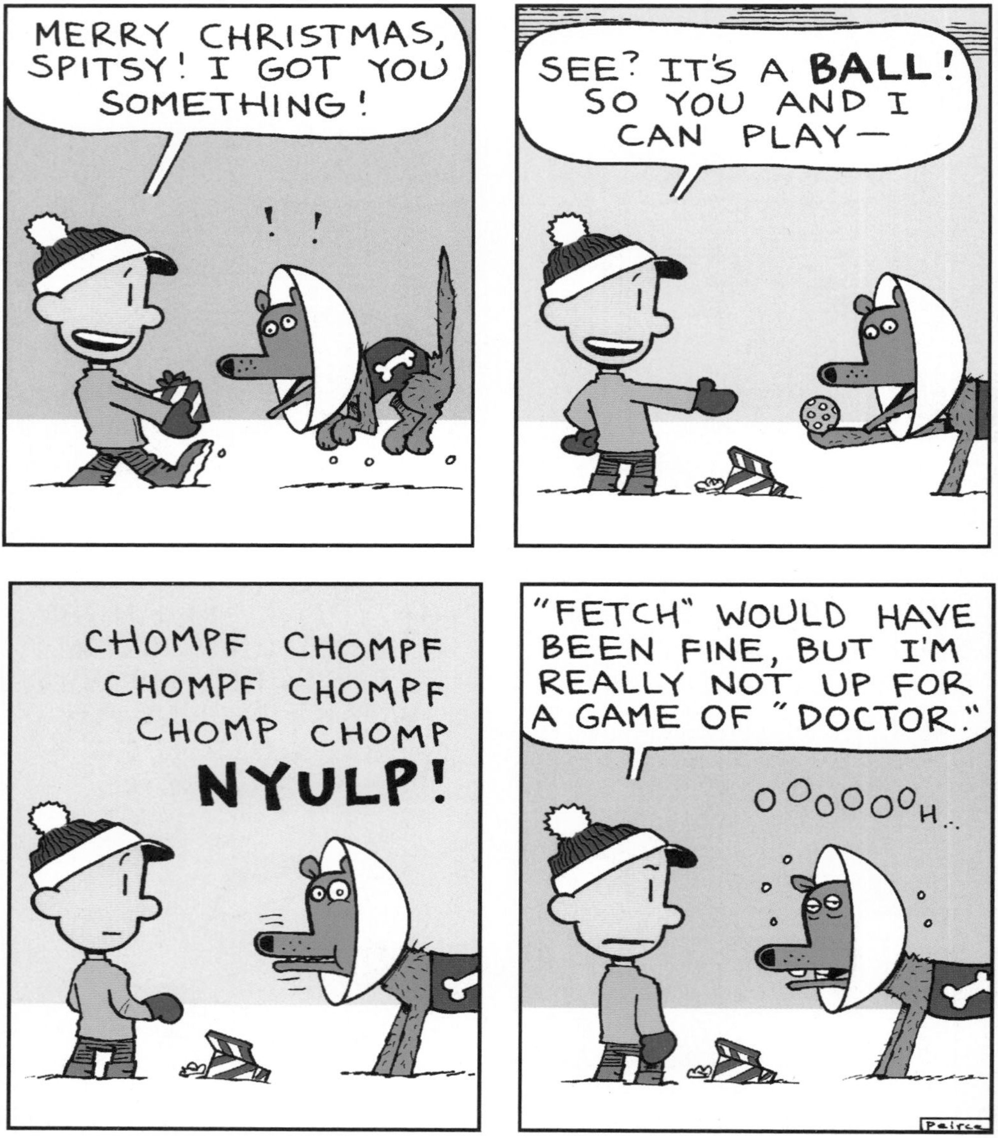
MERRY CHRISTMAS, SPITSY! I GOT YOU SOMETHING!
! !
SEE? IT'S A **BALL**! SO YOU AND I CAN PLAY—
CHOMPF CHOMPF CHOMPF CHOMPF CHOMP CHOMP
NYULP!
"FETCH" WOULD HAVE BEEN FINE, BUT I'M REALLY NOT UP FOR A GAME OF "DOCTOR."
OOOOOOH...
Peirce

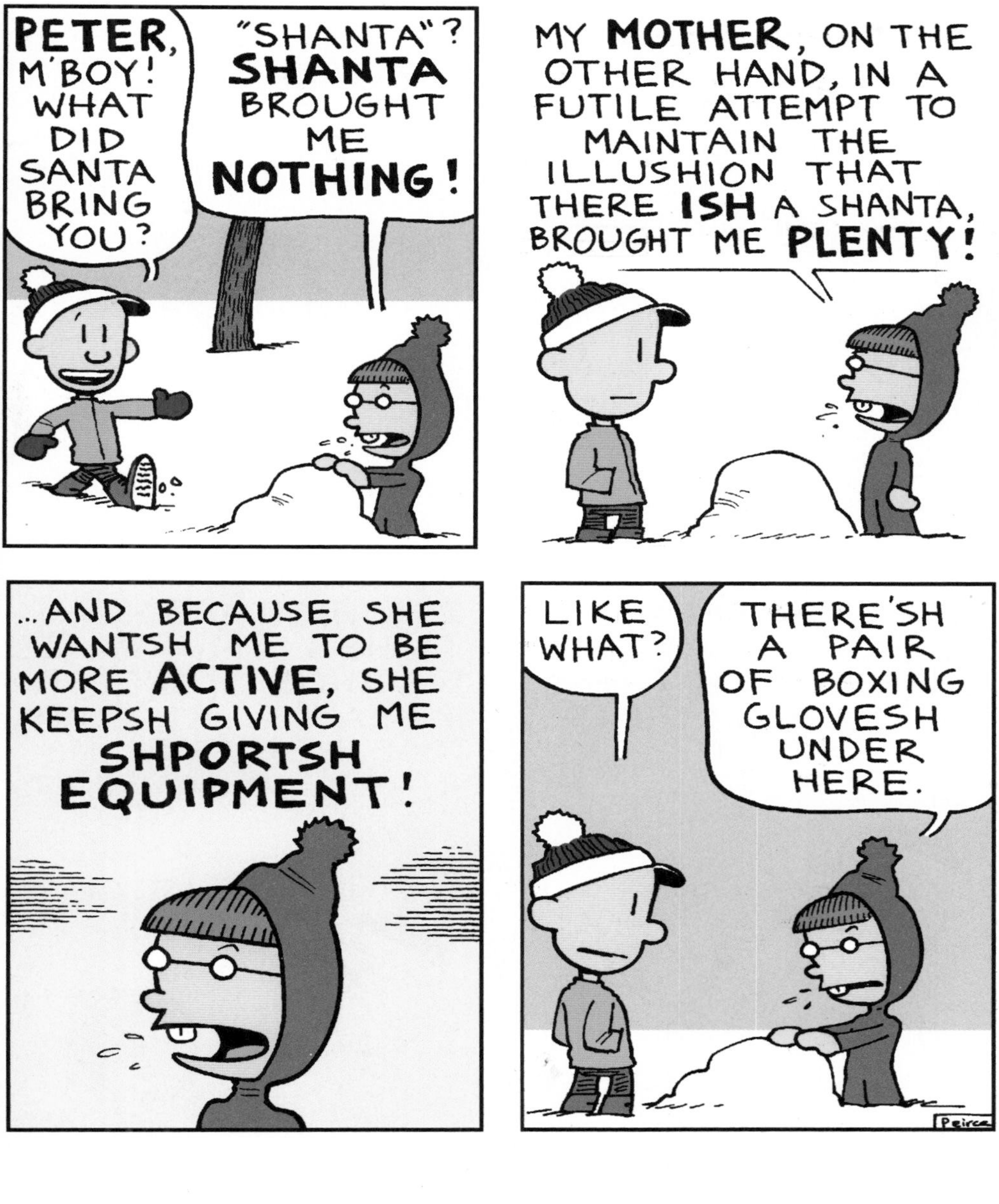

PETER, M'BOY! WHAT DID SANTA BRING YOU?
"SHANTA"? SHANTA BROUGHT ME NOTHING!
MY MOTHER, ON THE OTHER HAND, IN A FUTILE ATTEMPT TO MAINTAIN THE ILLUSHION THAT THERE ISH A SHANTA, BROUGHT ME PLENTY!
...AND BECAUSE SHE WANTSH ME TO BE MORE ACTIVE, SHE KEEPSH GIVING ME SHPORTSH EQUIPMENT!
LIKE WHAT?
THERE'SH A PAIR OF BOXING GLOVESH UNDER HERE.
Peirce

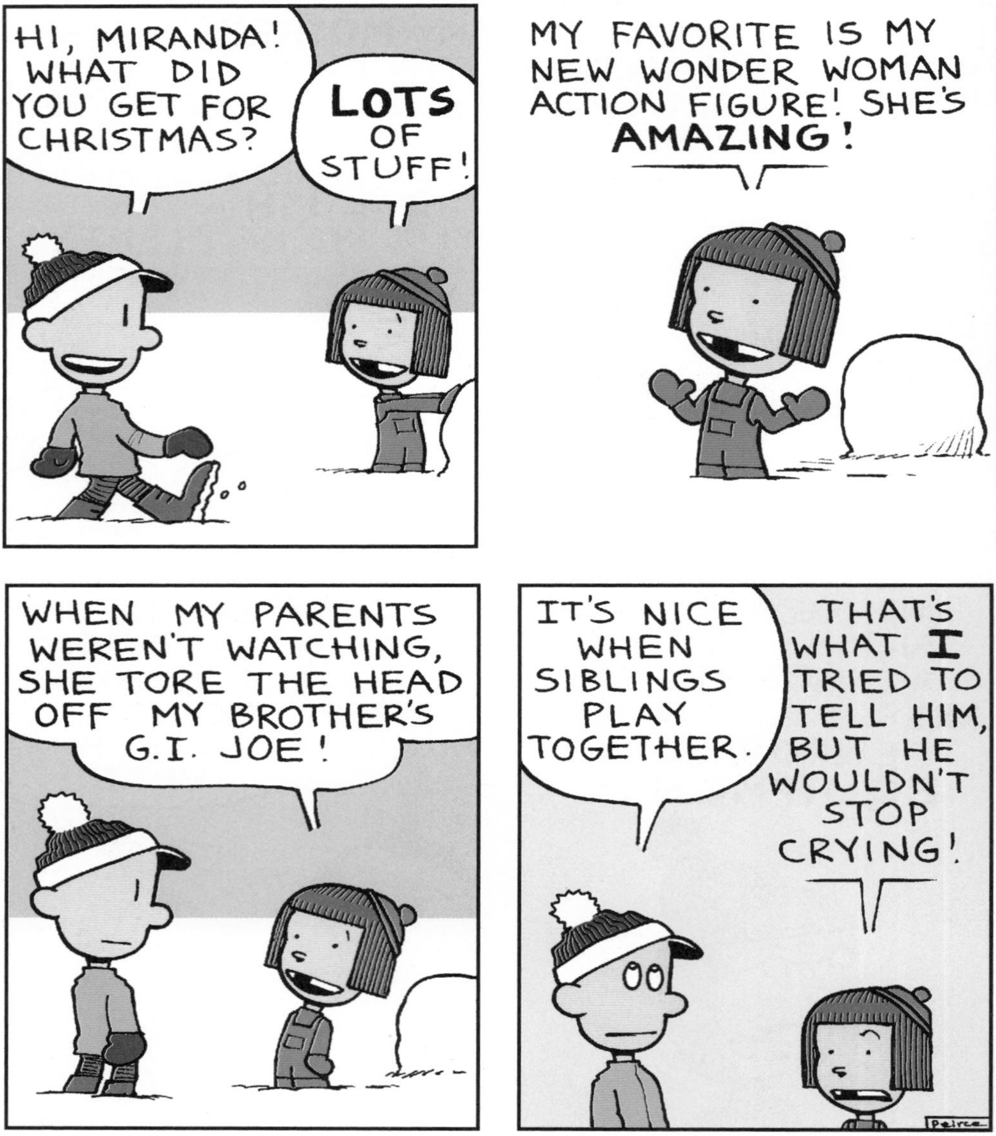
HI, MIRANDA! WHAT DID YOU GET FOR CHRISTMAS?
LOTS OF STUFF!
MY FAVORITE IS MY NEW WONDER WOMAN ACTION FIGURE! SHE'S AMAZING!
WHEN MY PARENTS WEREN'T WATCHING, SHE TORE THE HEAD OFF MY BROTHER'S G.I. JOE!
IT'S NICE WHEN SIBLINGS PLAY TOGETHER.
THAT'S WHAT I TRIED TO TELL HIM, BUT HE WOULDN'T STOP CRYING!
Peirce

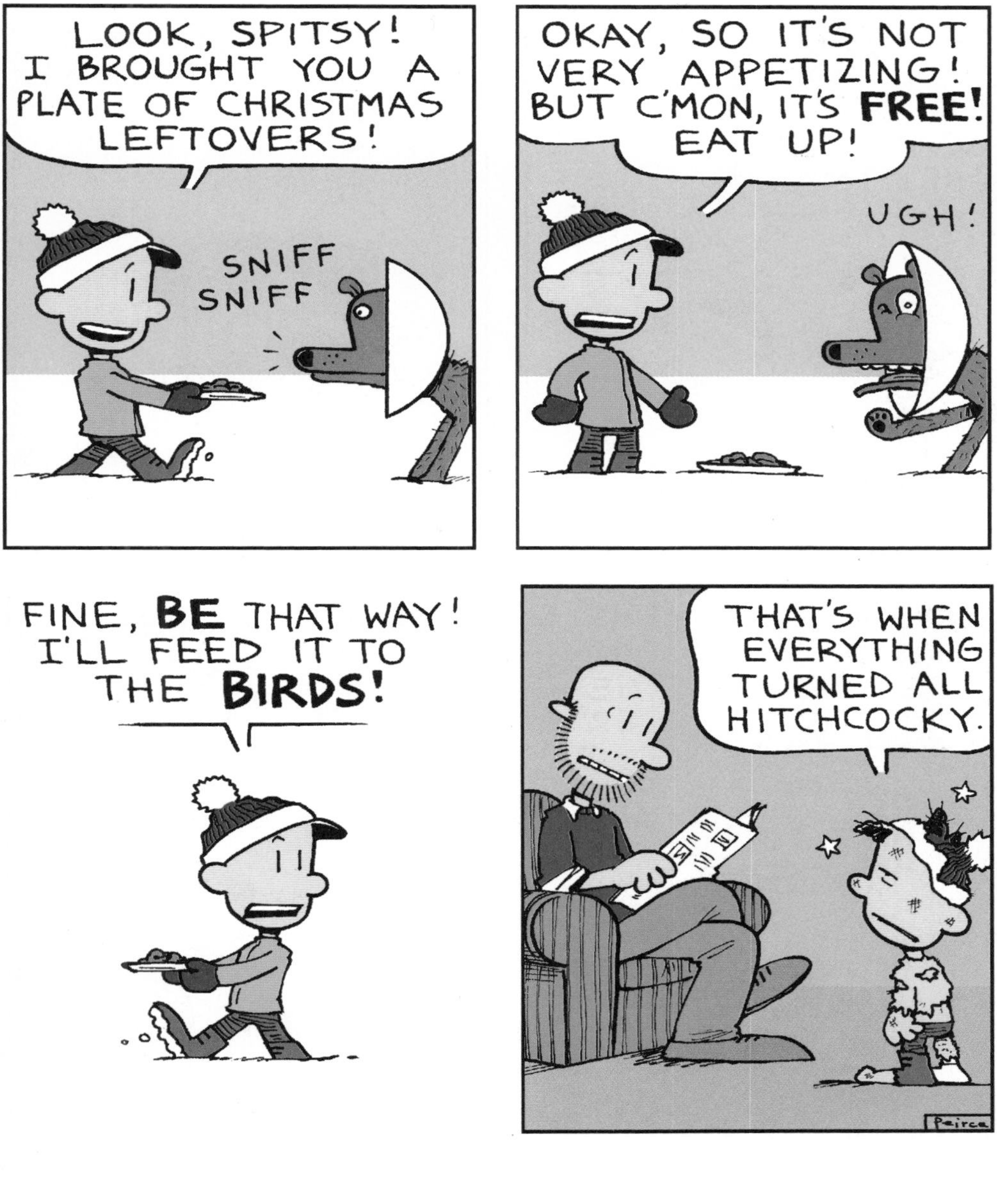
LOOK, SPITSY! I BROUGHT YOU A PLATE OF CHRISTMAS LEFTOVERS!
SNIFF SNIFF
OKAY, SO IT'S NOT VERY APPETIZING! BUT C'MON, IT'S FREE! EAT UP!
UGH!
FINE, BE THAT WAY! I'LL FEED IT TO THE BIRDS!
THAT'S WHEN EVERYTHING TURNED ALL HITCHCOCKY.
Peirce

DID YOU ASK FOR A DOG AGAIN THIS CHRISTMAS?

YEAH, BUT MY DAD GAVE ME HIS USUAL ANSWER:

"WHY DO YOU NEED A DOG WHEN YOU'VE GOT SPITSY LIVING RIGHT NEXT DOOR?"

MYOW! HEE HEE!

WEE HEE!

WURF!

PARENTS SAY SOME STUPID STUFF.

SEE, **HE'D** THINK THAT'S **CUTE!**

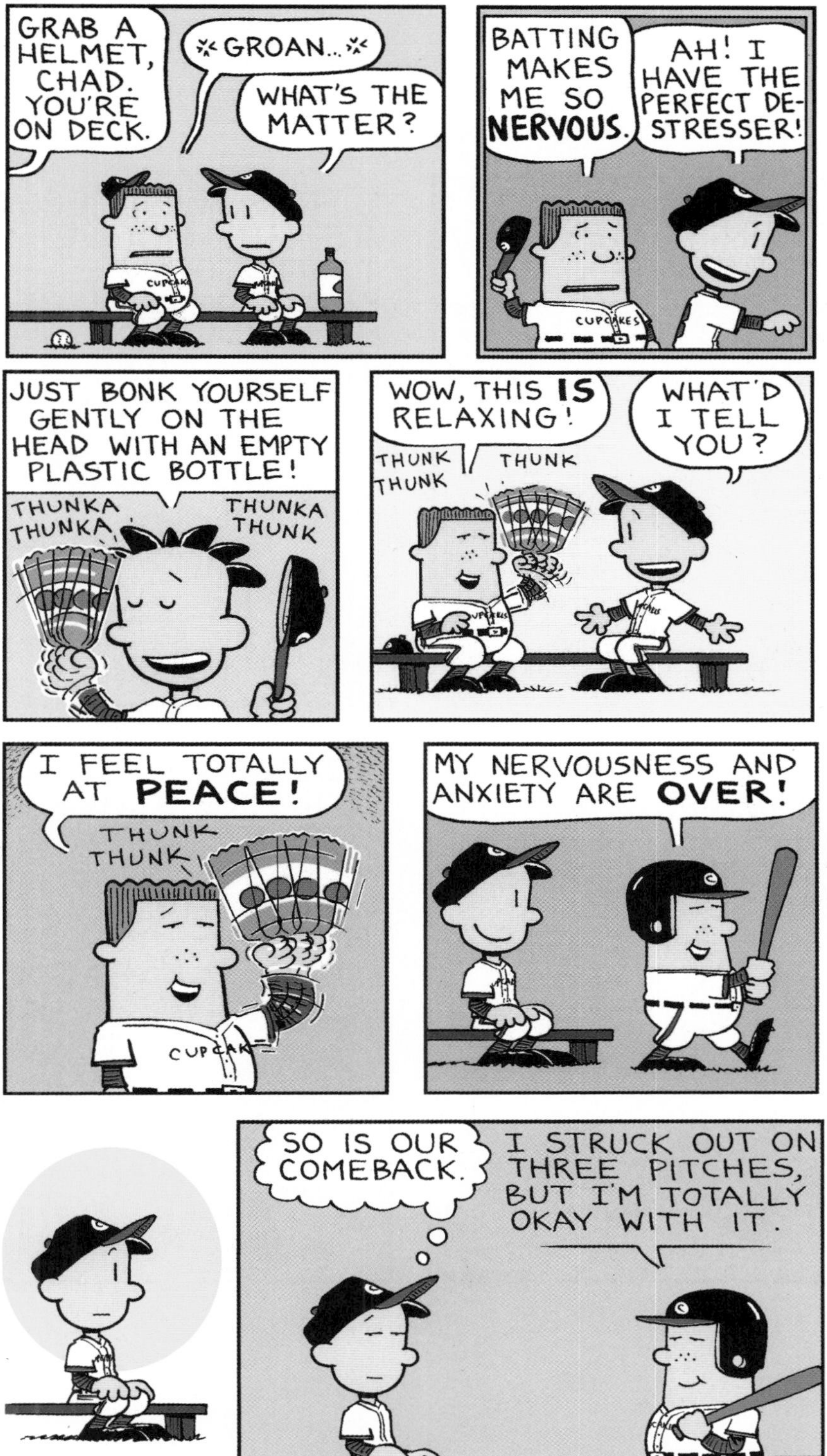
GRAB A HELMET, CHAD. YOU'RE ON DECK.
GROAN...
WHAT'S THE MATTER?
BATTING MAKES ME SO **NERVOUS**.
AH! I HAVE THE PERFECT DE-STRESSER!
JUST BONK YOURSELF GENTLY ON THE HEAD WITH AN EMPTY PLASTIC BOTTLE!
THUNKA THUNKA
THUNKA THUNK
WOW, THIS **IS** RELAXING!
THUNK THUNK
THUNK
WHAT'D I TELL YOU?
I FEEL TOTALLY AT **PEACE**!
THUNK THUNK
MY NERVOUSNESS AND ANXIETY ARE **OVER**!
SO IS OUR COMEBACK.
I STRUCK OUT ON THREE PITCHES, BUT I'M TOTALLY OKAY WITH IT.
Peirce

OKAY, THEY JUST PUT IN A NEW PITCHER. WHAT DO WE KNOW ABOUT THIS GUY?

HIS NAME'S ZACK.

I HAD A SLEEPOVER AT HIS HOUSE IN THIRD GRADE. HIS BEDROOM WAS REALLY MESSY, SO WE SLEPT IN THE LIVING ROOM.

HIS MOM MADE TACOS FOR SUPPER, WHICH I DIDN'T EVEN KNOW WHAT THEY **WERE** UNTIL I TRIED ONE, AND THEN I WAS LIKE: "WOW, I **LOVE** TACOS!"

OUR SCOUTING DEPARTMENT IS THOROUGH BUT UNFOCUSED.

THEN I THREW UP, AND I WAS LIKE: "ACTUALLY, MAYBE I **DON'T** LIKE TACOS!"

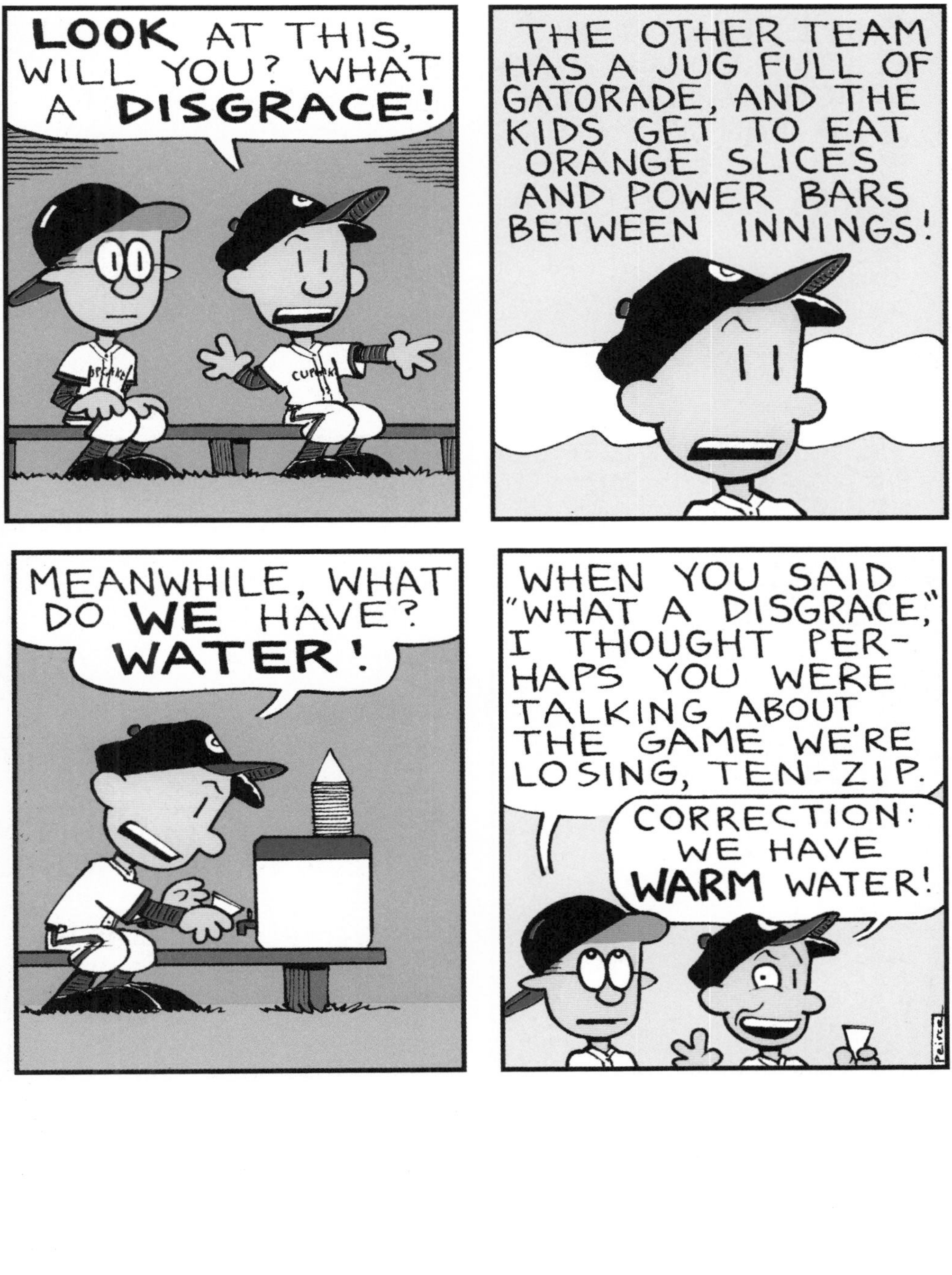
LOOK AT THIS, WILL YOU? WHAT A DISGRACE!
THE OTHER TEAM HAS A JUG FULL OF GATORADE, AND THE KIDS GET TO EAT ORANGE SLICES AND POWER BARS BETWEEN INNINGS!
MEANWHILE, WHAT DO WE HAVE? WATER!
WHEN YOU SAID "WHAT A DISGRACE," I THOUGHT PERHAPS YOU WERE TALKING ABOUT THE GAME WE'RE LOSING, TEN-ZIP.
CORRECTION: WE HAVE WARM WATER!
Peirce

I SEE THE OTHER TEAM'S COACH HAS BOUGHT A LOT OF FANCY SNACKS FOR HIS PLAYERS.

I **ALSO** SEE THAT HE'S BOUGHT THEM MATCHING BATTING GLOVES AND WRIST BANDS!

YES, I GUESS HE DOES THINGS DIFFERENTLY THAN I DO.

FOR EXAMPLE, HE DOESN'T DISCIPLINE HIS PLAYERS WHEN THEY MAKE SNARKY COMMENTS.

I'LL SIT DOWN NOW.

Peirce

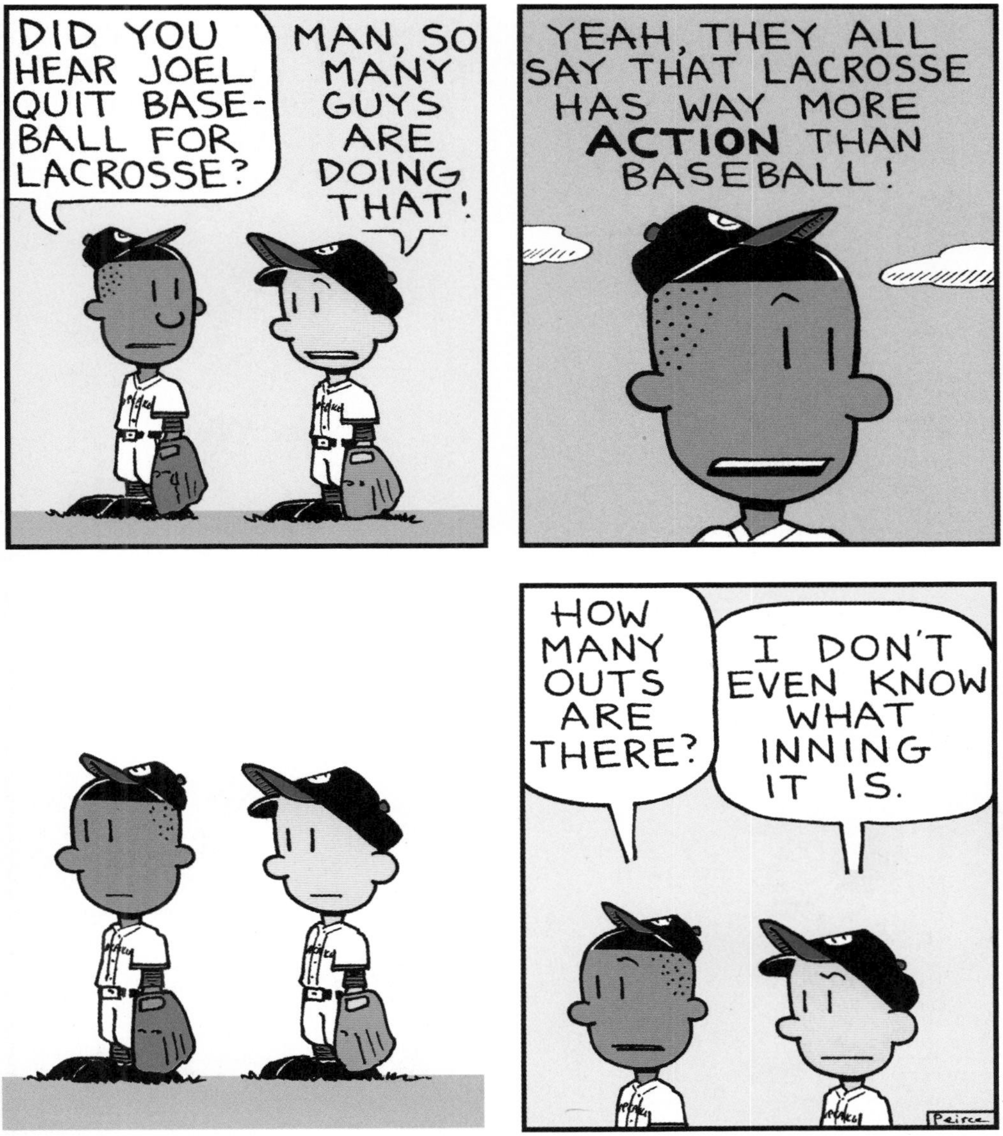
DID YOU HEAR JOEL QUIT BASE-BALL FOR LACROSSE?
MAN, SO MANY GUYS ARE DOING THAT!
YEAH, THEY ALL SAY THAT LACROSSE HAS WAY MORE **ACTION** THAN BASEBALL!
HOW MANY OUTS ARE THERE?
I DON'T EVEN KNOW WHAT INNING IT IS.
Peirce

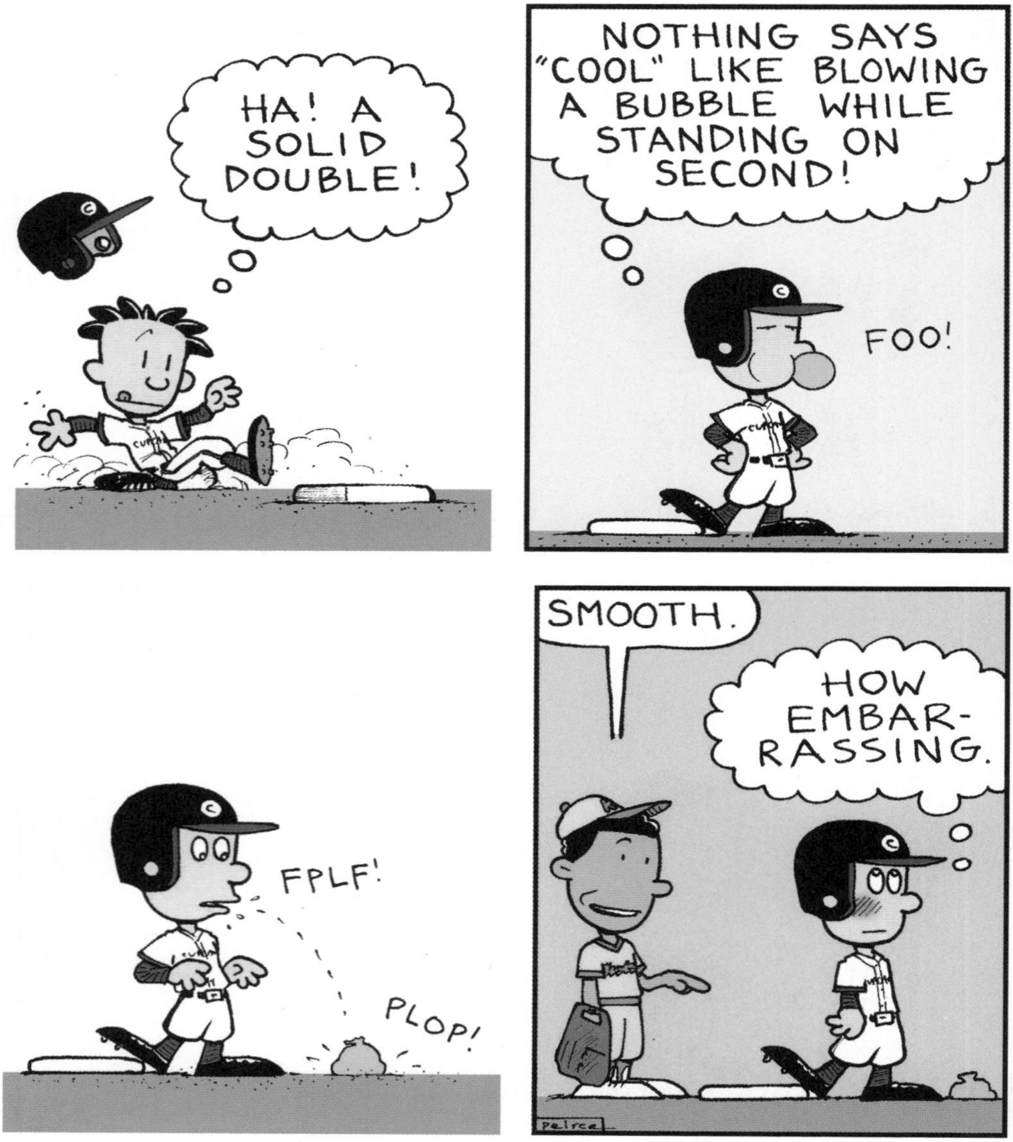
HA! A SOLID DOUBLE!
NOTHING SAYS "COOL" LIKE BLOWING A BUBBLE WHILE STANDING ON SECOND!
FOO!
FPLF!
PLOP!
SMOOTH.
HOW EMBAR-RASSING.
peirce

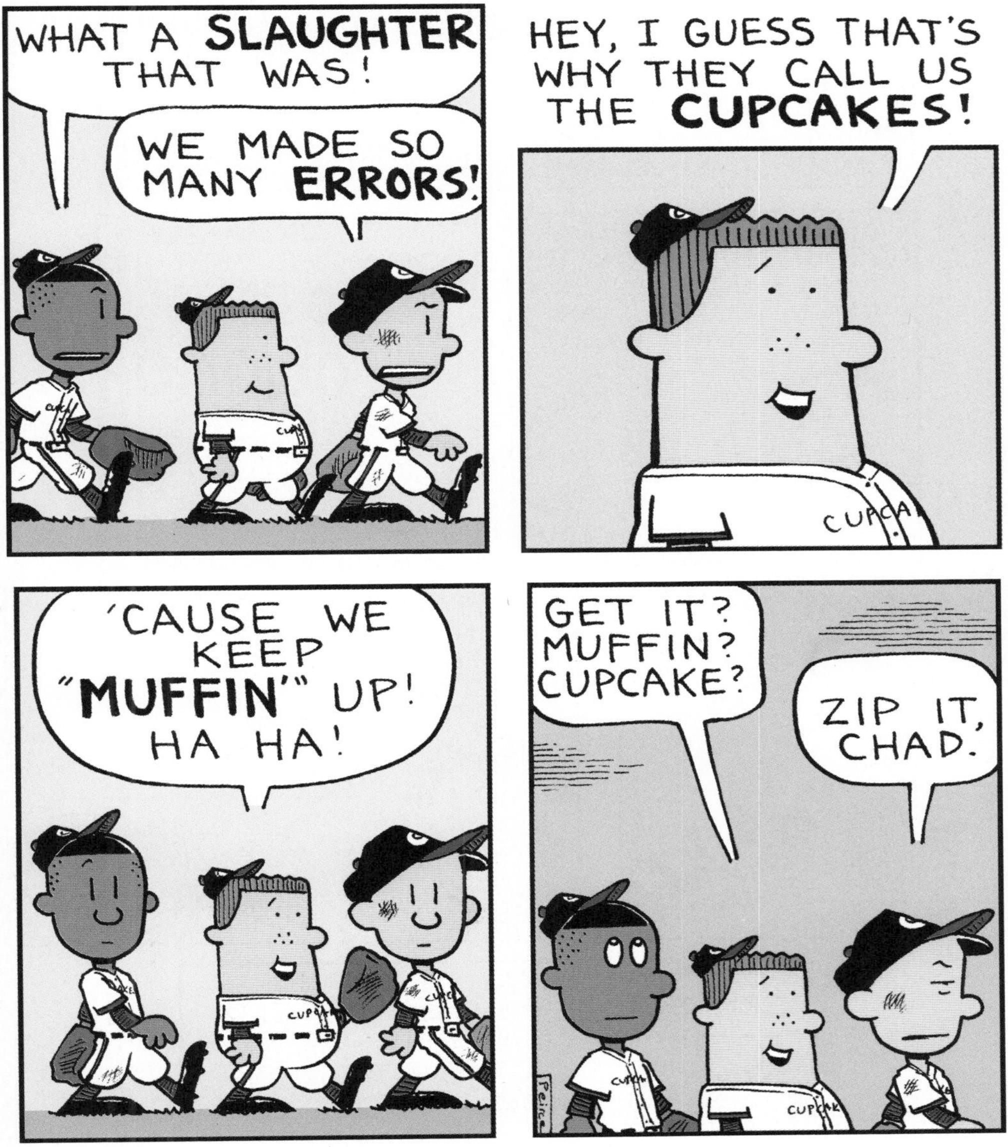
WHAT A SLAUGHTER THAT WAS!
WE MADE SO MANY ERRORS!
HEY, I GUESS THAT'S WHY THEY CALL US THE CUPCAKES!
'CAUSE WE KEEP "MUFFIN'" UP! HA HA!
GET IT? MUFFIN? CUPCAKE?
ZIP IT, CHAD.
Peirce

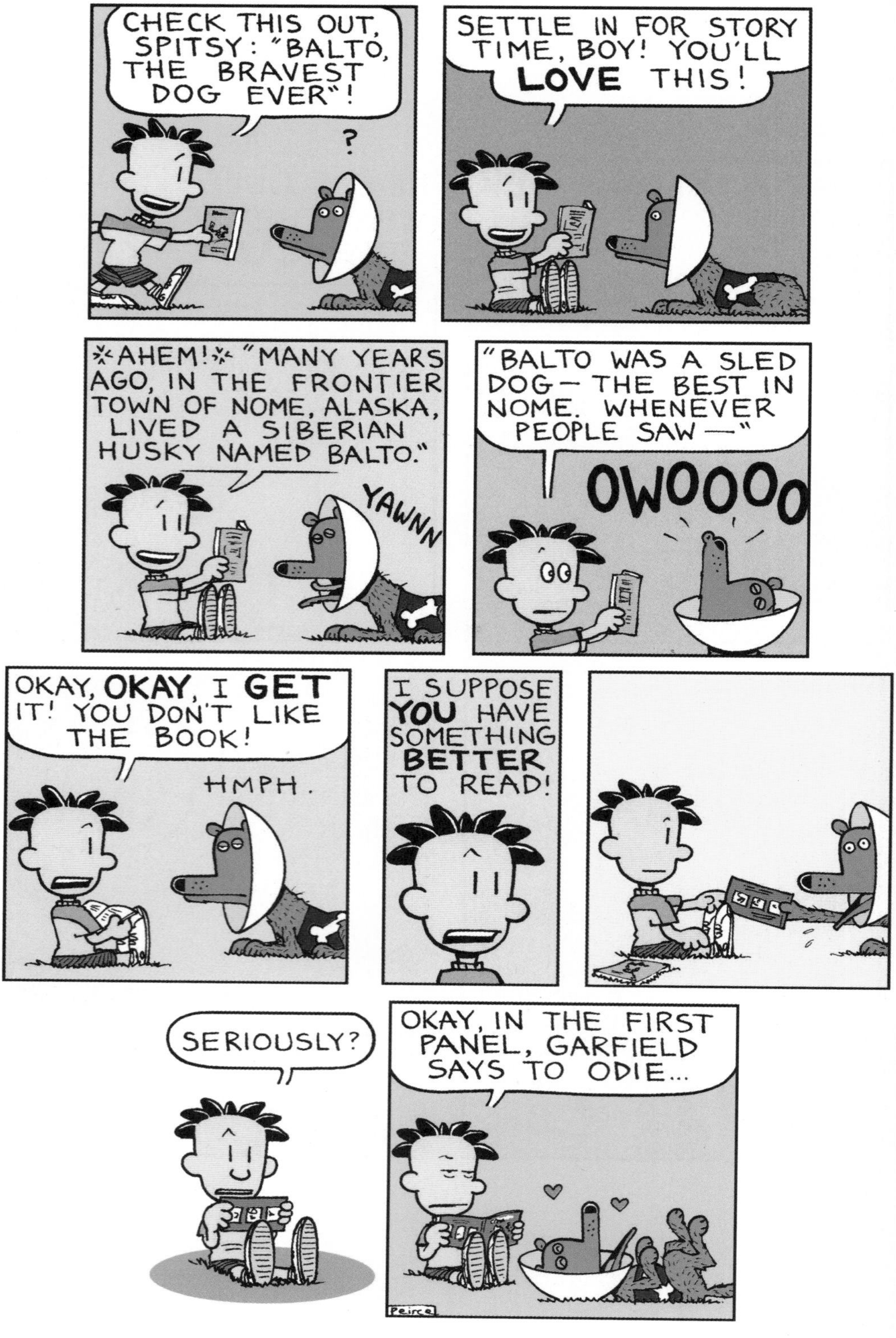
CHECK THIS OUT, SPITSY: "BALTO, THE BRAVEST DOG EVER"!
?
SETTLE IN FOR STORY TIME, BOY! YOU'LL LOVE THIS!
AHEM! "MANY YEARS AGO, IN THE FRONTIER TOWN OF NOME, ALASKA, LIVED A SIBERIAN HUSKY NAMED BALTO."
YAWNN
"BALTO WAS A SLED DOG — THE BEST IN NOME. WHENEVER PEOPLE SAW —"
OWOOOO
OKAY, OKAY, I GET IT! YOU DON'T LIKE THE BOOK!
HMPH.
I SUPPOSE YOU HAVE SOMETHING BETTER TO READ!
SERIOUSLY?
OKAY, IN THE FIRST PANEL, GARFIELD SAYS TO ODIE...
Peirce

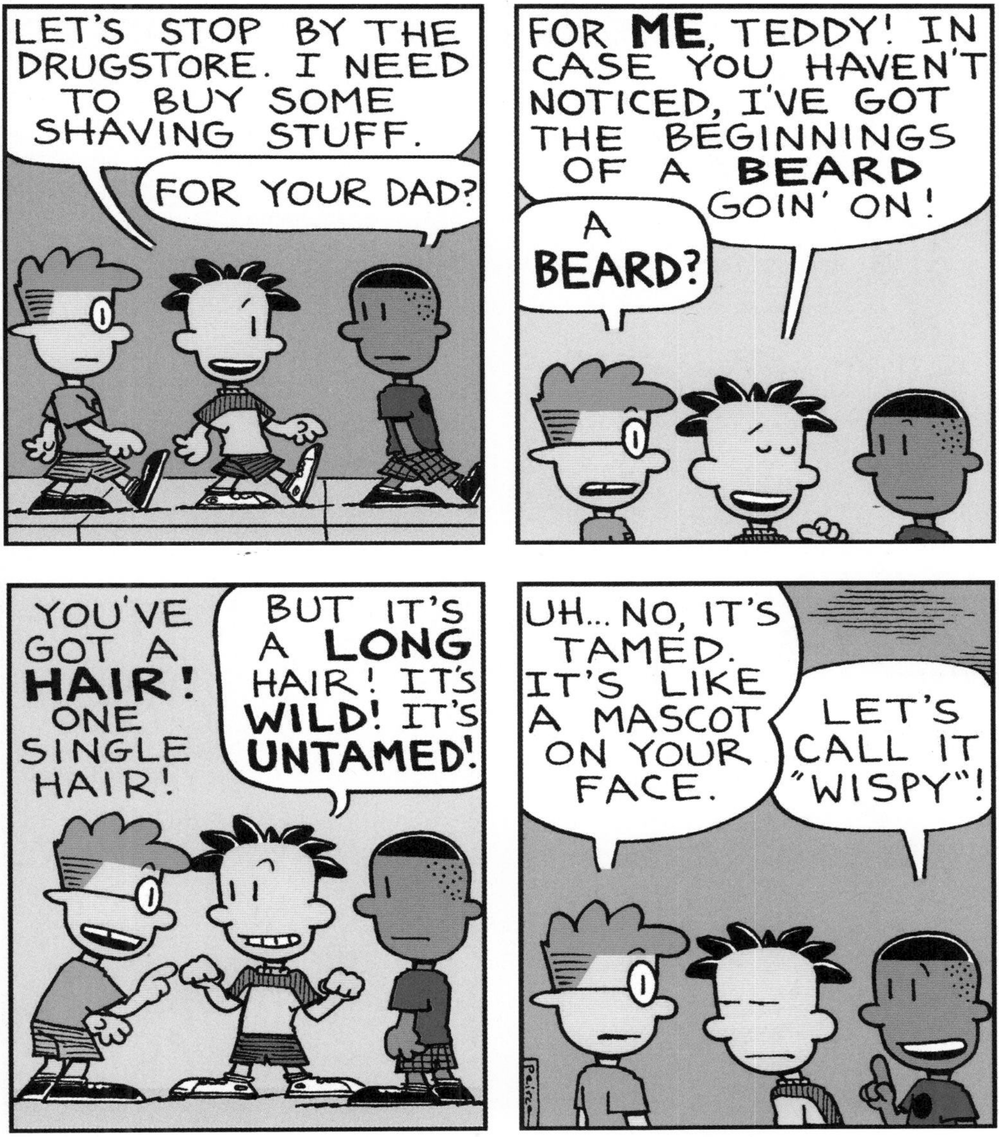
LET'S STOP BY THE DRUGSTORE. I NEED TO BUY SOME SHAVING STUFF.
FOR YOUR DAD?
FOR **ME**, TEDDY! IN CASE YOU HAVEN'T NOTICED, I'VE GOT THE BEGINNINGS OF A **BEARD** GOIN' ON!
A **BEARD?**
YOU'VE GOT A **HAIR!** ONE SINGLE HAIR!
BUT IT'S A **LONG** HAIR! IT'S **WILD!** IT'S **UNTAMED!**
UH... NO, IT'S TAMED. IT'S LIKE A MASCOT ON YOUR FACE.
LET'S CALL IT "WISPY"!
Peirce

NATE, HAVING ONE HAIR ON YOUR CHIN DOESN'T MEAN YOU'RE READY TO START SHAVING!
NOT TODAY, BUT SOON!
...BECAUSE PUBERTY IS JUST AROUND THE CORNER!
RIGHT.
IT IS! I CAN FEEL THE STIRRING IN MY SIRLOINS!
SIRLOINS?
WELL, IT IS GRILLING SEASON!
GUYS HAVE SIRLOINS, GIRLS HAVE HERLOINS!
Peirce

I HATE TO BREAK IT TO YOU, NATE, BUT I THINK YOU'RE STILL A LONG WAY FROM PUBERTY!
OH, YEAH? WHAT ABOUT THE HAIR ON MY CHIN?
IT'S **ONE HAIR!**
IT'S A **ROGUE** HAIR, THAT'S WHAT IT IS! YOU HAVE A ROGUE HAIR!
"ROGUE HAIR" SOUNDS LIKE A REALLY BAD STAR WARS MOVIE.
YOU WANNA SEE ROGUE HAIRS? CHECK OUT MY SIS-TER'S EYEBROWS!
Peirce

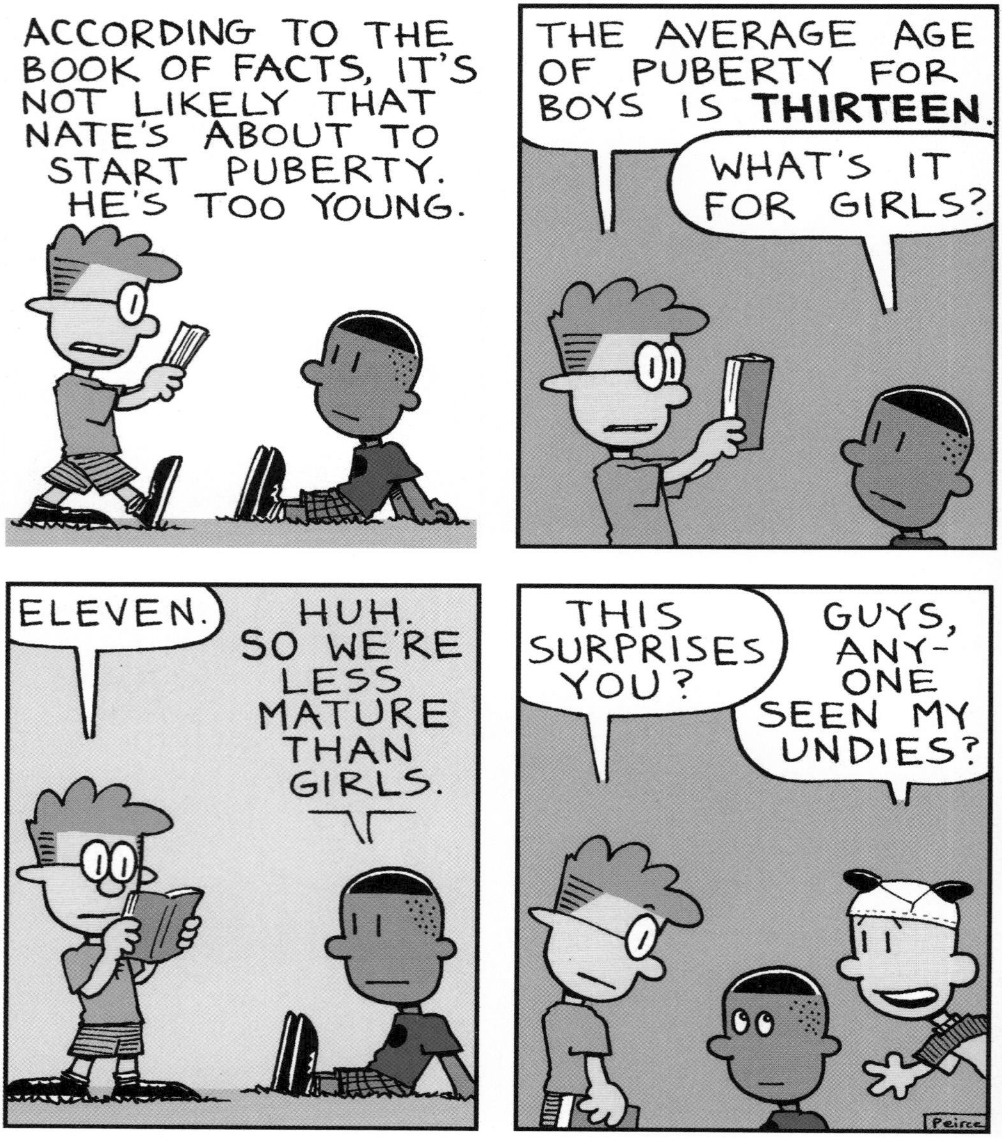
ACCORDING TO THE BOOK OF FACTS, IT'S NOT LIKELY THAT NATE'S ABOUT TO START PUBERTY. HE'S TOO YOUNG.
THE AVERAGE AGE OF PUBERTY FOR BOYS IS **THIRTEEN**.
WHAT'S IT FOR GIRLS?
ELEVEN.
HUH. SO WE'RE LESS MATURE THAN GIRLS.
THIS SURPRISES YOU?
GUYS, ANY-ONE SEEN MY UNDIES?
Peirce

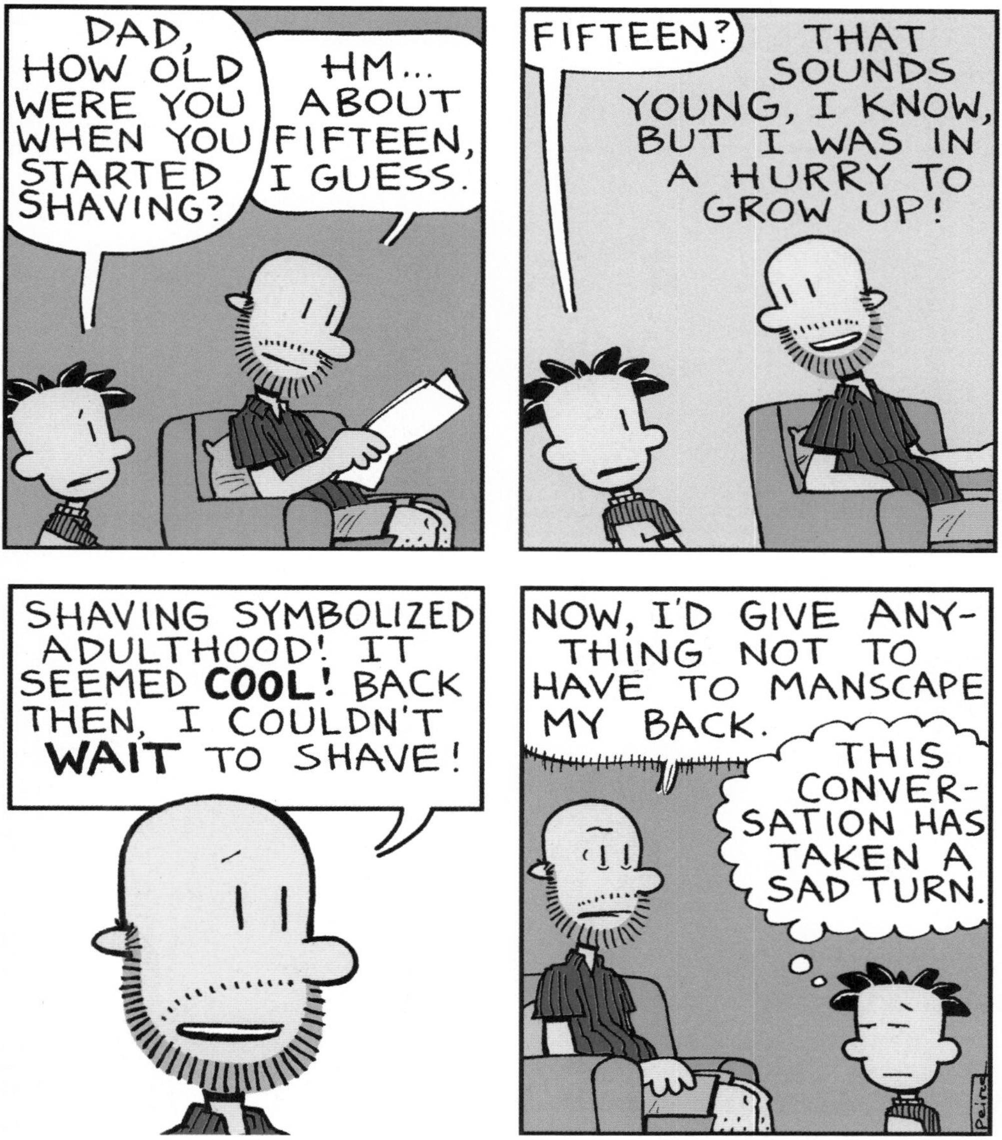
DAD, HOW OLD WERE YOU WHEN YOU STARTED SHAVING?
HM... ABOUT FIFTEEN, I GUESS.
FIFTEEN?
THAT SOUNDS YOUNG, I KNOW, BUT I WAS IN A HURRY TO GROW UP!
SHAVING SYMBOLIZED ADULTHOOD! IT SEEMED **COOL**! BACK THEN, I COULDN'T **WAIT** TO SHAVE!
NOW, I'D GIVE ANYTHING NOT TO HAVE TO MANSCAPE MY BACK.
THIS CONVERSATION HAS TAKEN A SAD TURN.
Peirce

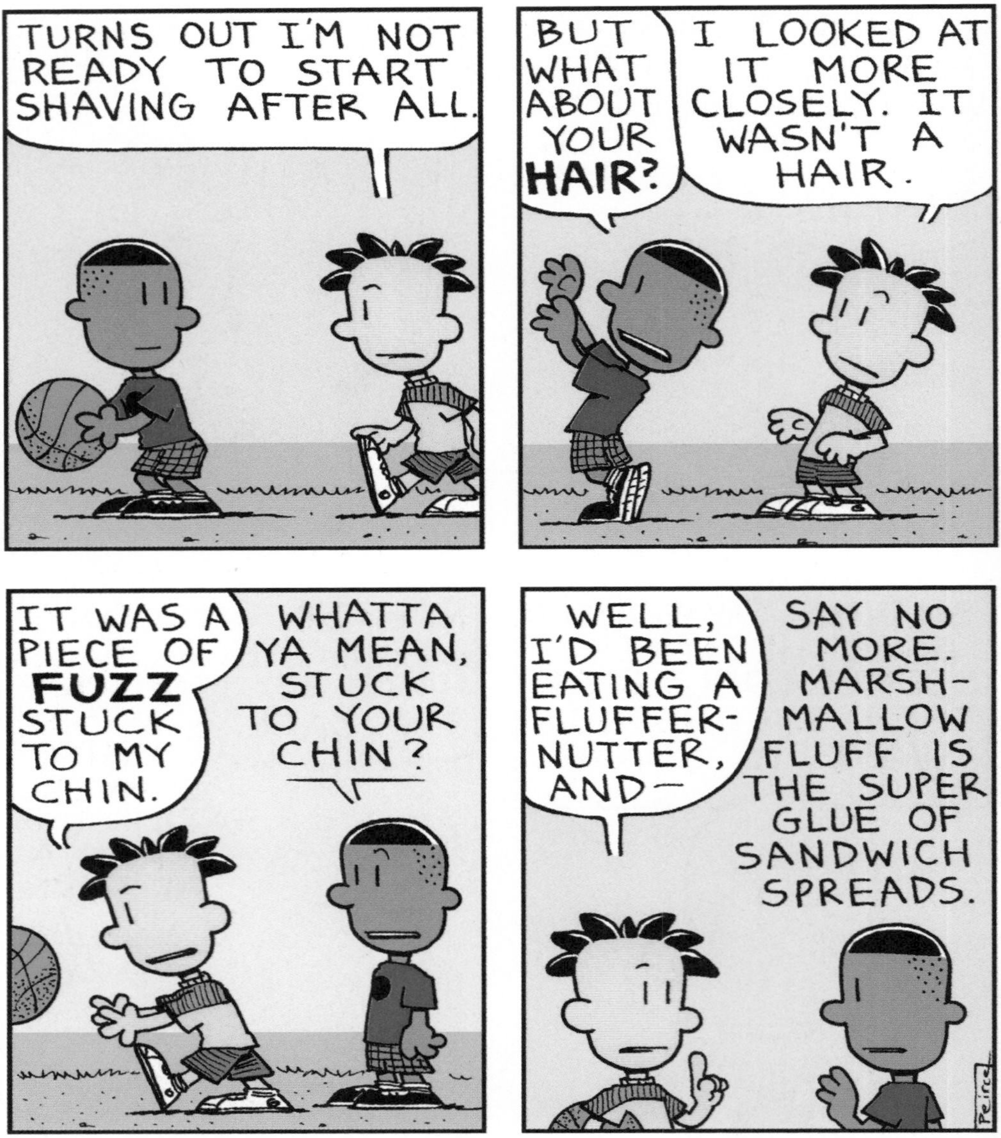
TURNS OUT I'M NOT READY TO START SHAVING AFTER ALL.
BUT WHAT ABOUT YOUR **HAIR**?
I LOOKED AT IT MORE CLOSELY. IT WASN'T A HAIR.
IT WAS A PIECE OF **FUZZ** STUCK TO MY CHIN.
WHATTA YA MEAN, STUCK TO YOUR CHIN?
WELL, I'D BEEN EATING A FLUFFER-NUTTER, AND—
SAY NO MORE. MARSH-MALLOW FLUFF IS THE SUPER GLUE OF SANDWICH SPREADS.
Peirce

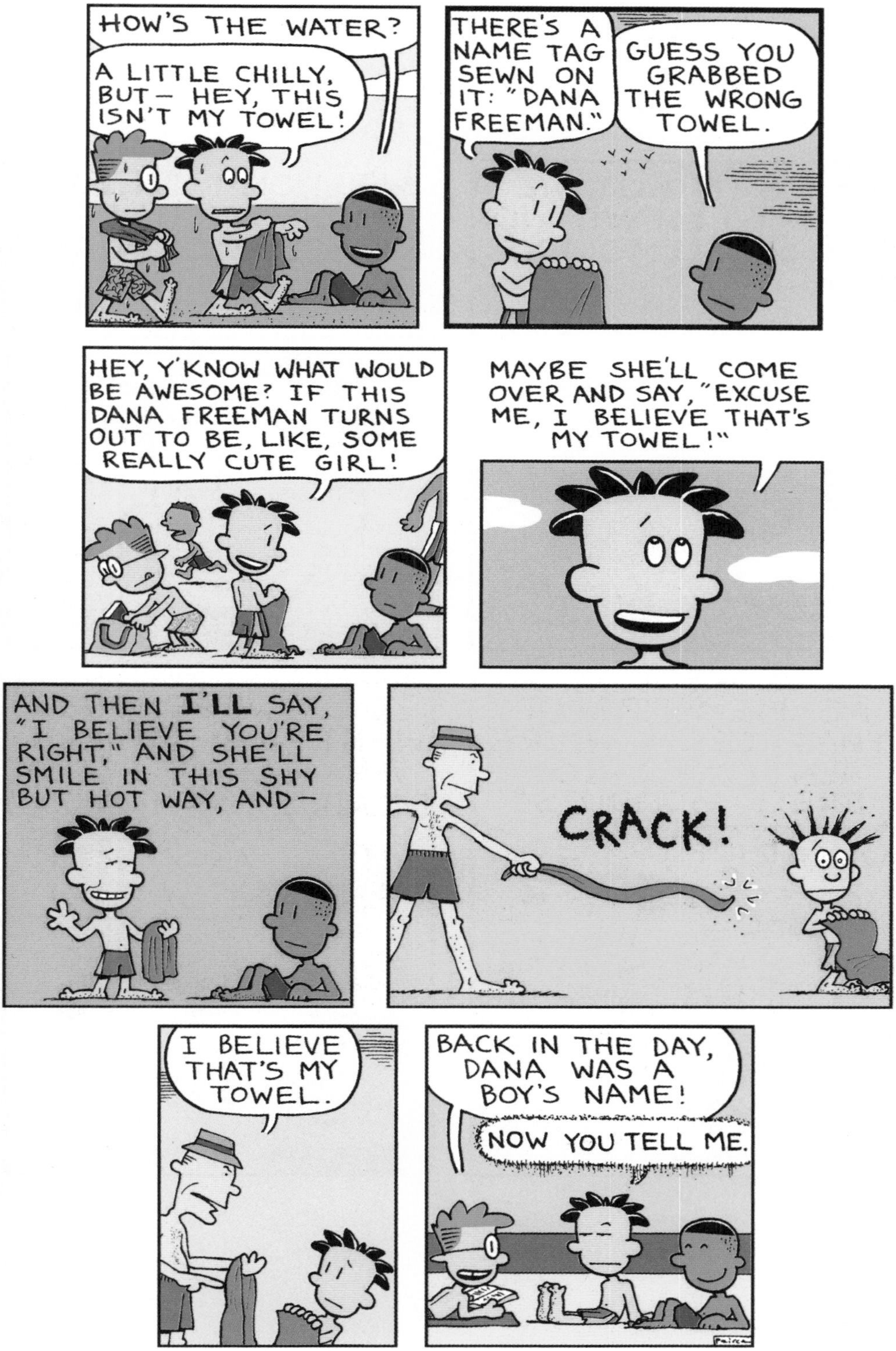
HOW'S THE WATER?
A LITTLE CHILLY, BUT– HEY, THIS ISN'T MY TOWEL!
THERE'S A NAME TAG SEWN ON IT: "DANA FREEMAN."
GUESS YOU GRABBED THE WRONG TOWEL.
HEY, Y'KNOW WHAT WOULD BE AWESOME? IF THIS DANA FREEMAN TURNS OUT TO BE, LIKE, SOME REALLY CUTE GIRL!
MAYBE SHE'LL COME OVER AND SAY, "EXCUSE ME, I BELIEVE THAT'S MY TOWEL!"
AND THEN I'LL SAY, "I BELIEVE YOU'RE RIGHT," AND SHE'LL SMILE IN THIS SHY BUT HOT WAY, AND–
CRACK!
I BELIEVE THAT'S MY TOWEL.
BACK IN THE DAY, DANA WAS A BOY'S NAME!
NOW YOU TELL ME.

LET'S GO INTO CRESSLY'S BAKERY!

BUT WE HAVE NO MONEY!

WE DON'T **NEED** MONEY, CHAD! CRESSLY'S SPONSORS OUR LITTLE LEAGUE TEAM!

AS MEMBERS OF THAT TEAM, WE'RE ENTITLED TO FREE GOODIES!

WE **ARE**?

I WANT AN ECLAIR!

WE'RE ONE-AND-FIFTEEN, CHAD. LET'S ASK FOR A SUGAR COOKIE AND WORK OUR WAY UP.

Pierce

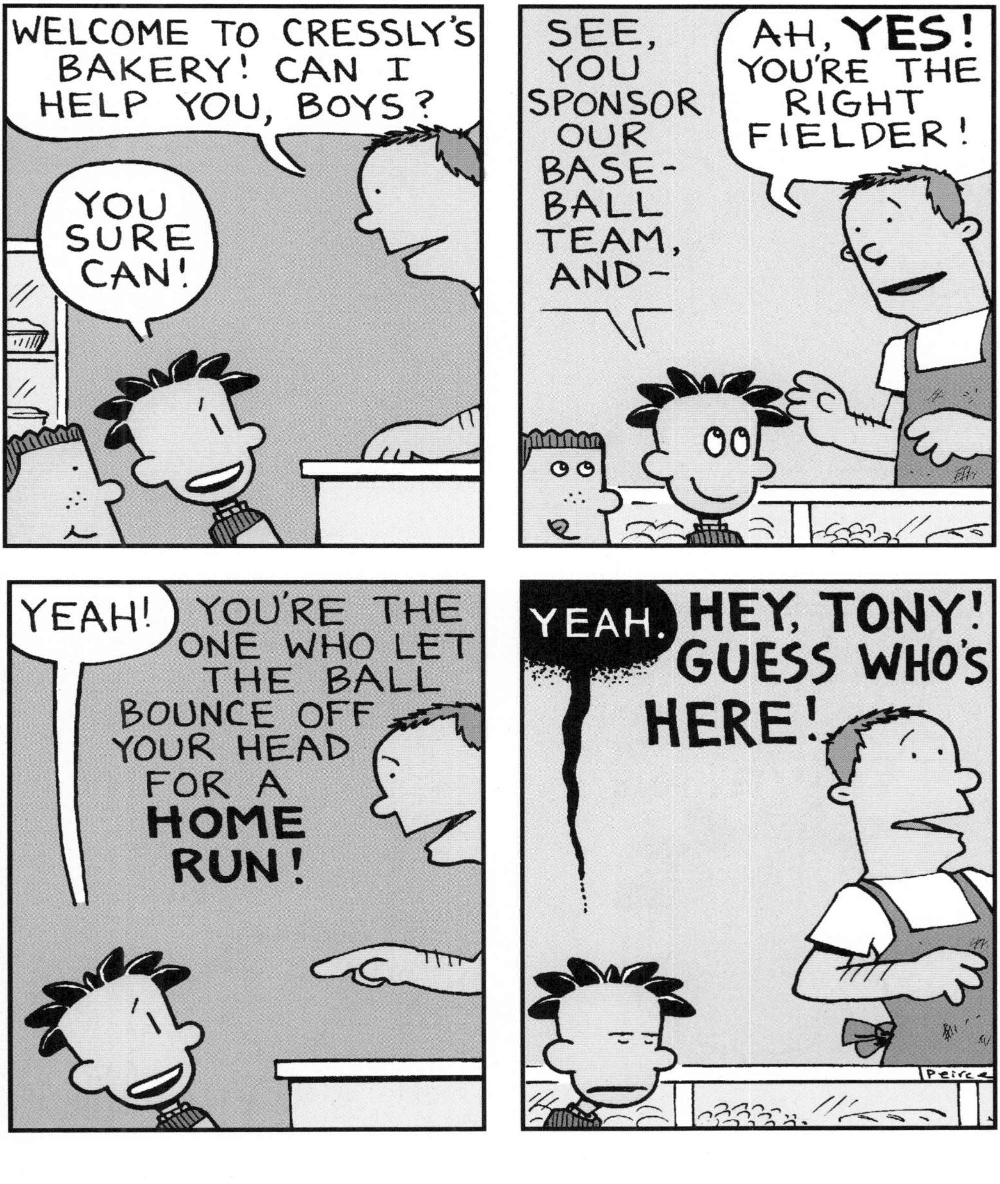

WELCOME TO CRESSLY'S BAKERY! CAN I HELP YOU, BOYS?
YOU SURE CAN!
SEE, YOU SPONSOR OUR BASE-BALL TEAM, AND-
AH, YES! YOU'RE THE RIGHT FIELDER!
YEAH!
YOU'RE THE ONE WHO LET THE BALL BOUNCE OFF YOUR HEAD FOR A HOME RUN!
YEAH.
HEY, TONY! GUESS WHO'S HERE!
Peirce

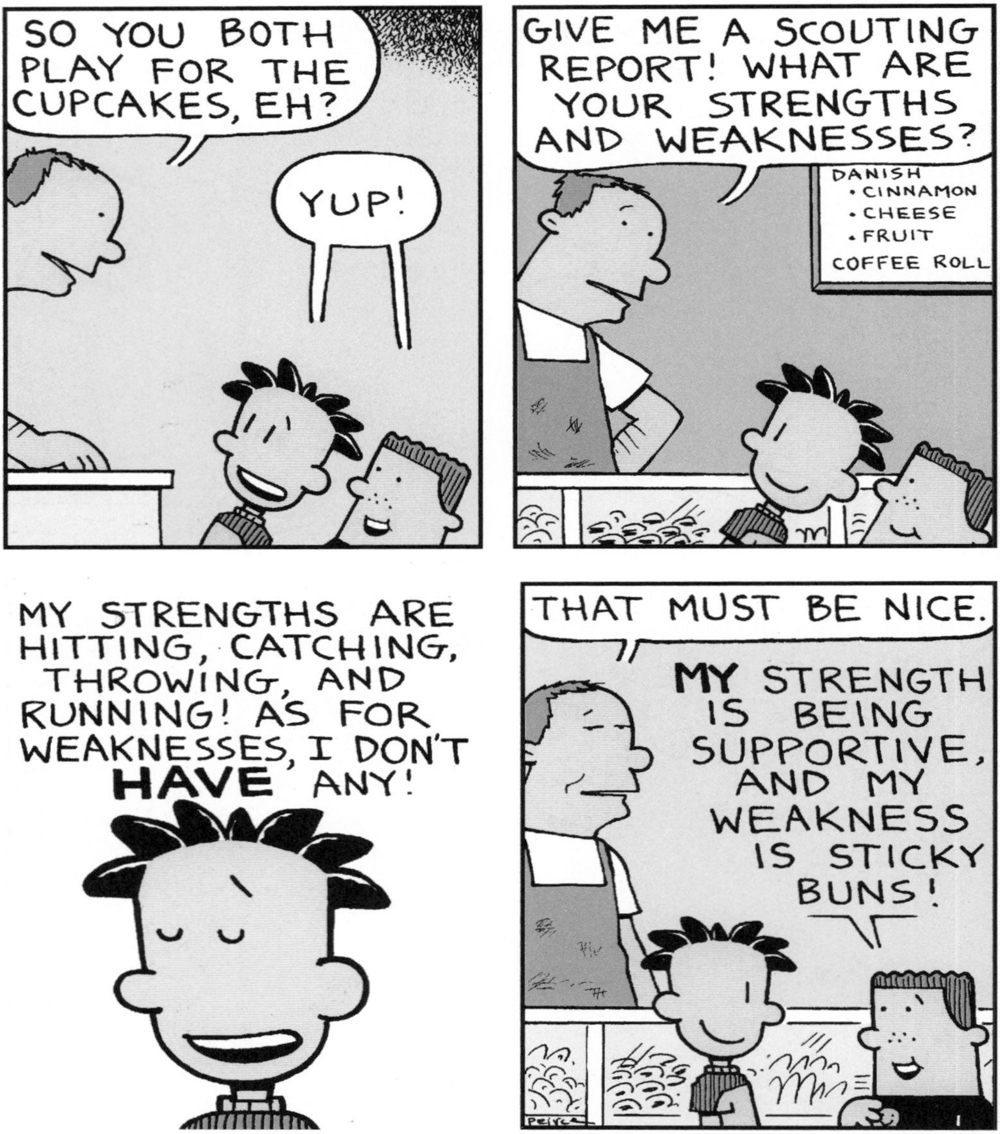
SO YOU BOTH PLAY FOR THE CUPCAKES, EH?
YUP!
GIVE ME A SCOUTING REPORT! WHAT ARE YOUR STRENGTHS AND WEAKNESSES?
DANISH
• CINNAMON
• CHEESE
• FRUIT
COFFEE ROLL
MY STRENGTHS ARE HITTING, CATCHING, THROWING, AND RUNNING! AS FOR WEAKNESSES, I DON'T HAVE ANY!
THAT MUST BE NICE.
MY STRENGTH IS BEING SUPPORTIVE, AND MY WEAKNESS IS STICKY BUNS!
PEIRCE

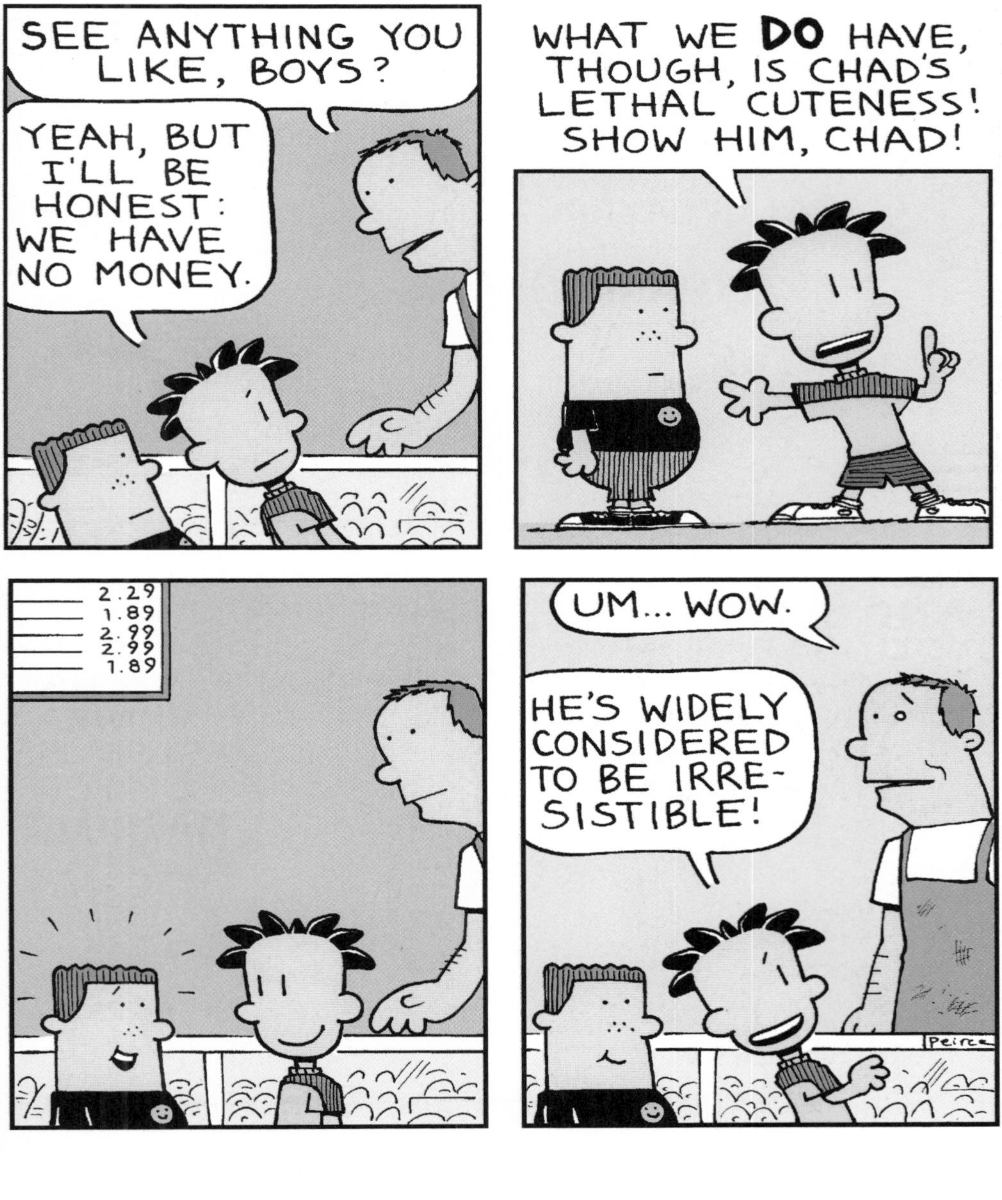
SEE ANYTHING YOU LIKE, BOYS?
YEAH, BUT I'LL BE HONEST: WE HAVE NO MONEY.
WHAT WE **DO** HAVE, THOUGH, IS CHAD'S LETHAL CUTENESS! SHOW HIM, CHAD!
2.29
1.89
2.99
2.99
1.89
UM... WOW.
HE'S WIDELY CONSIDERED TO BE IRRE-SISTIBLE!
Peirce

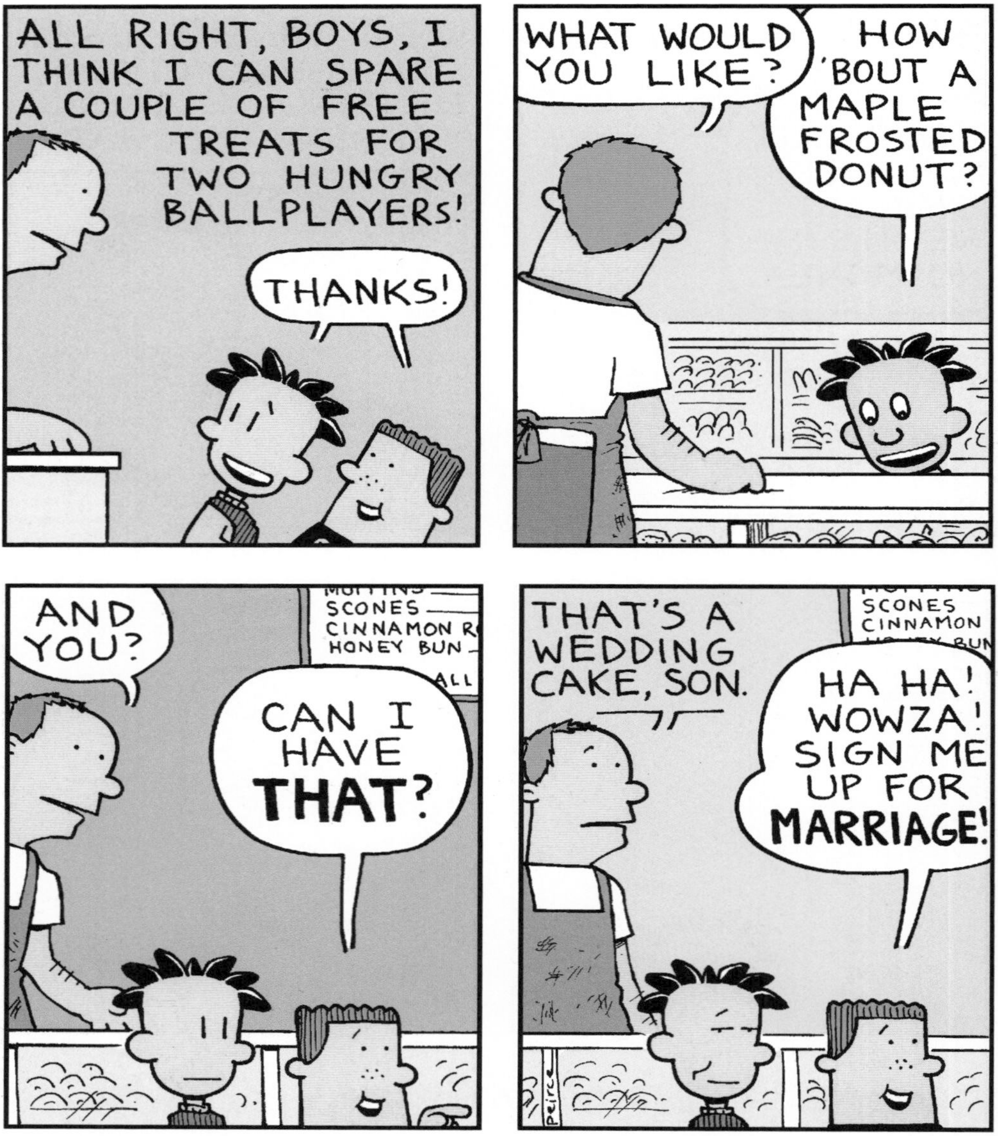
ALL RIGHT, BOYS, I THINK I CAN SPARE A COUPLE OF FREE TREATS FOR TWO HUNGRY BALLPLAYERS!
THANKS!
WHAT WOULD YOU LIKE?
HOW 'BOUT A MAPLE FROSTED DONUT?
AND YOU?
SCONES
CINNAMON R
HONEY BUN
CAN I HAVE **THAT**?
THAT'S A WEDDING CAKE, SON.
SCONES
CINNAMON
HA HA! WOWZA! SIGN ME UP FOR **MARRIAGE**!
PEIRCE

HEY, MR. CRESSLY, HOW COME YOU NAMED OUR TEAM THE CUPCAKES? AND BEFORE THAT, WE WERE THE CREAM PUFFS!
IT'S ADVERTISING, BOYS! I WANTED A NAME THAT WOULD REMIND PEOPLE OF MY BAKERY!
BUT YOU ALSO WANT A NAME THAT CAPTURES THE SPIRIT OF BASEBALL!
HOW ABOUT "LOAFS"?
...OR WOULD IT BE "LOAVES"?
SWING AND A MISS, CHAD.
Peirce

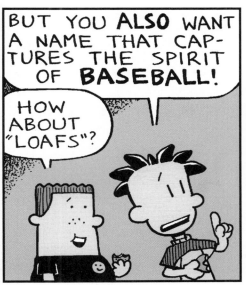

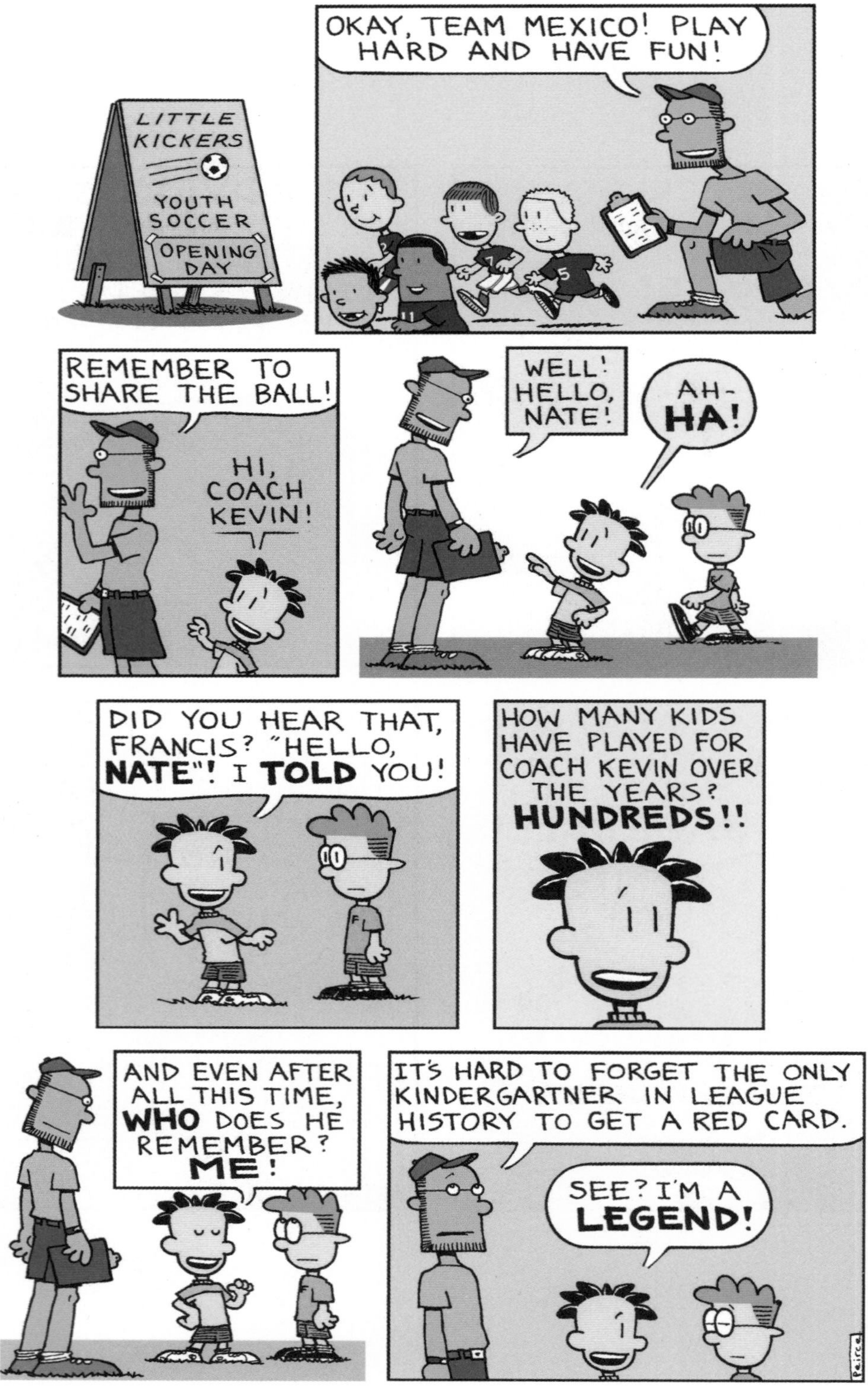
LITTLE KICKERS
YOUTH SOCCER
OPENING DAY
OKAY, TEAM MEXICO! PLAY HARD AND HAVE FUN!
REMEMBER TO SHARE THE BALL!
HI, COACH KEVIN!
WELL! HELLO, NATE!
AH-HA!
DID YOU HEAR THAT, FRANCIS? "HELLO, NATE"! I TOLD YOU!
HOW MANY KIDS HAVE PLAYED FOR COACH KEVIN OVER THE YEARS? HUNDREDS!!
AND EVEN AFTER ALL THIS TIME, WHO DOES HE REMEMBER? ME!
IT'S HARD TO FORGET THE ONLY KINDERGARTNER IN LEAGUE HISTORY TO GET A RED CARD.
SEE? I'M A LEGEND!
Peirce

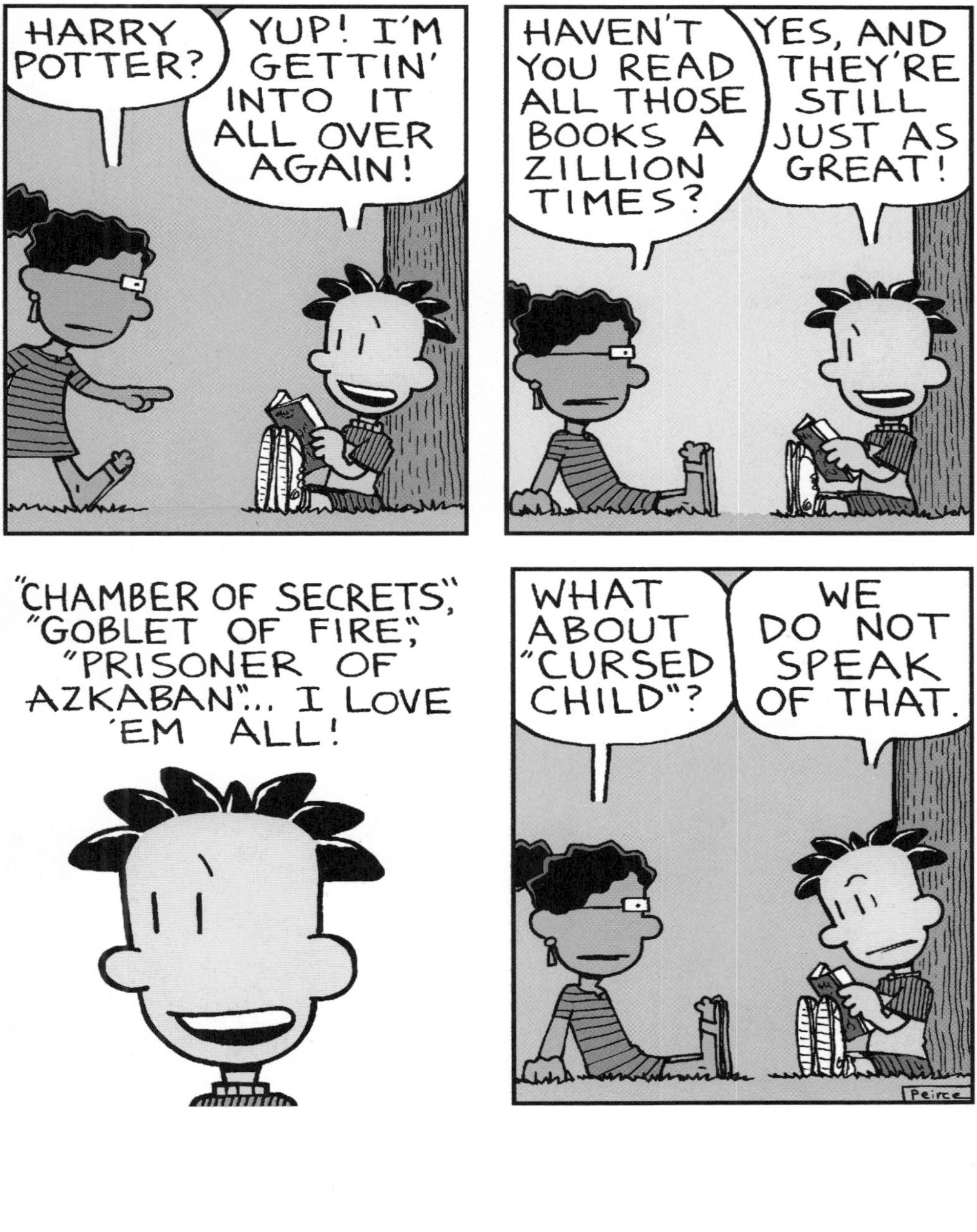
HARRY POTTER?
YUP! I'M GETTIN' INTO IT ALL OVER AGAIN!
HAVEN'T YOU READ ALL THOSE BOOKS A ZILLION TIMES?
YES, AND THEY'RE STILL JUST AS GREAT!
"CHAMBER OF SECRETS," "GOBLET OF FIRE," "PRISONER OF AZKABAN"... I LOVE 'EM ALL!
WHAT ABOUT "CURSED CHILD"?
WE DO NOT SPEAK OF THAT.
Peirce

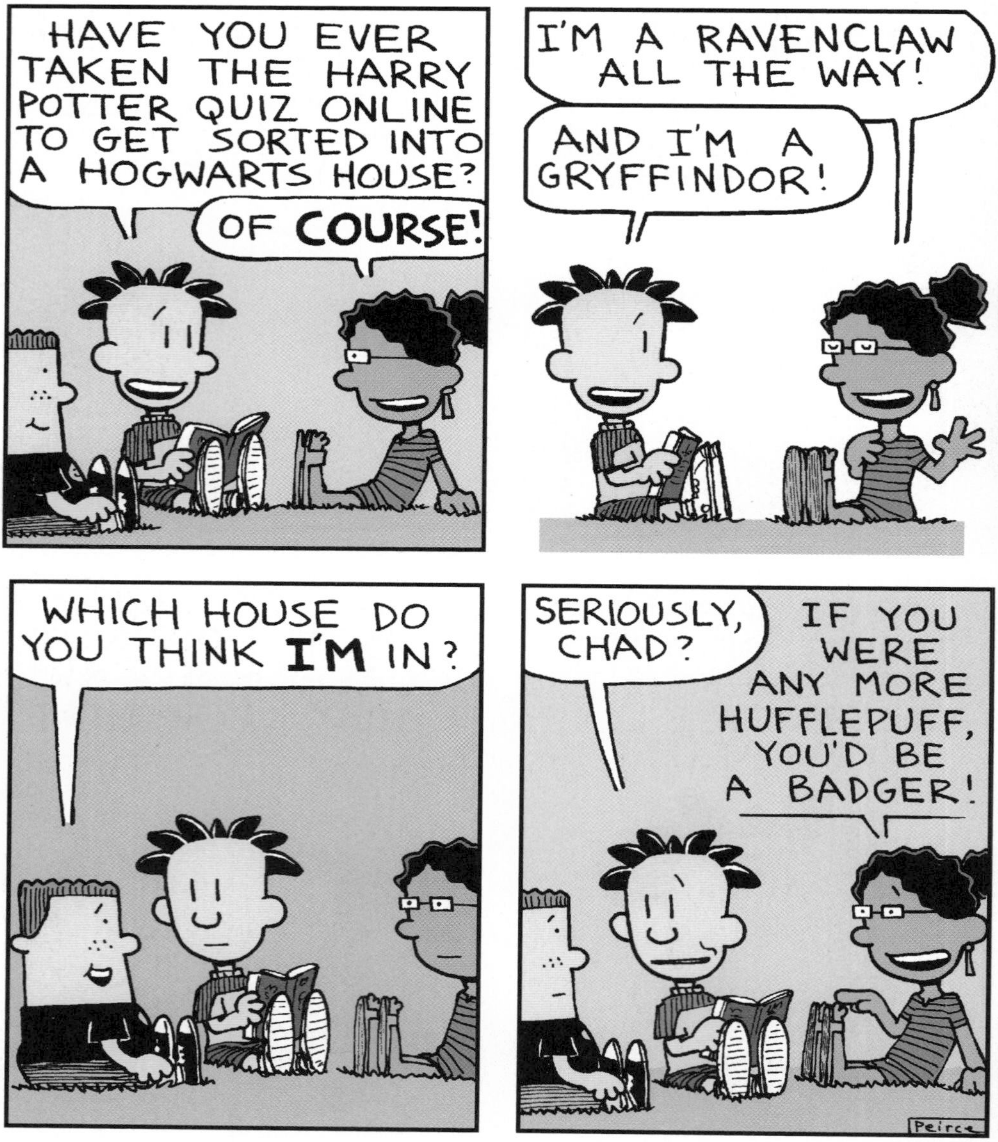
HAVE YOU EVER TAKEN THE HARRY POTTER QUIZ ONLINE TO GET SORTED INTO A HOGWARTS HOUSE?
OF COURSE!
I'M A RAVENCLAW ALL THE WAY!
AND I'M A GRYFFINDOR!
WHICH HOUSE DO YOU THINK I'M IN?
SERIOUSLY, CHAD?
IF YOU WERE ANY MORE HUFFLEPUFF, YOU'D BE A BADGER!
Peirce

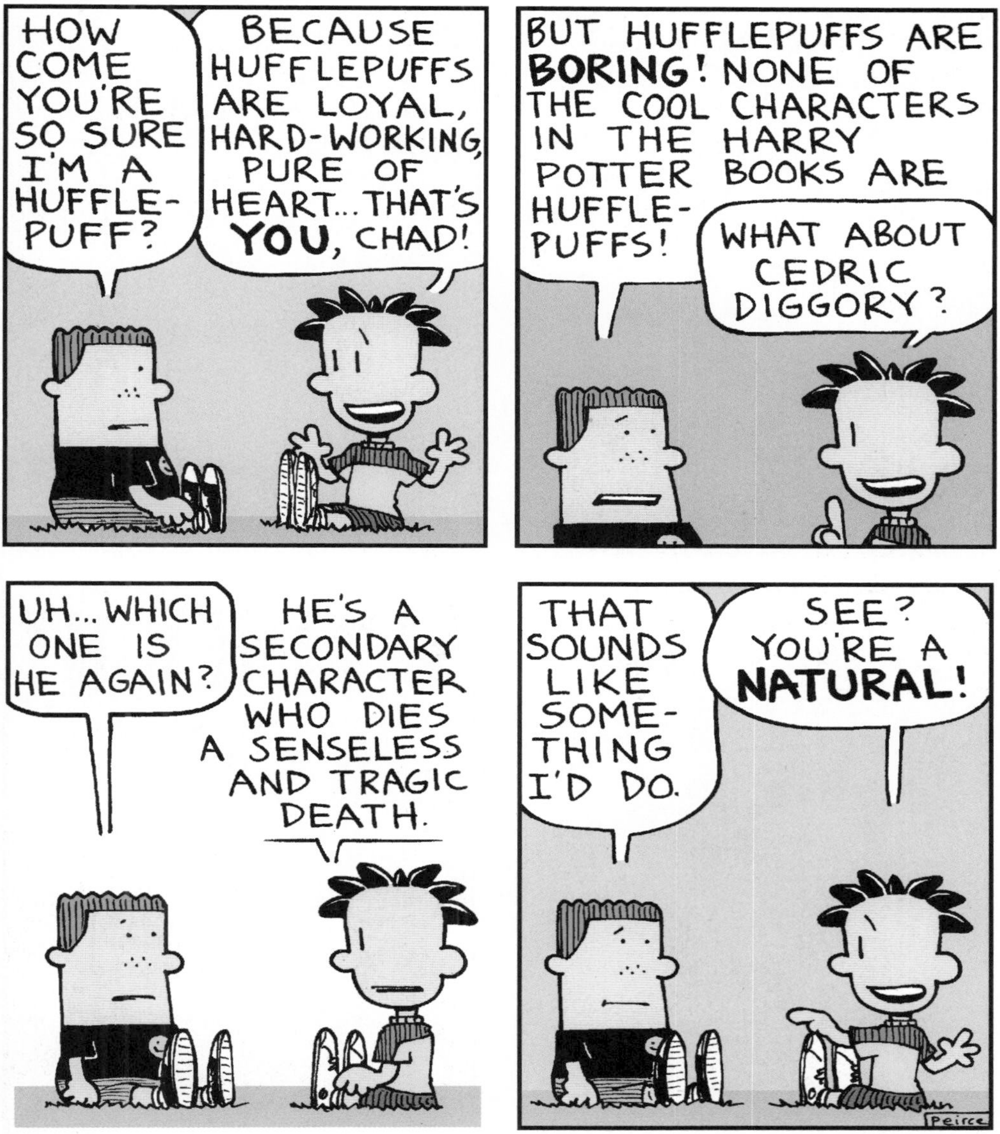
HOW COME YOU'RE SO SURE I'M A HUFFLE-PUFF?
BECAUSE HUFFLEPUFFS ARE LOYAL, HARD-WORKING, PURE OF HEART... THAT'S **YOU**, CHAD!
BUT HUFFLEPUFFS ARE **BORING**! NONE OF THE COOL CHARACTERS IN THE HARRY POTTER BOOKS ARE HUFFLE-PUFFS!
WHAT ABOUT CEDRIC DIGGORY?
UH... WHICH ONE IS HE AGAIN?
HE'S A SECONDARY CHARACTER WHO DIES A SENSELESS AND TRAGIC DEATH.
THAT SOUNDS LIKE SOME-THING I'D DO.
SEE? YOU'RE A **NATURAL**!
Peirce

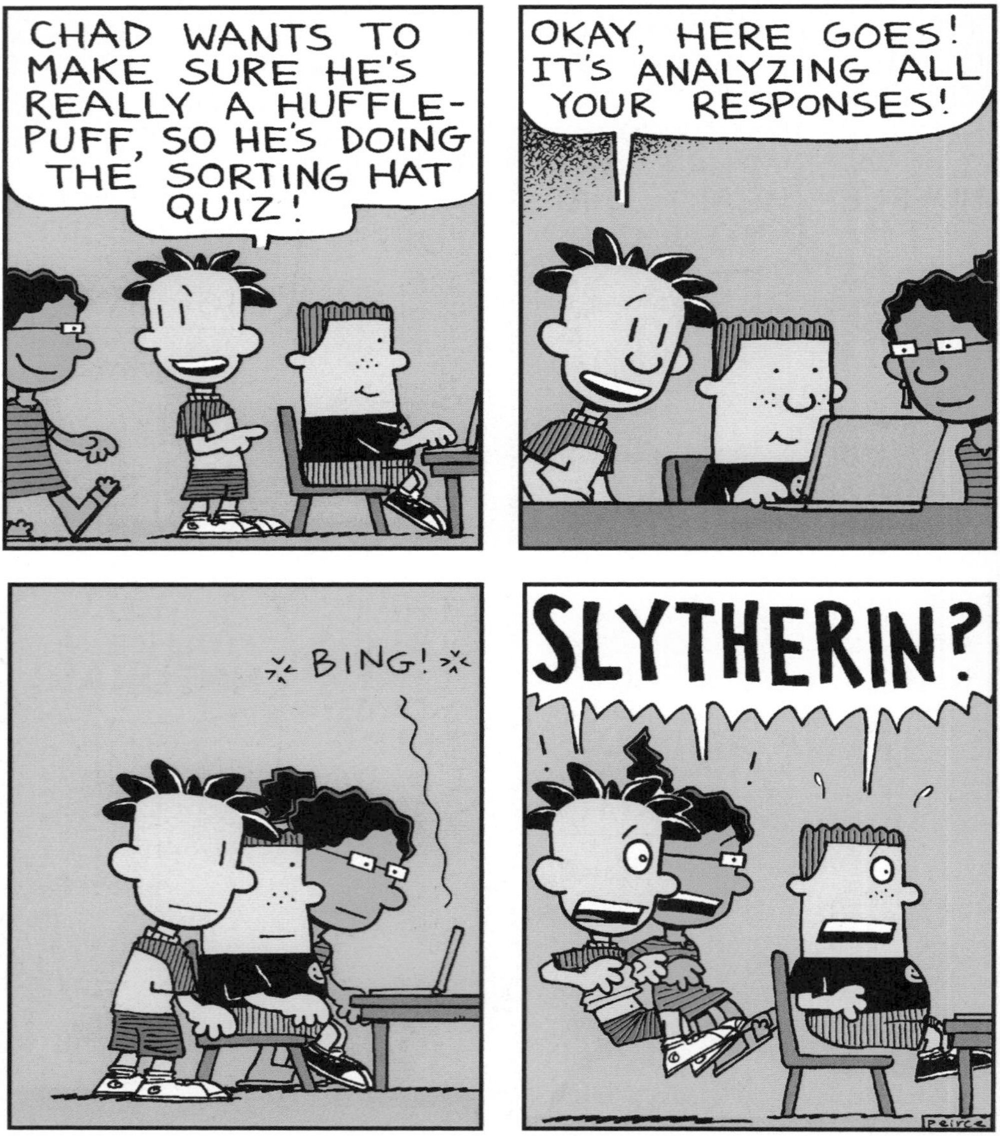
CHAD WANTS TO MAKE SURE HE'S REALLY A HUFFLE-PUFF, SO HE'S DOING THE SORTING HAT QUIZ!
OKAY, HERE GOES! IT'S ANALYZING ALL YOUR RESPONSES!
BING!
SLYTHERIN?
PEIRCE

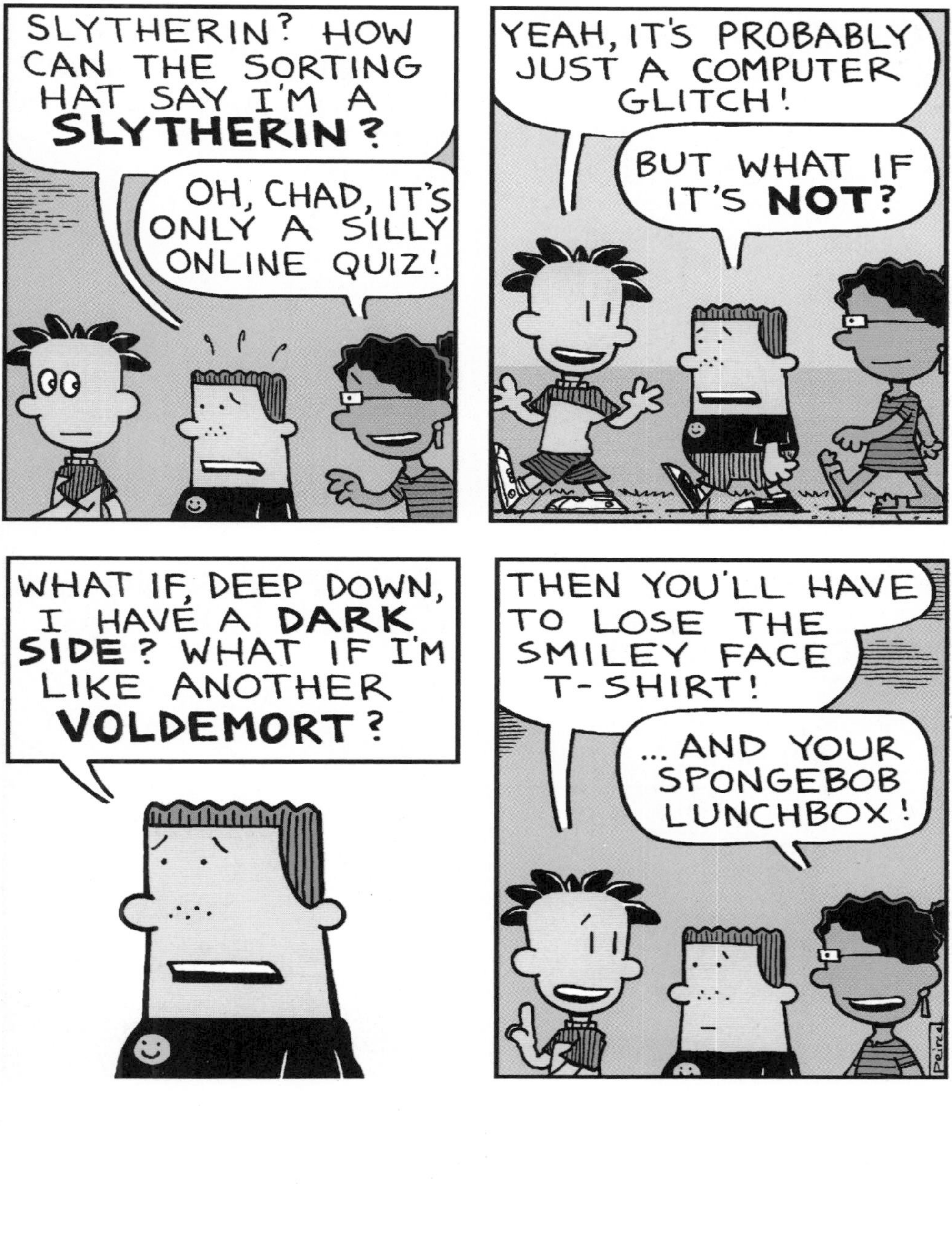
SLYTHERIN? HOW CAN THE SORTING HAT SAY I'M A SLYTHERIN?
OH, CHAD, IT'S ONLY A SILLY ONLINE QUIZ!
YEAH, IT'S PROBABLY JUST A COMPUTER GLITCH!
BUT WHAT IF IT'S NOT?
WHAT IF, DEEP DOWN, I HAVE A DARK SIDE? WHAT IF I'M LIKE ANOTHER VOLDEMORT?
THEN YOU'LL HAVE TO LOSE THE SMILEY FACE T-SHIRT!
...AND YOUR SPONGEBOB LUNCHBOX!
Peirce

HI, NATE!
CHAD! YOU LOOK HAPPIER THAN YOU DID YESTERDAY!
YOU'RE NOT STILL UPSET ABOUT THAT SORTING HAT QUIZ?
NOPE!
FINDING OUT I'M A **SLYTHERIN** IS ONE OF THE BEST THINGS THAT EVER **HAPPENED** TO ME!
HIIIIIII, CHAD!
TURNS OUT THE LADIES LOVE A BAD BOY!
Peirce

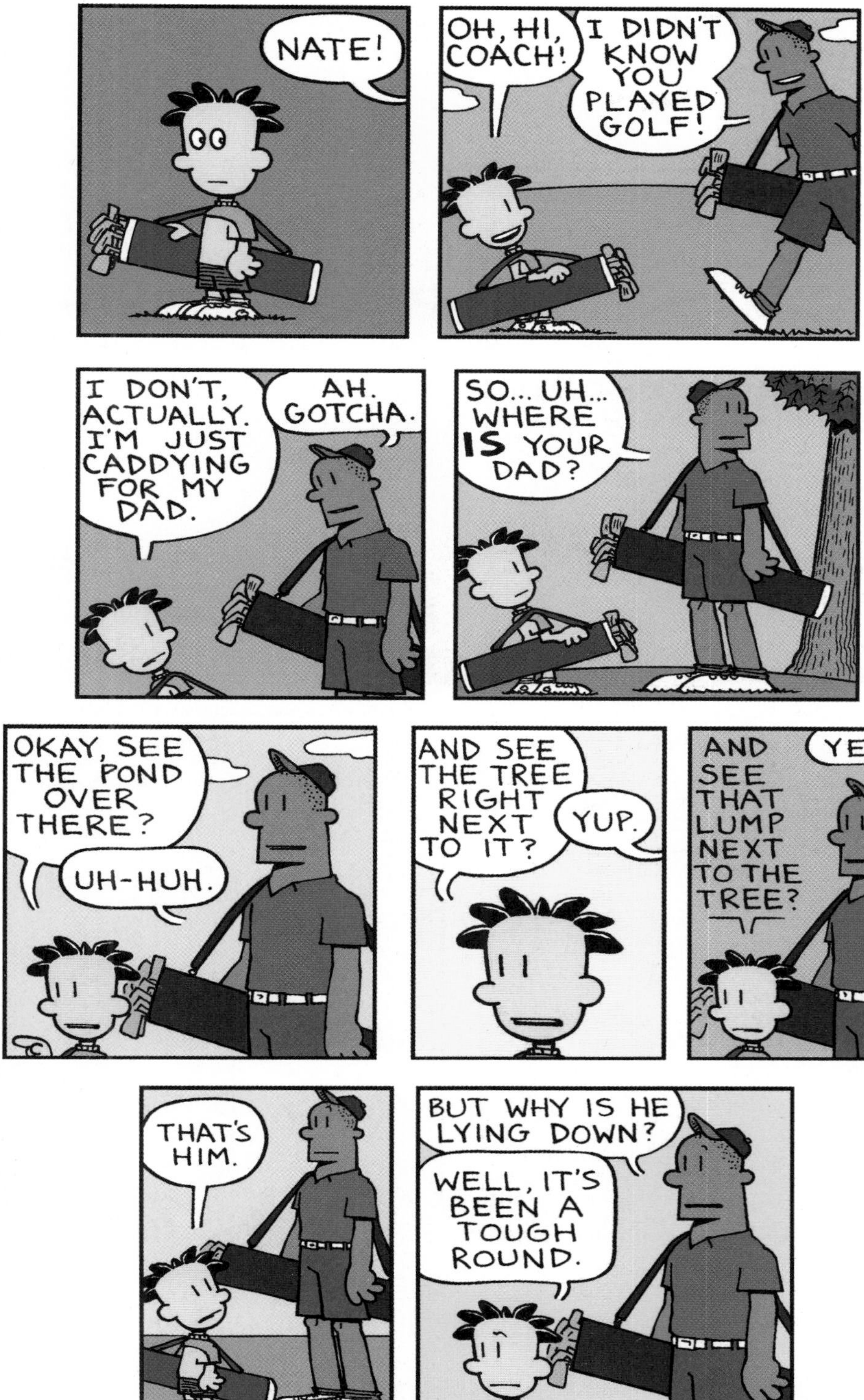
NATE!
OH, HI, COACH!
I DIDN'T KNOW YOU PLAYED GOLF!
I DON'T, ACTUALLY. I'M JUST CADDYING FOR MY DAD.
AH. GOTCHA.
SO... UH... WHERE IS YOUR DAD?
OKAY, SEE THE POND OVER THERE?
UH-HUH.
AND SEE THE TREE RIGHT NEXT TO IT?
YUP.
AND SEE THAT LUMP NEXT TO THE TREE?
YES.
THAT'S HIM.
BUT WHY IS HE LYING DOWN?
WELL, IT'S BEEN A TOUGH ROUND.
Peirce

WANT TO CADDY FOR ME?
NO, THANKS.
WANT TO CADDY FOR ME?
UH... NO.
WANT TO CADDY FOR ME?
HE TAKES A LOT OF MUL-LIGANS.
WHAT A **DAY!**
Peirce

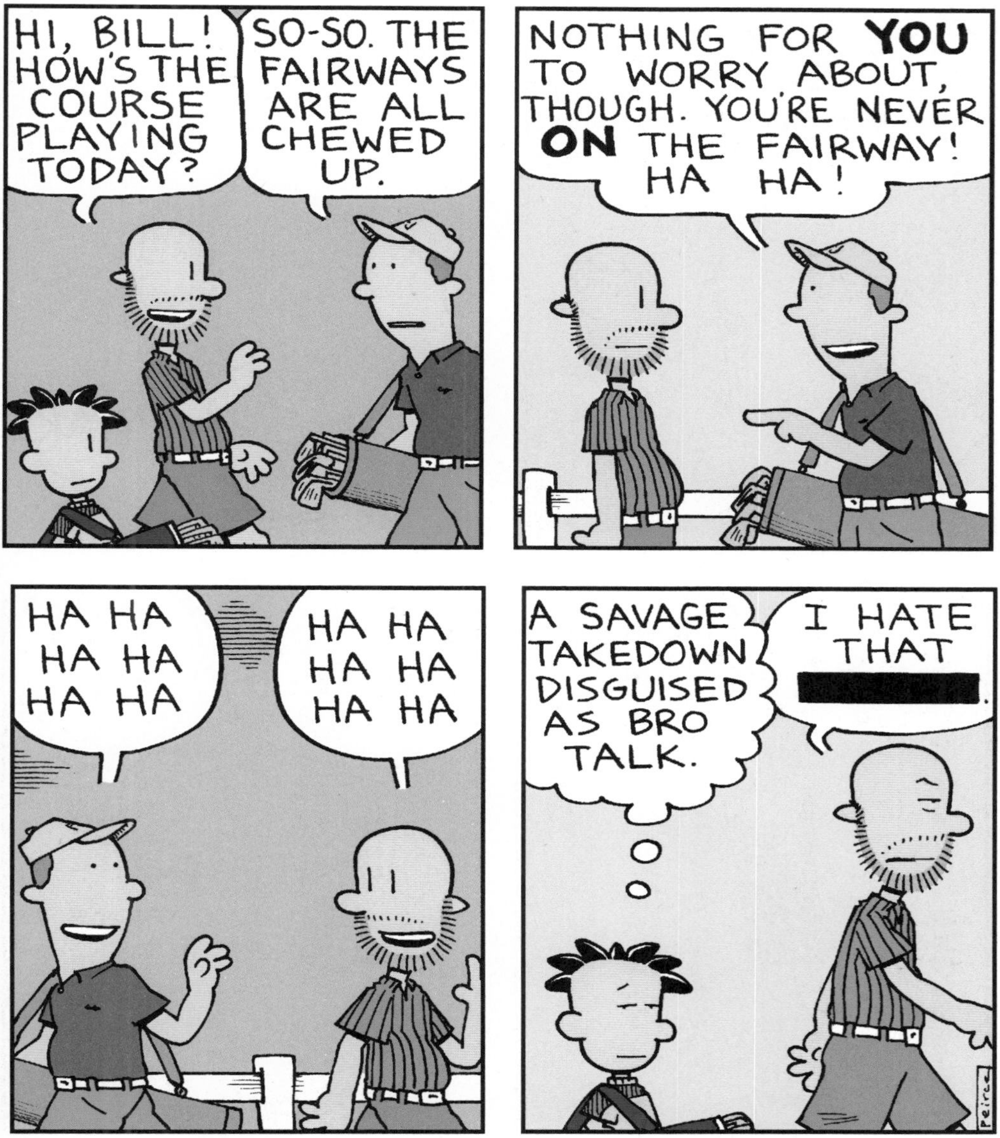
HI, BILL! HOW'S THE COURSE PLAYING TODAY?
SO-SO. THE FAIRWAYS ARE ALL CHEWED UP.
NOTHING FOR **YOU** TO WORRY ABOUT, THOUGH. YOU'RE NEVER **ON** THE FAIRWAY! HA HA!
HA HA HA HA HA HA
HA HA HA HA HA HA
A SAVAGE TAKEDOWN DISGUISED AS BRO TALK.
I HATE THAT [redacted].
peirce

TIME TO TRY OUT MY NEW DRIVER!
SMAK!
IT'S A LOT LIKE YOUR OLD DRIVER!
OH, COME ON!
Peirce

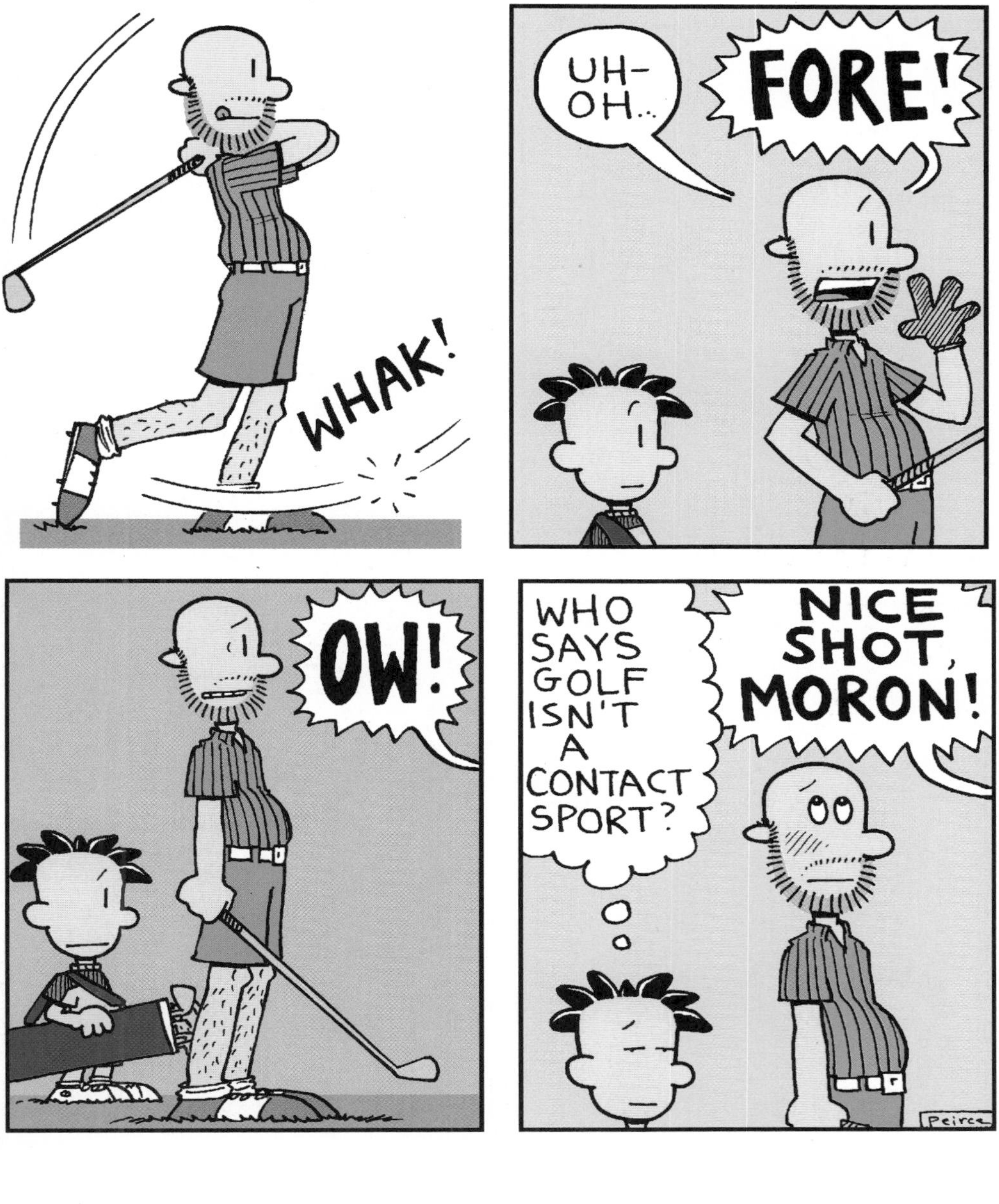
WHAK!
UH-OH...
FORE!
OW!
WHO SAYS GOLF ISN'T A CONTACT SPORT?
NICE SHOT, MORON!
Peirce

IT'S TOO HOT TO PLAY GOLF.
CAN I TAKE A BREAK TO COOL OFF?
SPLASH!
YES.
THIS IS SO REFRESHING.
Peirce

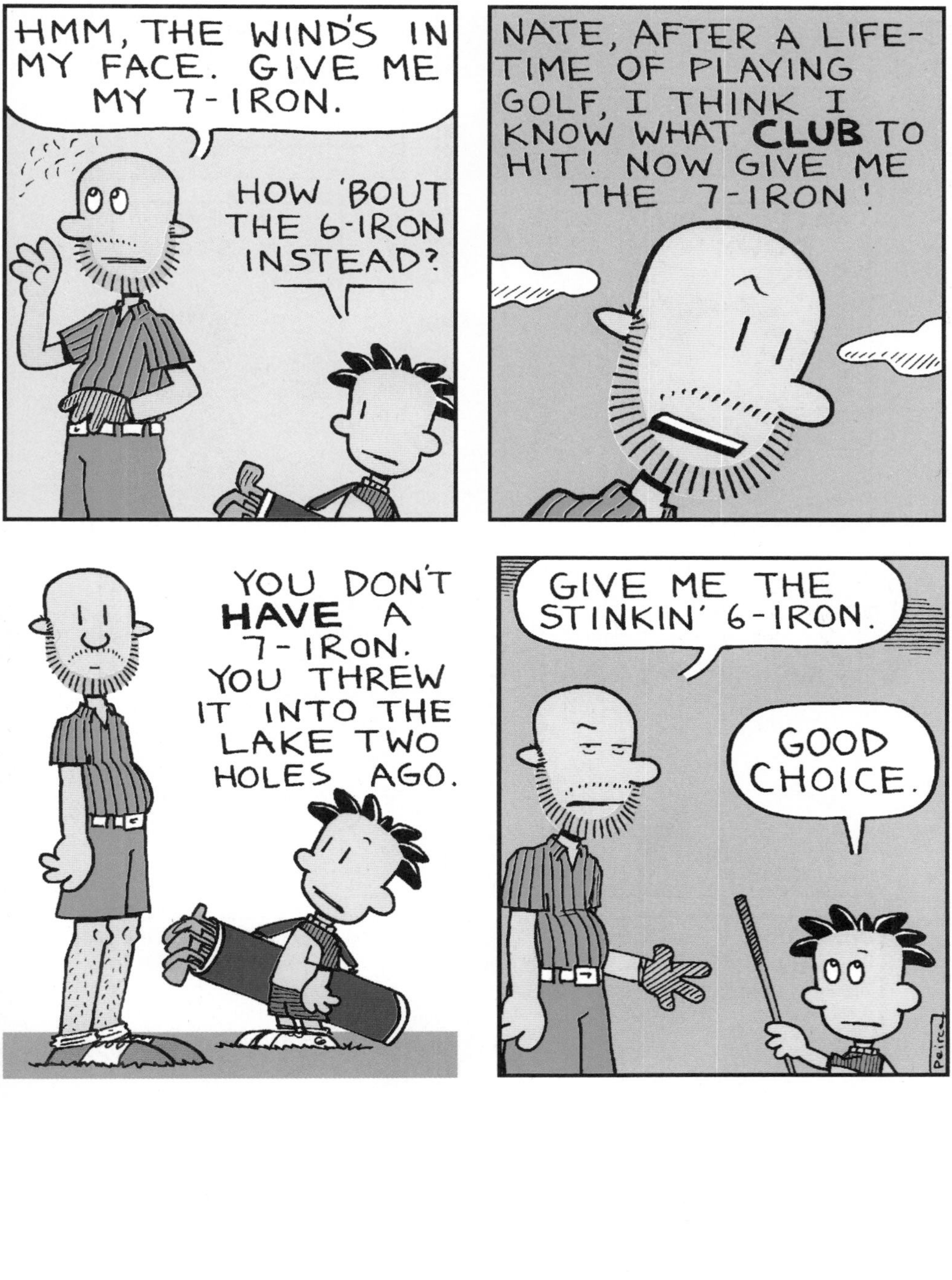
HMM, THE WIND'S IN MY FACE. GIVE ME MY 7-IRON.
HOW 'BOUT THE 6-IRON INSTEAD?
NATE, AFTER A LIFETIME OF PLAYING GOLF, I THINK I KNOW WHAT **CLUB** TO HIT! NOW GIVE ME THE 7-IRON!
YOU DON'T **HAVE** A 7-IRON. YOU THREW IT INTO THE LAKE TWO HOLES AGO.
GIVE ME THE STINKIN' 6-IRON.
GOOD CHOICE.
Peirce

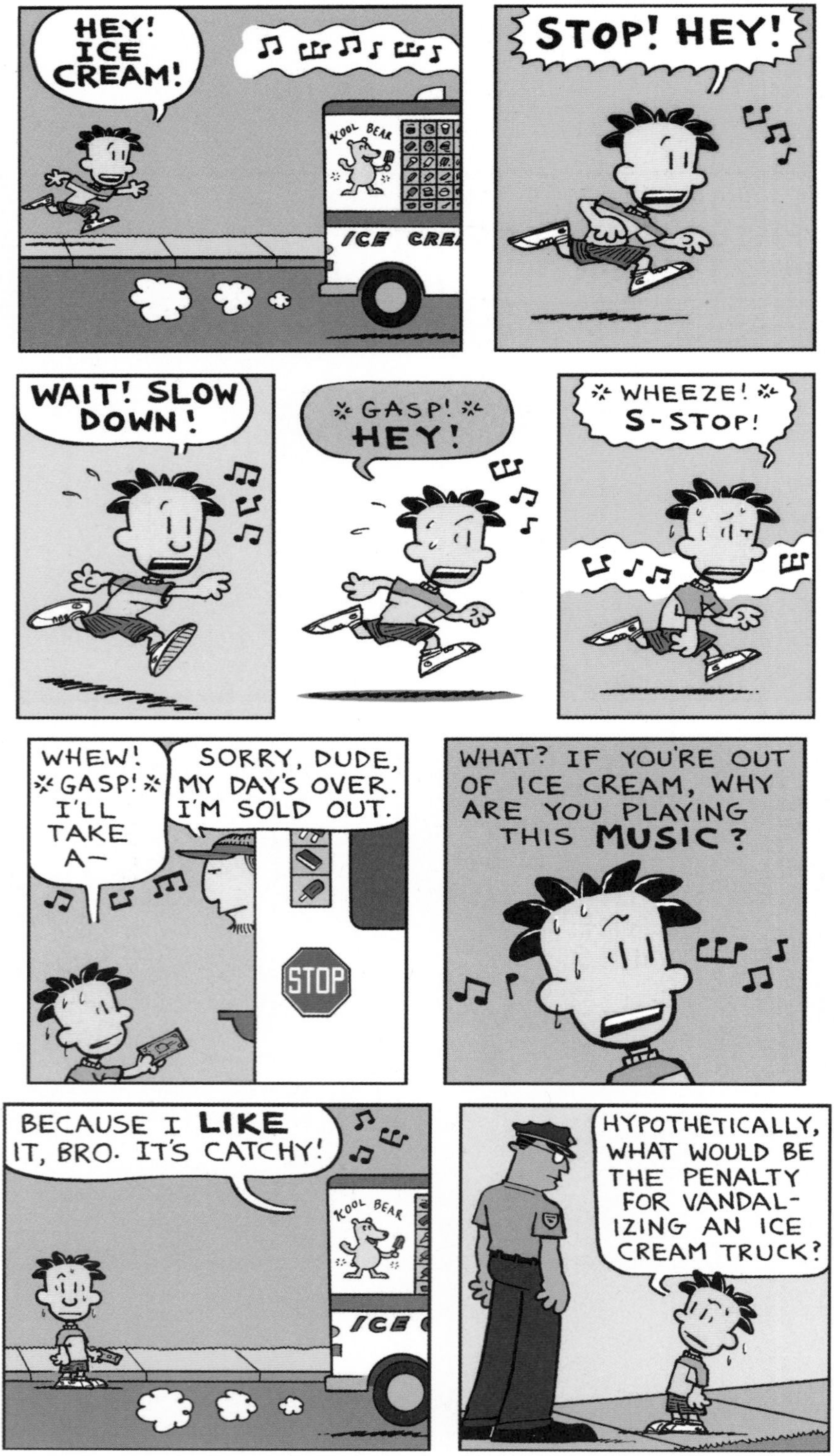
HEY! ICE CREAM!
KOOL BEAR
ICE CREA
STOP! HEY!
WAIT! SLOW DOWN!
GASP! HEY!
WHEEZE! S-STOP!
WHEW! GASP! I'LL TAKE A—
SORRY, DUDE, MY DAY'S OVER. I'M SOLD OUT.
STOP
WHAT? IF YOU'RE OUT OF ICE CREAM, WHY ARE YOU PLAYING THIS MUSIC?
BECAUSE I LIKE IT, BRO. IT'S CATCHY!
KOOL BEAR
ICE
HYPOTHETICALLY, WHAT WOULD BE THE PENALTY FOR VANDALIZING AN ICE CREAM TRUCK?

HI, GRAM!
HI, HONEY! WHAT A NICE SURPRISE!
WHAT'S NEW?
WELL, I'M TRYING TO EARN SOME MONEY TO BUY NEW SOCCER CLEATS.
... SO DO YOU HAVE ANY CHORES I COULD DO, OR—
CHORES? SAY NO MORE!
I HAVE THIS UNSIGHTLY PILE OF GINGER SNAPS THAT NEEDS TO BE EATEN!
BEST GRANDMA EVER!
Peirce

WELL! LOOK WHO THE CAT DRAGGED IN!
HI, GRAMPS!
HOW'S SCHOOL, M'BOY?
OH, IT HASN'T STARTED YET.
BUT WHEN IT **DOES** START, IT'S GONNA BE HORRIBLE.
THAT'S JUST HOW I FEEL ABOUT BINGO, BUT YOUR GRAND-MOTHER INSISTS ON DRAGGING ME THERE EVERY FRIDAY NIGHT.
I CAN HEAR YOU, VERN.
Peirce

GRAMPS, ARE YOU DONE WITH THE NEWS-PAPER?
GRRR...
GRAMPS? I SAID, ARE YOU DONE WI—
ARRGH!
TAKE IT! TAKE IT! TAKE IT!!
HE GETS CRANKY WHEN HE CAN'T FINISH THE "JUMBLE."
JUST AS WELL. IT'S TIME FOR "ELLEN."
Peirce

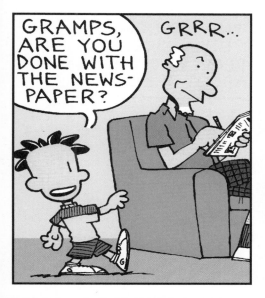

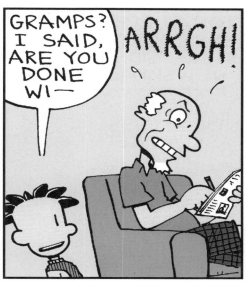

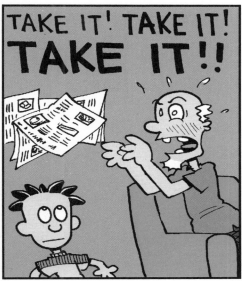

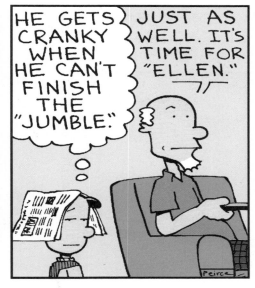

YOU SURPRISE ME, BOY. MOST YOUNGSTERS DON'T READ NEWSPAPERS.
I DO! I NEVER MISS "ASK ANNIE"!
THE ADVICE COLUMN? BUT THAT'S JUST PEOPLE COMPLAINING ABOUT THEIR PROBLEMS!
I KNOW! THAT'S WHY IT'S ENTERTAINING!
DON'T YOU LIKE READING ABOUT FAMILY DYSFUNCTION?
WHY READ IT WHEN I CAN LIVE IT?
SNACK UPDATE: WE'RE OUT OF CHEESE NIPS.

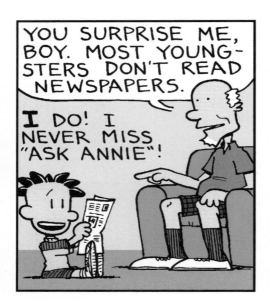

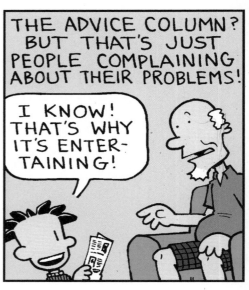

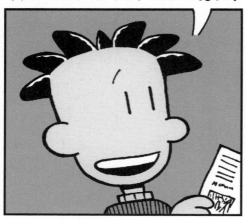

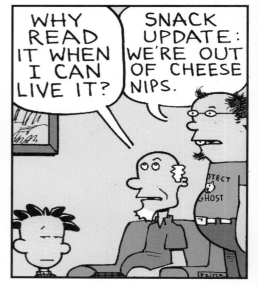

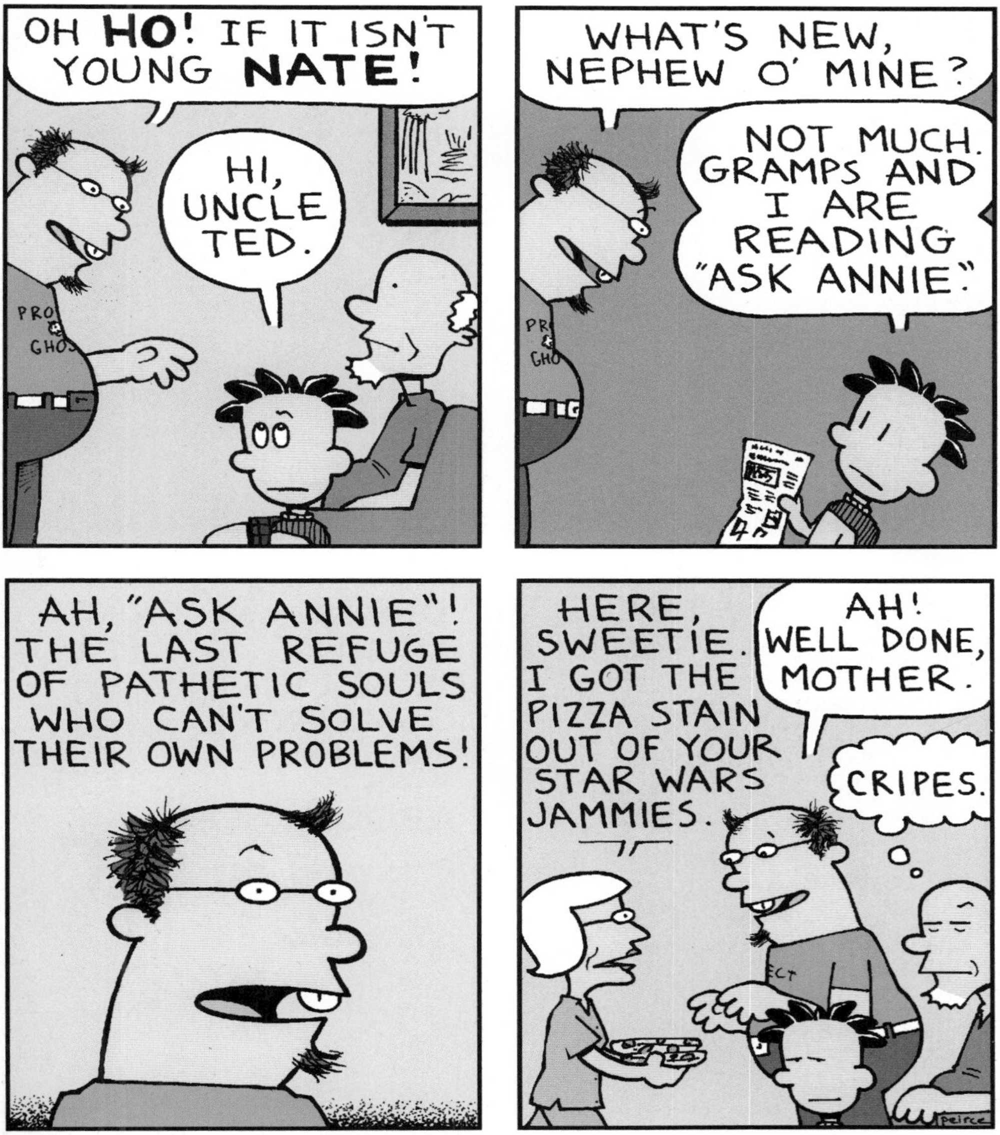
OH **HO**! IF IT ISN'T YOUNG **NATE**!
HI, UNCLE TED.
WHAT'S NEW, NEPHEW O' MINE?
NOT MUCH. GRAMPS AND I ARE READING "ASK ANNIE."
AH, "ASK ANNIE"! THE LAST REFUGE OF PATHETIC SOULS WHO CAN'T SOLVE THEIR OWN PROBLEMS!
HERE, SWEETIE. I GOT THE PIZZA STAIN OUT OF YOUR STAR WARS JAMMIES.
AH! WELL DONE, MOTHER.
CRIPES.
peirce

DO YOU THINK THESE LETTERS TO "ASK ANNIE" ARE REAL?
DUNNO. LET'S HEAR 'EM.
DEAR ANNIE: MY HUSBAND IS A MESSY SLOB, AND—
THAT'S FAKE.
DEAR ANNIE: MY HUSBAND NEVER LISTENS TO MY—
THAT'S FAKE.
DEAR ANNIE: MY WIFE IS ALWAYS NAGGING ME ABOUT—
THAT'S REAL.
Peirce

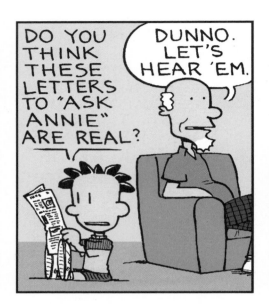

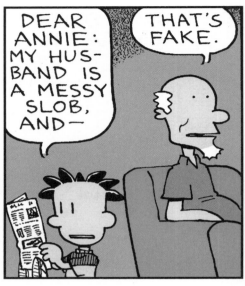

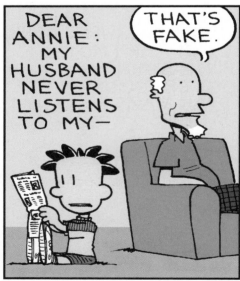

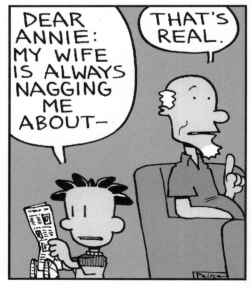

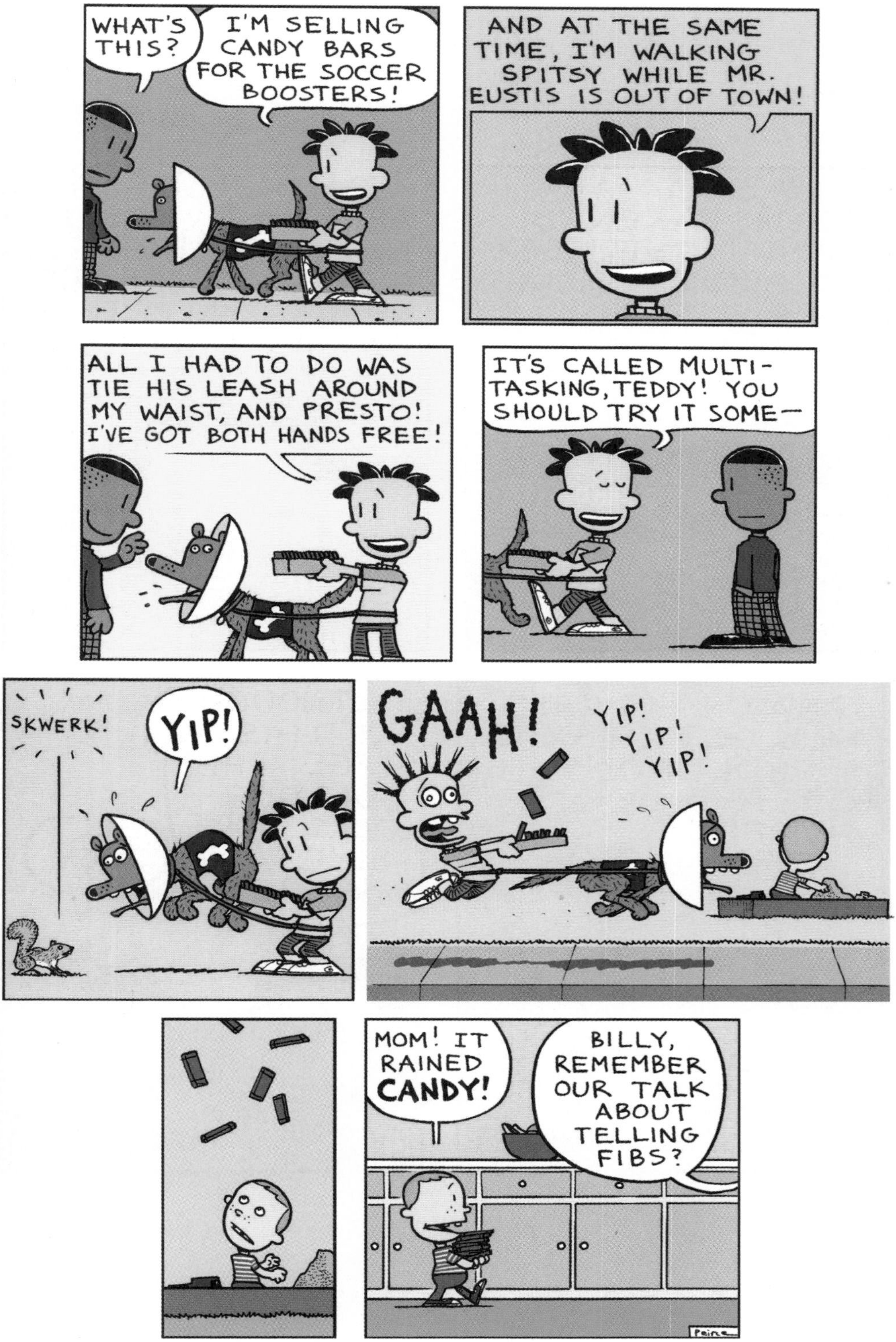
WHAT'S THIS?
I'M SELLING CANDY BARS FOR THE SOCCER BOOSTERS!
AND AT THE SAME TIME, I'M WALKING SPITSY WHILE MR. EUSTIS IS OUT OF TOWN!
ALL I HAD TO DO WAS TIE HIS LEASH AROUND MY WAIST, AND PRESTO! I'VE GOT BOTH HANDS FREE!
IT'S CALLED MULTI-TASKING, TEDDY! YOU SHOULD TRY IT SOME—
SKWERK!
YIP!
GAAH!
YIP! YIP! YIP!
MOM! IT RAINED CANDY!
BILLY, REMEMBER OUR TALK ABOUT TELLING FIBS?

I WAS AT MY GRANDPARENTS' HOUSE YESTERDAY, AND GRAMPS SHOWED ME ALL HIS TATTOOS.

HE HAS TATTOOS?

YEAH, HE GOT THEM WHEN HE WAS IN THE NAVY! HE'S GOT AN ANCHOR ON HIS ARM, A PALM TREE ON HIS SHOULDER...

...AND ON HIS CHEST, HE'S GOT THIS BIG BULLDOG!

...ALTHOUGH AT THIS STAGE, THE BULLDOG LOOKS MORE LIKE A SHAR-PEI.

OUCH.

I THINK IT WOULD BE COOL TO GET A TATTOO!
WHAT WOULD YOU GET?
A PICTURE OF MY FAVORITE COMIC BOOK CHARACTER OF ALL TIME: **FEMME FATALITY!**
BUT WHAT IF YOU OUTGROW FEMME FATALITY? WHAT IF SOMEDAY YOU GET SICK OF HER?
DO YOU GET SICK OF WATER? DO YOU GET SICK OF **AIR**?
NEVER MIND.

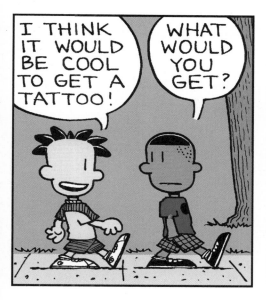

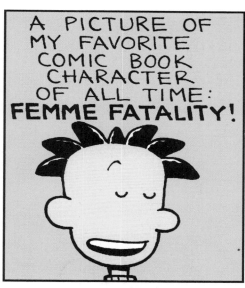

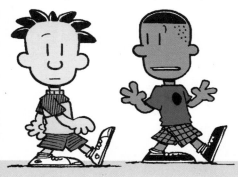

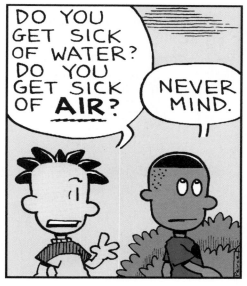

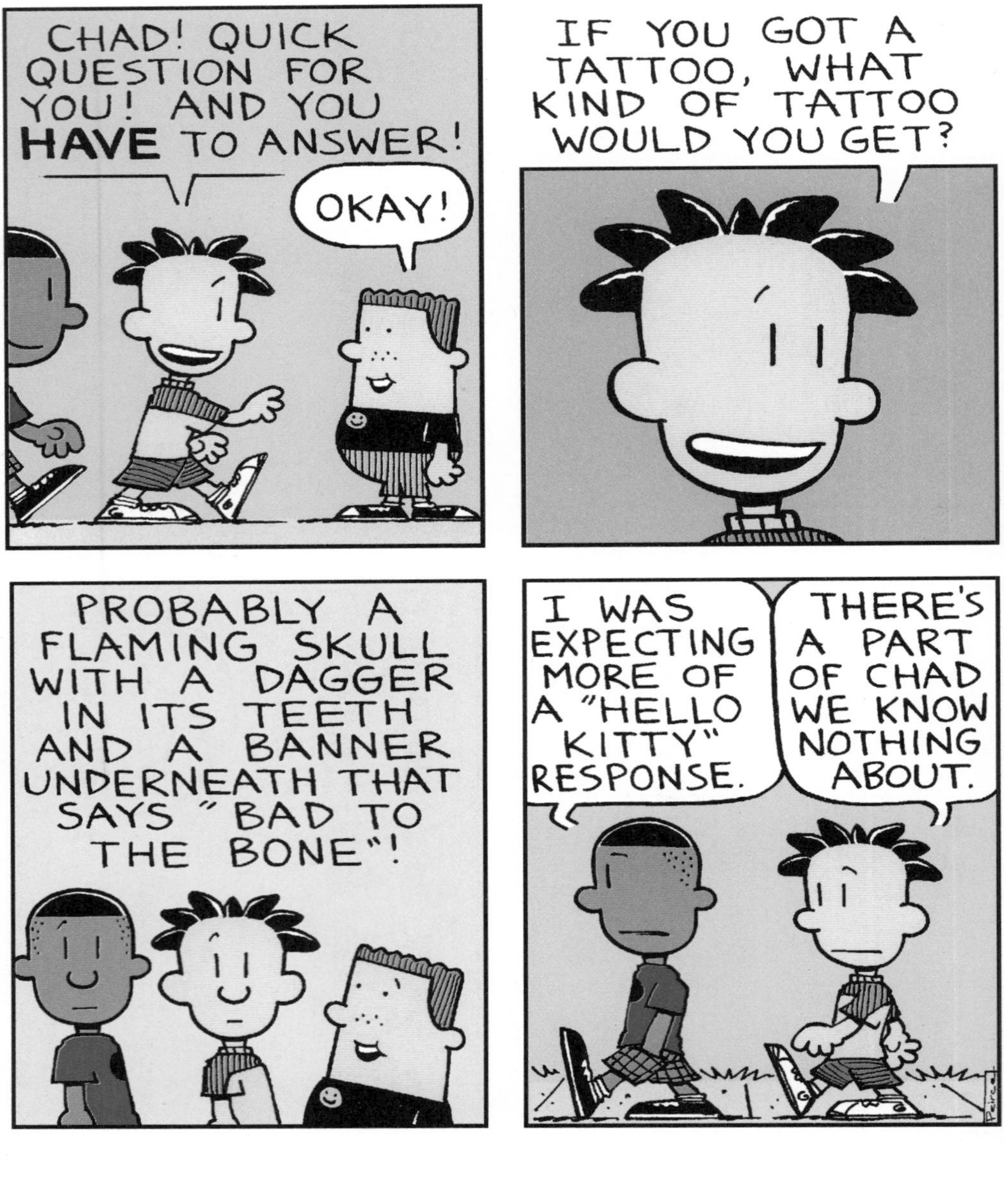
CHAD! QUICK QUESTION FOR YOU! AND YOU **HAVE** TO ANSWER!
OKAY!
IF YOU GOT A TATTOO, WHAT KIND OF TATTOO WOULD YOU GET?
PROBABLY A FLAMING SKULL WITH A DAGGER IN ITS TEETH AND A BANNER UNDERNEATH THAT SAYS "BAD TO THE BONE"!
I WAS EXPECTING MORE OF A "HELLO KITTY" RESPONSE.
THERE'S A PART OF CHAD WE KNOW NOTHING ABOUT.
Peirce

DEE DEE! DO YOU KNOW ANYBODY WHO HAS A TATTOO?
SURE. **BOTH** MY PARENTS HAVE 'EM.
WOULD **YOU** EVER GET ONE?
NO WAY. I ALREADY PRETTY MUCH KNOW WHAT IT'S LIKE.
BECAUSE OF YOUR PARENTS?
NO, BECAUSE IN FIRST GRADE, I DREW A UNICORN ON MY FACE WITH PERMANENT MARKERS.
EMPHASIS ON THE WORD "PERMANENT"?
WORST SCHOOL PICTURE EVER.
Peirce

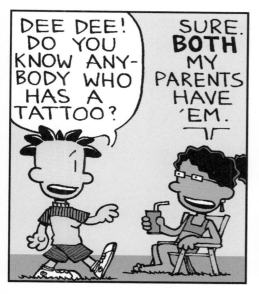

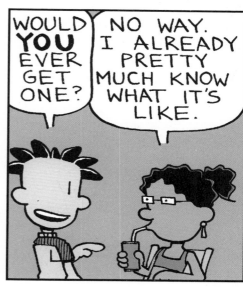

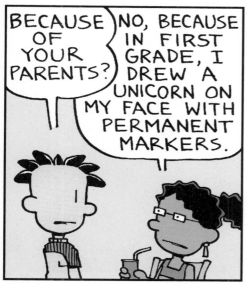

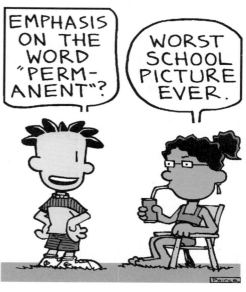

IF YOU GOT A TATTOO, WHAT KIND WOULD YOU GET?
I DON'T THINK KIDS OUR AGE CAN GET TATTOOS.
BUT IF WE COULD, WHAT WOULD YOU GET?
I'M PRETTY SURE YOU HAVE TO BE EIGHTEEN.
OKAY, FRANCIS! PRETEND YOU'RE EIGHTEEN! WHAT KIND OF—
PLUS, IT'S SUPPOSED TO HURT! AND CONSIDER THE HEALTH RISKS!
HE'S A WALKING, TALKING BUZZ-KILL.
I MEAN, HAVE YOU SEEN A STAPH INFECTION?
Peirce

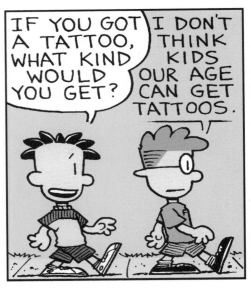

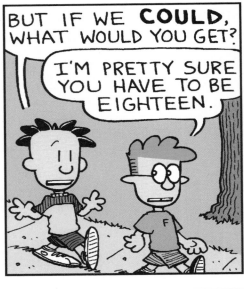

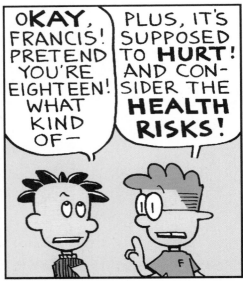

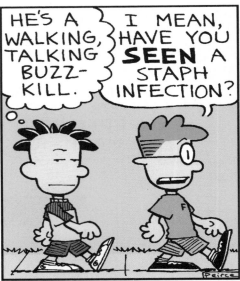

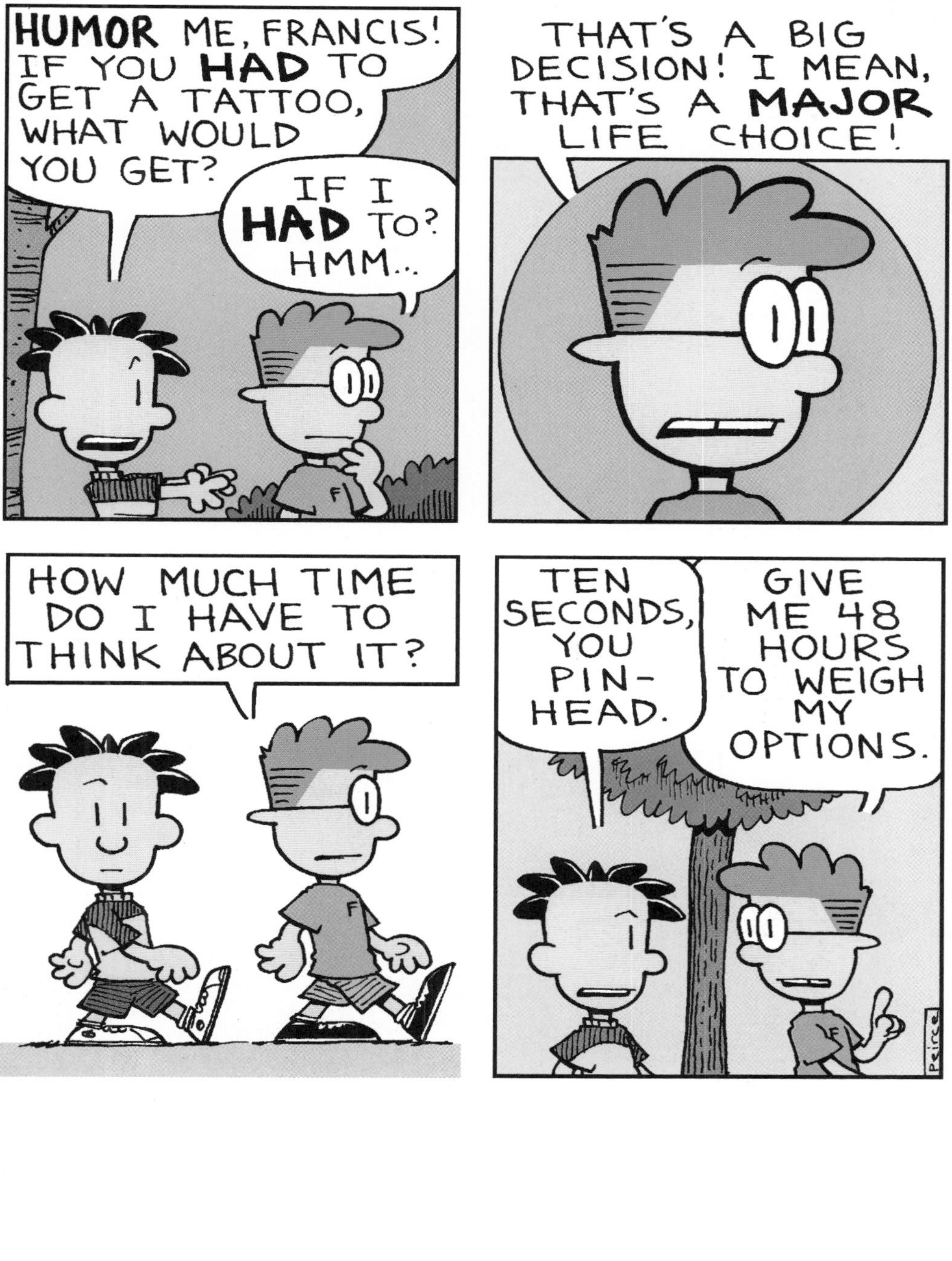
HUMOR ME, FRANCIS! IF YOU HAD TO GET A TATTOO, WHAT WOULD YOU GET?
IF I HAD TO? HMM...
THAT'S A BIG DECISION! I MEAN, THAT'S A MAJOR LIFE CHOICE!
HOW MUCH TIME DO I HAVE TO THINK ABOUT IT?
TEN SECONDS, YOU PIN-HEAD.
GIVE ME 48 HOURS TO WEIGH MY OPTIONS.
Peirce

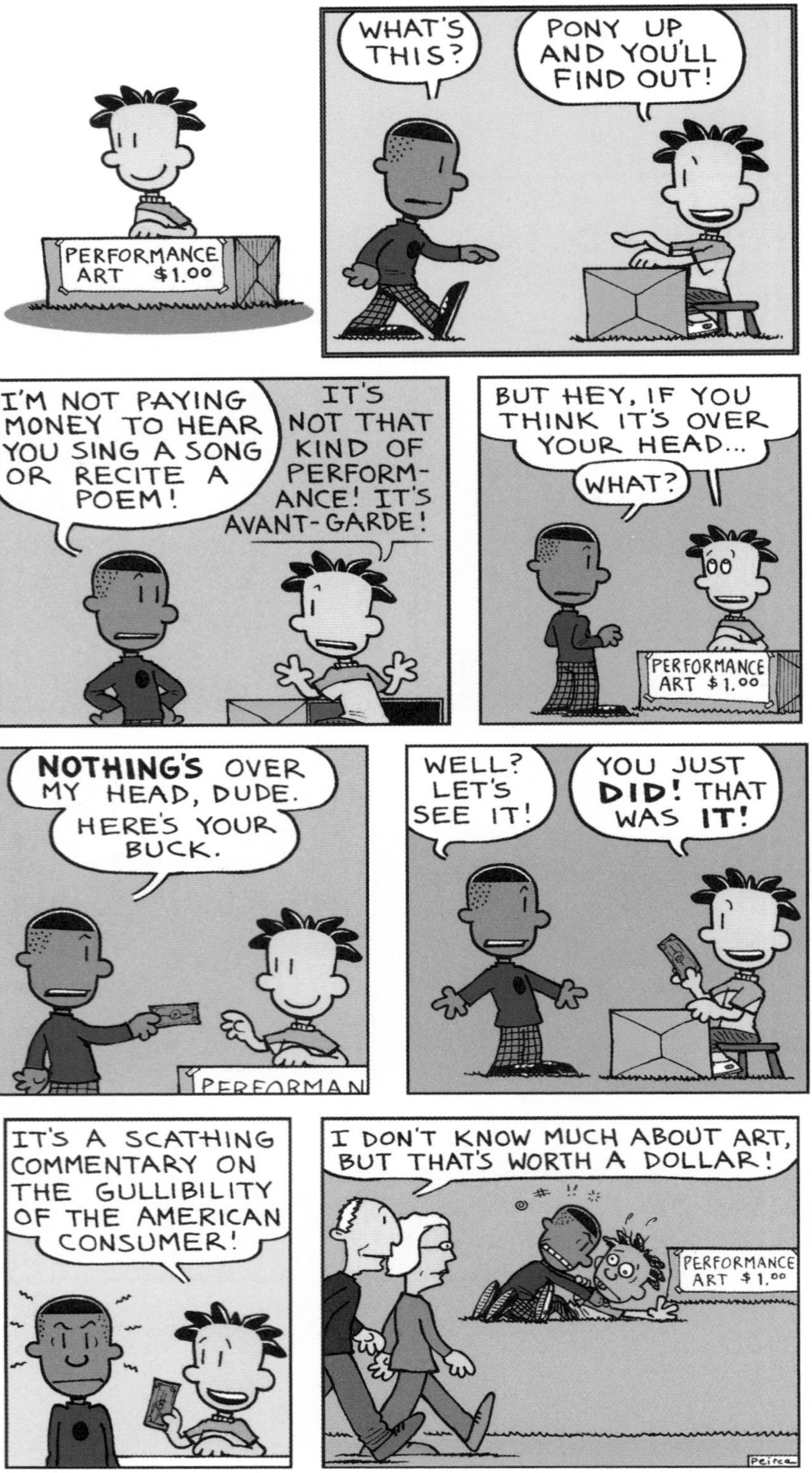
PERFORMANCE ART $1.00
WHAT'S THIS?
PONY UP, AND YOU'LL FIND OUT!
I'M NOT PAYING MONEY TO HEAR YOU SING A SONG OR RECITE A POEM!
IT'S NOT THAT KIND OF PERFORMANCE! IT'S AVANT-GARDE!
BUT HEY, IF YOU THINK IT'S OVER YOUR HEAD...
WHAT?
PERFORMANCE ART $1.00
NOTHING'S OVER MY HEAD, DUDE.
HERE'S YOUR BUCK.
PERFORMAN
WELL? LET'S SEE IT!
YOU JUST DID! THAT WAS IT!
IT'S A SCATHING COMMENTARY ON THE GULLIBILITY OF THE AMERICAN CONSUMER!
I DON'T KNOW MUCH ABOUT ART, BUT THAT'S WORTH A DOLLAR!
PERFORMANCE ART $1.00
Peirce

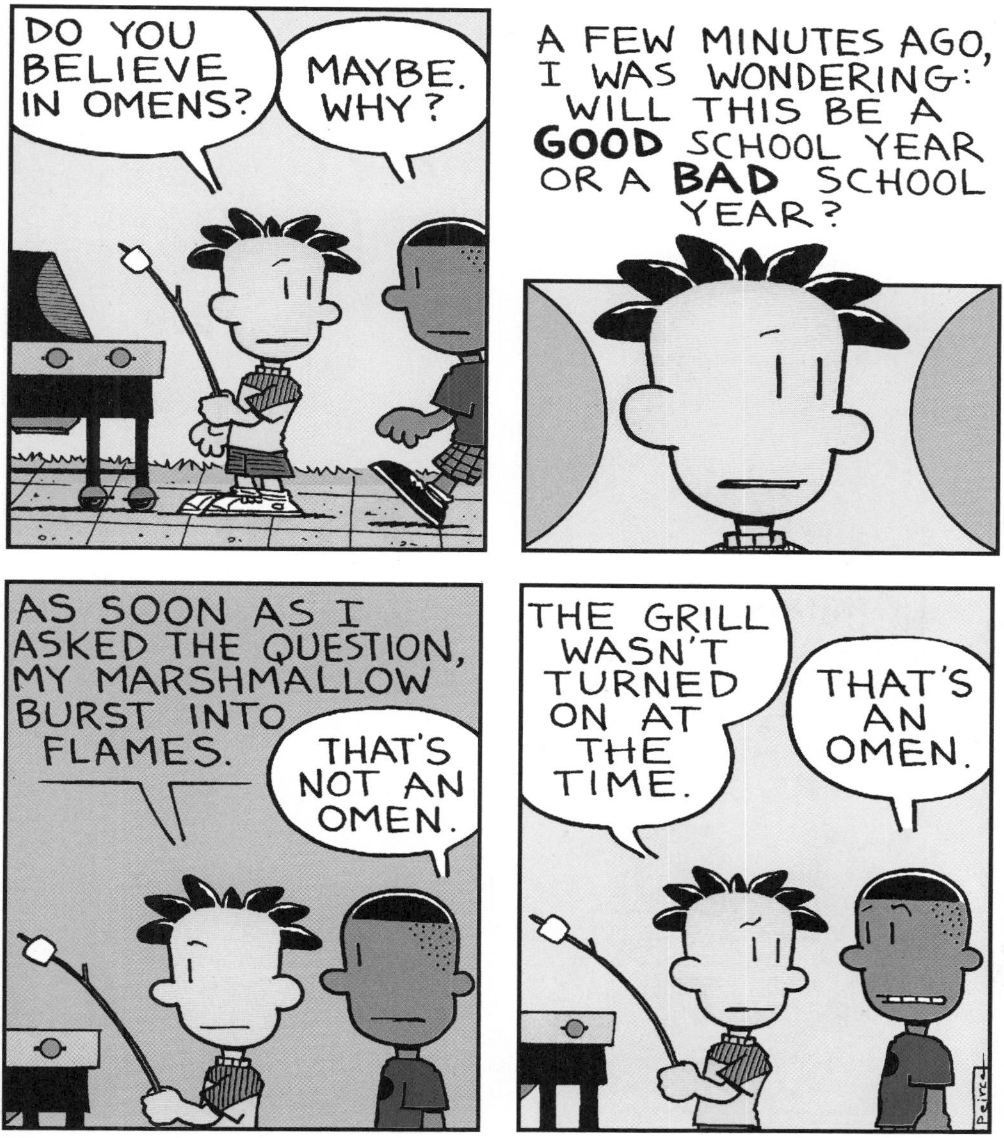
DO YOU BELIEVE IN OMENS?
MAYBE. WHY?
A FEW MINUTES AGO, I WAS WONDERING: WILL THIS BE A **GOOD** SCHOOL YEAR OR A **BAD** SCHOOL YEAR?
AS SOON AS I ASKED THE QUESTION, MY MARSHMALLOW BURST INTO FLAMES.
THAT'S NOT AN OMEN.
THE GRILL WASN'T TURNED ON AT THE TIME.
THAT'S AN OMEN.
Peirce

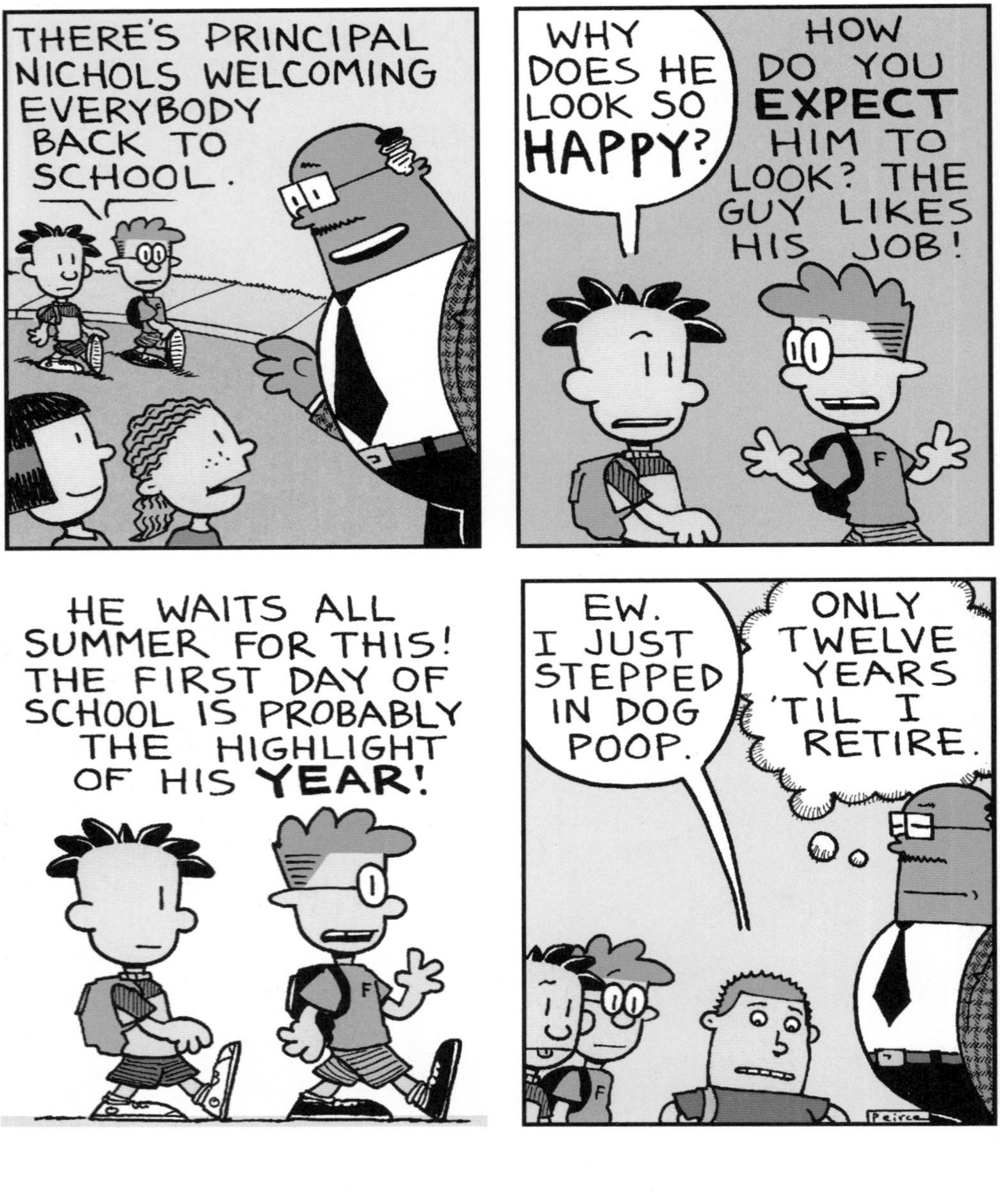
THERE'S PRINCIPAL NICHOLS WELCOMING EVERYBODY BACK TO SCHOOL.
WHY DOES HE LOOK SO HAPPY?
HOW DO YOU EXPECT HIM TO LOOK? THE GUY LIKES HIS JOB!
HE WAITS ALL SUMMER FOR THIS! THE FIRST DAY OF SCHOOL IS PROBABLY THE HIGHLIGHT OF HIS YEAR!
EW. I JUST STEPPED IN DOG POOP.
ONLY TWELVE YEARS 'TIL I RETIRE.
F
F
F
F
Peirce

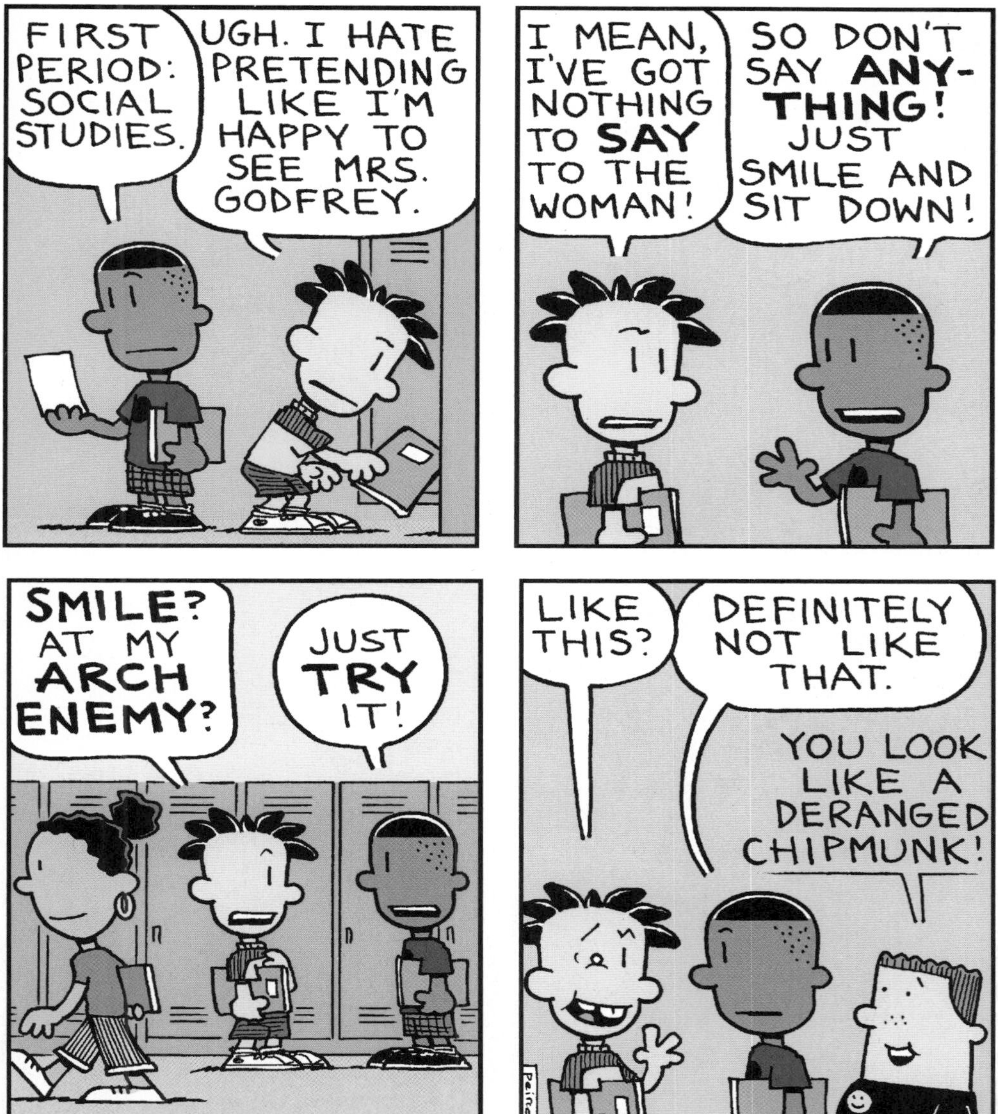
FIRST PERIOD: SOCIAL STUDIES.
UGH. I HATE PRETENDING LIKE I'M HAPPY TO SEE MRS. GODFREY.
I MEAN, I'VE GOT NOTHING TO **SAY** TO THE WOMAN!
SO DON'T SAY **ANYTHING**! JUST SMILE AND SIT DOWN!
SMILE? AT MY **ARCH ENEMY**?
JUST **TRY** IT!
LIKE THIS?
DEFINITELY NOT LIKE THAT.
YOU LOOK LIKE A DERANGED CHIPMUNK!
Peirce

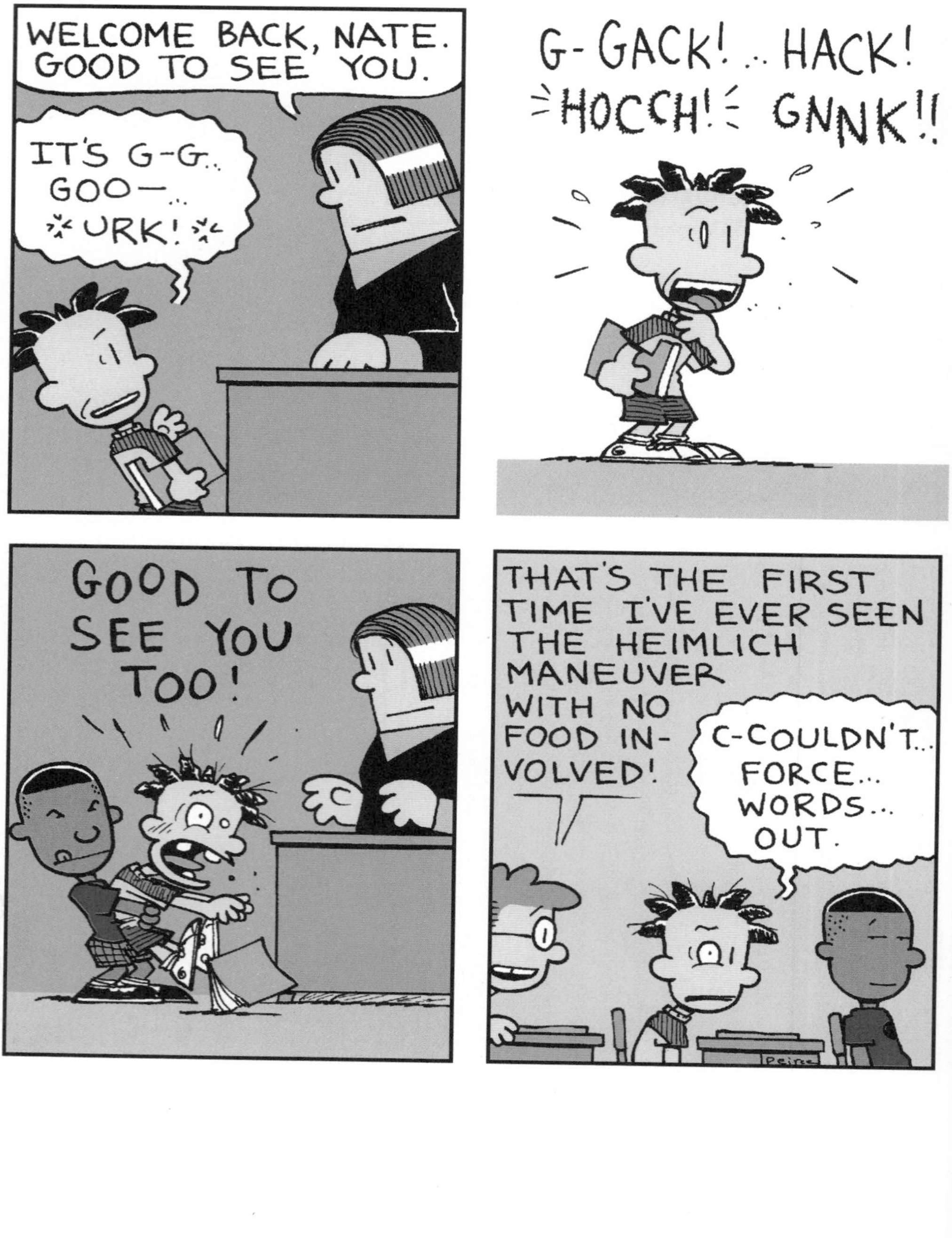
WELCOME BACK, NATE. GOOD TO SEE YOU.
IT'S G-G... GOO—... URK!
G-GACK! ... HACK! HOCCH! GNNK!!
GOOD TO SEE YOU TOO!
THAT'S THE FIRST TIME I'VE EVER SEEN THE HEIMLICH MANEUVER WITH NO FOOD INVOLVED!
C-COULDN'T... FORCE... WORDS... OUT.
Peirce

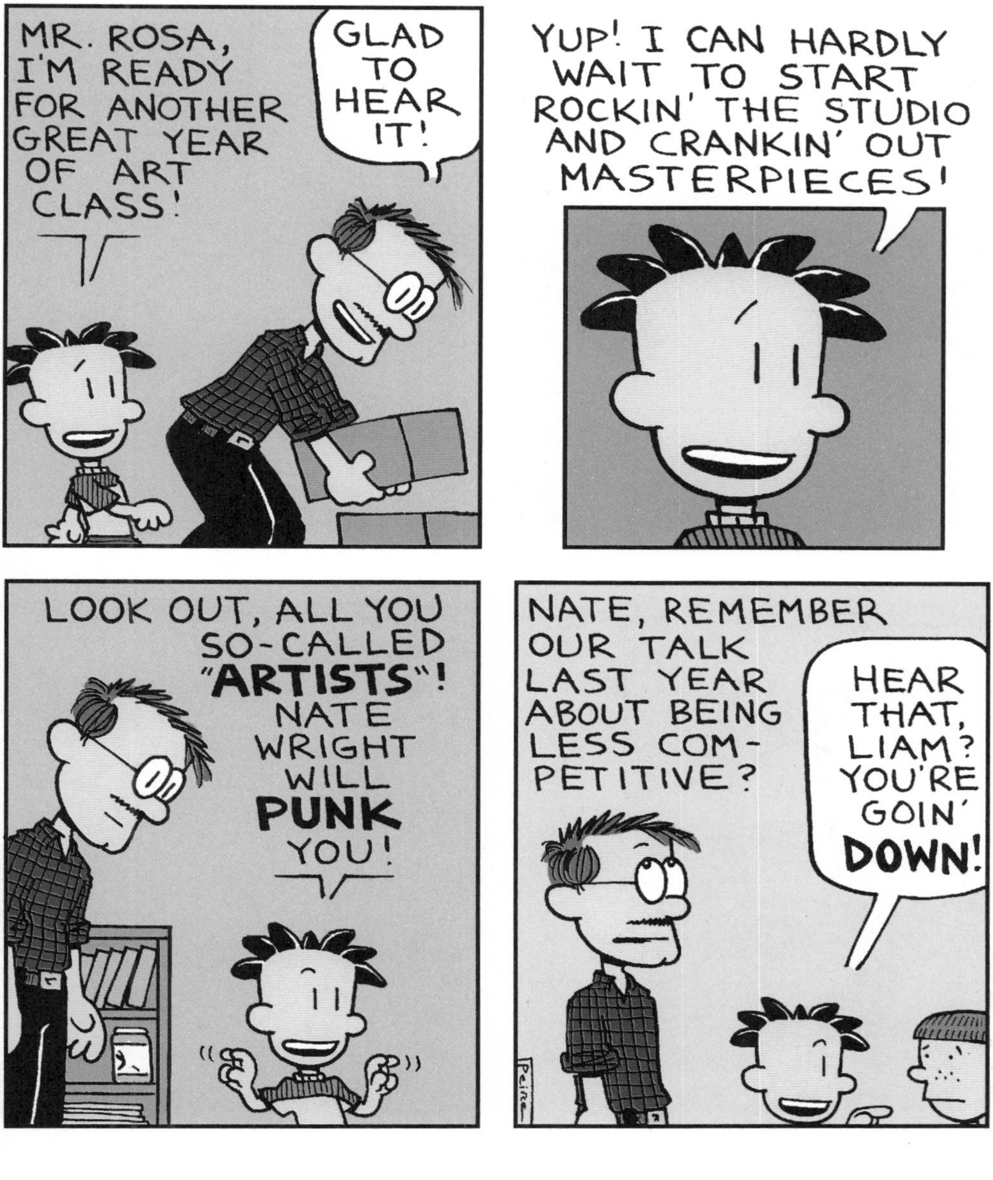
MR. ROSA, I'M READY FOR ANOTHER GREAT YEAR OF ART CLASS!
GLAD TO HEAR IT!
YUP! I CAN HARDLY WAIT TO START ROCKIN' THE STUDIO AND CRANKIN' OUT MASTERPIECES!
LOOK OUT, ALL YOU SO-CALLED "ARTISTS"! NATE WRIGHT WILL PUNK YOU!
NATE, REMEMBER OUR TALK LAST YEAR ABOUT BEING LESS COM-PETITIVE?
HEAR THAT, LIAM? YOU'RE GOIN' DOWN!
Peirce

MR. GALVIN, WHAT ARE WE GOING TO DO IN SCIENCE THIS YEAR?
LEARN ABOUT SCIENCE.
YEAH, BUT ARE WE GOING TO DO ANYTHING **COOL**?
DEFINE "COOL."
WELL, LIKE... Y'KNOW HOW IN MEDICAL SCHOOL, STUDENTS GET THEIR OWN CADAVERS?
THERE ARE NO CADAVERS IN 6TH GRADE SCIENCE.
...EXCEPT FOR THE ONE TEACHING THE CLASS.
SNORT
CADAVERS...
ZZZZZZ
Peirce

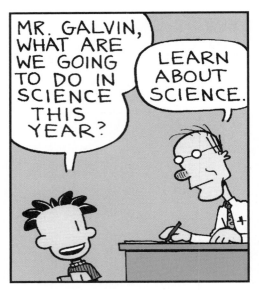

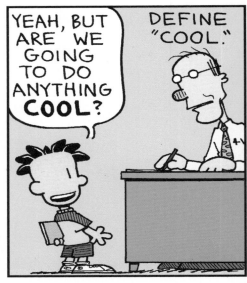

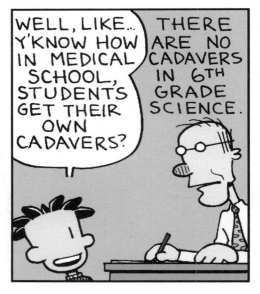

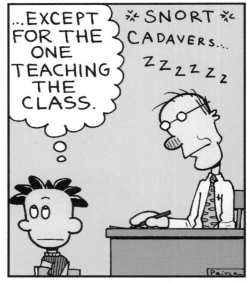

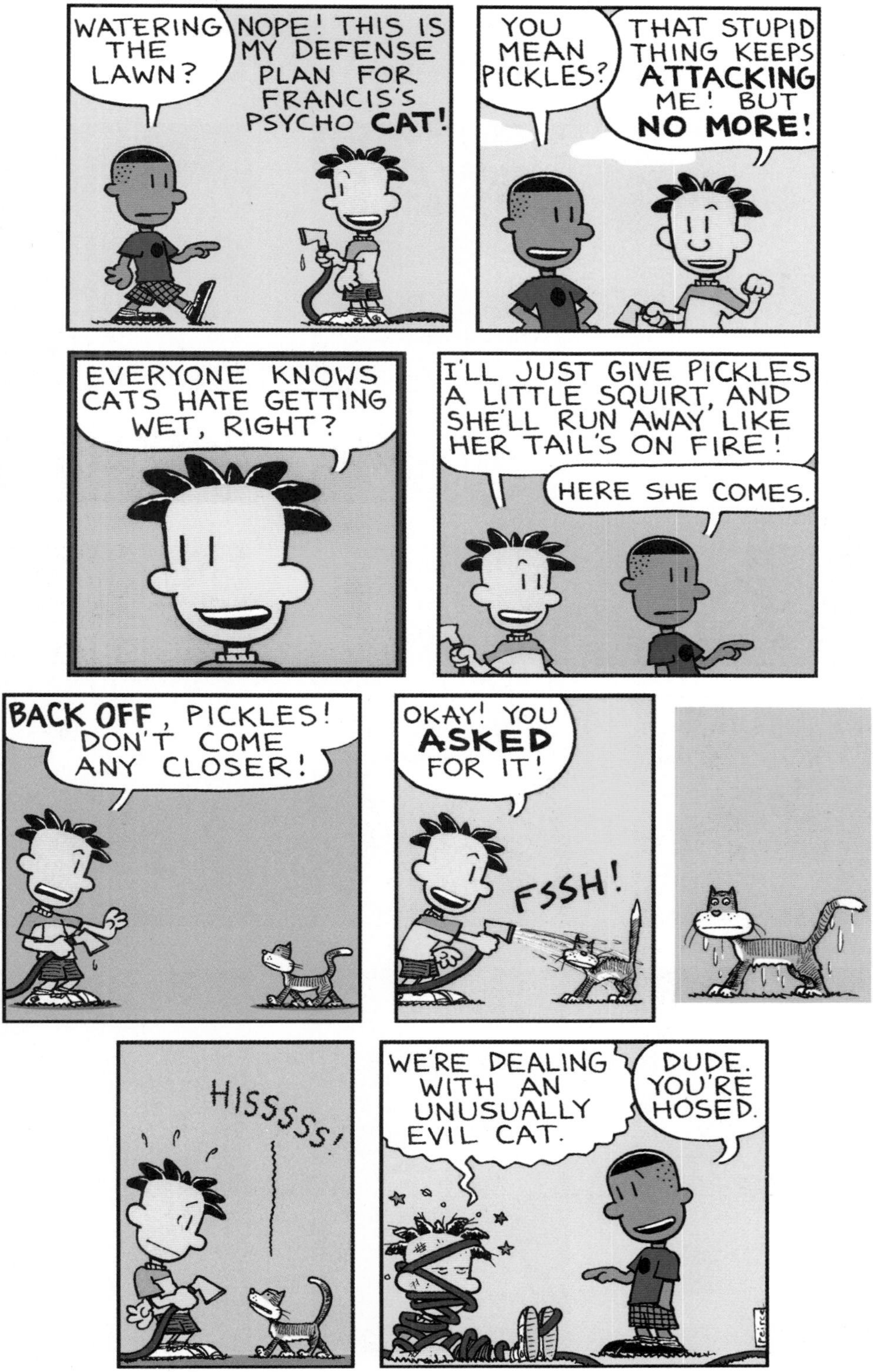
WATERING THE LAWN?
NOPE! THIS IS MY DEFENSE PLAN FOR FRANCIS'S PSYCHO CAT!
YOU MEAN PICKLES?
THAT STUPID THING KEEPS ATTACKING ME! BUT NO MORE!
EVERYONE KNOWS CATS HATE GETTING WET, RIGHT?
I'LL JUST GIVE PICKLES A LITTLE SQUIRT, AND SHE'LL RUN AWAY LIKE HER TAIL'S ON FIRE!
HERE SHE COMES.
BACK OFF, PICKLES! DON'T COME ANY CLOSER!
OKAY! YOU ASKED FOR IT!
FSSH!
HISSSSS!
WE'RE DEALING WITH AN UNUSUALLY EVIL CAT.
DUDE. YOU'RE HOSED.
PEIRCE

Look for these books!

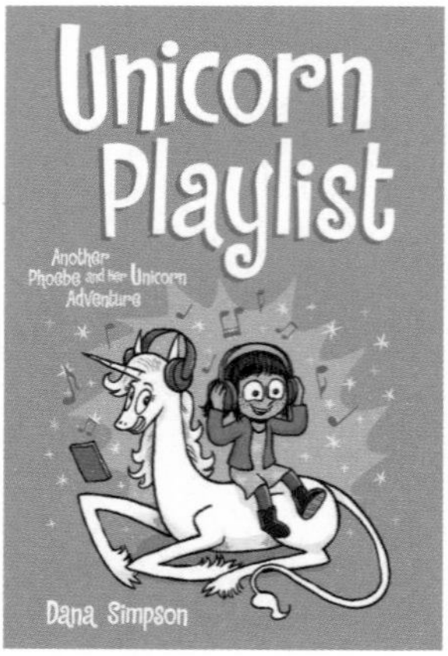
Unicorn Playlist
Another Phoebe and Her Unicorn Adventure
Dana Simpson

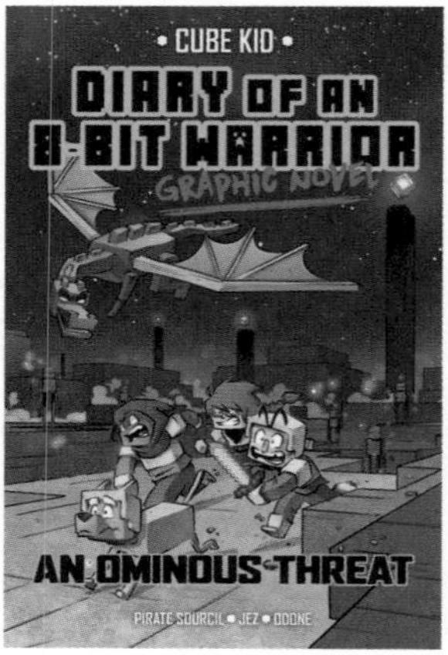
• CUBE KID •
DIARY OF AN 8-BIT WARRIOR
GRAPHIC NOVEL
AN OMINOUS THREAT
PIRATE SOURCIL • JEZ • ODONE

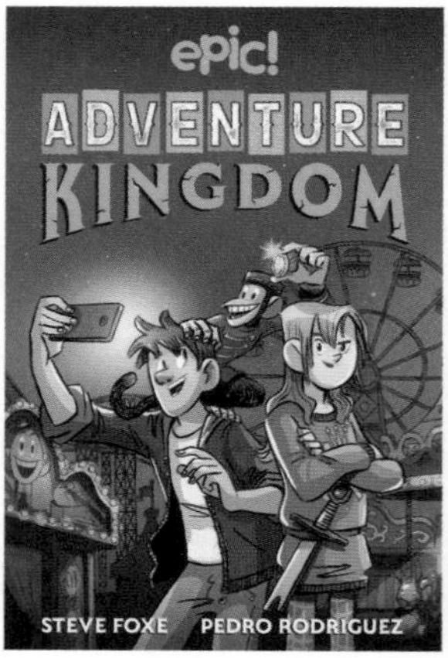
epic!
ADVENTURE KINGDOM
STEVE FOXE
PEDRO RODRIGUEZ

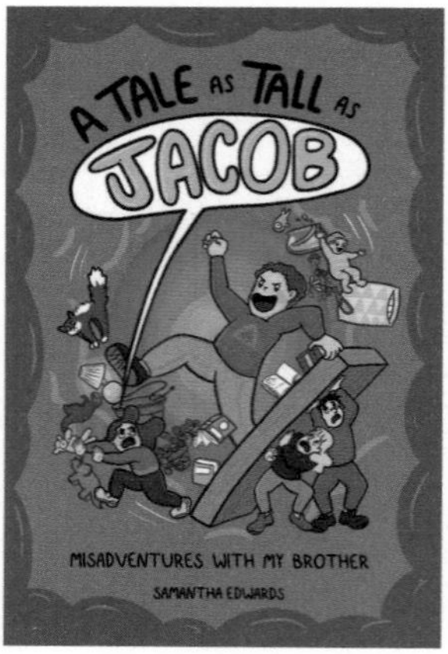
A TALE AS TALL AS JACOB
MISADVENTURES WITH MY BROTHER
SAMANTHA EDWARDS

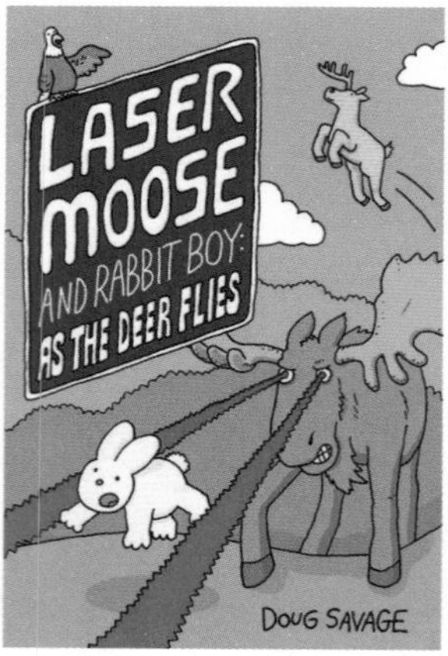
LASER MOOSE AND RABBIT BOY: AS THE DEER FLIES
DOUG SAVAGE

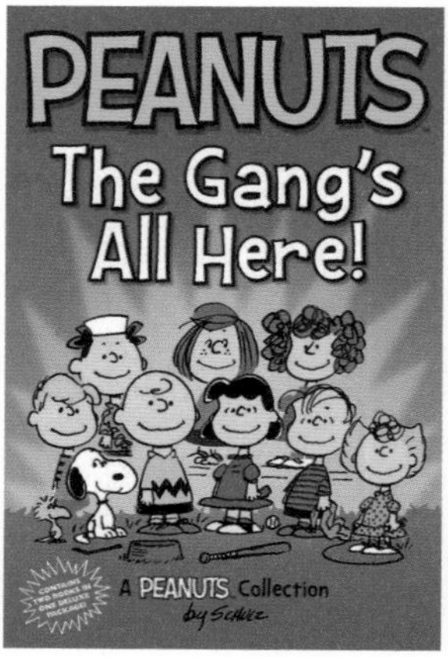
PEANUTS
The Gang's All Here!
A PEANUTS Collection
by Schulz

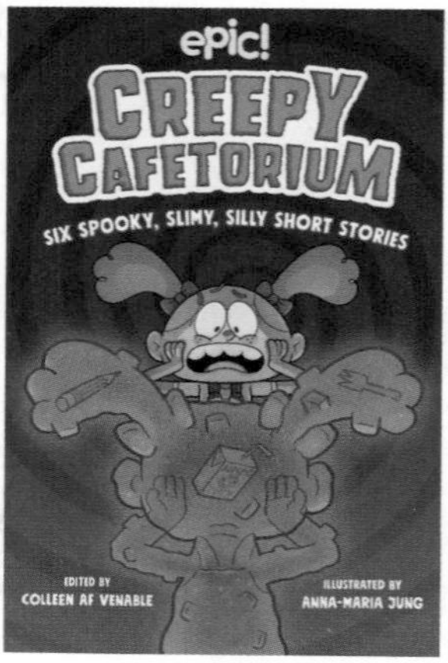
epic!
CREEPY CAFETORIUM
SIX SPOOKY, SLIMY, SILLY SHORT STORIES
EDITED BY
COLLEEN AF VENABLE
ILLUSTRATED BY
ANNA-MARIA JUNG

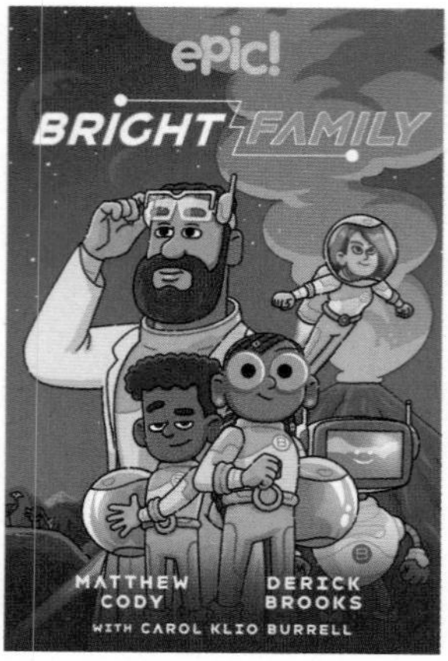
epic!
BRIGHT FAMILY
MATTHEW CODY
DERICK BROOKS
WITH CAROL KLIO BURRELL

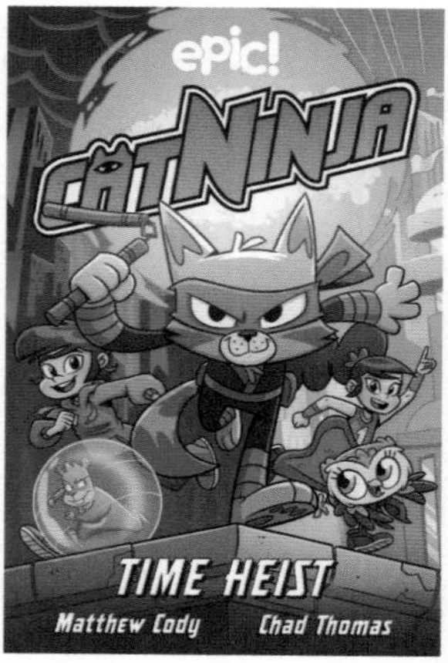
epic!
CAT NINJA
TIME HEIST
Matthew Cody
Chad Thomas

Big Nate is distributed internationally by Andrews McMeel Syndication.

Andrews McMeel Publishing
a division of Andrews McMeel Universal
1130 Walnut Street, Kansas City, Missouri 64106

www.andrewsmcmeel.com

22 23 24 25 26 SDB 10 9 8 7 6 5 4 3 2 1

ISBN: 978-1-5248-7157-4

Library of Congress Control Number: 2021945538

Made by:
King Yip (Dongguan) Printing & Packaging Factory Ltd.
Address and location of manufacturer:
Daning Administrative District, Humen Town
Dongguan Guangdong, China 523930
1st Printing—11/22/21

These strips appeared in newspapers from
September 3, 2017, through September 9, 2018.

Big Nate can be viewed on the Internet at
www.gocomics.com/big_nate.

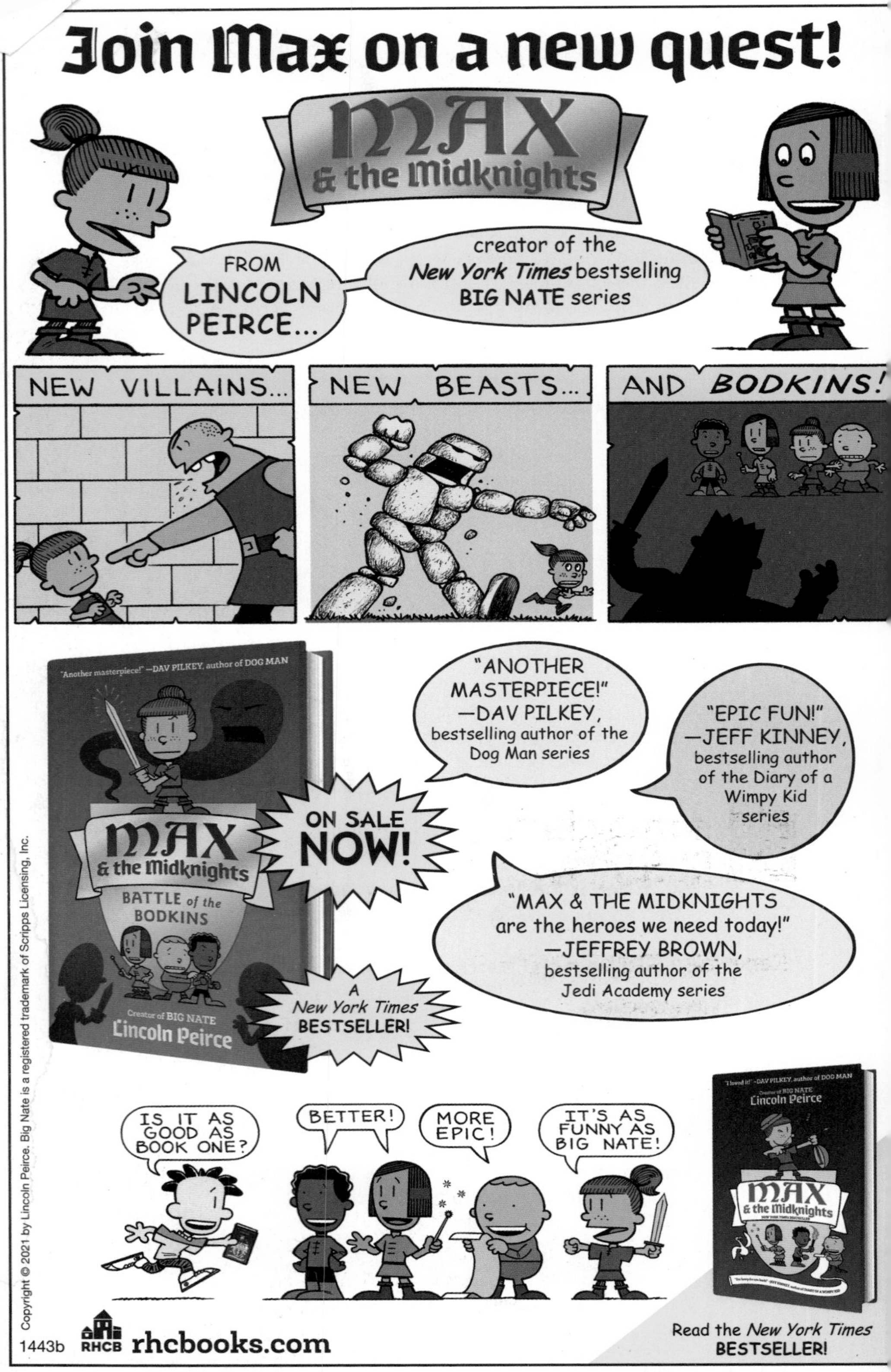
Join Max on a new quest!
MAX & the Midknights
FROM LINCOLN PEIRCE...
creator of the New York Times bestselling BIG NATE series
NEW VILLAINS...
NEW BEASTS...
AND BODKINS!
"Another masterpiece!" —DAV PILKEY, author of DOG MAN
MAX & the Midknights
BATTLE of the BODKINS
Creator of BIG NATE
Lincoln Peirce
ON SALE NOW!
"ANOTHER MASTERPIECE!" —DAV PILKEY, bestselling author of the Dog Man series
"EPIC FUN!" —JEFF KINNEY, bestselling author of the Diary of a Wimpy Kid series
"MAX & THE MIDKNIGHTS are the heroes we need today!" —JEFFREY BROWN, bestselling author of the Jedi Academy series
A New York Times BESTSELLER!
IS IT AS GOOD AS BOOK ONE?
BETTER!
MORE EPIC!
IT'S AS FUNNY AS BIG NATE!
Creator of BIG NATE
Lincoln Peirce
MAX & the Midknights
Read the New York Times BESTSELLER!
Copyright © 2021 by Lincoln Peirce. Big Nate is a registered trademark of Scripps Licensing, Inc.
1443b
RHCB
rhcbooks.com